WITCHES STEEPED IN GOLD

ALSO BY CIANNON SMART:

Empress Crowned in Red

WITCHES STEEPED IN GOLD

CIANNON SMART

HARPER TEEN

An Imprint of HarperCollinsPublishers

HarperTeen is an imprint of HarperCollins Publishers.

Witches Steeped in Gold
Copyright © 2021 by Ciannon Smart
All rights reserved. Printed in the United States of America.
No part of this book may be used or reproduced in any manner whatsoever without
written permission except in the case of brief quotations embodied in critical articles
and reviews. For information address HarperCollins Children's Books, a division of
HarperCollins Publishers, 195 Broadway, New York, NY 10007.
www.epicreads.com

Library of Congress Cataloging-in-Publication Data

Names: Smart, Ciannon, author.
Title: Witches steeped in gold / Ciannon Smart.
Description: First edition. | New York : HarperTeen, [2020] | Audience: Ages 14 up
   | Audience: Grades 10-12 | Summary: "Two enemy witches must enter into a
   deadly alliance to take down a tyrant who threatens both their worlds—with
   unpredictable results"— Provided by publisher.
Identifiers: LCCN 2020023309 | ISBN 978-0-06-294599-0 (pbk.)
Subjects: CYAC: Witches—Fiction.
Classification: LCC PZ7.1.S59443 Wi 2020 | DDC [Fic]—dc23
LC record available at https://lccn.loc.gov/2020023309

Typography by Chris Kwon
22 23 24 25 26   PC/LSCH   10 9 8 7 6 5 4 3 2 1
❖
First paperback edition, 2022

In loving memory of Megan Smart
and Sandra Lawson
And for you, mum, whose championing
melody never wavered

‖≡⁄ The Orders of Xaymaca ⅃⅄⁆⁊

ORDER OF ALUMBRAR

~~

JUDAIR CARIOT
Witches Council Doyenne
Métier: Stealth

JAZMYNE CARIOT
Witches Council Emissary
Judair's last living daughter
Métier: Healer

MADISYN CARIOT
Judair's late daughter
Métier: Healer

ORDER OF OBEAH

CORDELIA ADAIR
Former Empress of the Xaymaca Empire
Iraya's late mama

VINCENT ADAIR
Former Aiycan Navy Admiral
Iraya's late dada
Métier: Squaller

IRAYA ADAIR
Sole daughter and heir of Cordelia and Vincent Adair
Métier: Warrior

PART I

PLAY
FOOL
TO
CATCH
THE WISE

JAZMYNE

Though the night is flush with stars, the sky still seems like a lid of earth closing atop a grave.

It's a fate that could be mine, should anyone see me sneaking from my home at this hour—a fate reserved for criminals and traitors, rebels and liars. Not me, the doyenne's emissary.

Even if I am most of those things.

Ever watchful, the palace's hulking shadow looms across the Parade Court, dogging my nervous tread to the sweet-scented fruit grove where, as promised in the missive that drew me out of bed, my sand-prowler is tethered. In pursuit of blood eaters, Joshial bows a tree trunk with his weight as he flicks his whip of a tongue out.

At the sight of me, he jumps back to the grass on four thick scaled legs. Straining against his leash, he's more of a hound than a monster-size lizard. Cooing, I scratch the underside of his chin before mounting. There's no time to retrieve a saddle.

Who knows which eyes watch from the windows.

Adjusting my hood, I bend low against Joshial's wide neck. "Run fast for me tonight," I whisper. Always the loyal companion, he half sprints, half leaps, taking us away from the palace via the unguarded temple drive, and into a tangle of bush that conceals our descent into the sleeping parish streets at the base of the estate's mount.

We enter Ol' Town at a breathless gallop. In the day, it's a bustling street market. This late, no magi congregate to gossip, their musical patwah mingling with peppery jerk spice and opiate smoke. The slowing click of Joshial's claws on stone is the sole sound as we bear down upon the destination dictated in the missive. Wedged between vacant neighbors, and down a side street I'd never enter in the day, the building's windows are either shattered or boarded up; dark puddles, too murky to reflect light from fading witchlight lamps, seep before it, and trampled detritus litters its doorway—where a buguyaga slumps, blanketed in filthy rags. I guide Joshial right up to the snoring witch; his giant pink tongue unfurls and gives the side of her face a good lick.

"Cha!" Abandoning all pretense of sleep, Anya scrubs a filthy sleeve across her cheek. "When will you teach that beast some manners, mon?" Beneath her mucky camouflage, the toasted almond color of her skin is flushed with annoyance; it contrasts against wisps of straight silver hair peeking out from beneath her hood. "And why are you so late?"

"Wahan to you too. Whoever left the missive didn't wake me."

Straightening, she swaps her disaffection for the better-fitting militance of her Stealth métier. "I'll have a word with whichever fool was assigned. Some of the newer recruits could do with having more respect for our discipline." And who better to teach them than her, the best magically trained shadow I know.

"Can you keep Joshial with you?" I ask.

She shakes her head. "I'm on duty with the first battalion tonight, not the resistance."

Of course. At nightfall the magicless second battalion is replaced by those with magic.

"I'm undercover, obviously, but others in uniform are also making rounds. You'd better take your familiar inside before he licks the wrong face."

I look at the building's entrance, and nerves twist in my belly. Away from the palace I can no longer hide behind my mask of political envoy, a professional fence-sitter. In the meeting that waits inside, I'm part of a resistance working against the very structure I serve, and they have a question for me tonight. My answer won't please us both.

"You'll be fine as long as you remember to duck when the time calls for it," Anya says, knowing my expressions almost as well as she knows her own.

We two are bottom and bench. But while she might not fear the aim of Light Giver, the moniker bestowed to the grizzled resistance founder, my cheek smarts at the memory of the last time one of her slippers caught me in the face.

"Now go. I'll come find you later."

Joshial takes the entrance sideways, climbing onto the wall with whatever adhesive his clawed feet provide. I leave him in an empty room just off the doorway with plenty of dead insects to devour before venturing on. The building is a trap of endless corridors dimly lit by the soft glow of overhead witchlight orbs. It isn't a safe house I've been in before, which isn't unusual. The resistance changes location often to avoid detection. They all have the same feel to them, though: damp neglect undercut by a fetid heat—one that licks at my neck, my brow, and only encourages the creeping sense of unease working its way through my limbs.

I am not a liar by nature, but tonight I must sell the sky to magi who know it's free.

The resistance has tired of our leader, our doyenne. In the beginning, along with the rest of our order, they admired her decisions. Praised their bloom in the garden of her rule. But as time has passed, certain choices she's made have rankled, caused them to question how well they suit the spiritualism of our order. Enough that the resistance is prepared to prune the garden she's cultivated until it is barren, and she is no more.

I need to persuade them that she can change, that such extreme action is unnecessary, even as they hone their tools and discuss attack.

Soon snatches of patwah sound from behind a vast sliding metal door, but it's too quick for me to catch. I linger long enough to straighten my shoulders and fix a look of cool professionalism to my face before drawing the handle back. The door creaks awkwardly upon opening; behind, a small party of fourteen or so Alumbrar, now silent, turn to see who's entering. *Be measured. Be steady*, I will myself. Light Keeper is seated on a stool at the head of their gathering, straight-backed and formidable as any elder. Her eyes narrow.

"You're late, Emissary." Her tobacco-rough croak is full of reproach.

"The missive was late," I correct. Lowering my hood frees my silver afro of curls. Here it is a currency, a marker that I'm one of them. "Please, continue."

She watches me a moment longer, weighing up the trajectory of her aim and my distance, I'm sure, before her eyes, as dark as coal and just as incendiary, dart back to the standing speaker. "You heard her."

Nodding in acknowledgment at the attendees, I make my way to the back of the gathering while the witch I interrupted launches back into her report about numbers. This meeting is smaller than others I've attended, and yet not a single face is familiar to me. I'm again reminded of the size of this resistance and the power of its anonymity—the Nameless, as they titled themselves long before I joined, aren't as concerned with flaunting their membership as they are with the protection of our order from a leader sure to destroy us.

One they mean to kill.

My fists curl around the cotton fabric of my cape, scrunching up the delicate kaftan beneath. Remaining on the fence will make the upcoming conversation difficult, but not impossible. I have to believe that as the witch ends her spiel and Light Keeper turns her attention to me.

"What news do you have about the Yielding?" Our Aiycan accent is a song, like the music from cicada and cricket, but from her lips it's flat. Hard. "Last I heard, the Witches Council is still foolish enough to plan for it to go ahead."

"That's correct."

Murmurs of displeasure, annoyance, ripple across the room. I am not ignorant to their vexation. The Yielding, a sacrificial rite, sees seven pickney all about my age, on the cusp of inheriting their magic, compete for the honor of being offered to the Supreme Being in ritual sacrifice. It's necessary to provide the guzzu of protection wrapped around the island, an enchantment that keeps us safe from once-allied islands who have always craved the power imbibed in the mountains and rivers here, the earth and bush. But it's also the biggest blight in our order's history. The nature of Alumbrar isn't to kill. At least, it wasn't before the rite.

"But," I continue, raising my voice slightly, "there has been more discussion than ever before about the Yielding's merit now we've displayed our strengths to those who thought us weak, as well as facing so little threat from Obeah insurgents."

Light Keeper frowns. "Unfortunately, that's not a cancellation. I know how you feel about the decision to assassinate Doyenne Cariot, Emissary, but a *discussion* is not good enough after we've imparted our request through protests, missives, and she remains unmoved. Her lack of malleability isn't something we can afford to ignore any longer. Not this close to another Yielding announcement."

"If we wait until then, I'm sure she'll make the right decision."

Though I project confidence—I've been practicing in the mirrors in my rooms—resistance members exchange glances, and sweat builds anew between my shoulder blades. Some of my order shake their heads in pity at me, the fool they believe can't see her master is a monster. They truly think I'm turning a blind eye to a witch who has killed countless pickney throughout the years to ensure our order remains in power. But how could I be when they know that number includes my only sister?

Death isn't the answer, it's the problem here.

"If we assassinate her," I ask, challenging them now, "how are we any better? How will this island be less bloody *after* her than it was *before* her, when she earned her seat killing the last ruler too?"

The wrinkled skin around Light Keeper's mouth draws tight.

"The Ascension Festival is just six nights away," I push. "A mere moon phase—and when it comes, the moon will be New. A purifying blessing from the Supreme Being for our entire order, a chance to reflect and grow. It's the perfect time for the doyenne to announce a resurgence. One without the Yielding." My voice softens. "We should have faith."

Alumbrar are Healers, scholars, cerebrals, Artisans. We are not killers. The doyenne can remember that, if she's given the time. The resistance *should* remember that.

"Your faith is commendable, Emissary," Light Keeper says, her words chewed out slowly. "And you're right to exercise caution, to protect Alumbrar virtue. It's what will make you a better leader than the one we currently have. But know this." Her eyes narrow into a look as foreboding as the sky I left outside. "If the doyenne doesn't renounce the Yielding during the festival, indefinitely, she will be put down. And you need to be prepared to say goodbye when the time comes."

I swallow. Her message doesn't go unmissed.

The resistance will make their peace with ridding the island of a tyrannical leader with ease, but my relationship with the doyenne has always been more involved. She's not just the leader I work for—she's the witch who gave birth to me.

"Emissary?" Light Keeper pushes. "Do you understand?"

Should the doyenne be stopped? Yes. Replaced? Definitely. Killed?

Regardless of what she's done, she gifted me with life. I've struggled to endorse her assassination; though it's not sentiment alone that stays my hand. Ours isn't a relationship where she combs my afro at night, or I turn to her with my problems. She is my tutor. If she dies, I ascend. And I'm . . . not ready. A secret I can't tell the Nameless, not when they're looking to me as they are now, with pity, doubt, questions. Not when I *want* to lead, in time.

Sitting on the fence cannot cost me the respect of my people.

"Emissary Cariot, your answer?"

I inhale. "I'll be ready."

It's a harmless lie. This island, Aiyca, has been ruled by my family for a decade, and will be for at least a decade more. Nothing will bring about the Yielding this year, I guarantee it.

2

IRA

Six Nights Later

Nana would say that unlike storms, trouble doesn't give signs like rain, so we must always be ready for it.

Her words have been my constant companion, these ten years since I saw her last. More so than gods or goddesses, friends or lovers. Tonight I bind them to me the way a fighter wraps their fists for protection, curling the memory of her sage cadence around my palms and between my fingers. Her words will do as a favor to see me through what is still to be done. Not that I necessarily believe in such things. Hope may be for the faithful, but it is also for the focused, and what lies ahead means I must be dagger-sharp.

For all my preparedness, Carne Prison lulls in slumber around me. Not for the first time, I curse the lack of windows in this damp, stinking pit. Though, what's a prison cell if it doesn't torture the body as well as the mind?

It has to be close to midnight, goddess willing. I've already bathed and used the chewstick to clean my teeth, but my extremities twitch in demand for *more*. It's a chore to force myself to remain still on my pallet, to count the cracks in the too-close walls of stone, to track the indolent dance of dust motes, until one of the guards makes their way to my section of this block. For them, this night is routine, already lost to better memories.

For me, everything changes.

A soft intake of breath is all I permit at the sweet taste of its promise: leaving prison to inherit my ancestors' magic, becoming a witch, and finally being equipped to exact justice against those who tossed me in here, foolish enough to think me cowed.

After a long decade of imprisonment, tonight I'll be free.

No. Not free with the magical conscription that awaits me outside these walls.

But I suppose it will have to do.

"Up, Obeah!"

Officer Carsten, one of Carne Prison's guards, finally strides over to the lone glass wall of my cell. Her wheat-brown skin is already aglow with sweat. It gleams at the edge of her silver afro, a sign of status I am without, as a dark-haired Obeah.

"Yuh hear?" she snaps. "Move. *Now.*"

While I feign lethargy, as though still in sleep's clutches, my eyes roll freely at the way her piggy pair dart around for booby traps. After all this time, she's yet to realize the best trap stands before her. Another adage Nana Clarke was fond of saying, wise eyes narrowed under the unremitting fist of the sun, was that cows don't have any business in horseplay.

Satisfied by her preliminary inspection, the large golden coin hanging from a long leather cord around Carsten's neck illuminates with light, and the diamond glass wall separating us rescinds downward into the rock at her feet. She hulks in the opening, wide and squat, the deep green leather of her uniform militant. Her coin lights again, channeling centuries of her ancestors' magic at her will. She summons fetters; they lock around my ankles and wrists. Their jaws of oppression are a familiar weight, a stinging reminder of my reduced position.

They're why I make sure to never forget I wasn't made to kneel before her ilk.

"Tell me," I begin, amiable as ever. "How are you this fine evening, Carsten?"

"Don't talk."

"I'm well too, mon. Quite excited, actually. It's kind of you to ask."

"*Cha*. What did I say?" The coin around her neck is quick to pulse a warning of the magic basking at its surface, ready to be shaped and aimed at all threats—at me.

I'm flattered.

Magicless as I am, fettered as I am, her terror is still potent enough that I could inhale it like an opiate.

"Corner your mouth," she threatens, a delicious tremble in her voice. "And move out."

I do as she says, for now.

Outside my cell, I'm one of many brown-skinned prisoners

released earlier than usual to choke down a late supper in the block's canteen. Newly eighteen, we're all destined to receive our ancestral magic prior to starting twenty years' compulsory service to the crown. In theory conscription doesn't seem so bad, not when it involves working in fields like sericulture, healing, or energy, and we'll have homes of our own. But immersed in the small crowd of women, some yawning, others crying, whatever humor teasing Carsten instilled wanes in me.

I've longed for this day, but there's no denying it's not the pardon you hope for when leaving prison: it's a two-decade-long liberty. Obeah were leaders, an elite legion of magi, lethal and lauded for our skill in the arcane arts as well as our beauty, but now? Within this sunless fortress, skin that once gleamed has been robbed of its mahogany luster, its chestnut shine. Where we once walked tall, shoulders are bent and eyes downcast. We could be duppies, nothing more than a procession of lingering spirits en route to an afterlife in Coyaba.

It's easy to forget that we are the living, and we are the lucky ones.

I sometimes fail to remember that I'm not alone in having parents who didn't die at a ripe old age. Many Obeah in here have been orphaned, our parents murdered by the ruling Alumbrar because, at the dawn of our orders' creation, fate tossed a coin that sparked a perennial battle for sacerdotal power. It finally landed in their favor a decade ago in the aftermath of a surprise usurpation. Obeah call it the Viper's Massacre. Alumbrar, a long time coming.

A smirk tightens Officer Carsten's mouth as she notices my focus, the pall that's fallen thick around me. I'm quick to stop worrying my bottom lip between my teeth, but not enough.

"Wondering how such a bag of bones will fare outside?"

The steady plume of anger forever coiling in my stomach scorches my throat, eager to erupt.

Can't.

"Not so chatty now, are you?"

Don't.

"You look 'fraid, Obeah. It suits you better than your earlier conceit."

Carsten's laughter is a boot to the ribs, one that catalyzes my spite up and out.

"I wouldn't discount appearances if I were you, Officer. Even in that uniform, I wouldn't mind playing with *your* bones." My words are as sticky-sweet as molasses—as dark, to an Alumbrar who knows, even now, to fear an Obeah who speaks of bones.

The dead are our biggest allies, after all.

It's my turn to smirk as Carsten steps back, trembling fingers reaching for her coin, which blazes like a trapped sun. A wince cuts through my lips as three lashes land across the backs of my bare legs at her will, invisible lances that make them buckle with the sting.

"*Cha,*" she chides, freezing the hand I was about to use to rub across the tender welts. "To speak of the forbidden . . . I hope you try using that mouth outside these walls. You'll—"

"Now, Officer," a mischievous voice interrupts. "I didn't take you for one interested in sharing the delights of Ira's mouth." Kaleisha bumps my hip with the hard bone of her own.

Before Carsten can unleash the wrath of a dozen angry aunties on either of us, I drag Kaleisha into the growing congregation of Obeah queueing up at the food pass. Though clear of Carsten's vigil, other guards surround us. They take everything in with eyes fresh enough to tell me they recently exchanged with the day shift.

I take up a food tray and force a question through gritted teeth. "What was that?"

Undeterred, Kaleisha's generous lips stretch into a smile wide enough to expose the gap between her large front teeth. The left was chipped in a fight, turning her sigh into a whistle. "Me acting normally." She swishes her bob of narrow braids, looking far too pleased with herself.

A quick pinch to the soft flesh of her upper arm soon puts an end to that. And it's a good thing too. She's getting comfortable. Comfort means complacency, and complacency means death. She should know better. She should know *that*.

"It's like you want to attract attention," I grind out.

"I don't. I was trying to *help*."

"You could have fooled me."

Her dark brown skin puckers between her brows, tightening into a frown. "I hate when you do that."

"Call out your reckless behavior?"

"Talk to me like I'm stakki."

"Then how about you try acting like a sane person?"

Conversation halts as cornmeal porridge is slopped onto our trays, sans any sweetener, by an Obeah kitchen worker. Silence stretches between us when we sit at our usual table, save for the scrape of spoons. If I leave it a little longer, she'll break first. She's never handled silence well. But today something claws at my insides—granted, it could be the porridge. It did look a little suspect. There's a greater chance, though, that it's guilt.

Kaleisha has been my family in here since I was tossed inside, spitting like a cat and shrieking bloody murder. She calmed me, comforted me. Over the years we've become like two vines, inextricably tangled, thriving because of a combined strength. I might not have survived Carne without her.

"I don't think you're a fool," I mutter.

The dark stare she levels my way is like a well-crafted blade: balanced, acute, and underestimated only by the wotless, which I am not. Neither is she. Though such a side to the O Block's resident prankster, irreverent beloved, is little known to anyone but me.

"That's not what I meant, and you know it." Kaleisha leans in for the jug of water in the center of the table and breathes, "Do you believe me popping style will make any of the guards suspect we've planned a bruckout today? You need to relax, Ira."

I flinch at my moniker. *Ira.* The double syllable always feels abrupt, unsuited.

Kaleisha runs her keen focus down my face and across my stiff shoulders. Her eyes narrow to glistening pinpricks. "You've always been better than me at concealing your emotions, but you almost look a little . . . peccant."

"I assure you," I say, forcing indifference under her scrutiny, "I've yet to commit any sins this morning."

"How fortunate then that the day is young."

A smile cracks my resolve. "That line bore all my hallmarks."

"You learned from the best."

"True, mon. Your mistakes have been the best of teachers."

It's difficult to say who laughs longest, in that silent way that aches so much it pains. We are unnervingly similar, in some respects. Enough that everyone calls us sisters. The thought deadens my humor, entombing it somewhere deep. For a moment I consider confessing my doubts about her plans. That's one of the ways we differ. Kaleisha believes in everything.

Today she's confident that we're going to be successful in our fight to flee Carne and join the Obeah rebels, the Jade Guild. Named for the vibrancy of their stronghold, the Blue Mountains, which are actually dominated by green bush, to confuse matters.

They're working to reclaim our order's magical freedom every day. A life on the run with them would be better than the half-life offered by the Alumbrar, she said years ago, when this day seemed so far away. *Do you want to be watched by their soldiers every waking moment? To be afraid to breathe lest they accuse you of treason and lock you back up?*

She's not wrong. After today we'll no longer wake behind bars, but we'll still be prisoners.

"You needn't be afraid," Kaleisha says. Her fingers twitch like she means to take my hands, but touching is forbidden, and she knows I don't like it.

It's one of the few things I've shared with her.

She can't know that her wants aren't mine, that I have a *need*—magic. Her plan to escape, though clever tonight when there are fewer Obeah out of their cells, and so fewer guards on duty, doesn't guarantee I'll get my ancestors' magic. Inheritance has never been worth the indenture, to her. I don't relish the thought of conscription either, but it's always been a means to an end I've been willing to endure.

"Ira?"

In Kaleisha's face, long and slender, wise and patient, I see a friend I can't betray. But in her gaze, my reflection looms, and with my features, ties to a family they won't let me forget. Mama's bridgeless nose and wide-spaced eyes condemn. Dada's angular jaw clenches in silent resolve. The dead and the living each have a hold on me, and their contrasting wants are threatening to tear me asunder.

We both flinch as the deep pulse of drums echoes through the canteen. Conditioned to respond, Kaleisha and I jump up as the canteen tables withdraw into gaping mouths in the ground, and we join the throng that wends its way to gather around an aged platform.

One of the prison guards steps atop it. "Obeah, today you'll be escorted from Carne via prisoner galley to receive your ancestors' magic from your family trees." Her Alumbrar-silver afro glints like a steel helmet beneath the witchlight orbs in the ceiling. "After you're imbued with your inheritance, there will be a brief demonstration of your magical range before you'll receive your work assignments and prepare to reenter society to begin your conscription."

"I've heard the doyenne herself is looking for a new shield. Can you imagine working with our usurper?"

If I had the piqued ears of a jungle-prowler, they would've pricked up at the whispered patwah behind me. Our dialect is fast, demanding more of my attention than I should spare, but I can't help listening in.

"She called a new one half a year ago!" the second exclaims. "She can't need another already."

"She called two, mon!" says the first. "Apparently neither was strong enough to withstand whatever training she has them doing at that estate. Whoever she picks next will need to have the strength of more than two of us."

They stop talking as the weight of one of the guard's stares falls their way.

Rumors about the doyenne's personal cadre of Obeah, forty-nine shields that protect the compound upon which the palace sits, have circulated through Carne for years. Some doubt their existence, dismissing the idea of our two orders working together to protect the stronghold as hearsay, fiction, but just as many prisoners covet the idea of spending their conscription in the comfort of the palace, mitigating their guilt by keeping Aiyca, weakened by the usurpation, safe from outside threat. Better the enemy you know.

"There could be one," the first continues when it's safe to do so.

"Born back a cow." The second rasps a short laugh.

"I'm not stupid! She wasn't killed like her mama and dada were, and I've met Obeah who said she's been living in the mountains with the Jade Guild, biding her time to rescue us."

The derisive one kisses her teeth. "The Lost Empress is nothing more than a story spun by Anansi. If she lived, it'd be the Alumbrar in here. Not us."

I loosen the breath I was holding, slowly.

Anansi, the great spider god and brother to our matriarchal pantheon of gods and goddesses, all housed in our Supreme Being, the Seven-Faced Mudda, may be the most revered story-teller across Carne Sea, but he's also a notorious trickster. For centuries magi on my home island have hunted magical arti-facts, jéges, from his stories. Some, the spider's asserted, will gift power to whoever yields them. Up until now they've never been unearthed. As for tales of the Lost Empress . . . I've found it isn't wise to rely on stories, no matter how you may wish they're true.

The bite of a pinch on my arm makes me hiss.

"Not pleasant, is it, mon?" Kaleisha murmurs beside me. "You missed the first signal word in the speech, as well as the second." Her pause is filled with questions she doesn't ask.

There's no time to doubt my commitment. We have seven more words to pick out of the guard's instructions we're using for our coded countdown before all inheritors are shackled together, making any kind of fight—already difficult with the fetters—impossible.

Kaleisha rocks on her feet, fizzing with anticipation. "Take these."

My hands close around two thick batons—weapons, crafted from aged animal bone. I don't need to ask how or where she procured them. I've fought off my fair share of the four-legged vermin that lurk in the mountain beneath us, drawn by the scent of our despair as we're forced to sort and package coffee beans for trade.

"Don't lose focus now," Kaleisha urges.

A loss of focus has never been my problem.

Years of scheming have led to this moment. Her steps, so

familiar to me, pulse through my thoughts. And yet here, at the first hurdle, my nerves falter and stutter at its size. Everything grows and shrinks around me as my breathing shallows in my ears; the prison block's cavernous reaches suddenly feel chokingly intimate.

Past prison rebellions haven't worked, Kaleisha has said many times over. *We can't let this one fail.*

But now we're here, doubt gnaws at my will.

I know I can do it—*we* can do it.

I'm just not sure if I should.

JAZMYNE

The Festival of Ascension

It's avowed the first Alumbrar were born from the night sky.

Our origin story is one of many spun by Anansi. On this Ascension evening, from the First Family Alcove balcony overlooking the Courtyard of Moons, flooded with silver-haired Alumbrar, it's hard to doubt that my order began their existence as living stars plucked from the heavens, and molded in the Supreme Being's image. However untrustworthy Anansi is, I draw myself a little taller; tonight we do look fit to rule the dark, and all its denizens.

Obsidian bites at the edges of the heavens, ablaze with streaks of scarlet and mango. Alumbrar across the estate await its entire claim on the sky in reverent stillness. The wind is one of the few things that moves, stirring festoon lights strung between the courtyard's elegant columns and winding among the crowd carrying spiced notes of the awaiting feast. I can't help identifying another scent—anticipation. I'm not the only one desperate to learn if Doyenne Cariot will announce if she's abandoning the Yielding or continuing to embrace it. Speculation lingers amidst the peppery heat of evening, doubling its weight until it's almost tangible enough to choke on.

To think I nearly didn't make it here. Carne's conscript transfer happens to fall tonight this quarter. I've never missed overseeing one since my appointment to emissary. Thank the Mudda for Kirdan, however reluctant Doyenne Cariot was to let him go in my stead since he's the political envoy from a neighboring island and old enemy, Zesia. Her willingness can only mean she wants me here tonight, which suggests something must be different from previous Ascension Festivals. The Yielding's cancellation?

I can only hope.

Standing to the right of where she presides over the court-yard, so named for the moon phases our island nation uses to measure time, I sneak a look at Doyenne Judair Cariot. She's still enough in the light from the retreating sun that she could be a carving, like the gilded creation she sits atop. Before the usurpation, Obeah Artisans of Metal alone were permitted to work with conduit gold. The magical aptitude of the artist who created this throne is obvious, and yet it's easily eclipsed by the doyenne's severe beauty. Where its rounded edges are used to juxtapose its leviathan status, there's no such filtering in the doyenne's appearance. She was crafted with all her sharp angles intact—the cut of her eyes, the peaks of her cheekbones jutting beneath the glossy darkness of her skin. Not even the jagged scar responsible for taking the sight from her right eye mars the presence she commands.

I took after my father. He was killed, caught in a crossfire of magic during the usurpation, but in life, he was regular enough that no one would really look at him twice. Not like the doyenne. She isn't the first Alumbrar in our family's history, as the Supreme Being's first created, who's attempted to overthrow the Obeah. Our enmity is one that rivals time for agelessness. Nor is she the first to do so successfully, but she is the only victor in the century since the last failed attempt who has maintained her rule for so long—all while mourning Dada's loss. . . . Her mental strength is something to be respected. To Alumbrar it's far more admirable than the physical strength valued by Obeah.

"What is being forecast about tonight?" Doyenne Cariot murmurs, her accent as clipped and angular as she is. Though already erect, I stand taller. "Which decision does the island favor regarding the Yielding?"

I'm cautious to ruminate over my words before speaking. She taught me that.

"The Alumbrar feel safe, safer perhaps than they ever have before."

"Because of the Yielding."

"Because of you, Doyenne."

She taps a long red nail, filed to a brutal point, on the arm of the throne. Gold bangles jingle rhythmically on her wrist. Demands for answers strain against the leash of my title, our lack of relationship. Deference versus defiance, a familiar line I must walk with her.

"It isn't a leader's prerogative to be adored, you understand?" Each word is uttered with the clearest diction. Even as the sharp consonants drive me back, I can't help leaning in, drawn to her aphorisms about ruling. "We can't make our decisions with that concern. And yet, we can't ignore our people when we make decisions either." She doesn't turn my way; her eye, the sort of brown it's hard to see anything in, never leaves the Alumbrar beneath us. "Ultimately, though, there will always be those who are disappointed. It's a burden our shoulders must be strong enough to carry—one you must be strong enough to, if you eventually occupy this throne."

If. She doubts me still too.

"Should that burden cripple us, we never let people know. Those same adoring mouths will take eager bites if we show even the faintest weakness. That is ruling, Emissary, baring your teeth like a predator even if at times you feel more like prey."

The prescience of her words trails a finger down my spine.

"Is there anything you'd have me do?"

"Be my second eye out there tonight."

My shoulders droop, just a little. If we were in the kitchens, she would have handed me a pot, spoon, and no ingredients, toys to distract a bothersome pickney. She still doesn't think me fit for a real job.

Before she became Aiyca's ruler, Doyenne Cariot's métier was Stealth. She doesn't need me, or the skilled witches who form the crown's personal coven, the Xanthippe, who flank the throne at our backs. After decades of magical tutelage, with only the one eye she sees more than any of us. It's what will make her harder to overthrow than her Obeah counterpart, Empress Adair. Though magically rich, she didn't have the skill of deception Mama has.

"I will do my best." *Even though it's a waste of my time.*

"Be sure that you do." The doyenne looks at me then; not with the love one would expect from a parent. Never that.

When the Nameless and I overthrow her, part of me wonders if she'll be proud.

I take my leave with a nod, careful to hold up the delicate material of my peach-colored kaftan, ordained with hand-stitched golden birds. It's crowded up here. In addition to Cariot cousins, aunties, and uncles—Dada's family have kept to the Healing Centers across the island since his death—the six presiders who serve on the Witches Council also have access to the alcove. Tonight, two of the latter have brought along their firstborns. Passing one, who, like my cousins, is close to me in age, I keep my head down.

For as long as I can remember, it was Madisyn and me against them. They're both fiercely competitive about the Yielding, something I've never understood. Yielders compete to *die*, after all, regardless of the honor of becoming the Yielded.

The only one who would bother to pay attention to me, Javel, ducks out of the alcove. Tall and toned beneath a grand indigo cloak of silk, he swaggers forward with an irritating loose-limbed confidence, dragging an afro pick through the silver curls corkscrewing in a mohawk down the center of his head.

I dart behind a golden statuary before I'm seen. Anger flushes through my body. After Madisyn's death, he tormented me with whispered barbs about the shame she brought my family, dying first as she did in her Yielding. The only downside to the rite's cancellation would be his continued existence, a wicked thought if he wasn't hoping to be selected himself.

He inhales mightily. "Tell me you can feel that, mon."

Zidane, Javel's sidekick, stands close behind him, his broad brow scrunched up in confusion. "Feel what?"

"That everything is about to change."

"Really?" Lacking the status of being a presider's son, Zidane isn't as well dressed as Javel. His bulging muscles strain against the sleeves of a frayed tunic as he tucks into the small mountain of ackee and saltfish fritters on his plate. "You think she'll cancel?"

"The Yielding keeps us safe. To stop it now would put an end to that, surely."

"I think so too," Zidane says, parroting his bredren, as always, though that doesn't make what's being said any less true—to the masses.

It's maddening that many can't see putting an end to the Yielding wouldn't endanger our safety, it would simply mean we'd have to find it elsewhere. But in doing that, the doyenne would need to put her faith in others, something foreign to her. I'm not as skittish, as prideful, about putting my trust where it needs to be to protect my order. That's Dada's influence, my sister Madisyn's.

With Javel and Zidane moving away to secure more food, I keep my eyes on the doyenne from my hideout. Irritation twitches in her upper lip as she's swarmed by presiders across the balcony; one of them flaunts her pickney before her.

Tonight is one for finery, but Presider Mariama Antwi, of the St. Ann Parish, and her daughter Amoi have outdone themselves. Unlike Obeah, who scar their skin to broadcast their métiers, Alumbrar claim color. As Artisans, the Antwi family's dress is pewter; their specialty of gemstones means added sparkle reduces those who share their métier to mere gray phantoms, washed-out and lifeless in their wake, like Presider Ormine Phelony of St. Catherine Parish, Javel's mama. Though beautiful in a dove-gray installation accented with an indigo brocade, the reverse of her son's cloak, she pales in comparison, but only superficially.

Mariama is as useful as her jewels, a pretty ornament. But Ormine uses her Artisanal knowledge to design the uniforms for the doyenne's elite coven of witch guards, weaving guzzu amidst the threads that make them near impervious to attack. Hers is a skill Presider Antwi is without. And that's what métiers are, time-honed masteries with specific caches of enchantments, guzzu.

Almighty.

Realization strikes with the suddenness of a blood eater and just as little mercy as its stinger. I stagger back until the cool metal of the statue presses against my spine.

Ormine is a *Master*, the highest skill level a magi can earn. So is Presider Antwi.

The inheritance of their pickney, as firstborns, will dilute their mamas' magic, halving its capacity. Doyenne Cariot won't want that—won't *allow* that to happen. Her Council perpetuates that they pray about who to sacrifice, but past presiders have all lost their firstborns over the years. That's no coincidence. The doyenne needs their skills, and she needs the Yielding to make that happen. She won't cancel, she can't.

Curtains as light as spider's silk billow from the alcove beside me.

"Wahan, Emissary Cariot."

"Wahan," I murmur, barely sparing a look at the woman who's joined me.

I can't pull out of my thoughts, the string of words that twist and coil through my head like a great big snake. *They're going to kill her, and I will need to step up.*

Bony fingers pinch at the soft skin on the back of my arm, making me cry out.

"Pull yourself together before anyone notices," the woman hisses, her tone suddenly all too familiar. "Stand straight, look pleased, and wish me a Happy Ascension."

It takes a few tries with my throat dry, my thoughts racing. "Happy Ascension, Presider Finlayter," I just manage to repeat to the witch I know better as Light Keeper.

"The same to you, Emissary Cariot." Wearing one of the customary brown kaftans of her Wrangler métier, her hair as wild as the animals she seeks to train, she burns me with her customary stare. "Keep breathing, slowly. There's little to be done now except to wait for her decision." She presses against my side, bony and stalwart. "After that, we'll take our next steps."

Indeed.

And with the doyenne's decision all but pronounced, they will be bloody steps all the way to a throne I'm not ready for.

The ceremonial Kumina drums begin as night's jaws lock around the island.

In the courtyard below, Alumbrar split into two halves to allow a procession of drummers bearing the instruments around their necks, fire breathers, and dancers through their midst. The throbbing pulse of their footfall, their instruments, is flush with life, a heartbeat that jolts the stone beneath my sandals. But the song portends endings, portends death.

I scratch at the back of my hand until it bleeds.

Shadows swirl across Light Keeper's face where she stands beside me still, both from the sprays of fire and her past. She can't be thinking of anything other than her son. He was one of the early Yielders to die. Though I'm moved to take her hand, not all support requires touch. Sometimes it's knowing another person is there, as she has been for me, these two years we've plotted together. I don't want to let her down. But I will.

I'm not ready for this.

I open my mouth, prepared to confess my truth, when the drums begin to bleed away, and Doyenne Cariot rises from her throne to glide to the edge of the balcony, her elegant fingers curling around its balustrade.

I'm too late.

"Wahan, Alumbrar," she says. "From light we are born."

"*And to light we cleave*" is returned by all.

Doyenne Cariot's chin dips slightly. "Ascension has always meant the elevation to a higher plane of existence, one beyond the reaches of understanding for the few of you who've disagreed with how I've kept the Alumbrar in our reigning position for the past decade."

Light Keeper twitches beside me, no doubt struck by an insult that could only be aimed at the Nameless, more of an irritation to the doyenne than a threat to be respected.

"Contrary to what many believe, the Yielding isn't a rite that favors courage. It is selflessness that governs the participating hearts. An understanding that some roles reach their end sooner than others in what has been a bitter fight to keep Aiyca safe from the threat ever pressing at our borders."

These aren't words conducive to ending a sacrificial rite.

She's not canceling.

The crowd in the Courtyard of Moons below starts to move, to swim. Blinking for a long moment helps my vision clear, for the most part, but a section keeps moving—no, *shifting* as a witch wends her way through the congregation. Swathed in a dark cape, she could be a duppy intent on claiming anyone who steps in her way for the life after.

Wait.

Light Keeper's twitch.

She wasn't offended; she was *signaling* for the Nameless Stealth assassin slipping through the crowd like smoke. One who must be using her training to camouflage herself from the magi she moves between, guzzu of concealment and bewilderment, to prevent onlookers realizing the threat in their midst.

The doyenne continues to speak, unaware, which means the killer is masked from her too—but not me. I pat my sides. There, where Light Keeper pressed earlier, a rough-spun bag has been pinned. My fingers edge away from it, knowing that an animal eye sits within, one spiked with a Stealth guzzu to help me *see*.

And I've seen enough.

I can't stand here and watch the Nameless kill her. Not when I still need her. But no sooner do I take a step forward, open my mouth to cry a warning, than a hand clamps over my face and drags me back against a hard body.

"Don't," a voice I know as surely as my own murmurs.

Anya.

My eyes dip. Her hand is cold, hard, and painted *gold*.

She's been the statuary this entire time.

"You don't understand," I say, my words muddled by her palm.

"With all due respect, Emissary," Light Keeper whispers, "it's you who doesn't understand. You don't have to make the tough decisions alone. You don't even have to delegate them. Sage advisors will do what's necessary for you."

"No—*please*. Don't—"

"However," Doyenne Cariot calls.

I fall quiet, looking across the balcony with wide eyes.

"Decisions made at sea are often changed on land. Our voyage has been a decade long, and at times it wasn't entirely certain that the waters would still enough to permit us to sail home, but still they have. So it is with a heartfelt thanks to our previous Yielders, whose sacrifices defended our way of life, that we can now leave the tempests in our wake."

Anya inhales sharply behind me.

"Henceforth I have made the decision to put an end to the Yielding, until such a time as our order may have need of the enchantment again. It's time to beat a story on a new drum, Alumbrar." The doyenne flicks her wrist at the Kumina drum players, the dancers, to strike up their ruckus once more. "It is time to burn bright."

Slowly the crowd comes to life, unthawing with murmurs, and then cries of elation as hope sprouts, bursting through hard soil on a night in which I didn't think it could flourish.

Mercies bestowed.

After a lifetime of war, my order is finally at peace.

4

IRA

There's nothing like the potential betrayal of your oldest and best sistren, a friend closer to you than any other, to challenge any doubts about avenging your murdered parents.

The ways of Obeah in matters of vengeance are clear. It is *justice* to take in equal part that which was stolen from you, and my family would expect me to follow the teachings of Duilio, the god of Metal, Blood, and War. But to ignore the Jade Guild's fight Kaleisha wishes us to find and join outside would make the scarification on my forehead, and hers too, a mockery. One that would risk offending Clotille, the goddess of Warriors. Deities are like the dead; not seeing them doesn't mean they're not walking among us.

Our scarification drew Kaleisha and me together in here initially, though she possesses two of four vertical scars between her brows, and I just the one. They advertise our

Warrior métier to the world, the field in which we chose to specialize. It doesn't matter that we were trained in different covens; the scars bind us by Clotille's ancient code of honor, one that dictates we put our order's safety first and all other matters second.

"You'll soon be joined together," the prison guard continues from her platform.

The speech has been long and tedious, but *joined* leaves five more words until I need to make a decision that, frankly, should have been made months ago. Beside me, Kaleisha murmurs the words along with the guard, having heard the speech in Inheritance Days of the past, sure in her choice to fight at the end of our countdown. Confident that waiting until the moment before they connect our shackles will leave the guards vulnerable to attack. Dauntless in mind and body.

"Exercise deference and this can be over shortly," the guard drones.

Deference was the fourth word.

Obeah look equal parts frightened and relieved as guards move between them. Their eagerness to leave the confines of Carne is a tangible thing that cuts through the mire and grunge of a prison meant for the forgotten.

But while we may have been the unremembered temporarily, we didn't forget.

We remember how the Alumbrar feigned submission before eventually killing the Obeah first family and the majority of their most experienced practitioners of magic. We remember how fate allowed the same hands that trapped us to strip our only inheritance from us too.

My hands tighten around the bone weapons. Fate should know where she can stick it.

As the third and second signal words are said in quick succession, I look to Kaleisha and find she's already moved away from me and into position.

Ready? the tilt of her head asks.

"Yuh deh! Inmate!"

All prisoners flinch at the bark that cuts through the crowd like the curve of an executioner's scythe.

"What do you have in your hands? Are those *weapons*, inmate?"

A sea of Obeah-dark and Alumbrar-silver heads swivel to Officer Carsten and the cutlass she's stabbing in Kaleisha's direction. Usual moxie gone, my sistren is nothing more than a cornered animal. Brown eyes wide with fear, she opens and closes her mouth like the hand Carsten levels at her is wrapped around her throat.

"Lock it down!" the guard yells. "Them 'bout to bruckout!" Her comrades charge forward at the warning of imminent attack. Their will incites glowing shields to extend from their conduits like blown bubbles, forming a shimmering fence of magic around the inheritors.

Kaleisha's eyes dart to mine. In a second, that fear is replaced with an insidious smirk. I meet it in kind as I rotate the bones in my hands, revealing the sharpened edges I've been concealing in my palms. They're big enough and weighty enough to come from a forearm or thigh of one of the beasts that hunt in the mountain beneath the prison. I take a breath I haven't in a while, one by which I utter a prayer to Clotille to bless me with accuracy and intent. Twisting from my waist as I was once taught, I launch the bone baton above the shoulder-height shields with all my might. Carsten, focused on ordering guards, is caught unawares. She screams as my weapon sinks into her neck. Her cry burbles away in a cataract of blood.

"Now!" I roar.

The rest of the members in Kaleisha's Bone Orchestra propel their instruments at the wraparound mezzanine above, striking the overhead guards who didn't think to shield. Why would they? They believe the Obeah to fear were poisoned and defeated, their armies left to drown in their own sick, their allies fled, and their rule decimated.

Cows.

Horseplay.

When the first body smacks against concrete, chaos breaks loose on the ground level. Kaleisha only recruited ten Obeah to escape with her, with us. But rebellion is like wildfire—once it catches, there's no hope of escaping its reach. Before too long, the prisoners in their cells, the ineligible, are the only ones who stand and watch. Every one of my ilk outside engages guards in combat.

Fueled by a decade of hatred, women hurl their tired bodies at the Alumbrar guards. Ferocious snarls tear from mouths that've been silenced for too long; bodies smash onto the cracked foundations, grappling for dominion. Grayed brown skin gleaming with sweat, my order parry against magical shields with the Obeah's zeal for battle. For victory. I breathe it in, consuming the memory of who we once were—who we could be again. Rulers, innovators, victors.

A clash of steel sparks in my face; the only thing that saves me is a cross of bones in Kaleisha's hands. "Struggling to keep up?" she sings, slamming her shackled fists into my attacker's copious bosom. The guard howls in agony; her long silver twists squirm like they too are in pain as she flies back.

"Never." With something adjacent to a smile, I lunge, driving my shiv into the side of another guard's neck. Life gushes from her in a reverse fountain of youth. I skip over it, the pain of my shackles kept at bay by the thrum of adrenaline.

An amber spark flashes in my periphery—guzzu, one of suppression. I duck, taking an Alumbrar body with me as a shield. Relieving the now-incapacitated guard of her weapon, I also take her hand with a brutal thud of the blade, tucking it into the waistband of my undergarments. We'll need the magical glyph on her palm to pass through the warded doors.

Bone in one hand, cutlass in the other, I cleave my way through the guards. With just three years under my belt, before the Viper's Massacre, my Warrior training was insufficient. Kaleisha, who learned to use a weapon before she could walk, is responsible for this deftness.

My muscles remember her whispered tips for me to practice under the cover of nightfall in my cell, the times she aggravated the vermin in the mountain beneath so I was ready for this moment. Her eyes are triumphant as ours meet between blows, a proud teacher basking in her student's success—until a cry sounds from across the prison.

A dark, jagged hole sparks clean through the center of an Obeah's stomach. Only one guzzu results in edges that smoke red. Death. My breath catches.

The guards aren't trying to subdue us anymore.

They're killing us.

Kaleisha's still, gaping at the fallen body. Battle dulls in my ears. Most of the Orchestra don't notice we've just lost a player, or that, in turn, they'll be killed too before we can make headway. Without magic, they're powerless—*I'm* powerless. I'll die.

And for my parents, Empress Cordelia Adair and Admiral Vincent Adair, I have to live.

My decision might not have been simple, but it's never been clearer. Breaking for a clear door, I tug the guard's severed hand from beneath my smock.

"Ira!" Kaleisha bellows the two harsh syllables.

Once *Ira* was used by Dada as a loving moniker. Now it only serves to remind me that I'll never again hear him use it. I almost don't turn back, but I owe my sistren this much. She takes a step toward me, favoring her left leg. Blood gushes from a cut on her right. Still, her shoulders are thrown back, her eyes bright.

"What are you doing?"

A frantic rhythm beats across the summoning drums; it almost jolts the hand from my grip. More guards are coming. Too many.

"I'm sorry." I try for indifference, but the words lodge in my throat. "I have to live for my family."

"We're family." Her voice breaks. "*I'm* your family."

The crack in her voice threatens to undo me. I could tell her there's no way she can win here. Not if they're killing us. We need magic to match the Alumbrar.

"Ira?"

But I don't.

Hating me will make it easier for her to forget me.

"I'm sorry." I slap the bloody hand against the door; its magic absorbs me through the wards to the other side, a decaying labyrinth of shadowy corridors filled with easy pickings now I know the guards still haven't learned to fight like the Obeah.

That was the idea, anyway.

Instead, I find my chest one inhalation away from a golden conduit coin set into the snarling shadowcat-topped guard of a wickedly curved saber.

"Move and you'll lose a limb." The male's voice lands as effectively as I imagine his blade would. And if he doesn't favor the first, there's a plainer hunting knife in his left hand. It's topped with bone. "Drop the weapons. Now."

Benefiting from a power I cannot face as I am, I comply.

"Inheritor, your fate has long been set. Did you really believe we'd let you escape?" His stare's as entitled as a Warrior's tends to be. It's also curious. That makes two of us.

His eyes, lined in smudged black kohl, are a rich green, and his dark hair is straight and fine. Both traits are native to an island who would be foolish to send their ilk sniffing around here after the usurpation they offered us no help in fighting. If my mouth wasn't so dry, I'd spit.

"Nothing to say?" That emerald gaze drops to his blade, following a long chestnut-colored finger running across its length. I follow that finger, too. It's scarred enough to suggest it's highly skilled. "I have ways to loosen tongues."

My stomach tightens.

"If I tell you why I tried to escape," I whisper. "Will you promise to keep it to yourself?"

He scoffs. "Yeh mon."

"That lacked a bit of conviction—any conviction, actually." I tut. "Can't tell you now, can I? I don't go around sharing my secrets as it is." The smirk that lights my face welcomes challenge. "Especially not with traitorous lapdogs."

Those eyes widen in shock before narrowing to cold chips. The scent of rich spice and metal swarms between us as he steps closer. I tilt my chin up to meet that irritation—that interest—simmering in his stare.

"When the Obeah ruled this empire, your secrets would've had some sway. But this is a new age. There's no empire, no empress, and your order has fallen here." The Warrior steps closer until our chests all but touch. "How do you like that for a bark?" he growls. Seizing my upper arm, he jerks me away from the door. Devouring the corridor with lengthy strides, he never once stops to think that I'm the one who caught him.

If the doyenne's in the market for a powerful new shield, then fleeing a warded cell with a stolen weapon amidst a bloody riot should be enough to secure my place by her side. An Adair and a Cariot working together once more to protect Aiyca from threat, for a time.

And then I'll kill her.

I wanted to believe in Kaleisha's plan, but even before the guards snuffed out one of our own, deep down I knew it could never be more than a means to an end. No matter how different I wished it to be. Nana's advice about trouble taught me that an Obeah-witch is nothing without intentions.

Doyenne Cariot will learn too late how dangerous mine are.

5

JAZMYNE

Anya, Light Keeper, and the Nameless assassin vanished soon after the announcement of the Yielding's cancellation, but it isn't until Doyenne Cariot is converged upon by disappointed presiders and firstborns that I have the opportunity to go after my sistren. I know exactly where she'll have disappeared to.

Inaccessible to the masses in the courtyard, the palace is quiet enough that my thoughts fill its halls and nooks. Light Keeper's decision to act in my best interests isn't so surprising, not when I'm untested, but to set me up to be stopped by Anya? What does it say about my relationship with her that she would agree? Especially when she is one of two people who knows my doubts about my readiness to rule.

I make my way to my suite and fling open the doors.

The splashing of water becomes louder with each room I move through, receiving and dining, music, games, and finally sleeping and the adjoining bathing chamber. Anya didn't enkindle any of the witchlights, so the deep purple and gold of the furnishings, the walls, seems even darker at this time of night—or is it morning now? Forgoing the four-poster, I perch on the edge of a settee and wait. Fishing my locket out from between my breasts, I run a thumb back and forth across its plain surface, seeking comfort in the familiar.

"Figured you wouldn't mind me coming here" are her first words upon egressing the bathroom in one of my robes, chased by a specter of steam. "We needed somewhere to talk in private, and I needed to rid my body of all that paint. It was starting to itch."

"What's there to talk about?" Far from containing the vitriol I would have liked, my voice is a pale imitation, a cousin of the vapor lingering in my room. "Light Keeper was going to have the doyenne killed; you knew about it and didn't say anything to me."

Anya shucks her robe, knowing her nakedness will make me turn away. She doesn't want me to see her face. But I know her sleights of hand, and I won't be silenced.

"I've never defended the doyenne from your hatred," I say. Not after Madisyn died, and Anya was broken. Their relationship had been over for a while, but that didn't lessen her anguish. "I've respected your feelings. Why couldn't you respect mine?"

She kisses her teeth. "Are we still having this argument?" The question is muffled by whatever she pulls over her head. She's dressing. Good.

"We will until you stop expecting different from me. I'm not you."

"You're not a pickney anymore either," she snaps. "By now I'd have thought it easier to push your fear aside to step up and save your order from the witch responsible for killing your sister, not to mention countless others."

She's standing with her legs hip width apart and draped in the dark fabric of her métier when I turn around. Wet, her silver hair glints like thousands of blades in the moonlight filtering in through the floor-to-ceiling windows behind her.

"I need more time," I grind out. "And I won't let you or anyone else walk her bloody path to put me somewhere I'm not ready to be. Not when you're incapable of thinking clearly."

Anya's gaze drops. "You can believe all I want is revenge for Madisyn—" Her voice snags on my sister's name, hooked on the feelings of their past the way a loose thread catches.

And just like that, my *heart* catches.

Two years on and she's still hollow. I can't be mad at her when grief gutters through me with ease too, when it steals me of my reason at times. Contrite, I reach for Anya's hand, clasp it in mine.

"This isn't about revenge," she insists, blinking back tears. "The doyenne *needs* to die. Not just to rid the island of horrors like the Yielding, but for you to inherit. You're not a firstborn. You don't have the luxury of waltzing over to Carling Hill on your earthstrong, touching your family tree, and receiving your ancestral magic. They won't recognize you without her death." She clasps *my* hand now, ever the big sister. "When she's gone, you'll see that you don't need her. You'll see that you already know how to rule, with compassion, restraint, and wisdom. It's because of you that we will have a future to be prouder of than our past. But as long as she lives, we'll never reach it." She lays a hand to my cheek; I turn into it. "Tonight's decision means you have a little time to make peace with what must be done."

Must.

I stiffen; she pretends not to notice.

Reconciled, at least with one another, Anya and I make our way out to the Courtyard of Moons, where the celebration is in full swing. Pickney totter about, gummy mouths stretched wide in grins as they're permitted to greet the dawn. I smile too, pleased they'll grow without the threat of the Yielding. Ascension takes on new meaning tonight. There's a freedom in my order's movements, an unfiltered brightness shining from their faces. This is how our reign should have been from the beginning—it's how I'll ensure it remains, when I'm doyenne.

Mercifully, that's another few months off. If the doyenne will permit me to sit on the throne once I'm eighteen. Something Light Keeper and I will need to discuss again, at some point.

"You should join in," Anya says, a rare light in her eyes as she beholds our order. "Save me a dance." She presses a kiss to my cheek before leaving to track down the first battalion.

They're working security, tonight. Xanthippe tend to make people uncomfortable during celebrations like this with the stiff black and gold of their uniforms, their abundance of conduit metal. Aiyca's night soldiers are far more benign as Stealths dress for the shadows they occupy. Their subtle presence around the courtyard ensures the doyenne's personal vanguard won't need to leave the First Family Alcove unless it's absolutely necessary—so when two members of the coven shoulder their way toward me, my mind retreats to the worst places.

The doyenne knows about my involvement with the Nameless.

No. *She knows about the assassin.*

No. *She's changed her mind about canceling the Yielding.*

"Emissary," the first says, her silver hair twisted back from her face in two thick horns. "Your presence is requested in the palace." She takes up her position on my left; her partner stands to my right.

"Of course."

Be measured. Be steady.

The words form part of the Healer maxim we'd recite before making an incision or repairing a bone. Healing requires more skill than the Bush Magic practiced by Obeah. They always use the ancestors to guide their movements, but for Alumbrar our hands suffice. I unclench mine, letting them swing free by my sides. If it's merely suspicions the doyenne has about my involvement, I won't let my body confirm her Stealth-honed instincts. I have some too, thanks to Anya.

Once the Xanthippe have left me in the doyenne's study, however, it quickly becomes clear that her concerns have little to do with me. Standing before the fireplace, dwarfed by its high mantel, she clutches a journal I've seen her study from time to time close to her chest with one hand; the other touches her scarred eye like its long-dead tissue just squirmed, and the world stops turning—my world.

Something is very wrong.

"Doyenne?"

She doesn't give any sign that she heard me. She just stands there, a hand to her face.

She never told me what happened to her eye, and we've never had a relationship where I could ask, but there are hushed rumors that speak of Obeah-men invading her home when she was a pickney. They did *things* to her, to Nana Cariot; the shame drove Nana to take her own life, and Grampa to take the sight from one of the doyenne's eyes in restitution for being unclean. Madisyn told me the doyenne requested the delicate threading to hide the color her eye turned when her sight was taken—white.

Obeah white.

It's a color they wear in battle, in death, in celebration of life and love. It's a blazoning sigil of who they once were— infinite, both the surf of waters necessary for life and the wandering clouds that lorded over us.

How much of the story is true, I don't know. But white as a color has been banned from wardrobes and homes across the island, indefinitely; I suspect that if the doyenne could remove every grain of sand from Aiyca's iridescent beaches, she would. Her hatred of the Obeah made her do whatever it took to maintain the Alumbrar rule. Even if that meant killing pickney every year. Including her own.

"Doyenne?" I repeat. "Has something happened?"

She seems to come out of herself, physically drawing back from wherever her mind went. Her hand drops from her face as though burnt, and she zeroes in on me with a singular focus.

"There's been a bruckout in Carne Prison."

That's it?

My brow furrows. Why is she so concerned? Obeah riot every few months there.

"I need you to go to Carling Hill ahead of me with a phalanx of Xanthippe." She glides to her desk and exchanges the journal for a golden bell. It illuminates at her touch but makes no sound as it's rung to summon the guard. "Once I've made my excuses, I will follow."

"You don't need to come. I can oversee the inheritors myself."

"Carling Hill is adjacent to wetland area, Emissary," she snaps, with both her words and a temper she usually keeps leashed. I rear back, braced as they spring like feral prowlers in the bush. "Do I need to remind you who dwells in that territory? Obeah insurgents who walk across its bogs and marshes like duppies when Xanthippe are devoured in the sludge."

"F-forgive me."

"Think smarter and I wouldn't have to." Her eye bores into my own.

She's not wrong to chastise.

"The prisoner galley has yet to leave, but I want you sifted there. You are, as ever, to be the eye I rely on in my stead, Emissary. Do not let me down."

"I won't."

Fourteen or so Xanthippe have answered her magical summons. They're gathered in the hall outside the study. Standing between two, I grip both their forearms. The gold stitched into their uniforms, and the coins hanging from chains around their necks, flare with light; magic's hook snags my core, and then we are gone before I have too long to contemplate what about this bruckout is different.

6

IRA

Emerging from the darkness of a crevice at the base of Carrion Mountain, upon which Carne Prison precariously hangs, is like being born again.

My legs, weakened by the fight and all the stairs hewn within the sprawling range, buckle at the onslaught of fading stars, brightening sky, generating grumbles from the prisoners shackled in the line behind me. It's been so long since I've seen any natural light, I forgot how expansive the world is beyond Carne's walls. The air smells like salt and rain. Like possibilities.

"Why have you stopped, inheritor?" that nuisance Warrior snaps. Carne Sea laps at where he stands on the shingled shore. Shame it's not with a big enough tongue to pull him under. "Step fast, and step quick."

With a scowl, I shuffle forward. His comment grates all the

more so because he isn't wrong. Now isn't the time to stop and admire the view. Not when there's more to be done.

Ira, an unassuming orphan picked up by an Alumbrar patrol on the palace grounds when the Adairs fell, might be on the dossier for conscription, but *Iraya Adair*, who moved away from the palace under mysterious circumstances at the age of five, and, not being seen since, has become the fodder of Anansi stories, will be a wild-card entry, should the voyage run without a hitch. Though I doubt it will be smooth sailing with Kaleisha, cut and bruised but alive, thank the goddess, somewhere in the line behind me.

A mahogany galley, flying sails painted dark by the ebbing night, bobs at the end of an ancient dock seesawing in its moorings. Xanthippe line its sides, somber and ominous in high-collared uniforms of black, for the Stealth doyenne they serve, and gold, the color of leadership stolen from my family.

Carne's guards would have sent a missive requesting the coven's support. It's routine procedure after a revolt. Though they wouldn't stand against the legendary Obeah warrior covens of the past, the doyenne's chosen enforcement are mean and not wholly unimaginative with their magical punishments, I've heard—the only weapon they need. With the thick coins hanging from gold chains around their necks, and the conduit metal spliced through the piping in their uniforms too, even I wouldn't risk challenging them without magic of my own.

It's a relief when boarding passes without incident, and, sails engorged, the prisoner ship drifts away from Carne to cleave a path through wind-tossed waters. I don't look back.

Overhead, dawn flowers like a bruise. Pinioned against its backdrop, archipelagoes rise like monsters from the eponymous gulf separating the three largest islands in what was once known as the Xaymaca Empire, before the Viper's Massacre and subsequent dissolution into three independent islands.

Most of the smaller archipelagoes are uninhabited, home to mines, wild with creatures and bush, or outposts for Aiyca's coastal guard, but a collection are home to pirates: the Iron Shore. As steely and sharp as its name, the minatory spears of rock became a refuge of sorts for criminals and runaways escaping the rules of the empire. Were it not for their magicless existence, I don't doubt that empresses of old and Mama would have sunk them to unknown depths. As for how Doyenne Cariot is keeping them subdued, it can't be with the shields alone . . . she must be drawing muscle from elsewhere too. Perhaps Zesia?

It's the second biggest island after mine, Aiyca. And Zesia never let us forget it. Its people's existence was a constant whine for more territory, more trade, and more control across the empire. Doyenne Cariot must have promised an amicable emancipation if they didn't come to our aid, exchanging their independence for fealty. The presence of that bothersome Warrior from earlier tells me that.

He stands across the ship on the upper deck, surveying the line where sea meets sky, perhaps seeking the sand dunes and deltas of his home. His dark hair streams behind him in gods-damn silky tendrils. As if I didn't have reason enough to hate him when mine is stiff with dirt beneath a scrappy head tie.

As if he sensed my focus, his eyes flicker over. A potent surge of spite spikes through me; it's returned in kind by the narrowing of his gaze and the tightening of his brow.

Ready for round two? I can't help challenging with a tilt of my head.

"Before you get too seasick, listen up," he calls in a commanding voice, striding across the deck on his long, powerful legs. Xanthippe edge out of his way, their eyes wary. They bear more gold, but he is Obeah, and carrying a bone-hilted hunting knife. "You can see my weapons, my scarification. They're not decorative."

Peeking above the neckline of his shirt beneath a sweeping obsidian cloak, the coil of war rites climbs the wide column of his strong neck like thorn-laden vines—vines I wish I could choke him with. It's only the Alumbrar, after all, who honor their métiers with color. How can he have the nerve to stand before us and use his as a threat like most of us don't bear our own scars? Many unseen, at that.

"Take it from me." His eyes burn into mine like mutton hitting the bottom of a fiery Dutch pot. "An uprising won't work a second time. Once we dock in Aiyca, there'll be a short walk to reach Carling Hill. Once you've recited the Vow of Peace, as per the terms of your parole, you'll visit your family trees to be imbued with your ancestors' magic."

And magic means killing the doyenne, I remind myself.

There are many unanswered questions about the Zesian, but I need to keep a low profile, so I play the demure role and look away—right at a seething Kaleisha.

Well. I think, bracing myself for what's surely coming. *I wanted her to hate me.*

Switching from demure to irreverent, sure to irritate her further, I cock a hip against the ship's side. "You survived. I'm glad."

"No thanks to *you*," she snarls.

Those around us fall silent; even the sounds of retching fade.

"How could you leave us—leave me?"

Something twinges in my chest. Beneath Kaleisha's anger, there's a fissure of vulnerability, a weakness I could inveigle my way into with apologies and excuses. A longing to return back to the way things were squats on my chest, unignorable and vexing.

"We could have won," she continues when I don't proffer a response—can't. "But you secured our loss when you ran like a coward." She takes a step forward, forcing the other prisoners to jerk with her. The shackles rattle like an out-of-tune instrument.

Would it matter if I told her that by running, I drew the guards' focus away from her and the Bone Orchestra?

No.

It must be this way.

"Call me a coward again," I purr, more than spoiling for the chance to use fists and teeth instead of words and feelings. "I'll show you how unafraid I am." Which of us would win? She trained for longer, but she has taught me all her tricks.

"You tagereg," she spits.

Criminal. Liar. General cretin. She could call me worse.

"*Unlit* is better suited," another of the surviving Bone Orchestra members heckles.

I rear back, caught off guard.

That is worse.

Unlit is the lowest and most maligned status any Aiycan can carry. It's only bestowed to those who killed their own for nefarious reasons, selfish reasons.

That's what they think of me?

"Unlit doesn't work for her," Kaleisha says; for a moment I think it's in my defense, but her expression gapes like a wound and I know it's not. "They were stripped from their families, their magic, their métiers, and then left to die in the darkest parts of Aiyca. They didn't decide that. Ira chose to walk away from us." She takes a step toward me; a tear trails down her left cheek. "I trusted you. Do you have any idea what that means?"

"Enough!" the Zesian snaps. "Get back to your holds."

Danger flashes in Kaleisha's eyes; for a moment I think she'll risk the punishment, but she swipes at spilled tears and turns her back in another slight. I can only blink as the file uncoils, and I'm left with my neighbors, who angle away from me as if they wish they too could leave—Obeah I sorted coffee beans with, others who shared my table during mealtimes, survivors from a rebellion I used to secure my own success. . . .

This time, with Kaleisha's shoulders raised and shaking as she's comforted by mutual sistren, it's not so easy to exonerate my guilt. That earlier twinge flits through my core. Kaleisha's

55

name rises to the tip of my tongue, and so do apologies, reasons—the truth.

In the world before, I wouldn't have dreamed of fighting alone. I trained with a coven of sistren in arms, fellow Warriors-in-training. Had they asked, I would have found a way to banish night so there was only ever day.

But in order to see this mission through, friendship isn't a handicap I can afford.

I shake the stubborn regrets loose, letting the warm winds of the sea buffet them away as we storm east, to Aiyca, to Doyenne Cariot.

I didn't leave prison to be a hero.

We're not long into our journey before the rocking of the prisoner ship makes me think of Dada. Admiral Adair, né Clarke. It's not right that I'm on a galley without him.

Xaymaca was an empire of land, sky, and sea. While the standing army in Zesia and the aerial wing in the reclusive Skylands claimed the former two respectively, Dada's wisdom earned Aiyca's armada its esteem. Of course now there's only a coastal guard, with the Masters who sailed with Dada also killed by the Alumbrar, I assume.

My first time aboard a vessel was an introduction to his, *Cordially Yours*. Much to my disappointment, it lacked the obviously fearsome name of other famous galleons, like *Queen Anne's Revenge* and *Death's Handmaiden*, but that was Dada. He was always so measured; even his voice was nothing more than the stroke of a gull's wing against a wave . . . at least, that's how it feels in my memories. I no longer remember its sound.

I miss him so badly that, for a moment, I'm breathless with it.

A decade in Carne showed me that death isn't an absence that fades over time. It's a sharp stab that dulls into a persistent murmur. I turn my face into the spray launched upward from the ship's keel to hide the tears that managed to escape.

Typically, I'm adept at shuttering my feelings off. Mama taught me that.

Her opinions about life were polarized to Dada's sense of adventure. She found existence, our existence, synonymous with duty and little else. Her ancestors were empresses. They were bound by duty—anchors held in port interminably. I suspect that's why she and Dada were so compatible, and why, though I can't see her face anymore, I still feel the cold sting of her disappointment.

From a young age I knew I wasn't built to sit at a dock, to weather storms I could never chase. She didn't understand. Not when I tried to tell her, and not when I ran away from home shortly after my fifth earthstrong to live with my paternal grandmother, Nana Clarke, at her Warrior training outpost in the mountains. Mama never stopped trying to bring me home. Then I resented it; now I can't help feeling sorry that those moments—me cowering while Nana fought for my right to choose, and Mama shouting that for Adair women, ruling wasn't a choice—were our last.

I draw in a sharp breath, and another. Now isn't the time

to fall apart. At the very least, because I don't need Kaleisha to think me weakened. She'll only try to approach me again.

I raise a shoulder to wipe my nose against and inadvertently find the Zesian in my line of sight once again. He converses with the captain, gesticulating broadly. To think that those hands have a greater hold on Aiyca than my order is even more unsettling than the rocking of the deck beneath my feet.

When the doyenne chooses me to become her new shield— there's nothing like positive thinking—the Xanthippe won't cause too much of a problem for my magic. But the Zesian has skill they do not. He's the Genna here, for some reason. The coven fall behind him, which means Doyenne Cariot trusts him in some capacity.

It's a mistake.

His saber holds a lone conduit coin in its guard, one that's smaller than those worn by Xanthippe—and a lie. I know my ilk. Alumbrar believe magic usage is to be limited by the goddess Aurore, the Mudda's Face of Creation, hence the smaller quantity of gold they carry, but for Obeah magical expenditure is dependent upon its wielder's will, of which we have plenty.

Factoring in all the menial tasks the Zesian most likely uses his magic for, he'd burn through that tiny coin in a year, maybe less, wearing down his mind and body from the strain of channeling through such a small quantity of metal. And yet he bears no signs of magical fatigue. He can't be older than twenty; his skin is smooth, the muscles tight, and his face, however punchable, isn't entirely displeasing. If he's not burning through that small coin, he has to be hiding a surfeit of gold, and if he's hiding it, he's not to be trusted.

I rub my forehead, massaging away a headache. Looks like Zesia, still ruled by an Obeah first family I believe, is up to its old game of vying for power, something the Alumbrar might not have anticipated when they gave them their independence. Gods. What state of affairs am I sailing toward? Another usurpation?

Trouble doesn't give signs like rain.

I didn't listen to Nana's words ten years ago. Now I cannot afford to make that same mistake again.

7

JAZMYNE

We reach the foot of Carling Hill in that moment before dawn when duppies are emboldened and those who've yet to inherit magic should not go wandering in its deep, dark bush.

Gasping for air after the sift, I lean into my knees. Without magic of my own to regulate the speed of the travel, at first it feels like someone's wringing my lungs, then blades of air whet themselves against my body as it fragments and contracts all at once. Just when I feel like I'm about to die of suffocation, it's over.

Straightening, with some difficulty, I look to the hill's mouth. It's as far as magic usage is permitted here, in deference to the dead. Carling Hill literally means "where witches gather." It houses trees of immeasurable meaning to all Aiycans, for it's where our family trees grow. It's also where many of our ancestors linger, matriculating to the trees' roots—which I can already see are cloaked in shadows. Bulky ones that seem to pulsate and swallow what little light manages to penetrate the canopy of leaves overhead.

I'm not the only one in our party who makes no move to enter the twisting scion archway.

The Xanthippes' conduit coins blaze with golden light, like the gleam of gator eyes in the dark, before the knot of trees that chitter with activity before us—chitter with warnings. Even after years of coming here, the coven members still fear what's inside: angry spirits eager to disorient and distract; runaways driven mad by the dead, dehydration, starvation; pirates lying in wait to rob magi of gold . . . but none of them will compare to what the doyenne will do if we don't make it through before the inheritors arrive.

Bare your teeth like a predator even if at times you feel more like prey.

I raise my chin. "Onward."

Venturing into the bush, a snare of tension entangles itself around my spine. The weather doesn't help. There's no wind, no air, only the incessant stillness of heat trapped in a space with no escape, so its only option is to keep expanding.

Xanthippe grumble around me as the ground tilts and we find ourselves wading upward. Underfoot the earth's uneven. I turn my ankle more times than I can count, and, despite my earlier bravado, I flinch at every rustle of leaves above us as bough-prowlers track our movements through the dark.

Minutes seep into hours as we struggle to reach the top of the hill. Irritated and sticky, I lift my hair from the back of my neck when a humid tangle of wind stirs. It's the first breeze I've felt since we arrived, but stale and fetid, it's far from pleasant. As I pause to free a breast-length silver curl from where it catches in the chain of my locket, silence surrounds with a suddenness that makes my breath painfully loud.

It's not the quiet I seek solace in when I visit the palace temple to pray.

It's one armed with claws and teeth.

The Xanthippes' conduits seem to shrink as the encompassing murk swells. That sour wind masses, and the air thickens with the feeling of diaphanous forms. I'm turned this way and that, buffeted by bodies I can't see, only feel as they peal by with a blistering chill, zipping in and out of our formation. Several guards jolt back. Wide-eyed, they touch their faces. Blood drips from gashes on their cheeks.

It's not for us to limit the ancestors to our worldly understanding.

Those words might come straight from the Mudda's most mysterious Face, Aurore, but we all know the truth. Bargaining with the dead isn't an act of Alumbrar—it's Obeah territory. And the spirits, Alumbrar, Obeah, or indifferent, know it.

"Pray," I order as the dead continue to press in around us. "Start praying. Now!"

We fall into hasty veneration, offering our prayers up to the Mudda for aid. For protection. Eyes squeezed shut, I mutter the same plea over and over. Time drags by interminably with the spirits blustering around us, but eventually they stand down. I exhale a long breath before I open my eyes, my body crumpling with relief.

"Is it safe?" one of the Xanthippe asks me.

"Just keep praying." I breathe. "We're almost there."

My heart thuds harder and faster, almost seeming to echo through the hill's abandoned stadium when we reach it at last—without further incident, by the Mudda's blessing. Posts as tall as a river is vast jut out from the bordering Hendern Cliffs. A goliath of wood, the cirque rings the entire concentric glade of family trees. Once, it was packed with families who would come to witness their own inherit in monthly ceremonies. With the Obeah's magical inheritance controlled by the Witches Council, and my own order never gathering in the ostentatious stadium, it now squats, empty, like the skeleton of something left to rot.

Alone in its heart, beneath a wide palm frond held aloft with her magic's invisible hand, the doyenne already sits on a subtler throne of smooth, maple-colored wood—I say *already*, but we wandered the bush for so long that dawn has now been succeeded by day. She must have sailed in, taken the staircase up the cliffside at the stadium's back.

She's accompanied by even more Xanthippe than I traveled with. They've adopted sentry positions around the glade. Their conduits are ablaze, magic at the ready, and they hold cutlasses across their chests. They're not usually armed with the weapons. Magic has always been enough for them. What about this bruckout has the doyenne so on edge?

I dip into a bow when I reach her. "Is there anything specific

I should be prepared for?"

"Everything." Hand raised to her lost eye again, she looks haunted; she looks *afraid*.

I've never seen her fear anything.

"I don't know what we'll see this morning, Emissary," she says, her voice almost snatched by the stale winds that stole from the bush behind our party.

Behind the stadium, a stone's throw away, Carne Sea ripples gold in the steepening sunrise. From this vantage point, it's easy to imagine the blanket of water without its fists, but the sea is as violent as the monsters who hide in its depths— and, perhaps, sail toward us across its waters. For what else could the doyenne fear?

Nervous, I think of Kirdan, as close to me as Anya, overseeing the inheritor transferal. Unease builds, buzzing in my ears. My eyes drift to the Xanthippe below, their weapons. The locket's chain tangles in my fingers. A sixteenth-earthstrong gift from Kirdan nearly two years ago now, it's become something of a token, a secret he and I share along with the friendship we keep from the doyenne, and with it our plan to smooth the fractious relations between my order and the Obeah in Aiyca. Gripping it, I pray for his safety.

The guards aren't preparing for some*thing*. They await some*one*.

I just wish I knew who.

8

IRA

Late-morning light stains Aiyca's great Hendern Cliffs by the time they thrust into sight. With a sheer face beaten back each day by Carne Sea, the monolithic structure is often described by griots, revered storytellers, as the calcified shoulders of a sea monster who rose from unknown depths to conquer Aiyca thousands of years ago.

The heart of the old empire, Aiyca's built upon stories like this. Some fact, most fiction, they thread through the island like its lifeblood, suffusing my home with mysteries and terrors I've missed as much as sunlight and clean air.

"Brace!" the captain calls.

His crew move in a flurry of activity to bind sails and shift masts. Aiyca's wards push back as we sail through. I'd heard of the iridescent barrier of protection, an Alumbrar creation, in Carne. I had my doubts. The magic seemed a little excessive for the self-abnegating order, yet here it is, reluctant to grant us passage despite the glyph or guzzu the ship must have to permit ingress. My fingers, numb with sea spray, fumble to catch the ties on the ship's side as others around me are displaced by the depth of the magic. We heave to and fro alongside the accompaniment of magi hurling up their guts and others keening with thanks to be home.

Home.

It's been too long.

We dock in a tiny port. Xanthippe bark orders at us to climb steps that cling to the mountainside like mussels. The bottom third are smooth and slick with seawater, making our progress slow. My legs cramp with the pressure to stay on my feet. Any guardrail belongs to the sea now. As will we, connected as we are, if even one falls. I will the Zesian to slip the entire way, but the Seven-Faced Mudda doesn't listen. They haven't in a long while.

There's a sudden influx of sunlight that stabs with as little mercy as I remember, and an unwelcome increase in humidity as we finally alight at the clifftop to stand before *her*, Doyenne Cariot, seated high in the stadium enclosing Carling Hill.

Pictures surface, unbidden, bobbing in the murky waters of memory—a featureless figure walking beside Mama through the palace, whispering in her ear during dinners, laughing with her like they were the closest of sistren, sharing drinks in her suite in the evening when my governess would bring me to say goodnight. She's always been there, lurking at the edge of the mental pictures I have of Mama, this witch, this sleeping viper who slithered her way into my family's graces before betraying them.

My knees buckle as a sudden burst of pain lances through my left forearm.

Worry permeates the haze. *Has she worked out that I'm here?* It's soon eclipsed by a crescendo of fire. My teeth sink into my lower lip to suppress a cry. The burn is like being blanched with a white-hot poker beneath my skin. I squint at the other prisoners. They all writhe and cry out in a similar torment, clutching their arms. Fighting dizziness, I look down. Magically burned on the space below the bend in my elbow is the ancient Glyph of Connection, formed by two small triangles with intersecting points.

"You are officially conscripts now," the Warrior announces, and the title I've wanted—needed—warps into an insult. One that's so savagely lupine, I feel the full force of the bite. My neck's aware of every scrape of teeth against flesh.

I expected the glyph after meeting prisoners in Carne who bore them, but—I touch the triangles, wincing. Seeing it, carrying it, is another matter. Griots tell stories of times of war when magi shared their magic to defeat enemies. They scarred themselves with the Glyph of Connection before exchanging blood to open a channel of communication between their magic. Two triangles. A call and an answer. Like all Obeah scars, it was conducted during a ceremony of the highest esteem, under the watchful eyes of the Seven-Faced Mudda's Battle Faces, Clotille and Duilio.

"These magi," the Warrior gestures at finely dressed

Alumbrar seated in the bottom row of the stadium, "are your Conscription Officers. They too bear the glyph and will take your blood every two weeks at your designated workplaces' stations." He strides down the line of prisoners, now conscripts. "Should you act out in any way, incur suspicion about your activities at work or home, these officers have the power to use your blood to shut you down via the Glyph of Connection, before sending you back to Carne."

I press my lips together, holding in my disgust. Ingesting blood to connect channels between these scars is a marriage of total trust and the deepest kinship. The Alumbrar have inverted the glyph into something ugly: censure, control, fear. Kaleisha's eyes are heavy on me from down the line.

"Palms out for conduits!"

"Just a moment."

The Xanthippe about to distribute our coins pause, and turn up to the stands, to the doyenne. The woman behind her—a girl, I notice upon closer inspection—with a brilliant nimbus of silver curls, twists and knots her fingers in her lap.

They know I'm here.

"I understand there's been insurgence already, this morning." Her voice is rotund with an Alumbrar's lofty condescension. "Emissary, what do you have to report?" She looks to the Zesian.

I twist his way. He's his island's political envoy? I've never seen shoulders or scars like his on any errand boy before.

"There was a revolt, yes," he says, his deep voice carrying with ease. "Many of the guards on duty were killed."

"And who was responsible?"

Never one to miss my cue, I step forward before the Zesian emissary has time to speak.

"That would be me."

The doyenne leans forward, resting her sharp chin on bridged fingers. "And you are?"

I can't help smirking as I say, "You know who I am," in a loud voice. "Iraya Cordelia Adair. Blessed of Aurore, First Face of the Supreme Being, Arrow of Clotille and Duilio, Battle Faces of the Supreme Being." My voice strengthens as past years of practice take over. "Defender of Carne Sea, Heir of the Xaymaca Empire, her territories, and the Monster's Gulf; first of my name, and the only living heir of Empress Cordelia and Admiral Vincent Adair. Pleasure to see you again, Doyenne Cariot, despite the circumstances."

Chatter erupts in the stadium.

Those in the line on either side of me crane their necks to look, but I only have eyes for the witch before me. She hasn't moved—frozen in fear, no doubt. Perhaps she *didn't* know I was here, ruining my opening line somewhat. But never mind. Now she'll wonder how she missed me, how they all missed me. Sometimes I wonder too, but Carne showed me Iraya Adair has so many hopes pinned to her, she's become more of a symbol than a recognizable person of flesh and bone.

"Iraya Cordelia Adair." Doyenne Cariot repeats my abbreviated name slowly, like it's foul to the taste. I hope it is. She holds a slender hand aloft to silence the buzz in the clearing. It trembles, I note with a spike of glee. "You'll forgive me for neglecting to repeat titles you no longer hold any claim to."

"A matter of opinion," I quip.

The Zesian starts forward, his mouth tight and his saber drawn.

She waves him away. "It is *fact*, and something I can concede to you being ignorant of, having spent most of your life in Carne. Let me propose some additional facts: you instigated a bruckout, a bloody one, it looks like." Her lone eye runs a searing trail down my body, my ruined prison smock and filthy legs and bare feet. "That suggests you have much influence, Obeah, for a girl long thought dead. Which leads me to my final fact: there's no place for insurgent influence on my island." She tips her chin at a cluster of Xanthippe. "Seize her."

Coven members move in on Doyenne Cariot's command. I hold fast beneath their threat.

This wouldn't be any fun if she didn't try to kill me at least once first.

"Perhaps you'd like to hear the offer I have for you before matters turn nasty."

She laughs. Full-bodied and deep, it carries with ease. "Wait." The Xanthippe stand down an arm's length away from me. "What could you have that I want?"

"It's more about what you already have and would like to keep. Something I can help you with. Choose me to become your next shield, and this island will never be torn from Aiycan hands."

The humor in her face has disappeared. "You won't seek to take it yourself?"

"Surely you can't think I'm that big of a threat to your position, mon?" I turn to the Conscription Officers. "What do you think?" I gesture at the thinness of my frame, the dusty pallor of my skin, jostling the shackles deliberately. "It's as you said, Doyenne, my title no longer matters. What does is my wish to keep Aiyca in the hands of its own. What does is my power. You of all people should understand the magic behind the Adair name. Think of what it can give you, Aiyca."

Something flickers in her face.

The shackles connecting me to those on my left and right fall away. Releasing a small sigh of relief, I'm tempted to wink at the Zesian, but he isn't looking at me. I follow his line of sight back to the doyenne, and all triumph wanes. In place of the resignation I expected is the cruel stroke of her smile. Smugness reduces her full lips to a sharp line upon which blades could be whetted.

"Búku a," she grinds out.

Alumbrar don't use deep patwah is my only thought before the guzzu hits my mouth like a fist. I'm knocked back to the damp earth; air shoots from my lungs. The magic binds my body, stilling me as something weighty crawls across my face on legs that pierce my skin like needles. I will myself to roll, shift, *anything*. My body doesn't respond. I can't dislodge the entity that settles atop my lips. Sharp legs stretch to settle behind my ears, gripping the skin there and forcing a snarl from between my teeth.

The thing over my mouth twitches once more before it becomes immobile.

My head spins as hands snatch me up. Alumbrar laughter tinkles like death knells in the sunlight.

"All you can give me, Iraya Adair," the doyenne intones, "is your death. The glyphs incised on the muzzle's metal will ensure that urge to pop style will be tempered during your journey to Cwenburg Palace's holding cells, where you will await execution."

My outrage about the muzzle is minimized only by her threat of death.

"Not out of fear, Iraya Adair," she continues. "But justice for your ancestors' role in squashing my order's presence in Aiyca century after century."

Something uncomfortably close to fear rears inside. Everything I heard in Carne, the intelligence I gathered, pointed to her needing a shield with more magic than the norm. She *needs* me. She needs me just as much as I need her. I mean to say this, to issue promises, evidence, but bile bubbles up the back of my throat and chokes me.

My voice.

She's taken my voice.

For several fraught seconds, the only sound atop the hill is my breath whistling through the grates of the muzzle. Its metal hooks are sharp teeth that bite into the skin behind my ears. The glade tilts as consciousness tries to evade me; sheer stubbornness is all that keeps me standing.

"Take her back to the palace." The doyenne's voice is distant, muffled. "I want an accompanying escort to travel with her."

Faintly I register metal whispering against metal as cutlasses are unsheathed. The blades are followed by footfall slapping upon fallen fronds.

It can't end like this, not when I'm so close.

Somewhere removed from my body, my name's uttered in

the movement of leaves. Lush with all manner of them, some flowering, the ancient giants within the glade seem almost sentient as they bow and wave in the light morning winds. Realization courses through my limbs in a rush of adrenaline as I realize it *doesn't* have to end like this.

Magic.

I don't have my magic yet.

"I'll join you when all is done here."

I cling to the doyenne's voice, clawing my way toward it like consciousness is air, and I've been drowning. I break the surface, and my mind clears.

Before the guards can take me anywhere, I cup my fists and swing them into the stomach of the one to my left. She doubles over with a surprised *oof*—but not before I've swung up and thumped the guard to my right in the face. She stumbles back, both hands going to her nose. Her cutlass goes flying; I swipe it and drive its broad edge down between my ankles. The shackles spring apart with a clash, and I abandon the weapon.

"Seize her!" the doyenne bellows.

I've already taken off as if the wind itself lent me wings.

Something visceral and wild urges me on. Weaving to avoid bolts of guzzu from Xanthippe conduits, I bear down on the line of guards standing between me and the concentric landscape of family trees. A spark of suppression splinters a tree behind them. I duck, arms flying overhead. With any luck, their poor aim will split my wrist shackles too. Two more sparks take out a pair of guards—there's my opening. Every muscle screams in protest as my legs pump, driving my body onward until I'm within striking distance, at which point I divert, pivoting to the exposed side and plunging into the family trees.

Chaos explodes behind me, screams and bellows. It sounds like—it sounds like another revolt from the conscripts. *Kaleisha.* I offer up a prayer to Merce, the Mudda's Face of Compassion, to ensure this second attempt to flee will be a success for my sistren.

Driven by my racing heart, I leap over roots in the trees' close confines, flinging my body around wide trunks, ducking beneath low-hanging boughs as I tear a path to the center. The hard slap of the guards' sandals in pursuit pounds behind me.

Push. *Push*, I will myself each time I trip, eat dirt. Heavy with fatigue and light-headed, I run and run until I burst through a final thicket and find myself panting before the Adair family tree. It stands in the center of its smaller siblings, the One That Came First.

Gnarled, the lignum vitae tree impales the sky with its wide reach. It's Aiyca's strongest wood, and my family alone has the honor of calling it our family tree. Roots, large and twisted, plunge into the earth at my feet. The colossal trunk encompasses thrice as much space as the two trees on either side of it.

Invisible bodies swarm me—the spirits of the ancestors who've lingered by this tree waiting for their next heir. Waiting for me. They sweep me up and up farther until my feet leave the ground. I wish I could hear Dada among the whispers of the ancestors who coax my right arm forward until I'm reaching for the lowest-hanging bough. I can't, but I know he's here. Mama too. The waft of tobacco and fresh soap twisting around me is his scent. And the sweet coconut from the oil her attendants combed through her afro every night is hers.

An invisible hand wipes my tears away. Another knocks my elbow.

"*Arik na mi*," those voices whisper, ordering me to listen as they sing their ways in my ear. Above the growing clamor of guards, the sweet soprano of their rage is the featured soloist. Its melody is dagger-sharp and haunting. They too want justice, for the time that was stolen, the lives that were ended.

If I were an Obeah-man, Dada's magic would be all I inherit. But as an Obeah-witch, under the Seven-Faced Mudda's matriarchy, everything is mine. I stretch my fingers, the very core of me yearning for the command of my magic to show Doyenne Cariot—if she wishes to muzzle me like a beast, I won't just bite, I'll maul.

I touch the bough.

Its bark pulses beneath my fingertips, releasing a thrumming charge through my flesh that sinks deep into my bones. My limbs turn supple. My spine arcs back. Wind howls through the trees to join the ancestors' chorus; sunlight breaks through the canopy overhead to rain beads of light down on me in blessing. Eyes shut, I smile as even the earth trembles in this collision of the past and present, as magic meets witch in a furious flash of white-gold light.

9

JAZMYNE

An Adair still lives.

It's those words that ring in my ears, not the ruckus of her departure: rioting conscripts who push against Xanthippe who cast shields from conduits, bellow orders to fellow coven members to go after the small number who managed to escape. That's all secondary to the resurrection of a family name long thought dead.

Iraya Adair. Aiyca's first daughter. Xaymaca's Lost Empress.

Some Anansi stories depict her as an avenging messiah, biding her time to return and obliterate the Alumbrar for displacing her order. But that tale was meant to teach us caution, just as the one about the jéges teaches you not to hunt for fool's gold. Was it a mistake to believe it could ever be possible for such a legacy to be defeated? To be pressed between the doyenne's fingertips and extinguished forever? Seems so now.

Tension crackles around her where she sits. The tautness of her brow, her body, is the only visible sign that she's apoplectic with rage. She doesn't like surprises, especially not ones that pose a threat for the reign of Aiyca in lieu of just canceling the Yielding.

The Yielding.

Mudda above.

What if Iraya's emergence makes the doyenne renege on her word? She makes a decade of ruling look fragile enough to obliterate. And what of the Nameless's plans, *my* plans?

How will they stand against an infamous witch who would have been empress?

"Get down there."

I'm quick to rise from my seat. "Doyenne?"

"I want a report from Emissary Divsylar," she orders, her lips pursed. "I want the Xanthippe to bring me back those runaway conscripts." She hits the arm of her throne with a clenched fist. "And I want Iraya Adair returned to me. *Alive.* Go."

By the time I reach the bottom of the stadium steps, Kirdan prowls out of the tree line, sans Iraya and bearing a frown deep enough to carry a world of problems. Though, that's the expression he tends to sport when in the doyenne's company. I'm the only one fortunate enough to know a better side of him. Something that surprised us both, I think, that a bond could be formed between those from two polarized orders who've always hated one another.

I brush my hair behind my ears. *Are you all right?* the coded gesture asks.

He swats at his right ear, like he's ridding himself of a blood eater. *All is well.* The tension in my stomach unwinds some.

"The doyenne wishes to know how many guards were killed in Carne," I ask, professionally distant.

His eyes, a hue as verdant as the bush, also possess its dangers when he angles them up at where the doyenne watches. "The last count was thirty-three. Iraya took out at least five on her own."

"So many without magic?" I can't keep the revulsion from my tone like he does. He is Obeah, even if I've come to see him more as the rock I cling to, to weather Aiyca's storms. "How many others fought with her?"

"All those due to be conscripted. She wasn't the worst, though. There was another who took down almost twice as many guards before I got in there."

"Who?"

He jerks his head at the bush. "One of the prisoners who got away. Which reminds me, soon come." He strides toward a phalanx of Xanthippe. They wither as he issues clipped words, criticisms no doubt. Kirdan might only be an emissary, but to the guards his acumen is a reminder of Zesia. An island feared for its lauded standing army.

After Madisyn's death, during one of my early assignments as emissary in a neighboring parish to hear a report about Obeah insurgence, I followed a group of mourners to an early Nameless meeting run by a witch I was surprised to recognize,

Meritha Finlayter, presider on the doyenne's Council, as I knew her then. She spoke of many things that day, including the Simbarabo Fighters, Zesia's famed military of bastards.

Notorious for their strict matriarchy, in Zesia any firstborn sons are considered to have stolen the chance of inheritance from subsequent daughters. In Aiyca, they're enlisted in the first battalion whether they want to be or not. Zesia takes the slight of their birth one step further. Labeled *Simbarabo*— "fugitive"—the boys are taken from their homes, if not already abandoned, and sentenced to a lifetime in the standing army, where they would be at the front line of any conflict.

Light Keeper was trying to rally more Alumbrar to understand that the Simbarabo's training made them the most favorable solution to expunging the Yielding. There'd be no need for the Yielder guzzu protecting the island if we had a magical force three times as vast as the Xanthippe who could support Aiyca's coastal guard.

Kirdan prowls back to my side, leaving the Xanthippe looking thoroughly castigated. He rolls his eyes, too irritated to find their ineptitude amusing, as he typically does.

"They haven't had a lifetime of training," I soothe. Few Alumbrar served on Aiyca's Defense Force when the Obeah ruled. The latter order were always better suited.

"I suppose they didn't know who she was," he relents. "I didn't when I stopped her escaping. She's clever to have concealed herself all this time."

Dangerous.

And she wanted to become one of the island's shields. I can

hardly believe it. Even with the vow they agree to, its binding magic preventing them from rising against the doyenne, how could Iraya have thought the doyenne would permit her to live amongst forty-nine trained magical combatants?

I almost don't want to ask Kirdan, for fear of breathing its likelihood into the world, but— "Do you think that, despite what she told the doyenne, she's really here to take Aiyca back?"

Before he can answer, a cluster of Xanthippe stumble out of the trees. The glade falls silent, like all present magi are holding their breath. Even the bough-prowlers cease their chittering.

"Where," the doyenne begins, in a voice as soft as a concrete fist and about as calming as war, "is Iraya Adair?"

As if in answer, a charge of light, so white it's blinding, gushes through the canopy of trees.

It spreads outward like a flood. I squeeze my eyes shut. My kaftan flaps around my legs like a bird fighting to take flight with faulty wings. Screams sound, wood screeches against wood, and metal clashes like the gnashing of teeth.

It takes a moment after the light fades before I can open my eyes, in time to watch its iridescence rescind back to its original source—Iraya Adair. She bears no conduit. It pooled from *her*.

Mudda go with me.

If ever there was any doubt she is who she says she is, that proves it. The original three Obeah families allegedly selected by the Seven-Faced Mudda to rule each island in the empire were blessed with additional strength as a sign of Their favor—a naevus, like a magical boost. Zesia's ruling Divsylar family's strength is in the length of their hair. The longer it is, the stronger they are. But hair can be cut. No magi, past or present, has ever come close to extinguishing the power the Adairs carry in their eyes.

The doyenne is on her feet. Iraya is tall before her, proud. The line of her body is almost elegant. Her face wasn't much to look at before, covered in blood and filth, but now it's as if the magic has cleared away her time in Carne, exalting her until she looks every bit the fearsome magical juggernaut from Anansi's stories; far from humanizing her, the muzzle only adds to her otherworldly mien.

I long to gauge the doyenne's reaction, but Iraya possesses a pull that makes it impossible to look away. An age passes before words are spoken, and they're not the ones I expected.

"Will you permit your blood to be taken?"

Iraya holds out her arms, palms turned upward, and inhales with something like peace.

"Cut her," the doyenne orders.

One glance at Kirdan reveals little, but surely he must be as confused as I am. She means to bond with her magic? That suggests she's going to keep Iraya *alive*. Surely not. The threat she poses is too great. If the Obeah insurgents learn she's still alive, Aiyca will be on the brink of yet another bloody battle for supremacy.

Part of me wishes for Iraya to act out, forcing the doyenne to blast her to pieces, but she's still as the Xanthippe approach and gild her skin with the brightness of their conduits. She doesn't move even when one slices her arm with a small dagger, the skin parting in a sigh, her blood a crimson splash against the blade.

"To me," the doyenne says.

All eyes are on the Xanthippe running up the stadium steps to share Iraya's blood with her. There'll be no more appearances of the naevus now. Not when the doyenne bears the Glyph of Connection necessary for control. I touch the one I too have beneath my sleeve as she runs her tongue along the bloody blade, swallows.

"Foolish girl," she says with a smile—one as sharp as the glint in Iraya's eyes. "Can you feel that growing block, like a rising lump in your throat, preventing you from accessing your magic?" she calls. "It's now at my mercy for the short time you have left before your death."

Mercies bestowed.

Iraya doesn't move; she can't. Not with the blood exchange.

"Even in your final moments, you will never know the feeling of freedom." The doyenne might sound as imperious as ever, but when she sits, she organizes her bones like their density's increased tenfold in the passing minutes. "Emissary Cariot?"

I straighten.

"Take Iraya to Cwenburg, now. She's to be remanded in the holding cells until I return. No one can know her identity. And that goes for all of you." She gives the Conscription Officers a hard look. "Not one word about the Obeah rebellion in Carne is to reach the ears of anyone across this island."

"Yes, Doyenne," all chorus.

"I'm afraid this has been a waste of a trip. I can't trust these remaining conscripts to keep that quiet." She waves a hand in silent request; Xanthippe advance on the conscripts. Their conduits flare, and then death sparks are launched. Through the screams and roars of dissent, Iraya stalks toward me, stiff-backed and stone-faced, never turning. Not once. The steel, the hatred, in her face only affirms the intentions the spider foretold. Ones we almost share.

She wishes to destroy, and I to mend.

It's just as well she's to be executed.

10

IRA

Following a tense walk downhill, the Zesian emissary bundles me into a carriage at Carling Hill's nadir before slamming the door with enough force to rattle it. The noise doesn't really register, not when my ears already ring with the screams of the dying.

My fingers curl into fists on the plush velvet of the bench seat beneath me. Obeah lives taken, just like that, just for knowing my identity. Anger, pain, sadness, regret: they all sting my eyes with equal potency.

Even in your final moments, you will never know the feeling of freedom.

It was always a risk but—gods-damnit! I slam a fist onto the bench.

I didn't consider that her reasons to kill me would outweigh those to keep me alive. Not when she herself came to the palace as a prisoner of war, and deceived her way into Mama's confidence. Though, perhaps she of any would recognize a similar move.

Kaleisha wasn't among those who were just killed. Goddess willing, she'll have made it to some semblance of safety with the small contingent of Obeah who managed to escape. With the Zesian outside, his physique not conducive to paper pushing, whatever he wants the Alumbrar to believe, I can't.

For the first time since the guzzu, I raise my fingers to the cage around my mouth; sick surges with a suddenness that makes me gag against its leather straps. My fingers scramble north of the contraption to the security of the dyed vertical scarification between my eyebrows. I rub back and forth, tracing its smooth edges until the queasiness abates.

Almost a decade later, I still remember the pain of the heated dagger as it charred my flesh. The stink of it made my eyes water. But that pain was nothing compared with when Nana Clarke bled the mixture of white dye and molten conduit metal into the open wound. The measure of any Obeah undertaking their commitment mark in a scarification ceremony is in how long they can last before screaming at the intensity of the burn, the stink of their flesh as it bubbles. Some of the girls before me fainted. I didn't make a single sound. To this day, crescent moon–shaped scars line my palms where I'd tightened my fists to stop myself from crying out. They're a permanent reminder of what I can withstand in the process of acquiring what I want—what I need.

And I don't need seven faces to know I won't be dying by

Doyenne Cariot's hand.

I'll find a way out. I have to.

The carriage leans to the left. A clattering above announces the driver's presence. It's half a day's travel from Carling Hill to Cwenburg Palace—plenty of time to decide on a new plan. My nails settle into the scarred tissue on my palms one last time.

The two emissaries enter the carriage and just manage to sit before the sand-prowlers spur forward. I forgot how odd their scurry makes a carriage ride feel. It's like being attached to a pair of shuffling feet. The girl grips the window ledge as we skitter over some loose earth. Emissary *Cariot*, the doyenne called her: her daughter. She bears the same silken skin as her mama, darker than mine, healthier looking. Her figure is shrouded in reams of delicate fabric, like she's trying to disappear within its confines—a waste. The Mudda's Face of Fortune seems to favor her curves more than my flat chest. I drag a lazy gaze from the Alumbrar-silver afro spilling across her shoulders to her golden slipper–encased feet and back again. Like the rest of the jewelry she bears, the hundreds of little disks on the sandals are dull enough to repel all light, so not conduit metal.

For Obeah, not having a conductor wouldn't make a difference in magical status. Though firstborns alone inherit magic in both orders, some spirits have proven themselves benevolent enough, over the years, that if they're approached by an Obeah without magic who happens to be willing to part with an entire skin of rum, they can be quite altruistic. And then there are other methods in our arsenal: cursed artifacts, ensorcelled objects, homemade charms. All Obeah are magical. But for Alumbrar, only those who inherit practice, as they believe the Seven-Faced Mudda's will demands. So Emissary Cariot is magicless, and human, with all their vulnerabilities. . . .

If she feels me looking, sizing her up like a sacrificial lamb, she doesn't acknowledge it. Alumbrar are taught to reject the flesh, compliments, and everything else that's good in the world. The carriage teeters around a bend; she slides into the Zesian. He steadies her with a gentleness that belies his large scarred hands. While they separate almost instantly, is there something between them? They don't sit with the intimacy of lovers, though I suppose they wouldn't do that with me here. Not in the least because the Zesian doesn't seem able to keep those intent eyes off *me*.

"So you're an Adair," he says, like he's been dying for the right moment. "*The* Lost Empress."

Giving him my best eye roll, I cross one leg over the other and adjust my prison smock like it's spun from Aiyca's finest satins, not stiff with blood and sweat.

"Forgive me for my slowness, Your Highness," he says, dryly. *What I wouldn't give for words right now.*

Emissary Cariot flicks small eyes to me. It wouldn't take much to lunge across the carriage and incapacitate her, were it not for the Zesian. I let my gaze run between them suggestively. She looks away first, eyes lowering with embarrassment. Whatever they are, they're in each other's confidence. Enough that she doesn't carry any weapons. She relies on him, trusts him to keep her safe.

I'm pleased to find I can still snort.

The emissaries, not so much.

It's the only win I have now that my escape can't happen here, and the window of opportunity is narrowing. There might be a chance between leaving the carriage and my transfer to the holding cells, or the walk from the holding cells to my execution. It's not the solution I'd hoped for, but victory, if anything, isn't the defeat of loss.

It's the ember of hope in a fire thought to have long sat cold.

It doesn't take as long as I remember for the jade bush of Carling Hill to transform into the brick and steel of Aiyca's capital and mecca of trade, Queenstown. I never spent more time in the city than I needed to, growing up, preferring the island's wetlands and the Blue Mountains range defending the coast to the east, rising like teeth in a smile of challenge.

Only a knuckle-bone's throw away from Carne Sea, the accessibility of the vast port drew many foreign merchants—fair skinnned and light eyed—as well as disguised pirate ships eager to trade their wares for Aiyca's primary source of golden conduit coins. Drawn from an endless waterfall in a secret location only Mama knew, they're unique to this island. Near indestructible, the gold can be transmuted into almost anything. It made Aiyca the most profitable island in the empire, and, when my family reigned, the most powerful.

They were happy times, I'm almost startled to remember. Not just for Obeah, but Alumbrar too. For one of the longest periods of Xaymaca's history, both orders were amicable.

Enough that Mama reduced the number of peace-keeping sol-diers in Aiyca's towns and cities and instated monthly suppers to stitch together the edges of a relationship frayed by jealousy and bitterness.

Now I see Doyenne Cariot's hand in everything.

She convinced Mama to lower her inhibitions, must have planned for years—decades, even—how she would curl her way around Mama's heart inch by inch until it was too late to prize her away. And now she has done what she convinced her fallen enemy to stop.

Soldiers from the second battalion stand on most corners, armed only with staffs. There is no mix, as there was when Mama ruled, only Alumbrar. The ruling order trade and laugh as though nothing has changed. It's an affront to see them dressed in fine cotton and silk, the females with towering hair scarves in an array of jewel tones, the men smartly casual with pipes in the corners of their mouths, especially when I finally see what's been done to the "magicless" Obeah.

Where they once strode with pride, slapping hands with merchants and locals, slinging treats to prowler pups, they now hurry along, heads bowed as they pass the bloody scar-let of the soldiers' uniforms. My order once carried weapons forged from gold, majestic staffs and elegant swords, ban-doliers of delicately crafted daggers, pretty hairpins. Now their backs and hips are empty. So this is what peace looks like here.

"I can see your shock," the Zesian says, because of course he's watching me track the passersby. "Things have changed."

You mean that, as well as betrayal, stating the obvious is in fashion?

"Were you anyone other than yourself, you would have seen that your ilk live in neighborhoods guarded by the first battalion, under strict curfew. Frequent Xanthippe raids means there's little opportunity for mutiny. Any magi found with contraband, magical articles, or thought to be communing with the ancestors is sent to Carne. There are also executions of any thought to be working with Obeah insurgents."

The Jade Guild.

Kaleisha would foam at the mouth whenever they were mentioned, spewing facts in their defense whenever any prisoners challenged their ineptitude. A few riots here and a little fighting there hasn't reclaimed the island. Though, I suppose they're doing their best in a loaded fight without the primary weapon.

I briefly wonder why the Zesian's telling me such coveted information; then it dawns that he's showing off. He wants me to know those ineligible to conscript have no magic, and the conscripts have only the appearance of control.

The sight of my reduced order stays with me as we ramble out of the city, and begin the winding climb up to the mount on which the palace estate sits high in the center of St. Mary Parish. Behind the curve of a new defensive wall, unfurled like the gray tongue of some ungodly beast, wild grass waves its thin fingers. That, at least, is the same.

When I was a pickney, Mama would tell me to watch how the stalks remained anchored, despite winds determined to wrench them from their foundations. I'd always wanted to be the wind, unrestrained, unanchored, and wild. But this coup means it's finally time to become the grass, steadfast and immovable amid a turbulent storm.

Nothing will kill you faster, Nana Clarke would say, *than emotions in battle.*

I force myself to remain unmoved, even as the drive circles around and the sprawling Cwenburg Palace rises before us like a golden middle finger. Its entry gate is flanked by twin watchtowers. Also new, their dull gray brick is juxtaposed against the hills of green rising like whale backs behind the estate.

Realizing my mouth is open, I snap it shut. But not even Nana could expect me to be unmoved by this. When the galley first docked at the Hendern Cliffs, I didn't consider how it would feel to return home, only to find it isn't that anymore. It's a cold, closed thing, with black and gold flags rather than white and gold clapping in the winds.

The sting of my nails digging into my palms startles me. I can't recall when my hands clenched into fists. They remain that way as the carriage continues on the drive that curls past the palace gates; they don't unclench even when we stop at the estate's north access gate and the Zesian gives them a very pointed stare.

This is it, my escape. No Xanthippe wait on this edge of the seven-sided estate. It's hidden in the shadow of a border of tall trees. Perhaps, I think, as the emissaries exit ahead of me, I can run that way and use the low-hanging branches to swing myself up into the trees and over the wall.

But the moment I step out of the carriage, I know that won't be possible.

The holding cells' white stone is incised in an intricate artwork of golden glyphs, ones to debilitate and weaken; what little energy I reclaimed during the journey seeps from my body, making every step a battle. I teeter; my left side grazes the Zesian's right, just for a moment. He stiffens beneath my touch, recoils; I wish I could do the same, but my body isn't my own. Sweat gathers at my hairline with the effort it takes to stand. Gods-*damnit*.

"I'll meet you in my study, Emissary Divsylar," Emissary Cariot says, lingering by the carriage. They're her first words since we left Carling Hill. Her voice is soft, but her words scrape against the back of my neck like fragments of shattered glass.

The Zesian is a member of the *Divsylar* family?

I will my features blank as we descend the steps and enter the stretch of low-lit cells, but goddess almighty. He's related to Zesia's *first family*. A line blessed with a magical surplus, just as mine is. Unbound, his dark hair spills across his monolithic shoulders like a river of obsidian, advertising the strength those tresses bless him with. A prisoner groans from the dimness of the cells, startling me out of my trance enough to realize I'm staring, and the Zesian's staring right back, his almond-shaped eyes narrowed.

"Problem?" The nightmarish hue from the blue witchlight flames flickering on the walls throws the angles of his face into harsh focus. Forget emissary, he looks like a doyen, noble, unforgiving, and ruthless.

I shake my head, lost for words I'm not able to speak.

"Then look where you're going." He tugs me along. "Some of the stones are loose."

He doesn't seem to have any problem with his footing. His strides ripple with power beside mine, glyph-weakened and distracted. I can't believe he's a *Divsylar*.

He has to be a first cousin, and a firstborn at that if he's inherited his pupa's magic. I'm not as rote in Zesian practices as I should be after all this time, but I can't imagine the royals would send a second or third into Aiyca as a spy, for that must be why he's really here.

I'm not escaping these cells, death.

Zesia will never permit the empire's true heir, even in name only, to live. Not when they have more to gain from my death. Case in point, Emissary Divsylar is almost dragging me by the time we alight before an empty cell, he's so eager to dump me inside. It's small and dark with a suspicious liquid dripping down the stone walls. Many-legged creatures click-clack over the stone, emerging from cracks that most likely hide entire colonies. Wonderful. A wink from the emissary's conduit makes the barred door gape open.

Without his arm and magical support, I realize, my legs give just as I cross the threshold. The still-damp contents of someone else's stomach has the nerve to greet my knees and splash over my calves. I scowl up at Emissary Divsylar, sure he put me in here on purpose. Powerless, muzzled, and on my knees, I'm in stark contrast to his towering height.

"Empress Adair . . ." he says, the gravelly base of his voice echoing down the cells. "You would have left them behind, in Carne, your sistren."

The observation startles me. Why does he care?

"I heard stories about you when I was a pickney," he continues, as though he read the question on my face. "The Lost Empress whose mama stowed her away until a time when she was needed most by her bredren and sistren." He pauses, cocks his head to the side; his hair slinks around his right shoulder. "I suppose it's a mercy your order will never know you actually exist, because then they'd learn that you don't care a lick about anyone other than yourself."

My mouth dries; shame curls itself around my shoulders.

He looks at me a moment longer before turning back the way we came. My cell door remains open in his wake. I will my limbs to move, but they're as unresponsive as ever. I suspect he did it on purpose. The doyenne said I'd never know the feeling of freedom, but the Zesian means to make us familiar. Freedom, and with it, life, are only a short crawl away and yet inaccessible to me.

And so I sit, my legs becoming numb beneath me, with only the dark for company.

11

JAZMYNE

Anya's sprawled across my bed reading when I traipse into my suite, exhausted from all that happened at Carling Hill and dusty from the road.

"Wahan." I smile, pleased she's waited up for me.

She abandons the book, sits up. "Did I see you arrive with Emissary Divsylar?"

My smile falters.

"Don't tell me you left the festival early to meet with him and have a dance of your own? You know, mon, of the horizontal variety?"

"What? No!"

She knows it infuriates me when everyone automatically assumes Kirdan and I are lovers. But for all her humor, there's something in her face. . . . I've seen that calm intensity else-where tonight. It strikes me just as it did at Carling Hill when

95

Iraya emerged from the family trees, her body aglow with the alabaster glare of her naevus.

This isn't my sistren before me, sprawled with counterfeit insouciance.

This is an agent from the Nameless—a determined Stealth.

This is an interrogation. One that could only be about where the doyenne and I went.

"Even though I hate him, I wouldn't judge you if you wanted more with him," Anya says. "You'd have to keep it quiet though. He is Obeah."

Why does she keep pushing this inane subject instead of asking what happened tonight? Unless . . . unless we're not alone. A chill raises the hairs on the back of my neck. Pushing Kirdan at me, someone she knows is just a friend, must have been the only sign Anya could give me that the other Stealth hiding in here wouldn't recognize. Light Keeper wouldn't have trusted Anya to eke the necessary information out of me about where the doyenne went, not without witnesses, but she also knows there's no one else I'd be likelier to share tonight with.

"Kirdan i-is attractive, of course." I stumble over my words, not as accomplished at improvising under pressure as Anya is. "I have eyes. But I also have loyalty to the Alumbrar." My mouth is so dry, swallowing is like forcing down gravel. "I'm to be their doyenne. H-how would an affair with a Zesian look?"

Her head dips in relief that I've caught up, approval at my attempt of deception, and apology. The latter is the only indication I have of the assault that follows. I try not to reel as the questions hit me like tiny knives, one after the other with no letup.

"Then why were you together? Wasn't he overseeing the Carne prisoner transfer at Carling Hill? And where was the doyenne? She left too, I heard. Did something happen?"

Is there a danger in telling her about Iraya? Yes. The Nameless might anticipate Doyenne Cariot reinstating the Yielding, as I did. They cannot know. What was it Anya always said about lying? *Keep it as close to the truth as possible.*

"There was a bruckout," I begin, aware that everything I say will be reported back to Light Keeper. "It was bigger than the others, and—and Kirdan thought Doyenne Cariot needed to show her face so th-the Obeah would realize that they—"

"Need to stop acting out?"

"Yeh mon." I sigh, grateful. "I went ahead to gauge the situation before the doyenne arrived."

"And you didn't think it prudent for the entire Witches Council to be there?"

I shake my head, stalling for time. "It was . . . important to—to modulate our threat. If the entire Council showed for a bruckout, well . . ." I shrug, a little helpless.

"Where would you go the next time you need to discipline them?" Anya finishes.

"Precisely."

"That's reassuring to know. Light Keeper wondered if it was something more serious. But if you're telling me all is well, I'll leave now, share that with her." Anya straightens up from where she leaned against one of the bedposts. "You should bathe, Jaz, get some rest."

Allow the Stealth, maybe more than one, hidden in my suite to leave undetected.

"I had words with the witch who left that missive, by the way, for last week's meeting?" She pauses in the archway between my sleeping chamber and the adjoining corridor to the games room. Afternoon sunlight dapples the tile beneath her feet, but her expression is all shadows. "She won't make that mistake with you again. I've seen to it. Likkle more." Anya departs with a swish of her high ponytail, the threat hidden in her story more for the lingering eyes and ears than me. She wishes for them to know that no matter what Light Keeper orders, she has my back.

I make my way into my bathing room, worrying my bottom teeth between my lips. I don't begrudge the resistance leader's caution. She made all the difference in developing the Nameless from a small grief meeting to a movement of determined voices across the island in the last three years. Thousands of members in each of the seven parishes. And it's for that reason she can't learn about Iraya Adair, or the bruckout at Carling Hill. Just as Doyenne Cariot wouldn't risk the chance that the rebels might not defeat her, Light Keeper wouldn't wait to see if the runaways were caught; they're similar, in that way.

But the secret is kept. Iraya will die, and the doyenne will live.

Close to two phases after the Carling Hill incident, Light Keeper and I meet in my study under the guise of Witches

Council administration. Anya came by earlier to cast a guzzu of silence to prevent our discussion from being overheard, so we speak freely.

"In the next few months before my earthstrong," I say, "I'd like to shift the Nameless's focus from protesting and proselyting to something else."

As I hoped, Light Keeper sits back in her seat before my desk, interested.

"Parishioners are fearful about the safety of Aiyca without the Yielding. Now is the perfect time to open our doors with promises of support." I drop a hand on the pile of missives on my desk. "These are all from Alumbrar, secular Aiycans, in need of answers about what's next, something we've always known. With the doyenne's blessing, I'm going to visit parishes and hold assemblies to allay worry. All as emissary, of course. I need the Nameless working with me in parishes, pushing the agenda that I'll be doyenne soon."

Light Keeper nods, pleased. "A smart play."

Doyenne Cariot has taught me the importance of always thinking several moves ahead, and the Ascension Festival made it clear that I need to start winning my order around before I set my sights on the island at large.

"One that will involve the secular too, I hope." For too long, Aiycans who don't practice in the Alumbrar or Obeah orders have been lost in our skirmish. I hesitate—my next request is a gamble. "I think that one Nameless branch per parish will be enough to start with. We don't want to overwhelm the Alumbrar or trigger their skepticism. In St. Ann, however, I want all outposts offering comfort." I draw a small breath. "It's home to Carling Hill, we know runaways hide in the glade, and the Obeah are protected by its wetlands. Alumbrar there need to know, perhaps more than anyone else, that there's hope beyond the Yielding."

Especially since those runaways from Carling Hill have yet to be caught.

"Perhaps two outposts of the four instead?" Light Keeper suggests. "We don't want to show our numbers too early; not while the doyenne remains in power."

"Fair."

"Once the secular and Alumbrar have been suitably listened to and won over, we shall have to think about how to placate the Obeah. They will be the last bastion between Aiyca and peace. Which is ironic given that, as an order, they were far better at promoting unity across the island than Doyenne Cariot has been."

She isn't wrong, but she isn't entirely right either. Neither of us points out that Alumbrar were pivotal to the peace Aiyca enjoyed for close to a century, as they bided their time to rise and reared a leader who would be deft enough to front a successful coup—of the many, Doyenne Cariot has been the most successful.

Light Keeper sits forward, takes up her cup of ginger tea. "On that note, how are matters with the Jade Guild?"

I fold my hands in my lap beneath the desk so she can't see how they shake. "During Emissary Divsylar's negotiation last month, they were still happy to hold off attacking."

"Another success."

One I'm proudest of. At my request, Kirdan has held meetings with the Jade Guild Gennas on my behalf for the past year. Not only have we convinced them to cease insurgent behavior, ensuring the doyenne would cancel the Yielding, but they've agreed to sign a peace treaty in exchange for their order's magical freedom, with conditions I've yet to share, when I am doyenne. Though, that was before the escapees from Carling Hill potentially united with them and shared that they saw Iraya Adair, alive and well, being sentenced to death by the doyenne—an execution that has yet to happen for reasons I cannot determine, not when the doyenne has locked herself away in various parts of the palace where even her council hasn't been invited.

"What else have they asked for?"

"We gave them supplies, of course," I say, pushing aside my concerns about Iraya, the Jade Guild, the doyenne's inactivity. "And a little gold—not enough to risk them weaponizing, but enough to keep them compliant to commit to their end of the bargain."

"You have done what Doyenne Cariot has not, there." Light Keeper puts her cup back on its saucer; it lands with a hollow thud. "It's a shame she won't permit the treaty you plan to offer. After a decade of controlling them through conscription, she'll never stand for making them equals."

"They'll still have restrictions," I'm quick to argue. "Their gold will still be limited; the curfews already in place will stand. Forever, if need be." Though I hope not.

Light Keeper's shaking her head before I've finished. "You are too idealistic, Jazmyne. In the doyenne's eyes, they need to be punished for treating us as ancillary since we were created. Remember, you won't have magic until the doyenne decides she's ready to die. And who knows when she'll reach that decision. She can remove you from the throne before then, if she doesn't like the policies you put forth. Kill you."

Doyenne Cariot has spent my entire life rearing me to take her place. Why would she kill me? But before Light Keeper's stoicism, the question seems frivolous. The doyenne has already killed one pickney. What's to stop her killing me and having another?

Only her death, a small voice whispers.

"I commend you for the care you've taken, Jazmyne, the hesitation in making a decision the doyenne made with ease a decade ago, when she first brought the Yielding to the council. But you of all people should know that sometimes the best way to rid yourself of an infection is to cut it out."

The fire across the room blazes with a suddenness that makes me jolt. It spits a missive out onto the rug.

"I'll see about sending word to the outposts." Light Keeper pushes back in her seat and stands. "Think about what I said. Her death could never truly have been an *if*."

When she leaves, I turn my chair to the expansive bay window and the view of the island as it's set alight by the rising sun. I should have thought about an extreme reaction from the doyenne. If I was ready to occupy her seat, I would have. With a sigh I go and retrieve the fire message. Perhaps it's from

Anya. Hopefully with good news.

Jaz, the hurried scrawl reads. It is Anya's.

WE JUST RECEIVED WORD FROM A NAMELESS OUTPOST IN ST. ANN PARISH. THERE'S BEEN AN ATTACK—WITCHFIRE. IT TORE THROUGH AN ENTIRE ALUMBRAR VILLAGE BEFORE IT COULD BE EXTINGUISHED. MANY LIVES HAVE BEEN LOST. THE JADE GUILD HAVE CLAIMED RESPONSIBILITY. DOYENNE CARIOT KNOWS. LIGHT KEEPER WILL RECEIVE WORD TOO.

I choke out a strangled cry.

What Alumbrar call Witchfire, Obeah call Timbámbu in the ancestors' tongue. Born from Spirit Magic, the toxic green flame, infamous for being smokeless and killing with heat alone, hasn't been seen in years. And the *Jade Guild* used it?

They have to know Iraya Adair is alive.

Without warning, my study door flies open and Kirdan strides inside, cloak billowing in winds that smell of hot sand and spice.

"There's a problem."

"The Witchfire in St. Ann, I—I know."

"What?" He looks shocked.

"That's not what you were going to say?"

"No. I'm here about Iraya."

My blood runs cold. "Don't tell me she's escaped."

He shakes his head, impatient. "The doyenne's made her decision about the execution."

12

IRA

Rose-hued morning light streams in from the wide lunette window above the palace's imposing front doors, embargoing the darkness of the holding cells in the lofty atrium. My Xanthippe escort nudges me onward with whispered threats and taunts.

They're taking me to the doyenne, to my death, and I'd hate to arrive empty-handed.

The front doors are arched delicacies of incandescent conduit gold and lignum vitae wood, the latter darkly stained. Of the same species as our family tree, it was selected to ease the summoning of Adair ancestors, making this palace a stronghold for my family. In theory, anyway. For all their foresight, none of the previous rulers thought to guard against an intruder who was already *inside*.

Nana Clarke told my Warrior sistren and me that no

battlefield is as deadly as court, where everything from words to finials can be used as weapons. Snapping off even one of the decorative leaves flowering from the elegant dance of vines on the doors will widen my channeling pool, enough to take care of these coven members, perhaps even to burn this muzzle clean off my face, leveling a biased playing field. If I can get close enough.

Slowing my steps, I make a show of favoring my left leg, enabling me to veer close enough until all I need to do is reach out and—*ouch*. One of the Xanthippe clips my Achilles with a thick-soled sandal.

"Seems I stepped on a roach, sistren."

"I thought vermin did better jobs at scuttling out of the way," her companion replies. "This one needs a bit of *guidance*." With her last word, she snatches me away from the door, shoving me down a passage branching off the atrium.

My first instinct is to smash my head back into her nose, but the abrupt detour makes my surroundings spin. The absence of windows in the holding cells made measuring time impossible. Food deliveries were sporadic, when they came at all; the Zesian didn't condescend to come back to insult me further. My limbs had days, at the very least, to stiffen in the dark. Moon phases could have passed down there, entire weeks under the thrall of glyphs with the sole intention of beating my magic into a forced slumber. The surge that sparked like a storm beneath my skin at Carling Hill is a distant rumble now, a ghostly impression of what could have been, and what, if the doyenne gets her way, might never be again.

The passage widens into a gallery, one paying homage to some bygone war or other with instruments that could only belong to Obeah. Doyenne Cariot must have left these animal skin shields, the alabaster capes, splayed against the palace walls to remind all guests about who she defeated to take this domicile. . . . It works. In the unignorable face of it, I can't deny how easy it would be to cave, to curl in on myself. I'm so *tired*. Even as I think it, another cyclone of dizziness upsets my course, tilting me into the Xanthippe at my left. She knocks me to the right; my side slams into the second guard, whose size belies any softness. She's a unit, a stalwart wall of muscle. My bones rattle at the contact; so does my sore head.

"Wrong way, Obeah."

They laugh.

I stew between them.

As if I need leading. This was my home first. Doyenne Cariot might have torn down the handwoven tapestries immortalizing Obeah heroines and heroes, the vibrant colors of green, red, yellow, and black popping like the Scotch bonnet peppers Mama used to grow in her vegetable garden, and painted the once-white surroundings a dark woad, but she hasn't changed the palace's structural design. The Patio of Prowlers the gallery leads out to was a favorite hideout of mine whenever it came time to wash my hair, a nightmarish ordeal in which water would always make its way into my ears and eyes.

If my end is here, I'm glad this is one of the last places I'll see. Then, the gaping gold porticos fencing in the exposed stone sun-trap, the ornate fountain guarded by seven roaring jungle-prowler statues, made for a fun game between myself and the palace hands. Albeit one-sided fun. Beyond the courtyard, the palace cools beneath the shade of a roof, walls, again. My escort and I turn down Dada's hallway, the one with his study. Familiarity makes my heels dig in and my shoulders seize up.

No.

I thought my execution was to be made public! I can't die in there. I won't. Stopping, I lower my body to adjust my center of gravity so I can really dig in. But marble isn't as effective as dirt, or a rougher stone, and the Xanthippe drag me all the way to the open study door.

For a moment, Dada seems to sit behind his desk.

Dark shelves line the walls from floor to ceiling; they're filled with books and souvenirs from his travels. Giant shells from legendary crustaceans, a preserved tentacle from the sea creature that almost crushed *Cordially Yours* to splinters; his conduit weapon, a beautifully knobbled staff of lignum vitae spliced with gold, leans against the desk's side in anticipation of his next adventure. As a Squaller, he would have commanded it like a lightning rod, using his training to quell storms, summon winds, and master waves.

"Iraya Adair."

The voice claws Dada's memory away, replacing it with a dark-eyed, silver-haired monster. This witch has the audacity to wear one of Mama's diadems. A rose-gold halo band she would have seen enough to recognize as one of her favorites. She smiles at me from behind the desk, saccharine and superior. "Come."

The glyph on my arm flares with pain. I swallow a wince as the doyenne's compulsion takes root, forcing me out of the

Xanthippes' hold and across the rugs until I'm close enough to note that though mature, her face bears no lines. In Carne, Obeah scarcely older than me carried more wrinkles. I only have to look at the gold chains around her neck, the clips twisting her dreadlocks back from her face, and the wealth adorning her fingers to know how she stays so "young." Too little gold will drain life, but a quantity such as hers will replenish it.

"The first thing you should know is that you won't be dying here today."

Surprise would have made a lesser magi's mouth open, but not mine. That's not to say I'm not stunned.

"Heed this, Obeah: that can change at any given time." She draws herself up in her seat. "To ensure it doesn't, you and I need to have a conversation." A wave of her elegant fingers sends a tendril of sweet-smelling breeze across my mouth.

Weight lifts from my face, and the serrated edges of metal burrowed behind my ears disappear. *The muzzle. It's gone?* My hands twitch to check it's not an illusion.

"I must warn you," she continues, her accent softer than mine and without patwah, an affected attempt to elevate herself. I noticed it in her daughter too. "The thirteen days you spent in the glyphed cells will keep that naevus buried deep, and your ability to use any magic even deeper."

I was there so long?

"Let's not ruin what could prove itself to be a mutually beneficial meeting, you understand?"

Intrigued, I nod.

She inhales, sinking back into her seat somewhat. "During

my reign, I've only ever used execution as a necessary means to an end. The Order of Alumbrar are not Obeah, in that sense. We don't sanction the unnecessary killing of anyone, even our enemies, for that is what you are, Iraya. But your story doesn't need to end like so many others' have."

Like the conscripts back at Carling Hill, she means.

I clear my throat, determined my weakened voice won't break. "Why?"

"Your power." Her eye dips. "It seems I was too hasty when you first revealed yourself to me. It's as you said, I could benefit greatly from such a resource—Aiyca could benefit."

Still before her, shock leaves me without reply. Not so much at her rescinding the kill order. I'm to believe she's had a change of heart? If one beats in her chest, there's no compassion in that organ. History has proven this isn't a witch to be trusted, so what does she really want?

Relaxing for the first time since I was taken from the holding cells, I nod at the chair before the desk. She relinquishes her hold on my body. I sit, cross one leg over the other.

"What are your terms?" *Ask me*. I will. *Ask me to join your cadre of shields*.

"I don't enjoy murder."

"Naturally," I deadpan. "Alumbrar are not Obeah."

"No," she returns with the same faux lightness. "Which is why I've retained Obeah here, on the estate, to do that which my order cannot."

"Keep you safe?"

Her eyes narrow. "Keep Aiyca out of the hands of those who crave it, whatever the cost."

Perhaps she's not entirely ignorant to the risk the Zesian emissary poses.

"You are to join their number, immediately."

"Consider me flattered."

"And you can consider that mouth of yours warned." She leans in, that lone eye boring into my scarification. "You wish to know my terms, listen closely: you will live among your kin, serve among your kin, and they will have no idea that their savior is so close, for if you breathe one word of your existence to any Obeah, I will butcher them."

My mouth dries, but I hold her gaze.

"Aiyca might benefit from you, but that doesn't mean you are not expendable." She sits back and bridges her fingers. "You are but a little axe, and it's best to keep that in mind. If not for yourself, then for your order. You understand?"

I understand that a little axe can take down an entire forest, blow by blow, tree by tree.

"And those are all your terms?" I ask.

She watches me, ever calm and confident. "There's just one more. Or rather, three."

The skin behind my ears erupts in flame.

I slam both hands against my head, squeezing as incisions slice their way into existence, splitting open the burn blister wounds from the muzzle so blood runs freely. Doyenne Cariot blurs as my eyes fill with water.

"Two invisible Impediment Glyphs," she says. "To ensure your magic isn't so present. For the good of your order, of course."

"Of course," I pant.

Neither of us believes any of this is for my order.

"My newest shield needs to be taken to the Cuartel," she orders the Xanthippe. "The buddy coordinator has already been instructed to meet with her there."

"I'm not to live here, in the palace?"

She laughs, and it's the most genuine reaction I've seen from her since Carling Hill.

Taking that as an even *no*, I rise alone, determined that Doyenne Cariot doesn't see me as helpless, and find my ankles lighter than they were when we began this conversation. My wrists too move freely.

"No need for shackles. Or—" She waves a hand, and the blood running down the sides of my neck disappears, as do my clothes. They're exchanged for light silver sandals that lace up my all but bare legs; the black shorts take themselves so literally, the black tunic on my torso almost reaches their end. The latter's sleeves, fluted and loose, contrast against the tough hide of a black vest that clamps around my rib cage like teeth in a monster's maw—the doyenne's teeth, as she chews me up and spits me out into something unrecogniz-able, clad in her colors, save for the gold conduit coin that now swings between my breasts. She expunges the remainder of my identity with a light silver chainmail hood that covers my hair. "Anything else that marks you as different," she finishes with a cold smile.

I don't return it.

"If that's it, then I'll be going."

"The uniform wasn't the third term. There is a vow all shields take." She opens a desk drawer and pulls out a slim dagger; shafts of light reflect from its blade. "You may have heard about it. My final term is that you take it now."

"A blood vow?" This time it's not so easy to conceal my surprise. Alumbrar don't partake in such things.

"No. A Vow of Peace. Though it's more of a bargain. A Shook Bargain, in fact."

My focus shifts from her to the blade and back again. There is no blood in a Shook Bargain. It's a soul-binding act of magic. One that leaves a magical band behind, a manacle. Breaking the bargain results in the band tightening until it severs hand from wrist. And that's only if you've made the one. There are Anansi tales about magi who lost entire limbs when they failed to meet their end of the agreed terms, and they had bargains covering the lengths of their arms. So why the blade?

"What's the wording?"

"I, then you state your name," the doyenne says, "*agree to honor my end of this bargain, and hereby swear to uphold my duty as one of Aiyca's shields, to protect the named island from all threat, including the vulnerability of leaving said island bereft of its leader.* That would be me." She holds her right hand across the desk; her eye is bright with challenge.

She'll face none from me.

Shook Bargains are also known as Fool's Bargains, to those who know better. And only the foolish would mistake me for one of their own. I do not recognize Judair Cariot as Aiyca's leader. She is a squatter on the throne; one I mean to kick off promptly.

Maybe even today.

I take her hand, and the challenge in her eye widens to surprise.

"I, Iraya Adair, agree to honor my end of this bargain." As the words are spoken, the jewelry around her neck, her wrists, on her fingers, begins to glow. A sparking golden band entwines our hands. "And hereby swear to uphold my duty as one of Aiyca's shields." Squinting, to combat the brightness of all her conduit metal, the manifesting bargain, I seek out the blade she took from the drawer. "To protect the named island from all threat, including the vulnerability of leaving said island bereft of its leader. So I promise, so things do." The band tightens around our wrists; tugging her forward by the hand I hold, I lunge for the blade with my spare and plunge it into her chest.

At least, that was what I was hoping for.

Instead, I cry out as my assailing arm veers sharply to the left of its own accord, and my fingers fling the blade away.

The band ratifying the Shook Bargain pinches into my skin before disappearing, bigger on being felt than seen—but the threat of its presence is stamped across Doyenne Cariot's smug face. She flings my hand away and rises so that we are eye to eye with only the desk separating us.

"You can't have thought me stakki enough to not know your plans." She leans in, that lone eye boring into my scarification. "Why do you think I took the blade out? The bargain does not recognize you as a leader, and why would it when you've been indisposed for a decade? When you have no army, no family or friends, and your magic is all but *mine*. And so you cannot kill me. Not without leaving Aiyca vulnerable."

I could snatch her head down and slam it into the desk, goddess help me.

But I can't. Not anymore.

What have I done?

"I see you understand, at last." She exhales, with something I'd like to think is relief, but is really triumph. "You've been known as *Ira* in Carne, I've been informed. This will continue throughout your stay in the Cuartel. Farewell. Let us hope we don't meet again."

It takes all my pride to continue meeting her eye. "Indeed, Doyenne Cariot."

Under the Xanthippe's vigil, I must remain stalwart, but every step that separates me and Aiyca's *leader* raises more questions. She feared me, at Carling Hill. But today . . . Heat flares across my cheeks at what occurred—and why did it? She made such a strong case for killing me that her reasons for keeping me alive, even with the bargain, seem thin in contrast, a mere film she's using to conceal her true intentions . . . whatever those might be, and it's bothering me something chronic that I can't quite determine if she's brave or clever, given our families' history.

Surely many magi can't be both. If my past has taught me anything, it's that the brave act without thinking, and the clever avoid all acts of bravery.

It also taught me to trust few witches.

And definitely not any of the Alumbrar ones.

As we walk back out to the Patio of Prowlers, the conduit

coin clatters against the animal-hide vest. I grip it for the first time. Round and gold with an incised face, it's big enough to permit maybe a third of the dictated conscription. A deliberate measure to prevent conscripts from running away as soon as we receive our magic, no doubt. Is there anything that witch hasn't thought of? Gods alive.

The clearing of someone's throat draws the Xanthippe and me up short.

"One moment," Emissary Divsylar says to the guards. "I need a word."

Nodding their acquiescence, they march ahead, leaving us in the patio's shaded portico. They're stopped across the way by Emissary Cariot, who looks over at me with her small, dark eyes before engaging them in conversation, likely asking why I'm still alive. When I look back at the Zesian, I find myself being scrutinized by his customary curiosity.

"She let you live," he says, doing his best to phrase it as a statement, but his tone . . . he didn't know. For some reason, it improves my mood an indecent amount. "And she's making you a shield?"

"Something you seem elated by, mon. You know, I'm beginning to think you can't stay away from me."

"If you were thinking at all, you'd make the smart decision and keep your head down. But that doesn't seem to be the case." He shakes his head. "The stories didn't portray you like this," he adds, like he's unable to help himself.

"Witty in the face of conquering death?"

"Petulant and reckless."

"Aren't you a little old for tall tales and bedtime soothers?"

"Your stories weren't told to offer comfort, in Zesia. Though—" His mouth quirks in a sneer as he sears a burning trail down my new uniform. "They might have been generous. I'll have to see."

"Is that meant to be intimidating or creepy?"

Much to my delight, a deep flush mottles on his neck.

I feign surprise. "Don't tell me you were going for romantic?"

The splotches of puce stretch upward to his cheeks; he's quick to whistle the Xanthippe back over. "Don't forget what I said. I'll be watching." He marches off before I can think of a retort, but one comes before he turns out of sight.

"I'll be sure to wear something scanty then, mon!"

The stiffening of his shoulders and the thought of the embarrassment emblazoned across his entire face makes the blow the Xanthippe lands to the center of my back entirely worth it.

But then he is gone, and it is just me, my new uniform, and the confrontational realization that I have no idea how I'm going to kill the doyenne.

13

JAZMYNE

Having heard the Xanthippes' report, I was eager to learn firsthand from the doyenne what could have moved her to renege on her word to execute Iraya, given all we know about the Jade Guild—until Kirdan stormed past me, his jaw tight and his face flushed.

I didn't hear his discussion with Iraya, but I couldn't have missed what she yelled across the patio. My cheeks are still warm with the prurience of her tone—one that makes my concern from Carling Hill slam its way to the forefront of my worries with a bracing alacrity. *How will my plans stand against a witch who would have been empress?*

The vision Kirdan and I share for Aiyca is still so nascent in its timeline, so fragile, not even Anya knows its full extent. I can't help feeling all the more protective of it given Iraya's reappearance. The Zesian Obeah and the Aiycan Obeah did have a long-standing friendship of sorts for thousands of years. One that excluded my sect. Of course, Kirdan's told me that Zesia only ever tolerated the Aiycan Obeah, who, in occupying the empire's cradle of magic here, always thought themselves superior. But now that Zesia has all the power, the Aiycan Obeah need *them*. Is it such a leap to imagine my humble dream of doyenne being passed over for an Adair legacy?

Doyenne Cariot gave Zesia's doyenne the power she always craved, emancipating her island from the Aiycan Obeah's rule. But it's no secret Doyenne Divsylar's always coveted *this* golden isle. There are just as many reasons for Zesia's doyenne to seek Iraya out as an ally as there are to wish her dead. Officially, Kirdan was sent here to ensure Doyenne Cariot kept her word, replacing the last emissary who arrived not long after the Adairs fell. But unofficially? We haven't spoken much about what his doyenne may or may not have asked him to do.

I find him pacing back and forth in my study, his cloak discarded on one of the armchairs before the unlit fireplace.

"She affects you."

He stops abruptly. "What do you mean?"

"She's a legacy," I make myself say, however uncomfortable it is to speak so frankly. "One whose power almost comes second to her beauty. Given what she shouted after you on the Patio of Prowlers, I was wondering if it's irritation or . . . something else?"

"Whatever beauty she may or may not possess"—he coughs—"is negated by her lack of sanity. Carne clearly unhinged her. So." He's quick to change the subject. "Do you think the Witchfire in St. Ann influenced the doyenne's decision to spare her?"

I'm happy to oblige the conversation change. Matters of

the heart aren't my specialty.

"She wouldn't have made the choice without planning for all outliers." It's what a good doyenne does. What I keep failing to do. Irritated, I drop into one of the armchairs.

Moving his cloak, Kirdan sits opposite me. "But what about her reaction at Carling Hill? She looked afraid of Iraya."

"It must have been shock. We can hardly call this a rash decision, Kir," I say, trying to make him understand that nothing's wrong, because he seems to be intimating that something might be. "She's spent almost two phases considering it. She killed the witnesses at Carling Hill and swore the Conscription Officers to secrecy." With, I later learned, a Shook Bargain, a binding magical agreement notorious enough to stopper even the most loquacious of lips. "She'll probably tell the Witches Council now she's keeping Iraya alive, but outside of you, me, and her, they'll be the only ones who know."

"The escapees from Carne know she was at Carling Hill," Kirdan says in a voice low enough to elicit a shiver. "And they've clearly told the Jade Guild."

"I thought so too. You need to see them so we can fix this. For all they know now, Iraya's dead. We don't have to tell them otherwise to get them back on our side."

"I agree. There has to be some sort of new arrangement we can come to that won't mean war. Because not only is Iraya reckless, hell-bent on revenge, and *insufferable*"—he snorts—"she's the last Adair." He says the name like it's both a prayer and a curse. "Dead or alive, they're going to be vexed with how matters went down at Carling Hill. Honestly, I'm surprised the doyenne went back on her word. She knows what a threat Iraya is."

He's right. . . . Perhaps something is going on.

"I'll try and seek an audience with the doyenne now, allay some concerns."

He nods. "Meet for dinner?"

"Anya will be back from St. Ann."

Laughing, he rises and reclaims his cloak. "Another time, then."

I shake my head. The two of them will have to get along sooner rather than later. I wish to make Anya my first and Kirdan my second when I'm doyenne. The entire relationship will revolve around working to protect me, not sparring with one another because Kirdan made a remark about Madisyn's beauty. Anya's jealousy was an overreaction, especially given that she and my sister broke up half a year before her death.

Kirdan and I part ways outside the doyenne's study; inside I'm not surprised to find the entire Witches Council present.

"Emissary," Doyenne Cariot says from the head of the board table. "The attendant found you then. Good. We're just about to take a vote."

"Vote?" Taking my usual seat, I reach for the jug of coconut water in the center of the table and pour some into my chalice. "About what?"

"This year's crop of Yielders."

My hands jerk the jug. Water splashes across the table, my fingers.

"W-what?" I look to Light Keeper; she merely purses her lips.

Presider Phelony answers, "You heard about the Witchfire?" She nods across the table. Presider Antwi's sobbing quietly into a bejeweled kerchief. Of course. St. Ann is her parish. "We can't stand back after such an attack from the Jade Guild."

They must have approached the doyenne, demanded she bring the Yielding back.

I scramble to find my bearings, to help her avoid being forced into this decision. "D-do we know why the insurgents attacked?"

"Does it matter?" Doyenne Cariot remarks, like she doesn't know the Jade Guild fight for the leader they believe she took from them.

The one strutting about somewhere on this estate, alive, as we speak.

A frown creases my brow. Why hasn't she told them about Iraya? Is Kirdan right?

Is she hiding something? Or is she merely bound by the Shook Bargain herself, and unable to speak Iraya's name?

"However unnecessary this may seem, I don't wish to make assumptions for any of you." Doyenne Cariot sits upright, a hand on a book of the Seven-Faced Mudda's teachings. "All in favor of reinstating the Yielding, raise your right hand."

Light Keeper alone looks at me as her hand is raised with the other five presiders'.

I sit back, stunned and disoriented.

"Emissary?" the doyenne's first, Presider Magmire, calls. "Your vote?"

My arm is stone as it rises.

"Then it is unanimous," Doyenne Cariot says. "There's to be a Yielding this year after all."

14

IRA

The Xanthippe take me away from the palace on foot, along the path clinging to the estate's boundary wall, where the Blue Mountains range provides little shelter from the merciless reach of Aiyca's sun. Every degree of its heat wheedles into the new glyphs scored over the wounds the muzzle left behind my ears, near setting my head, already burning with embarrassment after my failed attempt to kill the doyenne, alight.

Surreptitiously, so as not to alert my guard, I survey the sprawling estate. Much of it is remains as it was when I lived here; the multiple courtyards and porticos, rich mosaic tile, fruit groves, and stretches of green guarded by palm and shade trees. This morning it's populated by milling Alumbrar playing games with pickney, reading, or hurrying along, busy with some task or other. None look at me twice. Not with the silver hood concealing my hair.

It's a shock to find few patrolling Xanthippe, and none manning the battlements in the seven-sided fortress walls rising high around us. That Vow of Peace must be absolute, considering the shields' base has to be somewhere close by— behind the palace compound, in fact, through a gate in the boundary wall that is manned by Xanthippe, along the drive that curls up the mount to the palace, and behind the villas where the doyenne's coven live. I commit the latter location to memory.

The Cuartel's seven walls are just as high as those around the palace; its great gray gates are flanked by sentry posts, through which the din of combat rings as clearly as birdsong.

I wipe my palms on my shorts, almost nervous at what I'll find behind the gates. The dinner Doyenne Cariot laid siege during, one my parents were hosting for the Obeah Witches Council, and the twelve most skilled Obeah métier Masters, ended with the death of all bar three of the latter. Whether by truth or design, the Master Bonemantis, a métier valued for their ability to read the future, managed to convince the doyenne to let them live on the grounds, and help her keep Aiyca safe from threat. I'm to understand that the doyenne insists on few Warriors and Stealths, Poisoners and Squallers, arguably some of the deadliest of our métiers. My appointment will attract some attention.

"Where's the buddy?" one of my Xanthippe ask the two standing before a sentry bohío.

"I'm afraid she's running late," a woman's voice murmurs. A witch steps through the side door beside the gates, and I bite back my surprise because I know her. "Welcome, newest shield, to the Cuartel. I am Omnyra, Master Bonemantis."

One of twelve, now one of the three. Close friend of Mama and one of the cleverest witches on the entire island, the third eye scarification between her brows tells me.

"Wahan." I bow my head, and keep my name to myself.

"Where's the buddy?" The Xanthippe repeats. "We're under strict instructions to leave this shield with them."

"Some of the shields are testing, this morning. The buddy will come as soon as the task is complete." With all the superiority her métier tends to foster, Master Omnyra reaches forward and slips a hand beneath my elbow and draws me toward her. "You can tell the doyenne I am merely standing in. Good day." With a gentle tug she pulls me alongside her.

What if she recognizes me? What if she's seen me coming?

The first worry is less possible. I was a pickney when I left and a woman now. As for the second . . . I'm less sure. Bonemantis scrying isn't as simple as looking and knowing. It's a complex art, and one those who don't practice know little about. Tense, I follow the Master through the side door; on the other side of the gate a wide courtyard separates two training fields where Obeah battle steals my attention.

Shields in uniforms like mine, though the Obeah-men bear longer pants, battle with guzzu shooting from conduits in yellow sparks, purple disks, and fizzing blue half-moons. Men atop great prowlers oversee the training, occasionally calling out victors, or admonishing those who fail to guard in time as partners duck and dodge with shields of metal, not conduit gold. I reach for my own coin. Once my ilk sported enough gold to call shields forth from them. But this is too small to bear the load of that will. We'd burn through it too fast.

Reconnaissance in Carne revealed that conscripts receive replacement coins after a year of respite within the prison, but new conduits won't eliminate any magical fatigue that's already set in. It leaves us like a weakened bone, one strenuous task away from snapping.

This was always a gamble, not ideal yet unavoidable. Watching the shields train, expending their will again and again, I wonder if I might find myself back in Carne sooner rather than later. . . .

"I see you've already noted the first major setback in your training here," Master Omnyra says. "The role of a shield is not isolated." She nods across the courtyard to the second training field, where shields work with Xanthippe. Aureate beasts project from their conduits, and shields shoot guzzu, hold spears aloft to fight back the monsters. "The Alumbrar coven members make up for magical shortcomings, just as shields make up for the gaps in their strategic knowledge."

I knew shields were trained to protect the mount, but after witnessing my order's diminished status on our journey from Carling Hill, to see this . . . "Wow."

"The circumstances that have brought us here are abhorrent, but the doyenne and we three Masters agreed to set our orders' obsessions with one another aside for Aiyca, and the coming threats that seek this island out. In your role here, shield, you must believe in that vow you took." The Master's focus sharpens on me with such bite that, for a second, I scare myself into believing there is recognition in her eyes and then—drums thrum through the earth across the Cuartel. "Come. The test I spoke of has just ended. Let us meet your buddy."

I have many questions as we cross the courtyard and bear right, away from the twin training fields, but the Master seems far from the Cuartel mentally, merely nodding at the shields we pass who greet her, and I don't mind her staying there if it means she doesn't think back to the pickney who used to sit, scowling, in meetings with her mama because she would rather have been anywhere else.

The schoolrooms neighbor a large infirmary I suspect I'll be visiting often in the coming moon phases as I try to figure out a way to get rid of these blasted Impediment Glyphs.

"We're educated here?" I ask the Master as shields pour from the cluster of small round buildings, discussing a test that was just given with their uniformed bredren and sistren.

"The Masters and I educate as dictated by the doyenne. There are lessons in—ah." The Master breaks off to wave at a small crowd of shields. "Here's Delyse now."

A slight Obeah-witch beats a hasty path our way. Beneath her right eye, the two horizontal scars, stained white like mine, identify her as one of the defunct Obeah Witches Council's eyes on the ground—a Stealth. She was two scars away from completing her training when our order fell.

Please don't be you. Please go past us to the friends you were waving at behind us.

"Wahan, Master Omnyra," she breathes.

Typical. I end up with a buddy who once worked as an intelligence operative.

"Be sure to settle this shield."

The buddy's clever eyes look me over before they dip back to her hands, which are clasped before her in obeisance. "We already have a bohío ready."

"Very well." With one nod, the Master leaves us.

"Wahan," the witch greets me, her musical patwah thick enough to tell me she grew up in the country. Those astute eyes run all over my face again, fixing on my mouth in a way that makes me want to check the muzzle is truly gone. "I'm Delyse. I'll guide and train you while you get settled here."

"And after that, will I be on my own?"

"You'll never be on your own." Her eyes lift to fix on the scarification between my eyebrows. I press my lips together so I don't tell her to look elsewhere. "The initial training will prepare you to keep up with our drills, but understanding your magic will be more of an ongoing thing." She squints at the position of the sun. "It's almost lunch. We can get a move on as soon as I know what to call you, mon."

I'm aware of the surrounding shields leaving the school-rooms listening in.

"Ira."

She raises a brow. "Just Ira?"

"So I've been told."

"Right. Well, follow me, Just-Ira." She turns on her heel, scattering those who linger with the threat of busha rounds. "They oversee our training here, make sure we do it," she explains, pointing at the silver-haired watchmen stationed about the Cuartel.

In matching silver uniforms, the busha sit astride great jungle-prowlers. Though fearsome, the oversize male cats are arresting. Their shaggy coats, some striped, some spotted, glisten beneath the sun. Ivory tusks longer than my arms curve from their mouths. They're the only weapons I spot in the bushas' vicinity, unless the spyglasses on their hips double as bats. . . .

"Why aren't they wearing conduit coins?"

"They're magicless," Delyse replies. "Second or third sons. I don't know. What I do know is that being here means someone else inherited in their families, and they're badmind enough to take it out on us. Don't be fooled by their lack of conduit. Honestly," she adds when she catches the disbelief on my face, "it'll be better for the prowlers to get you than them."

We alight at the top of a hilly rise. The Cuartel stretches beneath us, populated by shields going about their day with a lightness I didn't anticipate. They're almost *happy* in the work they're doing here, despite most of them coming from métiers that had little to do with combat, before. I only have to look at the varied scarification to see that these conscripts once lent their magical insight to melting down Aiyca's conduit coins to form weapons, the most skilled Artisans of Metal. Or Transmuters, who created magical fuel to power our homes and businesses, like the witchlights used across the island. There are Wranglers who once reared beasts in Aiyca's wilds, and Bush Healers; I do spot a few of my ilk, though we would have trained far from one another in the world before.

"A Warrior, huh?"

I drop my hand. I hadn't realized I was tracing my scar. "Yeh mon."

Delyse's dark eyes reveal little as she watches me. "Don't get many magi with your métier around here." She pulls deeply from a fat skin she carries on her hip, offering it my way when she's done. "But then, we don't get a lot from my métier around here either."

To my relief a deep drum echoes across the Cuartel, in a different sequence than the ones before.

"And that's for?" I ask, handing back the skin.

"Lunch," she says. "Come on."

Obeah join us on the verge, laughing and joking. Some build fires with refuse, frying aromatic salted cod and cassava on metal sheets. After Carne it stuns me, the verve, the lightness of spirit. The massacre might not have happened.

Delyse settles beneath the expansive arms of a shade tree. She unpacks a metal sheet and a few plantains. "Want one?"

"Please." It's been so long since I've eaten anything fresh.

Additional Obeah-witches join us while Delyse slices and fries the fruit until it's golden. One bite and I'm near melting with pleasure, enough that I don't mind answering questions about my time in Carne. It's a prime opportunity to dig for my own intel.

"How often does the doyenne visit the Cuartel?"

"Never mind that," Delyse interrupts, ever the nuisance I knew she'd be. "Can one of you sort her 'fro out?" Following the others' lead, I discarded my silver hood to eat. "All those curls will lock before too long. Unless that's something you want?" The question seems like a challenge.

"I'm fine with braids."

Liar, liar.

In Aiyca, locks and afros mean peace, pacifism; the intricate weaving of braids isn't simply a fashion statement. It's a symbol to prepare for battle. They united Jade Guild sympathizers in Carne. Could they do the same here? Most Obeah-witches I've seen so far wear them. Most of the Obeah-men too. In prison I could wear two thick plaits, straddle the line. Not anymore.

"You'll carry them well." Delyse's expression is crafty as she waves a witch over.

A face that looks like it's seen a thousand smiles beams at me with soft brown eyes—and a comb in hand. The older Obeah-witch begins tugging that wide-toothed comb through my hair, pulling hard enough to exact a wince from me. Two winces after, she raps my shoulder with the comb.

"Are all days like this, here?"

"More or less." Delyse toys with her own hair. It crisscrosses her scalp, in much narrower cornrows than there's time to give me, before cascading in twists down her back. Ribbons of yellow yarn wind through the black to add length as well as color. They're neat. Militant. "We're on a schedule, with a mixture of classes, training drills, and either a night or day watch on the mount around both compounds. You'll spend your first two moon phases training with me, and engaging in classes before you move on to a full schedule. We'll start your training tomorrow."

I squirm beneath the bony fingers digging into my scalp. "I'm ready to use my magic now."

The surrounding witches exchange knowing looks before they explode in raucous laughter; my skin bristles. Suddenly I'm a pickney again, forced to sit and listen to the gossip of women far older than me.

"It's not as easy as thinking something, Just-Ira. You'll be grateful for the privacy tomorrow."

I'm sure to keep smiling and laughing with them while they discuss the benign trappings of life here, aware of how phony I sound and hating every minute of it. It's a relief when the drums sound again and Delyse's sistren leave us.

"The tour's all but done, so I'll take you to your new home and you can rest before tomorrow. You should get as much as possible."

Busha stand about nattering at the base of the hill. I stumble over one of their prowler's paws.

"Watch where you're going!" one remonstrates as his beast snaps at me. "Cha mon!"

"S-sorry," I stutter. "Lost my footing."

"You should be more careful. Lost things don't often get found round here."

His companions shout suggestive slurs. Keeping my head down, I move on, tucking my stolen goods into the waistband of my shorts. We'll see how confident he feels tomorrow when he realizes his spyglass is missing.

"That swine was right," Delyse murmurs, as we cross into a more residential part of the Cuartel, its paths lined with flowering trees and benches. "Be cautious at night. The Xanthippe maintain a compass defense around the Cuartel perimeter, and there are glyphs etched in blind spots to prevent us from running, but they don't do anything to stop the busha hunting inside."

"Really?"

"We're partners in name only. They don't care about us otherwise, and the feeling is mutual." She snorts. "Do yourself a favor and don't sleep with your back to the window, or you might wake with fresh cuts." She lowers her tunic, exposing a soft pink scar across her collarbone. "I caught him before he could lick the blood, thank the goddess."

Realization sinks, heavy as a stone, in my belly. "The busha try to steal our magic?"

"Face the window," Delyse repeats.

So this is how things truly are here. My order may smile and laugh, but they're aware of the realities that lurk in this compound. What about who has made it so? Unavoidable, the palace crests the sky a mile away at the top of the hill, the Empress's Seat. All elegant turrets and bastions, rounded edges and light stone reinforced with a warm golden filigree of conduit metal, once it was the stronghold of an indomitable magical empire. And I know empires don't last forever, but Obeah were supposed to.

"How did the Alumbrar defeat us?" I wonder out loud.

"I think sometimes we forget that while the Mudda made us fighters, leaders. They made the Alumbrar to challenge us. Not with sword or staff, but with their minds. Their creation was supposed to make us better. More well-rounded." Delyse walks with ease beneath a low-hanging bough I have to duck to avoid.

Away from the training fields and classrooms, there's only vegetation to hear us talk, and the breadfruit trees aren't known for their prattling. Neither are the bough-prowlers who leap from branch to branch above us, following our every move with wide reflective eyes.

"*Aiyca's firstborn, the Obeah, come from one of the Supreme Being's ribs planted in rich clay.*" I recite the Anansi story of my order's origin. "*Them earthy origins mirror the strength emblazoned in the lightless hues of them dark-colored eyes. It's said the dirt made them hard, unforgiving. Me think the dirt inna them eye; that's why them always a scowl.*"

"Right." Delyse laughs. "I forget the beginning of the Alumbrar story, something about them being stars." She rolls her eyes. "But the important part is that '*Them origins gave them lofty temperaments and dreams of superiority above them earth-born Obeah cousins. Them not fighters, but it nuh stop them from fighting.*'" She shakes her head. "We turned each other into the worst versions of ourselves competing for supremacy in Aiyca. We might have acted like we were better than them, but they took it a step too far when they killed the Adairs."

I stiffen at my family name, but Delyse is too busy scowling to notice.

"I almost think a fight would have been better than what they did. Nobler. But our leaders became comfortable in their positions, lazy. The Alumbrar took the opportunity." She shrugs. "Now we're conscripted as if it's we who should be sorry, our conduits are taken the moment conscription ends, and the rest of our order lives in magicless seclusion—fear, because of the indolence of magi who should have known better."

"Are you saying the Adairs deserved what they got?"

As if aware of how cautious she needs to be with her next words, Delyse stops before a cascade of vines that rustle in the warm night air. "I loved the Adairs like I loved Mama. Despite the Masters releasing an edict that Obeah not fight the Xanthippe who came to take the firstborns to Carne, she died fighting them when they came for me. One of countless parents who didn't want their pickney punished for their supposed mistakes." Her features are delicate, pretty and doll-like. But when her sorrow sharpens into ire, she becomes fierce. "We don't have to like what happened, we have to learn from it. We need to make sure we're the better magi when the time comes. Because it will. *We* weren't made to be second." Her eyes rise to the top of my head, to the thick cornrows lengthened by dark yarn, before she sweeps the vines aside. "Welcome home."

On the other side, the first thing that strikes me is the light.

Hundreds of jars are strung up overhead to illuminate the village, far enough away that they could be trapped stars. Bohíos, the round huts, sit squat and low beneath them as though beaten from above by a mighty fist. We moved away from such rudimentary buildings decades ago, when stone became the more popular—the more temperate—option. It's another setback used by the Alumbrar to remind us of our reduced circumstances.

But the accommodation could be worse. The reeds forming the huts' walls fill the night air with a sweetness that's undercut by the grass and palm leaf thatch roofs. Memories of my Warrior sistren come to me. The moments between lessons when we'd lie in the stalks and track clouds as they drifted across the sky. Yes. These might not be the grand villas and great houses my order once occupied, but they're cozy, intimate.

"This is you." Delyse stops before a small bohío.

Behind the wooden door there's a low cot with a basket of fruit, and more supplies resting atop it, a mirror propped across from it, and a small pile of books on a rickety desk with an equally rickety chair. The stalks lining the walls smell clean, fresh. It would have made killing the doyenne easier, vow aside, but I find myself grateful I'm not in the palace, vast and cold without Dada's laughter to warm it, Mama's presence to fill it, family and friends to hide behind as my cousins and I sprinted through its halls screaming in some game or other.

Where might those cousins be now? Those aunties and uncles?

"Do you know anything about the rest of the Adairs, the Clarkes, who lived in the palace with the first family?" It's a risk to ask Delyse, but no one in Carne was able to tell me anything about them, and I won't sleep tonight without knowing.

She frowns. "The Masters are bound from discussing specifics, but I'd guess they died too."

As I thought.

"If anyone managed to escape, I suspect they would have fled. They might be in the Blue Mountains, with the Jade Guild."

More speculation, like that in Carne. It makes sense that both sides of my family would flee to the mountains, in a crisis, to the training bohío Nana Clarke ran, but I won't know for sure who did or didn't survive until the doyenne is dead.

"There's rum in that welcome pack." Delyse's voice pulls me out of my thoughts. "You can bring it along to tonight's kotch."

"It's been a long day."

"There'll be more food," she pushes. "And magi excited to welcome you."

That's what concerns me.

"I'm exhausted." I force a yawn for good measure. "Think I'll stay here."

"I'll leave you, then." She doesn't, though. "Actually, do you mind if I ask you something?"

My back tightens. Delyse's proven herself to be a witch who doesn't feel the need to ask permission.

"No doubt you've heard about the Lost Empress," she continues, proving my point. "I was wondering if you ever saw her, in Carne? Heard about her? She's about your age."

I nudge the cot with my foot, scrutinizing the thin mattress for any roaches. "I thought her an Anansi story."

"There's more truth in stories than many believe."

My responding noise is noncommittal.

"You didn't hear anything?"

"Nothing certain."

She looks disappointed. "Well, I was in Carne before coming here, and I'd definitely remember you if I'd seen you in there. I suppose it is a vast place. . . . But look, if you remember anything, you can let me know tomorrow. I'll be outside your door at first light. Likkle more, Just-Ira." Delyse leaves me with her promise of soon, but that was far too easy. She'll try again tomorrow, maybe the next day—*cha*.

Kaleisha would kick up dust in her haste to join up for the fight that must be brewing here, regardless of the vow. My fingers trace my scarification again. I can't think of her without being drawn to it, though I shouldn't be thinking of her at all. There are more pressing matters, like my plan to kill the doyenne. Now it seems riddled with as many holes as a sinking ship.

It won't be easy; at times I suspect it will be downright impossible—but no matter how many holes ruin this vessel, I won't go down until that witch does.

PART II

BLOOD
FOLLOWS
VEIN

JAZMYNE

There's an art to wrapping a head tie.

Two attendants hold either end of the rose-gold scarf. It's wider than my outstretched arms. My neck already aches with the promise of its weight. They pass their fabric ends to one another once, twice. I take what remains and twist it into a neat knot over which the silver coils of my afro spring.

For days like today the head tie is a necessity, an armor I wear to remind myself that this palace isn't home, and my rooms aren't a place of solace. They're an armory in which I prepare for battle. After a night of prayer with the Witches Council, allegedly, this morning the doyenne announces the start date of the Yielding, and its Yielders, in a public assembly.

Nothing makes a witch move like a lick of flame, and she, it seems, is no exception.

And now I too must be quick.

There was no time to talk after yesterday's vote, with the council going into immediate prayer. But I am going to speak with her this morning. How could I not after she allowed the presiders to believe the Jade Guild's attack was a coincidence? Something is amiss; I mean to learn what.

The magicless attendants bind me in a kaftan's silky confines. Blades of morning light from the windows scissor across the tile. On the lawn outside, noise from carriages drawn by sand-prowlers clatter over the stone on the drive. Some will belong to visitors who seek to visit the estate's temple this holy day. The doyenne risks insulting all seven of the Mudda's Faces announcing the Yielding today, which only makes her seem all the more eager to begin, once again making me revisit Kirdan's suspicion about her motives.

No one could reach for death like it's the sole option. It can't be as easy for her to bring back the Yielding as she made it seem. And if it is? In my dressing room, my reflections all worry their bottom lips between their teeth.

If it is, at least my attire is appropriate for what will follow.

I take the lesser-used west steps to the rear of the palace. My sandals stir dust and lingering roaches during the descent. A few turns through the narrow labyrinth of storage corridors positions me around the corner from Doyenne Cariot's study. After a quick knock, I enter.

Seated behind her desk, she looks up from a book—her journal. "Wahan, Emissary."

"Wahan." I close the door.

"I'm glad you're here." She returns to the notations before

her, browsing their contents. "I want to talk with you about Iraya Adair."

"About why you reneged on your word to kill her?"

The journal closes with a snap.

I wince internally. I should have practiced that line.

"Being a successful doyenne is about the very thing you do not understand—sacrifice." The doyenne's eye cuts its truth, even from across the room. "I was content to exchange love for respect when I first introduced the Yielding. Some Alumbrar would hate me, I knew, as they did when I introduced the Shield Initiative, but they would respect my ability to maintain our position—my willingness to do whatever it took to keep this island safe, so they wouldn't have to. The Yielding kills their pickney instead of war, instead of our enemies. Do you think I didn't consider the outcome of a fair fight? Alumbrar would be decimated by Zesia, by the pirates of the Iron Shore. Pickney across this island would die—more than a Yielding would take."

I don't understand what this has to do with Iraya.

"Tell me, Emissary." The doyenne's voice dips to a soft lull. "If I was ready to walk the Bone Road to Coyaba, to die for you to carry my magic as well as this crown, could you say that you would sacrifice whatever you needed to, whether it be your dignity or your people, in order to keep Aiyca from falling into the hands of those who don't deserve it?"

I shift on my feet. It's a question the Nameless have been asking for the better part of a year. One I haven't had an answer for.

"Sacrifice isn't easy."

"And what makes you think it's meant to be? It wouldn't have any meaning if you weren't willing to give away something that was important to you."

Like Madisyn?

Stomach churning, I reach for my locket. The doyenne's brows lower in twin scythes as she narrows in on the movement. I drop my hand, but it's too late.

"I've told you before that there's no place for sentiment in ruling," she says, as shrewd as ever. "It appears there's much I still need to teach you, child, before you'll be ready to lead." She smiles at me, but there's a dearth of any motherly feeling there. "And your first lesson is in asset management. Iraya Adair is your responsibility. She has been sufficiently warned to behave, but she is Obeah, and untrustworthy by nature. You are to watch her and report back to me if she goes anywhere on the estate, or otherwise, that she should not."

"But why—"

"Do you understand?"

I bite back the questions my place doesn't permit me to ask. "Yes, Doyenne."

It must be Iraya's power, her naevus, that's keeping her alive. What does the doyenne, her cabinet of scrying Sibyls, foresee that I do not? Does she see anything, or is she so used to conflict that she's creating her own to justify her choices? Whatever her reasons, it's clear, the clearest it's been to me, that our priorities are polarized. Light Keeper was right: I can't rule from beneath the doyenne's thumb. Hers has been a red ruling, and always will be.

"Now," she says, abrupt, "I take it you have somewhere else to be, dressed as you are?"

"Yes." I'm struck by a desperate urge to make one last attempt to seek anything worth saving in her. "Would you like to come to Mourner's Row with me?"

"Whatever for?"

I'm slow to speak. "To walk for Madisyn." She said my sister was important, just now. It was subtle, but it was there. "We never . . . we never speak about her." Something that may be my fault. I haven't been able to discuss my sister with the doyenne, but what if she wished to talk about her with me? "With the Yielding's return, we should think of her today. So, will you take the walk with me?"

Say yes, I will. *Use this final chance to prove I'm wrong about you, before it's too late.*

"And why would I do that when her death has brought me the comfort her life wouldn't have?" Doyenne Cariot returns to the journal, thumbing through its pages to reach her last. "You may continue to do as you see fit for now, Jazmyne. But I suggest you use these next three months before your eighteenth earthstrong to give up your juvenile indulgences." She waves a distracted hand. "You will sit by my side until such a time as when you can sit alone. I won't have your sentiment making us look weak. Close the door on your way out."

Tears rise hot and fast the moment my back's turned to her.

It was a fool's errand, but one I needed to complete. Now it no longer matters if I can do this; I *must*. And though it terrifies me, it is not a lesson I am unfamiliar with.

Even Healers have to be prepared to end a life at risk of doing more harm than good.

So while the very thought of going against the witch who gave me life should do more than make my stomach flip over, my heart thump . . . for the maroon Dada wore as Healer, the vow I would have taken before everything changed, and the life my sister should have lived, perhaps it's time to do whatever it takes to remove the doyenne from the throne.

Even if it means sitting on it myself earlier than planned.

16

IRA

Remiss of its usual vibrancy, dawn has yet to chase away the entirety of night the first morning I wake in my bohío. I allow myself a moment to relish the dappled sky, the freshness of the village's rich earth carried on a sweet wind. It stirs the curtains not fully covering the window; my body's unwound and indulgently loose knowing no prison guards will darken my doorway, but only for a moment.

If Doyenne Cariot is up to something, I must be too.

I find spare uniforms in the chest at the end of my bed, and dress in everything but the hood before slipping out of my bohío. Within the sleeping village, it's easy for the dark clusters of shadows to cling to my skin like spider silk as they make me one of their own. Years of early rising in Carne shunts my fatigue to the side, enabling my feet to dance across the dust, too quick to leave a trail for anyone to follow.

The busha aren't as skilled.

I come across half a dozen or so sets of prints. More than one lead right up to bohío windows. The thin line of Delyse's scar crests in my memory. Something wicked, something without remorse, wakes inside me. I memorize the location, planning to return later tonight to make that busha, and the rest, regret being so heavy-footed.

By the outer third of the village, I think, I wedge my foot in the corner of an empty bohío's windowsill and hoist myself onto the cane roof. The huts sit close enough that they almost touch, forming a path with their thatched tops. Like yesterday, no Xanthippe occupy the bastions along the boundary wall that separates the Cuartel from the rest of the estate.

Knowing now that the shields here are linked to this place by the Masters who worked with Mama, magi so willing to protect Aiyca from threat that they voluntarily swore an oath not to harm Judair Cariot, it makes sense that the Xanthippe wouldn't be watching. What need is there when my order here can't rise against the doyenne—wouldn't. Not without a suitable leader to replace her. If I find a way to kill her, will I be leaving this island vulnerable to attack? Justice can't be as simple as me against the rest of my order. Not when my parents were their leaders, surely. I have to believe that I exist in the gray, and if that means that I must walk alone then so be it. Walk alone I shall.

Provided with privacy by the undulating terrain in the Cuartel, leaving some bohíos higher than others, I can stand without being seen by the Xanthippe across the compound. If I am careful. But then, when am I not? Especially when navigating heights. The drop from the bohío's roof wouldn't be fatal, but one look down and queasiness punches through me all the same. Of all fears to have, one of mine has to be being far from the ground. *The Mudda doesn't give us trials we can't handle*, Nana Clarke would have said. So either the past ten years have been the longest test I've endured, or that axiom is a load of chaff. I'm inclined to believe the latter.

One breath is all I snatch before leaping to the next roof, and the next, repeating the pattern until I'm close enough to grab hold of the sweeping arms of a giant ceiba tree that stretches over the boundary wall from the neighboring palace estate. Nestled within the deep emerald of its leaves, I extend my stolen spyglass with a quiet click. The metal is a welcome chill against my skin. Even in the shade, Aiyca's heat maintains its bite so high up on the island. There are still no Xanthippe visible along the palace estate's perimeter to my left or right. That doesn't mean anything here. This might still be a glyphed blind spot.

My thighs grip the branch all the more to keep me secure. I've heard of glyphs that can shock you from the inside out; others, I've been told, are incendiary; some can even drive a person mad. Worrying my lip between my teeth, I turn my spyglass across the rolling estate. A mile from the Cuartel, the palace is positioned atop the highest point of the mount. A compound built to withstand battle, it's ringed by three defense points.

The outermost band consists of Xanthippe atop jungle-prowlers; they loop the palace and immediate walled private gardens, the stone and conduit gold too tall and smooth to climb without rope, as a scar on my elbow can attest from some childhood incident or other; atop, unattended battlements are lined with crossbow brackets.

My spyglass can't permeate the innermost ring. I mutter a curse. To think, yesterday I was close to that which I now seek behind its colossal wall of trees—an escape tunnel. A network of them run inside the palace walls, opening up all over the estate's mount. It's a smart bet that the doyenne knows about the main routes. They'll be in the floor plans. But there are others glyphed to allow only Adairs inside that she'll be ignorant of.

Being remanded inside the palace would have made accessing the tunnels easier, but—I draw a grounding breath that quickly turns into a yawn—I've never balked in the face of a challenge before.

I observe the guards' rotations until the bark beneath me loses all comfort, memorizing the number of steps their prowlers take, how often Xanthippe dismount to stretch or play with their familiars. No sentinels arrive to take watch on the battlements or in the private garden's tree line. I suppose they have nothing to fear—*had*. My snort frightens a mountain whistler from its perch above me with a disgruntled caw.

Today, I suppose, they'll be safe. I have business in the public gardens between the Cuartel and the new Alumbrar temple. Time to move.

With a deep breath, I climb higher up the tree and hoist

myself atop a thick branch. My arms quiver as I shimmy along the bough's length until I'm suspended outside the Cuartel. The tip bows with a groan. My teeth grit. *A bit farther*, I promise myself. Just until I'm a couple of yards outside the reach of whatever glyph might be concealed along the boundary.

BOOM boom-boom BOOM boom-boom.

The sudden rumble of an estate drum startles a cry from me. I fall.

Landing with a muted exhale, I wait, chest tight, hidden by tall grass. No alarms sound, and no Xanthippe come running. Shaking like a sapling, I place a hand over my frantically beating heart. *Thank the goddess.* My limbs are jerky, stiff, as I rise. Blasted drums. *That's something else that needs doing*, I think as I set off at a slow jog, *learning their timings*. My next fall might not end so well.

Cardio was difficult to achieve in Carne. Not even a quarter of a mile across the wild border of grass, when my jog becomes a wheezing lope, I regret not trying to find more ways to make it work. A stitch pierces my side and I'm sweating more than a witch who might not have time to change before classes and training later should. But regardless of the way my tunic clings to my body, I find it feels good to move again, to feel the tug of muscles awakening.

Despite the overgrown nature of this section of the estate, no doubt a deliberate move by the doyenne when she found herself unable to entirely erase the evidence that my family lived here first, I find what I'm looking for with a little difficulty. Its access marker, a trellis of roses, has been choked by weeds. By the time I've fought my way through the bush, cuts graze my legs from the snares, but the Adair Graveyard still stands, even if it's in disrepair.

In the shaded grove, all Aiyca's previous empresses are entombed atop raised daises, their golden encasements tarnished by the cruel duo of sunlight and time. My body is awash with reverence. My spirit, restless after the journey here, stills, and I am without doubt that this is where I am meant to be.

Forgive me, I beg the ancestors, despite the age of the bones and the fact that any lingering spirits would have matriculated to Carling Hill long ago. It's not like my absence could be helped, but still. Manners. The ancestors are always listening. I take a moment to respect each tomb, splashing rum from my welcome skin on their mottled surfaces in Jákīsa, the ritual of honoring the dead. A fragrant wind sings through broad leaves of the mighty ceiba and mahoe trees. I love that this graveyard is filled with music, but sorrow stabs low in my gut that my parents didn't have the chance to be buried here. Doyenne Cariot paraded their bodies through Queenstown, I heard, before lighting the pyre and sending them out to sea. There were worse fates she could have given them, I guess, but . . .

Don't think about that now. You can't.

There's work to do.

The upside of the doyenne leaving nature to claim that which I doubt she could remove magically or otherwise is that it's easy to forage for things in a scale of sizes I'll be able to practice my magic on. Sneaking in a few extra sessions without Delyse can't hurt. It isn't so much that I don't believe my magic will be difficult to call. With the glyphs behind my ears, it's promised to be. My naevus is the primary concern. I don't yet know how present, how *ready*, it is, and the last thing I need is for it to explode in Delyse's company.

The graveyard proffers several bruised mangoes, some green bananas, and a sheet of bark. Good enough. Focusing on the ugliest mango, I will a thread of wind to move it from its twenty-yard space into my hand. Either palm, I'm not picky. After at least five minutes of staring and muttering, nothing happens. Magic is about will, so surely wanting should be enough? And I've never wanted a fruit, never mind one I can't even eat, so badly in my life. I draw in another breath, doubling my concentration, and yet it doesn't shift.

Come on.

A headache brews between my brows. It might be dehydration. *Come on!* I urge, annoyed. Without warning, a tumult of energy roils through my body. White-gold light flares from my eyes, and all three mangoes hurl toward me at once. Blinking the light away, I dive to avoid them, but the ugly one smacks against my top. Its overripe skin bursts, smattering my uniform in cloying fruit pulp and maggots.

Cha!

I fall back against the mossy blades of grass. Overhead, the sky's obstructed by the wide casing of a tomb my head only just missed. The stone's incised in deep patwah.

"Not that I'm mad," I murmur. "But why give me all

this power if I can't control it?" My fingers trace the raised words; they're rough, even against my calluses. Some parts have eroded away, but what I can make out looks like it might be a—

"You shouldn't be here."

I start, almost knocking my head on the tomb again.

"Did you hear me?" Emissary Divsylar calls from across the graveyard.

Clothed only in loose sleeping bottoms slung low on the chiseled grooves of his hips, he folds his arms over a chest I'm not surprised is flayed with the puckered lines of scars.

"Shield!"

Rolling onto my side, I rise from the springy earth. It takes a substantial amount of my pride, nearly all of it, to contain a gag as I brush the remaining maggots from my shorts.

"I should have assumed you'd do something this stupid so soon, even after my warning."

"You've been thinking about me again." I swing my braided ponytail over my shoulder and blink up at him with wide-eyed innocence. "Should I be flattered?"

"You should be smarter." His pectoral muscles tighten. "Anyone could have seen you skulking about on the estate. The palace has windows, in case you didn't know."

"First of all, I don't *skulk*."

"You could have fooled me." Emissary Divsylar raises a single slug of a brow, and then, almost as if he can't help himself, he asks, "And second?"

Second, I think, *the temple prevents you seeing this dale from the palace, so how did he?*

"I know exactly what a window is," I say, dipping my eyes to my nails. "I plan on having a lot of fun envisioning myself kicking you out of one."

"Iraya—"

I tut. "*Ira*. We don't want to expose my identity, now, do we?"

His muscles twitch again. "You certainly don't want to, no."

"I meant we." I relish goading him. "I doubt my order learning about my existence would benefit you any more than it will Doyenne Cariot, because you both want the same thing, right, Emissary Divsylar?"

A mottled red flush blooms across his chest and neck.

"Looks like you've caught the sun there, mon."

"You're out of bounds," he grinds out, bristling. "By a significant margin. Do I need to fetter you, or are you smart enough to make your own way back to the Cuartel?"

"All you had to do was ask, Emissary Divsylar. I'm here to serve, after all."

I turn to go, leaving him looking very much like his head is about to explode. Perhaps that's the reason he tails me the entire way back to the training ground, and the long way at that, I make sure, to avoid exposing my way out. I'm thoughtful enough to swing my hips a little more than I typically would. It seems only fair that he has something to look at in exchange for his humiliation. After all, it keeps me in good spirits the entire way back to the village—though not to the point of distraction.

It's difficult to think of anything but the emissary's

all-seeing eye. I stand by my first impression now more than ever. His stealth, his speed, his spying: they all speak of an experience beyond his role of gofer and lapdog. They speak of palms calloused from gripping the elegant weapons he doesn't carry this morning, of weighted running drills until you feel as though your legs will fall off. My training with Nana Clarke's coven was short-lived with the usurpation, but I remember enough to recognize a fellow Warrior in arms.

Who is Emissary Divsylar really, I wonder, *and what might he be hiding?*

The doyenne is right to raise forty-nine shields when, undoubtedly, Zesia's sword is drawn.

Why, then, does their emissary appear to be working *with* her?

17

JAZMYNE

Outside the palace, in the public gardens, the soft peal of the Mourning Bell calls its somber song through the burgeoning dawn. Each note reverberates through me, soothing the static of my nerves after the meeting with the doyenne until I'm not thinking about what must be done next, the meetings I'll need to have with Light Keeper, or my own fallibility.

Together, the procession of Alumbrar and I make our pilgrimage along the meandering Mourner's Row, so named for the path's likeness to the life of those we gather here to remember. Though flush with visitors lingering among trellises romanced by fist-size flowers and ancient shade trees whose branches reach over the path to offer comfort, the garden also shows the negatives to life in its snares and blind corners.

A warm breeze carries wracking sobs from family members lamenting the loss of loved ones, whether it be due to natural circumstances, or the more nefarious, like the usurpation. Obeah alone call the Alumbrar victory the Viper's Massacre, but a massacre it has been to my sect too. Their cries sink into my chest like the tip of a claw. One tug and I'll split open.

As they always do, on these first Sundays in the month, internal voices encourage me to let go. After my meeting with Doyenne Cariot, the desire to challenge those voices doesn't come with the conviction it should.

But Dada's voice rises above the others.

To survive infection, he told me as a novice Healer, *the body* must *fight*.

I take this walk not just for Madisyn, or Dada, but as a reminder that if I don't step up, everything the Nameless and I hope to remedy in Aiyca will only worsen. The number of mourners, already great this morning, will increase. Girls of little consequence, who are impregnated young to make up for Yielders' deaths, will be even younger when used. They are the reason why I cannot let go. They are why I cannot give in.

The Row curves into a deep bend. Squinting in the sudden southern light, I think I spot Anya ahead. She missed our supper plans last night. I speed up, murmuring apologies as I overtake other mourners, weaving and bobbing my way through whispered snatches of my name, my title. Someone obstructs my path. We collide. By the time apologies have been made, blessing given, Anya—or the person who looked like her—is gone. But another face, just as welcome, cuts against the current toward me.

"Wahan," Kirdan says, his face softened by a smile. "I

received your missive." His shoulder brushes against my own. It's the most contact he'll permit in the storm of prejudiced eyes surrounding us, not quite repelled far back enough by his cache of weapons. "I was making good on my promise to keep an eye on our mutual annoyance."

Iraya Adair.

"You'll never believe what she was doing earlier."

"Not here," I say. It isn't safe. Not given the nature of what I too must share with Kirdan. "This way."

The Row's destinations rise like beacons atop two sister knolls ahead. Built from white marble, the first is a hemispherical structure. Sitting atop a dais of wide gilded stairs encased by four stone posts, the flat roof of the stupa is made of pure yellow gold; more of the conduit metal perches atop like swirls of cream. The second is the pale gold facade of the Temple of the Supreme Being's Chosen. A feat of columns entwined with golden leaf, each topped with lifelike banana fronds, it's almost half the size of the sprawling palace behind us. My unease dissipates at the sight of it. Through many a tempest have the effigies of the Seven-Faced Mudda kept me warm, standing tens of feet tall to welcome all their sons and daughters.

This morning I need Consuelo, the Mudda's Face of Consolation, more than ever.

"Doyenne Cariot charged me with watching Iraya," I murmur to Kirdan, though he was the one who had news to share first.

"Why?"

"I didn't get to ask after what she said next."

We venture left, away from the temple. Fewer magi wander around the stupa at our approach. Over two hundred feet in height, it stands like a giant amid the estate; inside, there are dozens upon dozens of skulls lining the bottom of the colossal glass vat. Past Yielders. Including my sister.

"She told me, in not so many words, that she doesn't regret Madisyn's death."

Kirdan sends a comforting swath of magic to encircle my wrist. "She is—" He swears. "No pickney should have that for a parent. I'm sorry, Jazmyne."

"Not as sorry as she's going to be."

"What does that mean?"

Accepting the doyenne's death always made me worry I'd undo all Madisyn's good work to ensure neither of us turned out anything like her. But the delay in my decision may have done more harm than good. Before the stupa, these skulls, the expansive space above them for more Yielders, thousands, I can't believe I *asked* for a delay.

"The Nameless might get their wish."

His brows shoot upward. "You don't have to rush this decision if you're not sure, Jaz. If you're not ready."

Looking at the skulls, I am sure.

After hearing how Doyenne Cariot spoke earlier, I must be ready.

"Leadership is about sacrifice, I've been told." My voice is resolute. "The few in favor of the many. In this case, it would only be the one."

Let this be the final lesson I learn from her.

"But there's never just one," Kirdan argues. "And now might not be the best time to kill the doyenne." His expression darkens. "Iraya was practicing her magic in the Adair Graveyard near here when I found her this morning."

"She's bound by the Vow of Peace." I shrug. "There's not much she can do."

"The vow hasn't taken her drive." He talks fast, his voice low. "The Cuartel is flush with insurgent sympathizers, whatever magical agreements the doyenne makes them swear to. The last image those runaways saw was Iraya making a break for her family tree. They won't know if she's dead or alive. We'd be foolish not to think their allies here have been told to look for her, and you know where that leaves our plans with the Jade Guild, don't you? Why would they believe anything we've promised them when we didn't tell them Iraya was at Carling Hill in the first place?"

My skin chills. Either way, they'll know we kept it from them.

"If Iraya were dead, this wouldn't be a problem," I whisper.

"But she *isn't*," Kirdan continues, his green eyes bright and concerned. "And it won't matter if she's bound by a vow, or if Doyenne Cariot threatened her order—just knowing an Adair was in Aiyca again could incite a rebellion on this island we might not win. And if they learn she survived? If she joins them? That will be it."

I don't have time to react to his words as a voice summons me. "Emissary Cariot."

I feel like I'm in a dream—no, a nightmare—as I turn to find a duo of Xanthippe approaching us, their silver afros braided into coronets at the top of their heads. "Doyenne Cariot has sent for you. It's time for the Yielding Assembly."

Daylight spools a buttery yellow in the gardens, but with the rite ahead of me and Iraya Adair at my back, I am cast in a shadow no light can reach.

18

IRA

Delyse finds me reclining on the steps leading down from my bohío, an hour or so after Emissary Divsylar left me outside the south entrance to the Cuartel with a stiff excuse to curious Xanthippe about where we'd been. Though it was no doubt his state of undress that raised their eyebrows, and sent their minds to places no Alumbrar's should go, poor dears.

"Oh—wahan!" Delyse's fine eyebrows almost greet her hairline, where baby hairs are swirled with an artistic flair. "You were up early, then?"

"Enough. I didn't realize it was a Sunday until I heard the bell."

In the distance, the dull clang of a Mourning Bell rings across both seven-sided fortresses. In Carne Prison, the same somber peal would echo through the walls from the Alumbrar half.

"The temple was one of the first things the doyenne made stone and metal Artisans build when she took over. Now Alumbrar across the island flock here to make their pilgrimage to honor their dead. They walk the public gardens all morning."

Outwardly I do not react, but inside something clenches.

That would be close to where the Divsylar emissary found me.

"The bell tolls the penultimate Sunday every month." Delyse rolls her eyes. "I'm surprised it doesn't rouse their dead, ugly-sounding thing. The ancestors would be better appeased with Jákīsa, mon."

I listen with half an ear, not quite able to believe my luck. If Kirdan hadn't arrived when he did, I might have bumped into Alumbrar mourners on my way out. They would have alerted Xanthippe that I was trespassing, and then what? With my silver hood forgotten, they would have informed the doyenne about a rogue shield. If she learned it was me, I doubt she'd believe I was simply paying my respects to dead family members. No, ever the Stealth, she would have assumed I was up to no good, and then acted on her promise to punish my order.

Still talking away, Delyse doesn't notice that I suppress a shudder. May the goddess bless that voyeuristic Zesian. I'm sure he's kicking himself for being so inadvertently helpful. Unless . . . unless he was trying to keep me safe?

I suppress a snort. Yeah. Right.

"I'm guessing the doyenne doesn't permit Jákīsa for Obeah mourning?"

"No." Delyse scuffs dirt with a sandal-clad foot. "But we have our ways of honoring our dead. Come by tonight's kotch, you'll see."

"Another one?"

"What else is there to do around here after training and classes, if you're not on watch duty, but drink? We should head off now to sneak in a bite before the first lesson of the day."

I rise with a barely contained groan. Sitting down wasn't the best choice for my muscles. "What is it?"

"History with Master Omnyra. The mess hall is this way."

Pain slices through the muscles in my legs as we walk; each step unleashes a fresh wave. A wince slips through my teeth. Delyse's focus shifts from greeting other conscripts hanging clothes out to dry, or braiding one another's afros, to my limp, which is determined to be noticed, no matter how hard I try to conceal it.

"Sleep badly?"

I make a noncommittal noise.

"There's a mere to the west of the Cuartel perfect for bathing. It's outside the boundary wall, but you can get away with a soak if you tell the Xanthippe it's your red week. Busha too, actually, though they take it worse." She laughed.

"Thanks for the tip."

"Oh, I'm full of them." She winks. "Here's another: don't complain about the consistency of the porridge or the cooks won't feed you tomorrow. After a while, you get used to chewing the lumps." She laughs again at the horror on my face. "You can meet my friends before they leave for their training drills, they've been dying to see you."

Poor choice of words.

"You know," I say, "I'll wait until lunch. I actually ate fruit from the welcome pack this morning." I lie.

"But we're close, and look, they're waving—"

I twist away under the pretense of rubbing my calves so I don't have to acknowledge anyone. After Kaleisha I don't want to run the risk of forming friendships I'll have to leave behind. "After what you said yesterday, I'm betting I have a lot to learn."

"You're not wrong," she acquiesces, though glumly.

Delyse leaves me outside one of the schoolrooms with a promise to return later to collect me for training. I take a seat at the back of the wide bohío, glance at the books and pencils for annotations, and wish I was outside running through magical drills with some of the other shields.

Magi filter in and greet me. I nod to be polite, but largely keep to single-syllable answers to deter any from striking up conversations. One Obeah-man isn't easily put off.

"Wahan." He takes a seat on the bench beside me with a broad smile that stretches the line of horizontal dots on his chin. "I'm Shamar." The scars are dyed white-gold, just like my scarification. He's the son of a Poisoner. Each circular scar represents Aiyca's deadliest poisons he had to inject into a cut over a period of time to inure himself. Mithridatism, though tough, is necessary to help inure his métier to the poisons they would have cured, and those they would have created, for the right price. "And you are?"

"Not a big talker," I say. His smile falters. I'm sure he's used to witches swooning with his afro shorn at the sides but high and curly on top, and his skin shining like a glass of rum sitting in a patch of sunlight. Suppressing a smile of my own, I turn to face the front resolutely as the Master enters in gray robes, her afro crowning her face.

"Texts open to four, shields," the witch instructs.

And that's the last word I heard her say for the next hour, having no interest in Alumbrar history. If this had been a class about guzzu, my attention would be rapt, but I don't see what there is to learn about them that I don't already know.

Alumbrar, avaricious and conniving. I think I've got it.

It's a relief when those around me begin packing their things up.

"So, what did you—"

"Have to go, sorry mon," I tell the magi beside me, Sham-something, leaping out of my seat and hurrying to the yard outside where Delyse is already waiting for me.

"How was class?"

"A waste of time."

"You never know what the past will teach you about the present," she says.

After explaining her role as my trainer to the Xanthippe by the south gate, we leave the Cuartel and descend the hill of a neighboring paddock just outside its walls. Concealed in its long grass, Aiycan tree frogs and crickets maintain a steady beat. A hot breeze chases us down the mount to a patch of scorched earth. With the Cuartel's walls blocking us from view, Delyse and I are all but alone.

She gathers fallen leaves from a palm tree from where they lie like drunks on the ground, creating a mini-pyre in the center of the charred earth. "The sooner you understand how to use your magic in the next two moon phases, the easier some of the other classes and your eventual training drills will be."

"Is that how long it typically takes?"

She shakes her head. "On average, it's at least two lunar months."

That's way too much time spent here, burning through this conduit.

"Once you get past the little gold we're given, the dangers channeling too much magic brings, and the struggle to generate enough at all, you still can't start using your magic until you've measured its bottom. The first thing I want you to do is to think of it like Aiyca's Great River." When I blink at her, she flaps her hands at me. "Close your eyes."

Nearly a hundred miles in length before it flows into Carne Sea, the waters of the Great River are near limitless. It's actually not a bad visualization for Obeah magic.

"Alumbrar, of course, obscure their river with a dam," Delyse continues. "Minimizing all that wild beauty into something more like a lake. They've extended that limit to us too, with the small conduits, damming our magic into something smaller, more *modest* than a lake—a pond. Imagine fencing in those waters, trapping a tiny area."

Wrongness settles in my stomach at the thick slabs of stone that thud into the Great River in my mind; water smashes against them, eager to be freed—deserving to be.

"Now we can't raise those dams without more gold, so we need time to rest for our ponds to refill naturally, or, well, you've seen what happens to fruit left in the sun. You can open your eyes now." Delyse props her hands on her hips, somehow dwarfing me even though I stand at least a foot taller than her. "Understanding your new limits is only half the battle, Just-Ira. I told you yesterday that magic isn't as simple as thinking something. Any fool can have wants. Only a Master can have a métier."

"Smooth."

"It used to be the first lesson Stealths were taught in magical theory." Her eyes turn sad, distant. It's a look I recognize. "Now you know what we're working with—"

"Or *not*."

"Right. There are three levels of magical intent that apply to all magi, no matter their métier. They all require varying strengths of will to work. The first, and easiest, is through *Self-Intent*. Our will can manifest tangibly through our conduits, projecting things like shields or weapons or sparks intended to suppress, even kill. Or we could, if we had a greater quantity of metal. It's not worth the cost with so little."

"And the cost is that the coins burn?"

"Yeh mon." She sighs. "Making it harder to channel the amount you need, which tires you out too. The second discipline tends to be safest because it doesn't require anything manifesting *from* the conduit: *Summoning Intent* is all about implementing will in the world around you, manipulating climate, fire starting, moving things. But they all have a cost, too. No matter how careful we are, they'll wear through our coins and tire us out, in the end."

I cannot stay here for two months.

"It's best not to use any magic for personal gain, and to save it for training, and eventually missions."

"What do they entail?"

She hesitates. "Mostly, we accompany Xanthippe to ports across the island to help them remove pirates who've managed to sneak past Aiyca's defense."

"Are they still attempting to illegally trade in conduit gold?"

"Yeh mon." She shakes her head. "Doyenne Cariot has minimized the amount shipped across to Zesia and the Sky-lands, so it's harder to come by. Our job is to make sure they don't get their hands on any of it. If they start offering Zesia vast quantities of gold under the table, their doyenne could break whatever agreement they made ten years ago with our doyenne not to intervene."

"Bringing war," I finish, and thus inciting the shields' interest to keep Aiyca safe.

"Right."

Does Doyenne Cariot send shields after the Jade Guild too? I don't want to open the topic up with Delyse, but I can't see the doyenne risking the vow by uniting Obeah with Obeah.

"The last level of magic is the most revered," Delyse continues. "The most difficult, and banned on threat of death. *Spirits*. I suppose it's better for us anyway. The ancestors are mercurial, to put it kindly. And you always better, mon, because they're always listening." Her eyes dart around, as if expecting a duppy to materialize. "But like I said, as conscripts we can really only rely on Summoning, and that still requires a wholeep of will, up here." She taps the side of her head, pauses, then frowns. "I just reminded myself of the Master Bush Witch here, Miss Agape, which means we can officially get started with one of the fundamental introductory tasks." She retrieves a leaf from a cane stalk. "Setting this leaf alight."

"That leaf? Not the pyre?"

"We'll see how you do with something smaller first. Will this leaf's combustion. Just like . . ." Her eyes narrow with concentration, enough to crease the smooth hazelnut skin between her brows before the conduit on her chest even glimmers, and only as though it catches the light of the sun rather than producing any of its own. "This!" Smoke spools from the leaf before a tiny flame sparks. Delyse pants before me.

I want to believe that Summoning isn't as hard as she made it look, but the mango stains on my uniform beg to differ.

"The real challenge is in limiting the magic, so you don't burn yourself out. You know, drain the pond we pictured at the beginning?"

"How?"

"To start a fire you need heat." She holds her hands out; waves of it pulsate around us.

"The sun. I'll manipulate a shard of its light."

"Good. In order to do that, you need to *become* that shard of light." Her expression grows seraphic. "Summoning is like an awakening of every sense, intensifying your body's reactions to what's always been around you, but inaccessible without the magnetic draw of magic. You're no longer a barrier, Just-Ira. You're a conductor with the capacity to harness energy. You just need to believe it, mon."

"A conductor?"

She nods.

All right, then. Feeling a little silly, I . . . conduct.

"Are you trying?"

"Sort of. Should something have happened?"

"Your conduit should have at least brightened. Remember, will is all about intent. The magic's inside you. You are it and it is you."

Several seconds pass. Nothing happens. I stride closer to Delyse, focus on the leaf again. The minutes slide by, like the beads of sweat at the back of my neck.

I exhale in an annoyed huff, throwing my arms up. "Look, is this really the best advice?"

"You think I'd hold out on you?" She chuckles. I flinch as it grates against my already frayed patience. "I told you it's not as simple as just wanting something. Intent is easy. I could intend on eating an entire cake; doesn't mean I have the *will* to see it through." She laughs again, her teeth white and straight. "Who am I kidding? I'd always have the will, especially if it's coconut cake. But I digress. Manifesting intent into will is where magic becomes challenging. Go back to basics and picture that power. Start with the Great River."

As irritated as I am, rushing waters slosh in my mind with little thought. My little pond develops a current, one that becomes rapid and dangerous.

"Your conduit just lit," Delyse whispers. "It's so bright. Keep it steady."

I'm panting with the exertion required to control my conduit. The metal's hot against my stomach, like a handful of fire. It makes Delyse's earlier attempt look even duller.

"That's good, Just-Ira. Great, actually. Now, as the Great River rushes, so does your magic. Imagine it as something malleable, something able to probe for the heat in the air."

A coil of smoke curls upward from the leaf. *Yes.*

The light around my neck doubles, enough now that I have to avert my eyes—to Delyse. The chip of metal reflects in her dark gaze; dual warnings, they pull me back from power's allure.

Stop.

Remember the naevus.

My body seizes up, magic rising until I'm sure I'll explode with it. Self-preservation clashes with will and wins. Before that surplus of magic can break its banks, giving away my identity, my body relaxes and lets go. My breathing steadies as the conduit dulls and fades. Shaking my head, like emerging from a dream, I touch it. The surface has cooled, the light extinguished. Delyse looks as dazed as I feel.

"You—you did well for your first time." She wipes her forehead. The degrees down here seem to have doubled. "Let's rest before you go again, get some food and drink in you. How about a story while we sit? One from Anansi? Have you heard the tale about the jéges? It's my favorite."

"Yeh mon, I've heard it, and my head's pounding, so I'll pass on the repeat." It's not entirely a lie. "I'll come back when it's lessened." Her face falls, but I don't hang around to give her time to protest.

We were having a pleasant morning, but I see the dangers of letting my guard slip all too clearly: my naevus erupts, and then the entire Cuartel is hearing *Delyse's* story about how the Lost Empress has returned to lead them to freedom. Unlike the mythical artifacts in Anansi's story, I exist, and I'll be benched on a throne instead of returning to the mountains.

Centuries of tradition demand the Obeah see me how empresses have always been seen, as symbols and figureheads. My scarification won't matter, and neither will my protests. No, distance is better. Not easier, after Kaleisha, I continue to realize, but better.

19

JAZMYNE

In the Assembly Room's doorway, the herald's conduit illuminates on his chest before he speaks. "Announcing emissary to the crown, and its presiders," he calls, his voice magically magnified. "Jazmyne Amancia Cariot."

I do my best not to cringe as all eyes turn to me. Kirdan slips away, leaving me to face the vultures alone. My eyes, focused ahead, don't shift from a spot on the wall. The witchlight chandelier cascading from the ceiling's center is fashioned after the constellation Alumbrar are said to originate from; it launches speckles of starlight around the Assembly Room, a cavern of dark marble and gold.

Typically it's bright and airy with floor-to-ceiling windows that provide the illusion of being among the treetops, but this morning, space is scarce. There must be close to a thousand Alumbrar in here, whispering and watching from pillars as I pass, leaning over golden railings on the balcony above, calling to bredren and sistren on the opposite side.

Stealing a steadying breath, I nearly choke. The air is thick with a cloying sweetness—offerings for Benito, the Mudda's Face of Fortune. Magi have bathed in honeyed milk, risking bites from blood eaters, and carry bags of sugared posies, all for the Mudda's favor to ensure their pickney are chosen, unaware that it's convenience, not divine intervention, that selects Yielders.

A long table stands close to the dais the six members of the council sit on, forever orbiting the doyenne, who sits at their center. Her eye roams over my mourning kaftan, her lip curling before she fixes on my hair tie. There wasn't the time to change into our family's official color. I hurry to assume my place at the front of the crowd in case I'm needed. My eyes remain on the floor, my distorted reflection there, until she begins.

"Wahan." The high ceilings carry the doyenne's voice with ease. "It seems like it was only yesterday that we last met, bredren, sistren."

The crowd chuckles. I want to leave.

"From light we are born."

"And to light we cleave."

"In circumstances I thought we'd moved past, the Obeah insurgents attacked St. Ann this phase, killing Alumbrar in a brutal attack. My council and I believe the attack to be an act of opportunity. They feel as though the Yielding's cancellation weakens us. They are not wrong. The rite is a gift bestowed on us, and I should have known better than to spurn such a blessing from our Supreme Being. They have sought to remind me of my nearsightedness through this test from the insurgents, and I don't mean to fail Them again. And so, Alumbrar, the Yielding will be reinstated, and we will honor the Seven-Faced Mudda the only way They have ever asked us to."

"*Flesh*," the crowd whispers, the word stretching to a hiss. "*Sacrifice*."

Some magi smash onto their knees and fling their hands before them; others shake their entire bodies, like they feel the Supreme Being's pleasure. Even as I recoil from them, I must force a smile, look pleased—excited. Wrongness churns in my belly.

"My folly has prompted the Seven-Faced Mudda to expedite proceedings. My council and I received visions about the Yielders all throughout the night. Never has this happened with such alacrity." Her eye dips, her brow relaxes. "We know They are pleased. And so must we be as we welcome this year's Yielders." She sits to stilted applause, the assembly not wanting to miss a word, and her second, Ada Caldwell, rises.

"As your name is called," she says, her voice pregnant with importance, "please come forward." She gestures to the high table positioned before the council's dais; the filmlike sleeve of her sage green kaftan wafts gently. "Amoi Antwi."

There's a squeal across the hall; Presider Antwi's daughter darts from the crowd. Her silver afro is twisted back from her beaming face with gemstone clips.

That's one of two presiders' pickney who will be called this morning.

"Next, Raeni Lawsome and Zidane Ryncer."

The first strides across the hall with her shoulders thrown back, her chin tilted up. In her green tunic and billowing pants, she is a victor to the crowd as a Recondite. The métier is renowned for their digestion of arcane knowledge, the facts the middling would never retain or recall. Even Ada can't contain a superior smirk, as a Master of the métier. Javel's sidekick looks less certain, in his Artisanal gray. His eyes dart about as if seeking escape. I'm almost sorry for him. He doesn't want this.

The next three Yielders are Alumbrar I've never met. The girl and two boys range from quivering with nerves to buzzing with as much excitement as Amoi.

"And this year's final Yielder," Presider Caldwell announces. "Javel Phelony."

That's two for two.

Both Ormine's and Mariama's pickney will die so their magic can thrive.

Javel materializes directly opposite me, from across the room. He winks. My lips press tighter as magi erupt into applause, whistles, shouts of praise, at the sight of the seven Yielders standing together. Some magi openly sob, fighting to reach them. Xanthippe move into action, iridescent shields springing from their conduits to buffer the overzealous back.

Doyenne Cariot holds a hand aloft. The crowd calms like she is a Squaller controlling their tide. "These souls are brave and noble enough to sacrifice their magic, their lives, so we can continue to sit among the greats, out of reach from those who wish to unseat us." She looks to them. Javel's spine arcs with pride. "Yielders, I now speak to you. Over the course of two lunar cycles, you will participate in four trials, one every two moon phases, assessing your dedication and knowledge of the Mudda's Seven Faces."

I never understood the allure of dragging out the deaths over an eight-week period. I asked Madisyn once; she told me the feat of surviving rounds, of working toward small victories, makes the Yielding seem like more of a quest, something exciting.

All of a sudden, I'm struck with the wildest desire to laugh.

"Each trial will consist of any number of those gods and goddess, be it one, two, or more. A lonely death awaits Yielders the Supreme Being does not deem worthy of sacrifice. Heed this: the only honorable death to be had is the one in offering to *Them*."

My thoughts return to the stupa, the lack of mourners there. The memorial serves as more of a cautionary tale than a place to honor the fallen. Again, how can anyone look forward to this?

"Those of you They see potential in, worthiness, will live to participate in the next trial. And so this pattern will repeat until the finale, when the lone survivor will be crowned the Yielded, and the Seven-Faced Mudda's blessings will be imparted to their family."

Gold. She means gold, jewels, land. A cache I have delivered before and most likely will again.

"Their sacrifice will take place on the last New Moon of this year—*the Sole*." The doyenne's smile is more of a smirk.

That's *pride*, I'm sickened to see. She's *proud* of all this.

How could I have missed that in previous assemblies?

"With many blessings to our Supreme Being, seven has always been a fortunate number for all magi. But the Alumbrar must not forget that *one* is also a number of great significance to us." She looks at the Yielders in turn, her eye ablaze with passion. "With the magic gleaned from the Yielded's bones during the Sole, we can keep the Obeah threat quelled for another year." That passion flares before the mural of obsidian at her back. "The Yielding begins during the New Moon."

My fingers dig into my sides beneath my folded arms. That's five days from now.

"The moon phase, and the power it provides, is our gift to you." Doyenne Cariot looks at each Yielder in turn. "Use the time you have between trials to study the Mudda's Faces. The challenges awaiting you are not for the faint of heart or weak of—"

Without warning, the Assembly Room doors slam open.

I jolt out of my skin as the doors collide against the walls with deafening booms.

Startled gasps ripple through magi; they fall back, repelled by *something* encased in a coruscating shell of golden sparks— an all-encompassing magical shield. I crane my neck, stretching on the tips of my toes to see what's inside, to no avail.

The Xanthippe surrounding the council's dais see

something, though. The guards drop to their knees before the council, shields spring from some of their conduits in shimmering walls of sparks; from others, great four-legged beasts manifest, paws slamming onto marble, snarling mouths roaring as whatever's encased in the golden shell, rounded like a bubble, is slowly funneled through the crowd.

When it emerges at the front of the hall, it's almost spat out, and I—I blink because it can't be *Nameless* inside that sphere of magic.

A waving hand captures my attention beyond them, across the hall. It belongs to a tall girl with a gleaming mane of silver hair. Anya. So slowly it can't be anything but deliberate, she winks. Far from being comforting, worry spreads around my rib cage like two hands.

What in all the Mudda's Faces do these Nameless protesters think they're doing?

Two of them separate themselves from the small crowd within, taking point. I know them. Younger than Light Keeper but older than me, Heather and Ivon are both parents of past Yielders.

I reach for my locket. Mudda go with me.

"It's a shame that the only way we could meet, after years of missives seeking an audience with you, is for a fraction of my bredren, sistren, and me to infiltrate your home. To bypass your guards. To interrupt you," Heather says. Her voice echoes musically through the Assembly Room, but there's a minor edge of spite that chimes louder. A twist of flats aimed right at the doyenne, like the fine point of a spear.

The space between them draws tight. Doyenne Cariot sits erect on the throne; her hands grip the roaring jungle-prowler arms, pulling the skin of her knuckles. I look for where Light Keeper sits on the dais with the other presiders, but she's distorted through the Xanthippe shields, their snarling conduit manifestations. Only she could have sanctioned this attack.

"Long have you tried to stifle our voices, Doyenne Cariot; to perpetuate your charade that Aiyca is united in the Yielding. But before you stands only a modicum of those who disagree with mass murder." Heather turns to face the room. "We are not the zealots she has sought to paint us as. We stand before you, all of you, as parents who've had pickney snatched from them in past Yieldings, and as parents who refuse to stand by and watch those in here suffer as we did, by *your* hand." She whirls back to the dais, stabbing a finger at the council. "Will you hear us now?"

That tight space between them frays.

"I believe I've heard you clearly. Tagereg."

Patwah.

Doyenne Cariot only uses that when she's too mad for propriety.

"You call *us* criminals?"

Someone moves through the crowd to my left—not Anya this time, Kirdan. He slips past magi beneath the balcony, a hand on the saber on his hip, a fierce focus pinned on me.

"Yeh mon." A vein ticks in Doyenne Cariot's forehead. "You challenge a rite the Mudda Themselves shared with me. How *dare* you."

"The Yielding is not the work of *our* most beloved Faces of the Supreme Being." Ivon steps forward, his voice a deep baritone weighted with scorn. "Does Aurore, goddess of Creation, approve of all the deaths of her pickney? Or her twin Merce, goddess of Compassion? And you can't argue that Sofea showed you this is the wise path, when *our* path has never been so bloody. If you wish to kill to retain power, rather than seek an alternative more suited to Alumbrar ways, you can't even call yourself Obeah. You are worse."

My left hand flies to my open mouth.

They didn't.

Doyenne Cariot's upper lip curls back from her teeth. "Arrest them."

"We won't fight." Heather shows the council her palms; behind, her cohort does the same. "We'll drop our shield if you promise you won't take us by force."

"Arrest them!" Spit flies from the doyenne's mouth. "By any means necessary!"

I don't know what happens first: the assembly making a frightened exodus; magical intent switching from shields to behemoth axes, spears, and mighty hammers from the surrounding Xanthippe's conduits; or Kirdan lunging for me, a shield springing around us as those colossal magical weapons, leaping beasts, slam against the protection around the Nameless.

The palace rocks; dust suffuses the air. When it clears, the shield stands. Kirdan's grip is tight enough to break bone as another blow hits, rocking not only the palace, but the world.

She's attacking Alumbrar.

She's attacking our own.

Overhead the chandelier clashes, seesawing on its wire. Magi fall from the balcony, and I cringe into Kirdan's shoulder, but the crack of bones rings through my mind, my core. More Alumbrar death, because of *her*.

"We need to move." Despite his words, Kir halts at the build of golden light. It refracts on the windows, catches in what witchlights remain on the chandelier. *Fire*. No. There's no crackling flame, no snare of heat. Its *light*. And it emanates from the doyenne—all of her. Not just her conduit. Her crown, jewelry, even the threads within her kaftan are ablaze with magic conducted by *conduit metal*. More than I've ever seen on any Alumbrar.

The shield encasing the Nameless explodes; sparks bounce off our shield.

She smashed it. Alone.

Kirdan's mouth is grim. My face feels just as tight. When did she arm herself with so much gold?

Xanthippe surge in to arrest the Nameless held to the ground by their golden beasts. The doyenne storms to the chambers behind the throne, her council at her heels, ignoring the wails of the resistance. My heart bleeds for them, but I have to run after the council. I have to know what the doyenne will do next, Light Keeper—*me*. Kirdan is by my side.

They all turn as the door closes behind us.

"You!" Presider Magmire's face twists in spite. Not at me, at Kirdan. "Treacherous Obeah. *You* let them in here!"

I step before Kirdan. "He did not."

"Of course you defend your *pet*." She spits.

"You can ask any of your court." Though I can hardly stand to look at her, I speak to the doyenne. In the low light of the chamber, her face is as hard as the surrounding stone walls. "We walked Mourner's Row early, and then came here."

"And before then?" Magmire pushes, ever the aggressive first.

It's Kirdan who replies, his voice respectful. "Your Stealth spies will tell you I woke late."

"Then how did those zealots get in?"

The council looks to one another, a clear panic awash as they defer to the doyenne.

The threads in her clothing have lost their sheen, but I can't forget the strength they advertised. Something the Nameless and I didn't foresee. Ivon may have condemned the resistance with his accusation about her being worse than Obeah, but only they wore such vast quantities of gold.

"That answer can only be discerned by visiting the tag-eregs," she at last murmurs. "Emissary, I trust you can handle matters here until we return?" She doesn't wait for my reply before she leaves, her council behind her.

I start for the door too, but before I've reached it, it opens and Anya slips inside.

"What did they say?" she asks.

She's expectant, not surprised. Not fearful for the Nameless. It's as if she knew what they planned; her wave . . .

"I *did* see you in Mourner's Row. . . ." I shake my head. "*You* let the Nameless in."

She bites her lip, eyes brimming with apologies.

"Why couldn't you have told us what you were planning?" Kirdan cuts in.

"I don't owe *you* anything," she snarls.

"What about me?"

"The plan unfolded quickly, Jaz. Light Keeper managed to send our outpost in Queenstown a fire message last night. We weren't to tell you because . . ." Her voice peters out.

Because they thought I'd object. So they went behind my back. Again.

I turn from her, kaftan flying out at my back, and pace away.

"It's why I found you out there," she calls after me. "So you'd know you weren't alone."

"She wouldn't have been," Kirdan says. "*I* was there."

"A great comfort, I'm sure."

"Stop that," I chastise, spinning to find them a yard away from squaring up. "Have either of you noticed Doyenne Cariot wearing extra conduit gold before today?"

"We wouldn't have protested if we knew she'd light up like a damn solar flare."

One glance at Kirdan confirms we're on the same page.

Iraya Adair.

The doyenne wasn't wearing as much conduit gold before her.

"We've learned something, this morning," Kirdan says. "She's too powerful for the Nameless to overwhelm, whether it be to imprison, or to kill." He glances my way. "Before the day is out, that information will have made its way across the island. *Doyenne Cariot, history's most powerful Alumbrar-witch.* There's no way your order will believe indentured Obeah managed to assassinate her now, even if your Stealth assassins *could* kill her. Which I doubt."

Anya puffs up, and then deflates; he's right.

History's most powerful witch . . . I've heard something similar about one other before. The island wouldn't believe the doyenne's assassination capable of a regular Obeah, no.

But they might if I told them Iraya Adair was behind it.

20

IRA

Delyse's request for story time made me so worried about accidentally exposing my naevus that by midmorning I haven't managed to illuminate my conduit again, never mind spark an actual fire.

"Perhaps we call it a day." She packs away the leftover breadfruit she fried me to refuel. "We still don't know your limits, and I don't want you to burn out when you have another class later, and we have more days of training ahead. Plus"—she throws me a look—"yellow-heart breadfruit is my favorite, and you just ate most of my ration for this moon phase."

"You can have my ration, all my rations, if I can go one more time."

She raises a brow. It would be smarter to stop, but a niggling part of me can't face returning to the Cuartel, my bohío, a failure. Not after my meeting with the doyenne yesterday.

There isn't time to slowly emerge from my comfort zone. I have to smash through it, *now*.

"Seriously, mon," I continue when Delyse doesn't voice her thoughts. "I only lit up once. A final try won't risk too much. Think about the breadfruit."

She laughs. "Not just any, it has to be—"

"Yellow-heart, I know. So?"

Her head tips to the side as she takes stock of me. "Drink more coconut water. Your lips are a little chapped."

Lifting the fruit that's twice the size of my head makes muscles twinge in my back, my core. Though I suppress all discomfort, I don't do so fast enough.

"Don't think you're slick," Delyse says. "I saw that." She crawls over and sits behind me, rubbing my shoulders without asking. It's so glorious, I fall back against her.

"Thanks, mon."

"Thank me by being *careful*. Knowing your limits is an important part of magic management." She circles her thumbs on the tops of my arms and I nearly pass out with satisfaction. Burning out risks returning to Carne."

Doyenne Cariot knew what she was doing, sentencing me to a tenure out here. My shoulders tighten.

Delyse's fingers press harder. "I know," she murmurs. "I know. But we can manage this. You were close, this morning. You can get close again."

I roll my neck, luxuriating in her advice as much as the palms she kneads in the center of my back. "I suppose being a Stealth helps you know so much about people," I say. In part, it's a compliment, but it also serves as a greater warning to myself, a reminder of what Delyse trained to be, who she is. Because baking beneath the crushing weight of the sun hasn't been so bad with her by my side. Under different circumstances, we might have been sistren.

"It didn't hurt." She releases my shoulders, rises, and sticks out a hand to pull me up. "But I've always had an interest in people. The rest of my family worked in medicine, would you believe. Mama was one of the finest Bush Healers in our town. But when I was meant to be learning which herbs helped specific maladies, I was busy watching her customers."

It isn't common to abscond from family métiers. I can't suppress my curiosity.

"How did your mama react when you chose a different path?"

"She loved it." Delyse's smile turns sad. "I'd sit and tell her which clients were lying about symptoms and which were taking what she'd brew to sell for themselves. We were quite the team, when she lived. . . . What about you?"

I turn away and retrieve a leaf. "What about me?"

"Were your family all Warriors?"

"The witches on Dada's side were." Nana Clarke came from a strong line of female fighters who worked alongside Adair empresses to protect the island. Mama and Dada's union would have been arranged, but they met without their parents' meddling and fell in love.

"Sounds like an interesting tale."

"For another day, perhaps." I rub my hands together. "Let's start now."

"As you wish." She pretends to let me get away with withholding my story.

I pretend not to notice.

"What's the first step?"

"Picturing the Great River."

This time, I don't close my eyes to imagine the vast reach of the water. I need to keep my conduit in view to avoid repeating the same mistake as last time. My body, relaxed from the massage, actually feels at one with the mouth-drying humidity, instead of fighting against it. I pluck a strand of light, feeling it pulsate through every muscle, every follicle.

"You've got it," Delyse whispers.

She may as well have shouted.

Reminded of her proximity, and my naevus, the thread snaps.

Irked, I stalk away from her and into the burnt cane stalks before I combust, wishing I could burn this estate down, wishing I could smash the dam around my magic and let it drown that witch in the palace, wishing—

White-gold light rises in my eyes, swallowing my vision.

I reel, blinking away the power, pushing it down, tucking it away. No. *No.*

Panic swells at the crackle of flames, the dark stink of char. A towering blaze greets me when I turn around; tongues of flame and heat lick the earth by my bare feet. Delyse isn't visible—the entire patch of exposed earth isn't visible.

"Just-Ira?" she calls. "Stay there, I'll go for help!"

Oh gods. Already the flames spread, curling fingers set on destruction around more stems. What if she doesn't make it back in time? No shield can put this out, not without damaging their conduit, and the little water we carried up here won't put it out—we need more, or I will set this hill alight and the doyenne will learn of it. My panic crests into something greater, and my power manifests in another alabaster burst.

No.

I slam my hands over my eyes, my head throbbing with the urge to let go, to release.

And then something does.

Water splashes against my hands. One drop, two, and then too many to count as the sky opens and Aiyca reminds the estate we are in the midst of rainy season.

"Ira?"

At Delyse's out-of-breath shout, I lower my hands, the light gone. Though my heart pounds and my breathing is shallow, I school my features to look self-congratulatory, boastful, as the flames shrink. When they're below shoulder height, an impressed Delyse stands a little ways from where I left her. The Obeah-man from my history class stands beside her.

"Thank the Mudda for the rain, but you did it!"

"You sound like you doubted me," I mock-scold, blinking through the cooling shower of water and trying not to think too hard about if I called it too, further risking my conduit.

Shamar chuckles and crosses the space between us on legs as slim as a newborn colt's, but limned with muscle. He doesn't emit a single wince despite the earth smoking beneath his sandals. I'm not so busy checking him out for any signs that he saw something that I don't miss the appraising look in his dark eyes when they take in my braids.

"For a greenie, that was notable," he says.

"Thanks—"

"This is Shamar, Ira."

"We met earlier. Call me Sham." He sticks out a large hand; the fingers are calloused enough that I'd believe him a Warrior but for his Poisoner scarification.

"Impressive," I all but purr, nodding at the horizontal line of dotted scars across his chin and giving him the reaction I didn't earlier. The surest way to distract any Obeah is to compliment their scars.

He laughs from his belly. It's a deep, unapologetic sound.

"Stop flirting, Shamar." Delyse approaches us, knocking him in the chest, where she just reaches. He's well above six feet, slouching. "We're done for the day, Just-Ira. After your class, head back to your bohío and rest—no complaints," she adds with a wink. "We had a deal."

"Blessings, for today."

"No worries, mon. There's another kotch tonight. I can look in on my way there?"

"If I'm feeling rested, I'll come."

"We'd love to have you," Shamar adds.

And I'd love to learn what you saw.

I leave them in the charred grass stalks with a wave, but my thoughts linger. Did they really not see any light, suspect the timing of the rain, or are they both talented in the art of deception? One thing I did learn today, without a shadow of a doubt, is that any and all magic I use puts me at risk of exposure—and fatigue, I think, as my legs buckle.

"You good?" Delyse shouts up the hill, because of course she's still watching.

Waving her off, I tread with more care. Is the chance of discovery still worth the reward of the doyenne's head? While she'd be dead, my order's desire for my leadership won't be.

JAZMYNE

It takes the majority of the day to restore peace to the palace after the Nameless's ambush.

The earlier rainfall helped to cool the frenzy. It's why I love wet season most of all; the way the water lingers on the palace stone. There's something cleaner about the air, the senses.

For once I know immediately what needs to be done. By my order, an increased number of Xanthippe march about, conduits glaring around their necks. I also sent for the palace griot to take up residence in the Patio of Prowlers. She holds center stage beneath a shade tree alight with witchlights shaped like flowers, distracting Alumbrar with some tale or other. Everyone lingers to be the first to learn the outcome of the doyenne's interrogation.

Cwenburg hasn't been breached these ten years. The Nameless embarrassed her, in more ways than one. She'll make an example of them, and this worries me. Passing through the floral arcade, with blooms as large as dishes growing on the walls, I bite my lip, my thoughts with Heather and Ivon. They're both Growers whose hands provide life. Will she kill them?

They shouldn't have confronted her as they did, but if I'd hopped off the fence sooner, they wouldn't have been desperate enough to go behind my back. I must do better, *be* better, as their soon-to-be leader.

"Evening, Jaz." Javel spins a scarlet poinsettia flower stolen from the wall, newly minted in his Yielder role, and even more puffed up with his own sense of self-importance.

I don't need to look around to know that we're alone. He'd never forgo my title in company. My steps falter. With the sky dark above the glass roof through which sunlight streams during the day, and no additional light along this arcade, it might be wise to turn back.

"Aren't you going to congratulate me, mon?"

I swallow. "I'm a little busy, so if you'll excuse me."

"Sure you're not a little jealous?"

"Of not dying?" I can't help saying.

"Of knowing you'll never be in a position to do anything to save our island yourself." His eyes, a lighter brown than mine, gleam with intentions an Obeah would be proud of.

I shouldn't have taken the bait.

"Of knowing you'll never have the chance to redeem the shame of your sister's failure."

His words tug a loose thread, but after all that's happened since I saw him last, it isn't sorrow that seeps out.

"You'll be long dead by the time I become doyenne," I say, thrusting my chin up. "But that doesn't mean you can disrespect me while you're still alive. Not in my home, and not when I have better things to do than pander to your ego."

Stunned, he gapes at me.

"And don't pick any more of my flowers," I say, striding toward him.

My shoulders tighten when I draw close, but he edges aside without further comment.

I'm shaking when I leave the arcade, but oddly pleased— *rejuvenated*. Too often, when I've been faced with confrontation, the words to defend myself haven't come. But that, that was too good not to do again. I hope we see each other once more, sooner rather than later. That's only if he doesn't die early in the Yielding, which I doubt. Cockroaches tend to thrive in chaos, and this catastrophe is one I can't help feeling responsible for.

Had the Nameless's timeline gone ahead without my interference, the doyenne would be dead, and the Yielders would have lived for many years. Instead the very thing we hoped to avoid is happening. Unless the plan that's been percolating since this morning can come to fruition within the next five days.

Iraya Adair, the Alumbrar's ruin, might just be Aiyca's savior.

Turning a corner, I ascend a floating staircase. An attendant is crossing the landing when I alight. I charge her with telling as many of the palace hands as she can, all of them if need be, that I'm looking for Emissary Divsylar. They'll find him faster than a fire message can given that I can't guarantee he's in the rooms he keeps here.

"When he's found, he's to meet me in my study immediately."

Hands clasped before her, she nods and hurries away.

I've been waiting for less than half an hour when Kirdan stalks inside my study.

"I was trying to learn the Nameless's fate," he says, closing the door with a snap.

"Here." I hand over the glass of rum I've had waiting for him. "You might need this," I warn, before launching into my plan to use Iraya Adair to kill the doyenne. "What do you think?"

Kirdan crushes the tumbler in his hand.

"You're bleeding!"

His conduit flares; the wound on his palm knits itself back together, leaving behind a splash of blood and a faint red line. "All better. Now, can we go back to the part where you suggested *working with Iraya*? Because I must have heard wrong."

"You did."

He huffs a laugh. "Thank the gods."

"I suggested *using* her." I take the seat behind my desk. "She has power the rest of her order do not. Using and then blaming her for the doyenne's death will be the perfect solution to all our problems."

"Or become the cause of a greater one." He pours another tumbler of liquor and knocks it back. "If we ignore the Vow of Peace that prevents her from harming the doyenne for a moment, what's to stop her taking Aiyca when all is said and done?"

"We barter with the Obeah's conscription, of course." It's so simple I can't believe he didn't think of it first. "I'll offer them a shorter tenure, and they can retain their conduits once they've paid their debt to the island. Can't you see? Everything I want, *we* want, can still be achieved if she takes the fall. Killing the doyenne will make her a hero to the Jade Guild, and I can pretend to honor her in her death by giving them a life I always planned to, when I become doyenne." I sit back, pleased. "But you're right about the vow. I don't have a way around it."

"Exactly. Involving Iraya adds another problem without a solution. I can kill the doyenne. I have skills beyond my title as emissary. All Zesian Obeah do."

"No." Aghast, I can only stare at him. "*No.* Zesia can't be implicated in an overthrow." We've had this talk before. "It will be classed as an act of war, one that will call the terms of your treaty with Aiyca, the Skylands, into question."

"I'd rather take that risk than watch you kill another."

"Don't be ridiculous." I can't help laughing. "*I* wouldn't be doing any killing."

He flinches from me. The violence of his action severs all humor.

"Kirdan—"

"So should you find a way around the vow, Iraya will have Doyenne Cariot's blood on her hands. And who will have Iraya's blood on their hands, then?" He flings his before me. They're still stained from the glass incident earlier. "The

Simbarabo?" His face is harder than I've ever seen it, the set of his jaw stubborn. "Who else but they are strong enough to face Iraya Adair and walk away? And how many will have to die for you to get what you want with this plan, Jazmyne? Have you thought about that? Or has your only thought become ascending to some gods-forsaken throne?"

I lean across the desk, the wood feeling like an acre between us. Before I can even think of what to say, we're interrupted by a knock at my window. He gets up, shaking his head, and crosses over to the bay by the bookshelves.

"What is it?"

"*Who*." He opens the window and steps back. Seconds later, Anya is climbing onto the bench, trampling my decorative cushions.

I rise, round my desk for a second time tonight. "What's the matter?"

Her sob stops me dead. She hasn't cried since Madisyn.

"Light Keeper's dead."

All the blood rushes from my head.

Anya's eyes are swollen, the white striated with veins of red. "Doyenne Cariot was going to torture the Nameless—*torture Alumbrar*." She draws a wracking breath, one that makes me reach for my chest, the locket chain. "She wanted to know everything, and she would have used every guzzu in a Stealth's arsenal for extracting information. There are enchantments that dig into the mind and make the victims spill all their secrets. She would have had everyone's names, so Light Keeper gave herself up. She admitted to plotting against her and using the Nameless to discredit her so that *she* could become doyenne."

My skin is too tight for my bones. I claw at it, needing space, needing *something*.

"Stop that!" Anya is before me, her hands around my wrists. She shakes me. "What are we going to do about this?" Her voice is thick. "What are *you* going to do about this?"

"That's enough." Kirdan's voice sounds from far away. His hand comes between us. "Can't you see she's in shock?"

"There's no time to be in shock!" Anya's voice breaks. "Doyenne Cariot killed her like a dog down there in the dark. She sent the Nameless who stormed the palace to Carne. She won't be so forgiving next time now there's no Light Keeper to take the fall. It's over!"

Because Light Keeper's dead.

Doyenne Cariot killed her—killed her *too*.

"It is not over."

Kirdan whips around to look at me. I don't sound like myself.

"We'll send fire messages warning all outposts to dismantle. But I—I want the Gennas to come to Queenstown for a meeting." My legs are like blocks of ice as I begin to pace. "The Nameless must become Faceless too." I won't let Light Keeper's dream for Aiyca—our dream—die as she has done, in the dark.

Gods. I squeeze my eyes together, fighting back tears.

But even if I find a way around the vow, Iraya might not be enough.

"I have another card we can play," I mutter. One with enough numbers to keep the rest of the Nameless safe from the fray. "If they agree to work with us, it's not over." And for that to happen, I will have to call in a two-year-old favor.

"Jazmyne," Kirdan starts, his voice filled with concern. "We can do this later. There's—"

"Don't say *time*." Light Keeper's death has shown us there's none to spare.

Back at my desk I scrawl a pleading note requesting a meeting with a friend, of sorts.

"This fire missive needs to reach its recipient within the hour."

"Who's it for?" Kirdan asks, suspicious.

I wipe my face against my sleeve. "A friend of Madisyn's."

"Which?" Anya's also suspicious now.

"No one you know. Either of you." I can't look at them. They'll see the growing dread making itself comfortable across my shoulders, for all my earlier confidence.

Good Alumbrar don't kill, they don't engage the services of Aiycan Obeah, and they definitely don't consort with their sister's pirate ex.

But if there's one thing I'm learning, it's that the definition of a good Alumbrar has changed.

22

IRA

On our way to the kotch, I fill Delyse in on the guzzu the third
and final living Master, Fayard, one of Stealth, taught in his
class—one that was far more useful than Master Omnyra's
history lesson this morning—when she begins to dance to the
lively beat thrumming through the earth in the village.

"Is there a holiday?" I've long since lost any sense of notable days, but there should be some as the year ends in the next
couple of months.

"It's more of a celebration," she says—*dances*. "Something
we do for all new arrivals. A welcome kind of thing."

Startled, I pull Delyse up short before she can brush aside the
curtain of vines. They still glisten with droplets of rain. "You
said this was just a kotch. The doyenne?" I near shout, having
to raise my voice above the clank of steel pans. "Xanthippe and
busha? The Masters? They allow things like this here?"

"Technically this is our home! The Xanthippe don't mind if we keep it down. As for the Masters, they stay in the palace, but even they can appreciate that we need to blow off steam after the drills and classes. And most busha will be drunk enough that wandering over here won't be on their minds until later."

"I—I'm too tired."

Delyse's look tells me I'm just as lame as my excuse.

"It's been a hard day," I insist, nevertheless. "I don't think I rested enough earlier." It's not a lie. Exhausted though I was, lying on the cot in my bohío after my first day of magical instruction, all I could think about was practicing more. Maybe sneaking around the estate to probe for weaknesses, learn where the doyenne sleeps, throw stones at her window—boulders.

"I'm not accepting that." Delyse reverses my hold with a quick twist, winks at my scowl, and tugs me after her.

It's less of a welcome and more of a jump up, with the drums and pans, dancing and food. The conscripts have tented the center of the village, and strung up more of the witchlights in jars. We could be in the parish below, not on the palace estate. I'm greeted by so many magi, at least two thirds of the forty-nine shields who aren't on duty tonight, I won't recall their names later. But I won't forget how those who have been here longest have grayed skin that makes them look like negatives of themselves. Nor the drawn look in their eyes, even as they beam in welcome.

"Everyone, this is Just-Ira." Delyse directs me to a stool close to the firepit, where magi grill fish and meat. "Just-Ira, this is everyone."

A warm wooden bowl is placed in my hands. It's brimming with shredded chicken, the skin glossy with burnt sugar sauce, and a mound of dark green callaloo seasoned with rich spices that makes my stomach roar.

"Wahan." Handsome, with skin that's dark and dented by two deep cheek dimples, the magi who handed me the bowl winks. "I'm Ford."

"*The fool*," a pretty Obeah-witch adds, shunting him aside with a narrow hip before he can sit beside me. "I'm Nel." A brilliant blue scarf draws focus to her near-black eyes that sparkle beneath the jars of witchlights above. "You're the Warrior. We'd hoped to see you last night."

"Yeh mon." I resist the urge to touch my scar. "It was a long first day."

"Not as long as others you've had, I'm sure." Ford toys with the dark twists atop his head, nodding at my forehead. "I bet you have a few stories to tell."

"Ira doesn't like stories." Delyse sniffs. "Not hearing them, anyway."

"Maybe you'll prefer telling them." Sham rests on the spare wooden stump to my other side, two bowls balanced in one of his large hands. "Where are you from?"

I was supposed to be conducting the interrogation, figuring out what Shamar and Delyse did or didn't see, not finding myself at the center of their smiling scrutiny. Stalling for time, I shovel fingers filled with chicken and greens into my mouth and nearly groan in pleasure.

"It's good, nuh mon?" Ford digs into his own bowl. "Carne didn't have food like this. The doyenne knows that to keep us sweet, she needs to appeal to our bellies."

"I can't believe she wants to keep us sweet."

"It's all part of the bargain." Delyse rolls her eyes. "She can't pretend to be a benevolent ruler for it to stick."

"Back to the stories," Nel says. "I'll go first." She tugs her uniform top down, revealing a lone scar shaped like a paw print just above her heart. Ford whistles; she flips him a finger. "Both mamas were Wranglers. Familiars had a place in my heart before I could walk. My dream was always to earn my second paw and travel to the Skylands, to apprentice under one of their Master trainers. They have the best beasts up there."

It's the first time I've heard mention of the reclusive northern island.

"My turn—"

"Sorry, Ford," I interrupt. "But where do the Skylands stand in all this?"

"Where they've always stood." Shamar shrugs. "Neutrally north of Aiyca, Zesia, and our continued rivalry with one another. Xaymaca turned its back on us, gave in, but we're readying our blades."

"As wonderful as that imagery was," Ford drawls, "I'd rather not wash my meal down with talk of blades and where they're being buried. If you don't mind. As I was *about* to say, my métier's the worst." He splays large hands. Two leaf tattoos curl around his index and middle finger on his right hand. "But it permits jokes like, what did the earth say to the Grower? Can you give me fing—"

"Ford!" Delyse throws her bowl at him. While he catches it, the chicken skin inside flies up and slaps him in the face. I snort into my bowl, surprising myself.

"If you wanted to show me a little skin, D, you only had to—"

"Just-Ira, tell us your story before I *kill* this Obeah-man."

Once again, they look to me. I must have been hungrier than I thought; my bowl's already empty.

"My nana was a Warrior," I'm forced to admit. "Our coven lived and trained close to the Strawberry Hills." I jerk my chin in the direction of the fruit-filled knolls cloaked in night rearing in the distance behind the estate, weaving a little dishonesty in with the truth. "At five, I started my training." Late for most métiers. None of them make comment, though. "At eight, the Alumbrar attacked. We came here to help." *I* came, against Nana's orders. "I was captured and brought to Carne. That's all."

Ford whistles again. "What happened to your parents?"

"They died fighting this."

"The same thing that happened to ours." Shamar indicates to himself, Delyse. Ford and Nel sit quiet. Their families still alive, no doubt, somewhere across the island.

Though I can't see it through the trees, I feel the palace as keenly as the blood eaters that lurk in the dark. And within, the witch responsible for why Mama, Dada, and I can't regain the years I spent training in the mountains, not the hills.

Good food won't make me sweet.

"You might not like stories, Ira, but you sure know how to tell a sad one."

Nel and Delyse gape at Ford; Shamar fidgets, uncomfortable. I can't help huffing a laugh; it's not too long before Ford snorts, and we're all suppressing sniggers, lightening the pall my story instilled.

"Well, I have a story," Delyse starts. "But not about me. I have it on good authority—"

"She means she overhead a conversation," Nel interrupts for my benefit.

My shoulders tense. "I bet she did."

"And you'll be grateful when you hear this." Delyse leans in and lowers her voice. "The Jade Guild attacked a settlement of Alumbrar in St. Ann, the day before yesterday."

There are demands for more information while I'm busy doing the math. Doyenne Cariot rescinded my execution the day before yesterday. Her excuses, already flimsy, all but dissipate. Why free me in the face of a rebel attack?

"Was there much damage?" I ask, louder than the others.

Delyse is near giddy. "They used Timbámbu."

Witchfire.

"The Jade Guild haven't sought the ancestors' aid before," Ford muses. "It's always a risk. It's not like we all carry the respect of the Adair name to just summon the help of the dead."

I stiffen at his reference to my surname.

"I think they're finally ready to fight back." Delyse looks at each of us, the implication of her words clear.

The group is silent, but it's a silence that's replete with meaning. Retribution has taken its time, this past decade. It feels like coming full circle to use the spirits of the dead to avenge that theft. It's the return of the knife they stuck in our backs, like Shamar said earlier.

This time, I can no longer avoid my curiosity about the Jade Guild.

"Have any of you been sent on missions after the rebels?"

The group exchanges a look.

"She doesn't send us after them," Shamar says. "Doesn't trust us. Even with the glyph, the vow, she prefers the Xanthippe, but . . . some of us have returned from missions unable to recall what happened."

"What do you mean?"

"We leave for a mission with the Xanthippe." Delyse twists her fingers in her lap. "And when we return here, we have no idea what we've done. I've spoken with all shields, and none of us have been able to recall what's happened. She's never been there when we've left for the missions we can't remember, but she's the only one with our blood, and the only one with enough gold to evoke the pinnoco guzzu."

I lean forward. "What's that?"

"An enchantment that turns you into a puppet on a golden string. If the magi controlling you tells you to jump, you jump, if they tell you to forget, you forget."

"It's a violation." Nel shakes her head. "And she knows it's wrong, which is why she makes us forget whatever it is she's had us do."

The food we ate turns to stone in my stomach.

Is this why she's kept me alive, to go after my own order in a mind-controlled state? It's sick. But, arguably, the Jade Guild will leave Aiyca vulnerable to threat if they kill her, so, technically, she's still trying to do the best for Aiyca. . . . Gods-damnit.

Delyse turns her attention to me. "What are you thinking, Just-Ira?"

"Hmm? Oh, just that it's about time the Jade Guild has done something definitive," I lie.

"And what are your thoughts about the Jade Guild? Did they recruit, in Carne?"

The others might not have Delyse's intensity, but they're all staring.

This can't be an initiation, can it? Not when no shield can kill the doyenne.

"I'm glad someone is doing their part to rectify our situation." My eyes lower to my lap. "But I didn't want any trouble in Carne, and I don't want any now." *Liar, liar.*

"Fair enough," Shamar says, his voice resolute enough to draw the focus of the others away from me. "It makes sense that the rebels would rely on Spirit Magic in St. Ann—it's so close to Carling Hill—but why use it now? Do you reckon something changed?"

The others murmur their speculations.

I do my best not to draw attention, because goddess almighty. How could I have been so *slow*? What are the chances Kaleisha found her way to the Jade Guild and told them about *Empress Adair's* reveal? Knowing her as I do, I'd say rather high. And it looks like Doyenne Cariot might want to use me to fight fire with fire.

I stand abruptly. "You know what? I'll leave you to your discussion."

"Ira—"

"I'm going to bed," I continue, not giving Delyse an inch.

"It's been a trying day."

Ford nods. "If you were with this one, I'm not surprised."

"That's it!" Delyse launches herself at him.

While they grapple with each other and the rest debate who'll win, I slip away, another shadow within the village.

"Iraya Adair."

My heart near stops as an Obeah-witch emerges from a patch of darkness ahead of me.

"What did you call me?"

"Follow me," she says in a flat voice.

Awash with dread, I edge closer, cautiously curling a fist. Her face, sallow and pockmarked, is blank. Her eyes stare unseeingly ahead. On her exposed arm, her Glyph of Connection flares a raw red.

My gods.

Someone is directing her magic, using her through it.

This is that guzzu Shamar spoke of, which can only mean one witch is behind the enchantment.

"Follow me, Iraya Adair," the shield repeats.

If only to shut her up, I do. Several steps behind, I follow the Obeah-witch through the village, past the empty training grounds, and out to the southern entrance, where two Xanthippe are on watch and four more are visible through the window of the left sentry bohío. She walks right out of the Cuartel; neither Xanthippe makes a move to stop her.

"I know you're there," a soft voice, as melodious as birdsong, calls through the night.

Not the doyenne's.

Emissary Cariot moves into the glow of a witchlight lamp,

golden details shimmering in the dark. "Come out, we don't have long." She turns to the sentries. "Tell your sistren inside to actually patrol this area," she orders. "I'm commandeering this sentry box to speak with this Obeah. Alone."

The coven members exchange a look but comply. Emissary Cariot strides over to the bohío and up its steps. A hand on the door, she pauses and looks back at me.

"Aren't you coming?"

Half in the shadow of the gates, I stare after her. Something about her demeanor is . . . different. A steel I didn't notice before lurks beneath her skin.

Abandoning the security of the Cuartel, I follow her inside. The sentry bohío is bigger than those in village. There's a table with cards and additional accoutrements; the emissary must have interrupted a game as well as undergoing a complete personality change—almost. Not entirely foolish now, she stands by the window in the line of sight of two Xanthippe who linger outside. They're not who I'm worried about.

"Where's your pet?"

"I'm here alone." She reaches for her neck almost passively, like it's something she does often. A gold chain disappears into her décolletage. "And with a warning." She wears a golden wrap around her silver curls. So much gold. My family's color, once.

She should have worn something else.

"Don't cause trouble, don't kill any of the doyenne's coven as I did guards in Carne, and stay out of the public gardens on a Sunday. I think I've got it, mon." I wave an unbothered hand.

"Let me return the favor and give *you* a warning, one I have a feeling you've heard before too. Keep the Zesian close, enough to see his betrayal coming before it lands."

Her mouth tightens like my words are sour to the taste. "And why do you think he's going to betray me?"

In truth, I don't particularly care if he does or doesn't, as long as he doesn't get in my way. Emissary Cariot shouldn't have come here trying to throw her position around. And that guzzu she used to get me here hasn't helped her case.

"Common sense." I shrug, continuing my charade. "Or perhaps it's my understanding of history. Zesia wanted Aiyca for a long while—perhaps as long as your order. And we both know you weren't willing to wait forever to take it. Now, I'll never be one to tell another woman who she should or shouldn't give it up to, but do ensure you're protecting yourself. Emissary Divsylar looks like a heartbreaker. And you, Emissary, look prone to shattering."

Doubt ripples across her face. *There she is*, I think. There's the girl from Carling Hill, nervous and uncertain. But just as soon as that vulnerability makes itself known, she fixes me with a look that's more hateful than afraid.

"And what about you, Iraya?" Her hand drops from her neck. "Unbreakable, I suppose?"

"I wouldn't have been nearly so narcissistic, but I'll take it."

"No one is unbreakable," she says. "We all have weak spots. Yours trains in the Cuartel, sleeps in bohíos, eats dinner around a fire with friends."

"And yours," I murmur, more than happy to return the

threat, "sports a blade on either hip, though his tongue might be his deadliest weapon." I straighten from the wall fast enough to make her flinch. "My scarification should tell you that I have skills in weaponry, Emissary."

"Your uniform should tell you that you're not in a position to use those skills." She walks to the door, never putting her back to me. "Seems like something you should remember."

Half surprised, half amused, I don't respond.

She leaves; I don't have long before the Xanthippe come back and throw me out into the night. Charged after that strange meeting, I jog back into the Cuartel, to the village. Doubling back on myself confirms I'm not being followed by any more ensorcelled shields. Stopping before an empty bohío, I hoist myself onto the roof and crouch low as I listen to the estate. The sky presses down like a palm, no doubt harboring more rain. I wish people were as easy to read.

Though, Emissary Cariot's strange visit, Doyenne Cariot sparing me *after* the rebels attacked—an act that should have guaranteed my death—both tell me something big is afoot in the palace on the hill. My magic needs to be ready for whatever that is, because I will find a way around the bargain.

I lie in wait for a long while until the first busha steals into the village, the magic-seeking thief armed with a blade in hand and intentions as dark as the sky overhead.

23

JAZMYNE

For days after my meeting with Iraya I could think of nothing else.

I whiled away hours lost in what she was thinking, doing. Who she met with, spoke to. Could she have confidences among the shields already? Hers isn't a spirit that would be shaken by the doyenne's threat to keep her head down, behave. It most likely amused her, as I'm sure I did. I should let her underestimate me, and yet . . . I want her to see me as a threat, a worthy opponent. But as I soon learned, the devil makes work for idle hands, because days after our parley, the announcement for the first Yielding trial stole first place in my thoughts.

With the sun long gone, a sickly moon casts its dim light on the streets of Ol' Town. A sickness, one that has little to do with the tangential motion of my curtained litera, thrashes inside me. I've yet to receive a reply to my missive, and now life will be lost tonight.

The entire island, it seems, has flocked to Ol' Town to witness the opening trial. With trembling fingers I peel back curtains as fine and iridescent as dragonfly wings to peer out at Main Street. It heaves with chittering Aiycans dressed in their finest kaftans and robes. Alumbrar and Obeah conscripts bear conduits, polished and shining, around their necks.

Inebriated and jovial, islanders spill out of taprooms and eateries, fueling an atmosphere redolent of the Ascension Festival's. The busha who carry me atop their shoulders are knocked hither and thither. I grip the sides of the golden box with my free hand, feeling exposed and at risk physically as well as emotionally.

The warehouse doors leer open in the night, like a gateway to some forsaken place—the Rutz *is* just that. The fighting pits within began illegally. A group of secular graduated from pitting cocks against one another to their ilk, for the same reason a pickney reflects sunlight at an ant, I suspect. Instead of shutting them down when the doyenne learned of what they'd started, she didn't object, no doubt to keep the largely ignored minority happy.

Madisyn hated it. Even Kirdan refuses to set foot inside, and he is familiar with the Mudda's Battle Faces, as this trial no doubt means to test the Yielders on. With Anya working a private job for some wealthy witch in Queenstown, tonight I stand alone.

Once inside, the busha let me down. Xanthippe move in to ensure I am untouched by the fray. Above the din of the crowd, bones audibly shatter in the pits where fights already occur. Kaftan aloft around my ankles, I pick a careful path to the waiting Witches Council and doyenne. They sit high up in the stands packed with spectating Alumbrar. Artisan, Stealth, and Recondite families sit closest, as the métiers the doyenne values above all others. Most hold delicate handkerchiefs to their noses to block the heady amalgam of sweat and copper suffusing the air. I reach for my own as Doyenne Cariot rises, a golden beacon in her flowing ceremonials.

"*Wahan*, Yielders."

Like good Alumbrar, the gathered seven in the pit below place a fist over their hearts in salute to our leader. Our doyenne. Our ruin. Though I suspect I'm in the minority who think so tonight. There's a glaze to the expressions of those gathered around her, sweat at their temples. It exposes them for what they are: fanatics. Magi as eager for the Yielding as she is. No doubt they are damage control for the assembly and the Nameless who protested.

Light Keeper.

My lashes flutter to hold back tears. Something wrenches inside.

"The rules of this trial are simple: win." The doyenne's voice rings clearly through the Rutz. "There will be two rounds of combat. Those battling in the first round will be randomly drawn. Subsequent rounds, however, will be determined by victors and losers until the weakest can no longer continue."

This is barbaric, even for the doyenne, and not something I would have thought her capable of before Light Keeper. I glance out at the crowd of silver and black hair, my throat tight. How many more of my ilk will die if I fail?

I am not down in the sand with the Yielders, but the uncertain purchase of its grains shifts beneath me too.

"You couldn't have picked a closer hideout for the Nameless Gennas?" Kirdan sits across from me in the carriage, focusing on the city outside the windows.

It's several days after the first Yielding trial. With the afternoon sun blazing down on Queenstown, the city ringing with patwah, music, and arguments between vendors and buyers, it's easy to forget what I witnessed in those fighting pits.

Until I close my eyes, and then I remember all the red, the screaming spectators, the doyenne's eye never leaving the carnage in the pit below. Two Yielders' lives were taken, that night, in an event that only confirmed my decision to remove the doyenne from the throne.

The carriage collides with another, jolting my eyes open. Road markings are loosely followed in Queenstown, where we combat with poorly trained prowlers. Jungle and sand alike, they leap over each other in a bid to defeat congestion; smaller carts attempt to squeeze themselves by too, encouraging much cursing between drivers. Even the Cariot sigil on the carriage doors goes unnoticed in this free-for-all.

"Seriously," Kirdan gripes. "I would have sifted us here if you'd given me notice."

"The next time Doyenne Cariot kills one of the Nameless and remands a wholeep more to Carne, I'll let you know what I'm planning earlier so you're not inconvenienced."

There's a beat of silence.

"Sorry, mon. That's not what I meant."

"No, I'm sorry." I sigh, frustrated with the Yielding, Vea's lack of reply, and my own inadequacy.

Kirdan's forehead furrows with concern. "You've been out of sorts for a few days now."

Since I met with Iraya. Something I'm reticent to tell him about, for obvious reasons.

"Is it the mysterious recipient of that missive I sent for you?"

To say yes wouldn't be an all-out lie. Our timeline is still as soon as possible, and if Vea doesn't respond, I'll have no choice but to go to Iraya. All roads seem to lead back to her.

"Are you ready to tell me who it was for?"

So many secrets, but he wouldn't be happy to hear about Vea either.

"No time." The carriage comes to a stop before a row of stores. "We're here."

The clothier is a prosaic building, with a smart typeface on its sign, and an even smarter Artisan of Cloth working behind the counter. She glances at the two Xanthippe who follow Kirdan and me inside, a necessity given that Jade Guild members are likely to frequent the city.

My smile is broader than usual, to put her at ease. "Wahan, Cardil."

The witch bows. "Both here for fittings?" she asks, for the Xanthippe's benefit. "This way."

The coven members remain in the main body of the shop, incongruous and militant amidst the bolts of fabric, florid kaftans, and handsome tunics. Cardil takes Kirdan and me around the back, past the measuring station and dressing rooms to the cavernous storage unit, where the Nameless Gennas have been flocking to hide since Light Keeper's death. Kirdan goes ahead; I pause in the hall.

"Blessings," I tell Cardil. "And I'm sorry." It's our first time speaking as well as meeting; our communications have mostly been through Anya. "Light Keeper burned brightly on this island."

"Our sky is darker without her." She bows her head. "But I trust you'll ensure her vision for Aiyca doesn't fail, Emissary."

"It's *our* vision."

Elegant, with her head tie sitting high and proud atop her forehead, her head dips again. "Of course. I was wondering about her Nine Night. I know she's been deemed a traitor, but there are only two days left to honor her. Does Doyenne Cariot really plan on ignoring them?"

Without the nine days of jump-ups and dinners to remember the newly departed, to honor the life they lived, Aiycans believe their spirit will linger and cause trouble in the community.

I try not to fidget. "St. Bethann is currently having a Nine Night for the Yielder they lost. As it was Light Keeper's parish, I think that—I think—"

"The doyenne is using that poor dead pickney's wake to ensure Light Keeper doesn't come back to avenge her death."

I look away, unable to coax the words to convey how ashamed I am of Doyenne Cariot's actions, how disgusted I am that *I* have to be the one who carries that message—and, worst of all, to hide the part of me that wonders if she manipulated the trial's outcome to manufacture this very scenario.

"Light Keeper will be honored through us, and what we do in Aiyca."

Cardil looks at me, really looks. "We're all hoping so. I'll be back within the hour."

Already feeling the weight of what she clearly expects from me, I enter the room where twenty Gennas, including Anya, look at me as she did.

Here we go.

"Wahan, Gennas."

Magi nod, a few wave. I don't know them all by name yet. Light Keeper did, and she also handled the speeches. Her absence fills this warehouse with an air of despondency; the lack of windows, to protect the bolts of fabric, some of which have been unspooled and turned into beds, makes the vast space feel all the more morose. This will not do.

"I want you to return to your parishes. Today."

That enlivens the Gennas; they sit up, murmur among themselves.

"Given Light Keeper's sacrifice that day, I am instilling some precautions." I clear my throat. "You will no longer proselytize. From this day onward, the Nameless will become the Faceless."

"Excuse me, Emissary?" a witch calls. I recognize her half-shaved hair, the long spirals of silver that spill across her shoulders on the opposite side, from a previous meeting. "How will our numbers grow?"

"Naturally. With one Jade Guild attack, and the potential

for more, Alumbrar will want places to go, and our outposts will be those havens—threat-free havens. Light Keeper did a brave, selfless act, standing up to save us. But if you're seen out trying to build Nameless numbers, the doyenne won't be so forgiving twice, and I won't risk losing more of you."

"So what happens now?"

"Doyenne Cariot dies." Anya steps forward. "And Emissary Cariot takes her place. She's already working to secure alliances, in addition to the Simbarabo, Emissary Divsylar. They will rid the palace of that witch, freeing our Light *Seeker*"—she nods at me—"to deliver a new dawn to this island. You get to return home, Gennas, and wait for the next missive, the one inviting you to Cwenburg for our new doyenne's coronation."

"So we do nothing?" an Alumbrar-man asks, a Healer, in a maroon kaftan in a style once favored by Dada.

Another victim of the doyenne's, however inadvertently. She has killed almost everyone I've called dear. No more.

No more.

"You wait," I instruct. "You survive. You prepare."

"For what?"

"Change."

24

IRA

In the past moon phase I've been conducting these rooftop stakeouts, Emissary Cariot be damned, a busha's telltale meandering gait is a warning sign I've come to know intimately.

Unaware he has two shadows, the overseer teeters past bohíos, leaving a stinking trail of sweat and rum in his wake. Every now and then he pauses to peer in through windows. This late, workers who share the morning watch with me will already be fast asleep, the perfect prey to a thief such as him and others of his ilk.

Finding a target he likes the look of, he hoists himself onto a bohío window ledge with thick forearms and wriggles his way inside the hut with a surprising dexterity considering I've seen no evidence he can walk in a straight line. Lowering to a crouch, my body tenses in preparation for the first screams. They come sooner than most of the others.

The bohío door flies open, and the busha rolls down the steps, landing on his back in the dirt with a groan. His blade sinks into the earth between his splayed legs. The shield he tried to get the jump on steps into view. Dressed for bed, she's armed with nothing but her tiny fists and a scowl I believe could cut through anything—metal, flesh. At the sight of her, he rolls onto his side and surges to his feet, near tripping over them in his haste to get away.

Witnessing a busha's humiliation never gets old.

You'd think they'd know better than to try to steal magic from shields who train to use their own against threats, but for every conscript who can fight them off, there are others who've woken to cuts, their blood stolen in their sleep so some busha can purloin them for a night and wield their magic in the parish below—unless I've gotten to them first. When the fleeing footsteps fade, I peer over the edge; the door is closed, and the girl's would-be attacker's trail through the dirt leads deeper into the village, which is worrying. In some cases, injured beasts will fight even harder than they would otherwise. I flip myself down from the roof, pleased to find that I execute the maneuver even better than yesterday, and stalk after him.

Guided by the dim light of the jars strung up overhead, I race around and ahead to intercept the busha, calling forth the image of Aiyca's Great River. Its vast waters ripple like molten granite before two dam walls cordon it in a small pond, and my conduit flickers to life. Training with Delyse by day and target practice with the busha by night has made this far easier, but the true test is always in exercising control.

The night enables me to tuck and dart through its folds unseen until I emerge behind the busha. He leans into another window. Fury makes my conduit flare as my magic crests its surface, eager for command. Lowering my hair tie over my scarification, I pad toward the busha, coaxing a thread of wind to do my bidding. Guzzu, Master Fayard keeps telling us in class, are easy in theory. In practice, when you're under pressure, it makes more sense to exert your will around you. But it's hard. The effort tightens my core and dampens the back of my neck. The pursuit of control shallows my breathing, almost to the point of light-headedness. I will that thread to extend outward. He slaps his neck, swatting his hand around for the blood eater he thinks touched him.

Not enough.

I will more, for the wind to loop around the busha's neck until he finally abandons the window with a choked cough, his fingers scrabbling against his rich skin. I drive the magic to tighten, but I'm the one panting now, loud enough that he stumbles around.

He blinks, his eyes small in his rum-bloated face. "Night Prowler," he gasps.

Who?

My surprise makes my control slip; the conduit fades against my chest. The busha breathes deeply; his hands relax their grip around his neck. I step back, desperately clawing at my magical control.

Great River. Dam walls.

Too late. With a crooked leer, the busha charges for me. Reverting to combat instead of magic, I drop into a crouch and sweep my right leg at the back of his left. He hits the ground hard but reacts with far more haste than he did back at the first bohío. A hand darts out and grabs my face. My shout is muffled against his filthy palm as I'm snatched down, onto my stomach. Before he can straddle me, I twist and kick out, catching him in his throat. He chokes. My hands scrabble through the dirt. I chuck a fistful at him in an underhanded tactic Kaleisha loved. He splutters, hands cradling his neck and eyes squinted. Stumbling to my feet, I draw my leg back, ready to end this, when a hand seizes my upper arm and yanks me away.

My back's flattened against a bohío, and Emissary Divsylar is before me, a finger pressed to his mouth as I struggle beneath him.

"Listen," he hisses. "*Listen*."

It's then that I hear whispers from what sounds like three or four busha heading toward my attacker. They exchange muffled dialogue. Something clangs—weapons. Are they hunting—are they hunting for *me*?

When I meet Emissary Divsylar's eyes, his pupils are large, the black devouring the green until it's nothing more than a thin ring. He jerks his head, demanding I follow. He cuts through the village like the deft strikes of a cutlass, the anger rippling from him as tangible as the dark cloak he wears. In fact, the potency of his temper is so heady by the time we reach my bohío—it doesn't surprise me that he knows where I sleep—I seem to have inhaled some, because one look at his face and I am ready to fight for the second time tonight.

He slams my door, dislodging a handful of cane reeds. We both speak at the same time.

"If you think I'm letting you stay the night—"

"Of all the foolish—I can't believe you'd be so *stakki* as to—" He kisses his teeth. "Night Prowler?"

"*That's* what this is about? The busha said the name too, I've never—"

"It's you! You've been sneaking around this village using your magic on busha, and they've clubbed together to take down the magi who lies in wait for them. You—" His insults merge into an incensed mess of patwah. "Why were you attacking them?" he demands. "If you've been watching the village then you know your order practically has everything under control."

"And *practically* having things under control makes busha stealing our blood acceptable?"

He drags his hands through his hair, tugging on the strands. "Nobody said that."

"It sounded like you just did."

"Why do you even care? You left your order in Carne. You *ran*."

The cicadas' song is the only sound for the several minutes I use to find the control necessary not to fly at the emissary and smack his head against the wall.

I smile, amiable, deadly. "Don't presume to know me, Zesian."

A familiar curiosity tightens his expression.

"And why are *you* here?" I ask.

"I told you—"

"Of course."

"—that I'd be watching." He shakes his head slightly, and that earlier curiosity shutters off. "Fear of admonition might stop the busha from reporting Night Prowler, but if you don't quit interfering, Emissary Cariot and I *will* tell the doyenne what you're doing here. Don't expect another warning." He bangs out of my bohío without another word, probably going to tattle to the Cariot emissary.

My hands loosen by my sides, the bones in my fingers cracking at the release of tension.

"I heard shouting—is everything okay?"

I flinch to my window. Delyse peers through it, her eyes bouncing around the inside.

"Just . . . yelling at the moon."

"And does he always shout back?"

My shoulders stiffen. "There might have been some busha around. You shouldn't be out."

"And you shouldn't provoke them by shouting," she counters.

"I'll rig my traps and sleep facing the window."

"I can stay?"

I'm taken aback by a deep ache of longing for company in my core.

"I'll be fine," I say, ignoring the feeling. "Goodnight, Delyse."

"Same to you, Just-Ira."

After checking she's gone, I fling myself on top of the cot.

It's a strange paradox, to hunger for companionship while also fearing what it can cause. But between the two emissaries and Delyse I'm never alone, not truly.

They're never going to let me win, and she's not going to leave me alone.

25

JAZMYNE

"Light Seeker," I say to Anya. "Have I mentioned how much I like that title?"

"Only about a dozen times the entire journey home, mon." She closes the door to my study, removes her traveling cape. "But you can say it a dozen more. You earned it today. I wish you could have seen yourself. Light Keeper would have agreed."

The smiles we exchange are equal parts fond and sad.

"You were every bit the leader she hoped you'd become when she was tossing her slippers at you."

We both laugh, without much humor. The coldness of the sound is amplified by the gloaming that dusts the estate outside my study windows. Blinking back a sudden rush of tears, I remove my own cloak and hurry to turn on witchlights, eager to keep the chill at bay.

Life has rushed past at cyclone speed since the Yielding Assembly. I haven't given Light Keeper the space in my head she deserves. Today's success with the Nameless Gennas was due more to her tutelage than the doyenne's. Of course there were some who decided to step back, fearful of the palace's reach, but the majority haven't lost their faith in me. *She* never lost her faith in me, though she exercised about the same amount of patience as the doyenne. I laugh again and it chokes off into a sob.

Determined to light a fire, I toss my cape at an armchair and miss. It falls to the rug—where a scrap of paper lies before the hearth. I stand there staring for long enough that Anya calls out to me, her voice thick.

"Jazmyne? What is it?"

Suddenly I'm moving in a flurry of awkward limbs. I catch a side table with my hip, cry out, and dive for the missive.

"Jazmyne!"

Out of breath, I scan the spiky scrawl.

"Has there been another attack?"

"No." I breathe, offering up a quick mental prayer of thanks. "She's agreed to see us." I hold the scrap up to the light so that Anya might read. "She's agreed to see us, *tonight*."

Anya hoists me up with her spare hand. "Who?"

"We need to hurry. Mudda knows how long the carriage has been waiting outside. Why didn't we see the note when we came back?" Snatching up Anya's cloak, I shove it at her.

"Will you send for the Zesian?"

"No, he has work to do here." He traveled ahead of us,

from Queenstown, to watch Iraya. From a distance. "It'll just be the two of us." I retie my cape at the base of my throat and lift the wide-brimmed hood to conceal my face. The length and weight of it will ensure my identity is protected wherever we're going. "We'll have to sift to the carriage from here."

Anya's forehead wrinkles. "You hate sifting."

"Yes." I take a bracing breath. "Just as much as Vea hates tardiness."

"Vea?" Her confusion doesn't last close to long enough. "Not *Captain* Vea?" Whatever she finds in my face incites her anger. "*Wanted pirate captain Vea?*" Anya kisses her teeth. "What were you thinking?"

"I was thinking," I say, my voice small, "that we lost the time to be picky, and that we need numbers."

"You can't tell me Divsylar is on board with this?"

"He doesn't know."

She snorts. "I bet."

He didn't want Iraya. When he learns about Vea, he might regret that decision. She's not worse, exactly, but pirates abide by different laws than Aiycans. She'll be unpredictable, and he won't like that.

"*Please*, Anya, we have to go." For a moment I think she'll refuse to take me, but her conduit flares and we're sucked through the tiniest of gaps between my study and our destination.

We blink into being amidst vegetation that's dark and clicking with creatures. I try to mask my panting breaths as someone emerges from inside the waiting glossy carriage. Unfolding himself to stand just as tall as the cab on vast wheels, the pirate rolls shoulders built for raising sails.

"Wahan." His accent is indiscernible, an amalgam of inflections from across the seas. "I was under the impression you'd be with another." He eyes Anya, who stares right back, coolly assessing every year he's been alive, no doubt. "Permission to help you inside, Emissary?"

Worry flutters in my stomach as his gaze transfers to me with an arrogant indolence. Partially obscured by the dreads escaping from the pile atop his head, his eyes are as golden as the conduit coin glimmering around Anya's neck. *Molten*, I think. My cheeks flood with heat.

"I'm fine."

"And I'm Roje," he says. The smile playing about his mouth reveals a golden grill covering his bottom line of teeth. At the sight of the sharpened incisors Anya angles herself slightly before me. "It'll be four hours or so in the carriage." He opens the carriage door. "The roads wind. There are sacks in there. Just in case."

"Where are we going?" she murmurs.

"Black River Port."

That's in St. Jayne Parish, to the west of this one. In four hours? That explains the faster jungle-prowlers at the front of the carriage. Their loping sprint will demand the sick bags more than the winding roads. My stomach turns at the prospect. I'd rather we sift, but Roje has no magic, as a pirate, and Anya should retain her strength, just in case.

"Specifically?" she demands. "That parish is almost as big as this one."

"A taproom."

"Which?"

"It doesn't matter," I cut in. "Let's go."

Inside the carriage, Anya sits heavily when she enters after me.

"Hold on to something." Roje grins, snapping the door closed.

"Grand," she remarks, gesticulating at the decadent velvet interior. "But then, I'd expect no less from the self-proclaimed Queen of Carne Sea. Jazmyne—"

"Don't." I grip the bench as the carriage leaps away. We bounce over a pothole; my head smarts where it smacks the back of the seat. "You need to trust that she won't hurt me. I told you, she was going to help Madisyn escape her Yielding."

Just like I helped Madisyn keep their relationship secret.

I wait for Anya to make the connection, but she continues her rant.

"And do you know what she demanded from Madisyn in exchange for her help?"

Love makes no demands. That's what my sister told me when I asked her the same question two years ago.

"I don't know," I lie, and not without guilt, but it's not my secret to share. "What she did say, before—*before*, was that Vea would help me too, if I ever needed her."

"Let's hope she remembers making that promise. Two years ago, when Madisyn still lived." Anya sighs through her nose, visibly calming herself. "I can't deny that Vea, her crew, will make formidable advisories," she says, stilted. "Especially with their trappers."

Trappers, carnivorous slugs, are harvested from the deepest parts of the sea. Worn on a thong of leather around pirates' necks, they siphon magic from magi.

"I know." They could make all the difference in a fight against the doyenne. Though, I confess, I was more preoccupied with Vea's thirst for revenge.

The carriage rounds a corner, tipping onto two wheels. Anya grabs my arm, saving me from slamming against the side.

"If this pirate doesn't kill us with his driving before we make it there, you know what she'll ask for, don't you? Pirates don't call Aiyca Gúdu Téretere for nothing."

Good land—*golden* land.

Pirates are born from lust. They enter this world unwanted, and as they grow nothing changes. Most can't trace their origins to family trees. But even if they did, they're not permitted magic under the Alumbrar rule, just as they weren't when the Aiycan Obeah ruled the empire. It doesn't stop them from stealing conduit gold from the magi sailing trade ships on their way to Aiyca's ports, though. Or bargaining for it from desperate Alumbrar.

"I've thought all this through."

"Let's hope so," she mutters, looking to the window.

Slipping out my locket Kirdan gifted me, I seek comfort in the egg-size pendant in his absence, hoping its gold is enough of a favor to beseech Benito for His luck so everything goes accordingly. And not just with Vea. Light Keeper's death makes bringing Anya onto the same page as Kirdan and me all the timelier. And then there's the matter of Iraya Adair.

You don't have to make the tough decisions alone, Light Keeper said.

"What I'm about to say," I start, not quite able to look at Anya, "will, I'm sure, make you want to interrupt. But I ask that you listen until I'm done, please. Can you do that?"

"Wait." She mutters something unintelligible; her conduit flares. "I've cast a silencing guzzu. Go ahead."

And so I tell her.

I tell her about the dream Kirdan and I share for Aiyca. To repair the relationship between orders, to make the secular feel part of the community, to prevent further bloodshed. That Kirdan will swear his fealty as my second and how I long for Anya to be my first. She doesn't interrupt as I share my grandest ambition, sailing the Simbarabo here not only to protect Aiyca from an Obeah retaliation, but to force Zesia to sign an edict recognizing my power here, and, once and for all, putting an end to any hopes they have to one day make Aiyca theirs when their standing army becomes mine.

And then I tell her about Iraya.

"You intend to do *what* with *who*?" she yells, in a good enough likeness to Kirdan's reaction when I first told him about my plan to use Iraya that I can't help wincing. "Let me make sure I heard you right, because that was a lot, mon."

I look at her for the first time. She's pinching the smooth hazelnut skin between her eyes, breathing through her nose.

"Not only is that group of magi you said could help not magi at all, they're the *Pirate Queen's crew*, and *Iraya Adair* is here? *The* Lost Empress?" She draws breath and finds a second wind before I've responded. "But she has been for almost an entire *month*, yet this is the first you're mentioning her?"

"Anya—"

She flings her spare hand up, stopping me. "To add insult to injury, you actually contemplated using her to kill the doyenne!"

Were it not for the silencing guzzu she cast, I'd worry Roje might hear her—I'd worry the Black River Port might hear us coming.

"That's not the worst of it either. You've allied with *Kirdan*!"

"He won't double-cross me."

"And you're sure of that?" She battens down, the set of her mouth an angry blockade, impervious and unavoidable in such close proximity. "The Simbarabo were always a risk; we'd be giving Zesia's strongest arm license to wrap around this island. If you give Kirdan the proximity a second demands, before you have any magic of your own to make the position binding, the Zesian doyenne could order an attack. How do you know he won't listen to her? How do you know it isn't her plan to let you think he's on your side, so she can take Aiyca for herself?"

Her words are uncomfortably close to Iraya's, though their motivations are oil and water.

"I trust Kirdan."

"Then you've bet on a lame prowler. Cut your losses now, Jaz, I beg of you." Anya leans forward and clasps my hands between her own. "Think of our order, of Aiyca."

We're disrupted by shouted expletives from several magi.

Above us, Roje parries with matching gusto, his insults corrosive enough to burn my ears and cheeks.

"How far out are we?"

Anya checks behind the curtain. "A few minutes, perhaps."

Blessings bestowed.

"Jazmyne—"

"Enough about Kirdan." The needles of truth she forced beneath my fingernails are why I want Anya to be my first, but to walk away from Kirdan is to walk away from my entire plan to dismantle the Yielding, to protect Aiyca. It wouldn't be a separation; it would be a disaster—an unnecessary one, because I trust him. "There are more pressing matters this evening."

The prowlers' pace didn't make me sick, but the reality of meeting with Vea might.

I look out of my window. We're adjacent to the bustling port now, navigating craters in a fractured road that rears up from a ground polluted with sludge, rubbish, and Aiycans cloaked in mystery and wrongdoing. Even the shadows scuttle to watch the carriage slow to a stop with carny eyes.

Boots slap against stone and the door opens, ushering in the most stomach-turning odor of rotting fish, blood, and familiar excrement.

"For you." Roje proffers a large kerchief that's clean enough for me to accept. "Welcome to the Black River Port."

Too many ships to count are docked—it's Aiyca's second-largest pier. Obeah and Alumbrar alike scuttle about with wares, or free the ties of grand galleons with flags of crimson and aubergine. Even at this time of night, it's busy.

"The taproom's just here. Can't say the smell will improve inside. You'd better keep my rag. Mind the shit."

I clutch the length of the cape, my kaftan underneath. Wedged between sagging buildings, damp with spray from the sea, the metal roof propped atop the shack looks like a weak gust of wind could blow it off. Inside, my sandals stick to the taproom's floor, where I keep my eyes as I follow the tread of Roje's boots through the cramped, riotous inside, up an unsteady flight of stairs, to a private room in the back.

He sticks an arm between Anya and me. "Past experience has taught me it's best that exes with partners in common don't meet—not the ones Vea shares, anyway."

I wince.

Anya's brow furrows. "Not Madisyn?" Her entire face drops. "*This* is who she left me for? Jazmyne—no. Do *not* walk away."

Juxtaposed beside Roje's grin, Anya's face is stone as I disobey her and close the door. I've barely exhaled, pushing my guilt aside to deal with later, when a voice addresses me.

"Consorting with pirates?" Vea's voice is deeper than I thought it would be, but as musical as all Aiycans' accents are. "Perhaps you have a little of your sister in you after all."

Inside the scantly furnished room, a solitary witchlight does little to illuminate its dinginess. All I see of her is a pair of over-the-knee boots propped atop a rickety old desk. Lowering my hood so that she might see the resemblance between Madisyn and me, our small dark eyes and heart-shaped faces—albeit mine's a little fuller—I force my voice not to shake. "I hear the cannons you release for her earthstrong every year. Blessings."

"I don't want your *blessings*." Vea drops her boots. My neck flushes with heat as I see what ensnared my sister.

She possesses the alluring yet terrifying grace of the sleek shadowcats that lurk in Zesia's sand dunes at nightfall. Her high cheekbones and slanted dark eyes are underscored by the large cat's calculating spite. Beneath the wide brim of her hat, coils of inky hair spill over her exposed slender shoulders.

"What is it with you Cariot witches and your penchant for flirting with danger?" She rises and moves toward me with the hypnotic ease of Carne Sea before the tides snatch you under.

I shake my head, as though clearing my ears of water. "I—I have an offer for you."

She keeps moving. Prowling toward me. My feet clip the door at my back.

"You said as much in your missive."

I'm so focused on the moon blades on her hips that I don't notice the dagger she's freed until it's pressed against my throat.

"Regardless of invitation, how could you walk in here like I haven't earned every single black mark against my wanted name?" She purrs, her body flush against my own. "If Syn was here, she'd floor you for your lack of common sense." I snatch in a breath at my sister's moniker. "Where are your weapons?"

"I don't have any. And my sister never would have hurt me."

Vea's laughter shakes both our bodies. "Your sister had a mean right. It caught me out a few times." Her eyes roam across my face, shooting up to the top of my head. My hair, silver, like Madisyn's. Abrupt, she releases me and retreats. My legs buckle.

A dagger thuds into the wood an inch from my sandals.

"Keep that. It's all you'll be getting from me."

"What do you mean?"

"You've come to offer me a chance to kill your mama." Returning to her seat, Vea places her boots back on the table. I notice she angles them to the side, so I can see her this time. "Instead, you should have considered why I didn't retaliate immediately after Syn died."

"I thought you needed help getting your fleet into Aiyca. I thought—"

Vea throws her head back and roars with laughter. "I'm Queen of Carne Sea. Captain of the *Invisible Lady*. Bane of the empire, moratorium on the ports here or no." She waves a dismissive hand. "What need I of help? For Syn, I would have demolished this island and chained her killer to the mast of my ship to greet the waves as my figurehead. But I made a promise." Vea runs the tip of another dagger beneath her fingernails.

My eyes bounce from her dexterity with the blade to her face and back again, worry mounting. It sounds a lot like she's saying no.

"She said power made your mama stakki and she didn't want any part of it. She wanted out. For you and her."

This I know. She died in the Yielding she meant to run from, and we never got that chance.

"These past few years I've honored the life of peace she

would have lived." Vea shrugs. "Aside from the occasional pillaging and murder, of course. Nothing will tempt me to wade into the affairs of this empire. Not anymore."

"If you had no intention of helping me, why did you agree to see me?" Why build my hopes only to spike them atop an anchor and dash the entire thing to the bottom of the sea?

She lingers on my unbound curls, my face. Lust, sadness, and anger fight for dominance in her expression.

I leave, no longer needing a response.

"I thought she'd say yes. I hoped she'd say yes. It's been so long since I've held my axe in battle." Roje lifts his tankard, losing himself in its contents.

Anya nudges my drink out of reach. She needn't have worried. A leak from the ceiling has been steadily dripping into the murky brown rum since we took a seat in a corner of this hovel. If I were to drown my sorrows, I'd sooner fling myself into Carne Sea outside. As it stands, I'm close.

The fight against the doyenne seemed like the wild adventures I've heard of the queen embarking on. Madisyn loved recounting how Vea came to steal the *Invisible Lady* for her, lose it, and reclaim it. A wild exploit of deceit, costume, and dancing in the mists rolling from the rear side of the Blue Mountains.

"We have gold," I try. "And there'll be titles available once all is said and done."

Roje examines an octopus tattoo splayed across his left hand. "Vea will kill me for saying this—or try to anyway—but she's sick."

"She looked well." My cheeks warm.

Anya crosses her arms over her chest and snorts. She saw Vea too, when I exited the room. If they were without their shared history, I know she'd agree. The queen carried her beauty like an unsheathed sword. One wielded with expertise.

"It's a wasting sickness on the inside," Roje explains. "Those closest to her call it grief. Her enemies, karma." As quickly as his smirk comes, it goes. "After a lifetime evading Death, I think she wants to meet Her as a friend."

A scuffle breaks out over a game of cards a few tables away. Roje watches the magi; I watch him. Time with Anya has taught me enough to identify the telltale signs of grief that linger beneath his eyes, in the corners of his mouth. He already mourns her. She and Madisyn can find one another again, in the afterlife, but . . . no matter what I do to get ahead in this race, I remain behind.

"Everything good?" Anya queries.

Roje nods, eyes sliding away from the roistering.

"What will happen in Vea's absence?" I probe.

"There'll be a race for the next queen." He runs a scarred mahogany hand down his face. "Candidates already sail for the Iron Shore."

I can only imagine what'll be taking place on the pirate archipelago closer to Carne than Aiyca. "Perhaps we can proposition the next queen," I think out loud. "Offer her what we would have Vea."

"The next queen would sooner gut an Alumbrar than ally with one. Vea was—*is* special. I don't see what else can be done. It's not as if you can be doyenne and queen, is it?"

A table's upturned; cards and coins go flying. Roje downs the dregs of his ale with a grimace. I eye mine, rethinking the distance to the waters outside.

It really is a no.

"I should get over there before Vea comes down. She gets headaches. You can take the carriage back," Roje adds as an afterthought.

Anya's laugh is without humor. "And have its owner come for us rather than you? No, mon. I already clocked that you stole it back at Cwenburg."

"You Stealths see everything." Roje tips his head at her, and a few dreads spring free; one falls in his eyes as he looks at me. "Walk good, Genna. Keep my rag and think of me often." His mouth quirks in one corner, then he's gone.

Genna? How can he call me that? What sort of general fails to recruit an army?

Anya isn't quick enough to stop me from snatching up my tankard and drinking at least half.

"Jazmyne," she tuts.

"No. *Iraya.*" I wipe my mouth with Roje's kerchief. It glides across with a softness I didn't anticipate. "Do you think she'll work with us—*for* us?"

"Are you sure you want her to?" Anya counters. "If we approach her, there'll be no turning back. No way out. And then there's the vow. I don't know how she'd work around it."

Kirdan would say the same, if he were here. Vow aside, it's not like I don't have my own reservations about her. She could demand gold, among other things, in return for her aid. And then there's the personality she smacked me with the last time we spoke. She's arrogant, spiteful, a goad—I sigh. One I need. That much is clear, even if the rest of my head is a little foggy.

"I don't want a way out."

Water smacks into the windows of the drinking house; the entire building seems to lean, teeter, and then readjust. The patrons don't miss a beat. Someone hollers for more drink.

"In that case," Anya says, her focus on the window nearest to us. "from what you've told me, I think she'll do whatever she can to get what she wants." She shakes her head. "People have been known to wriggle out of Shook Bargains, and she might be easier to manage than the Kirdan situation."

"Enough." My eyes bounce across her face, or maybe her face is bouncing across my eyes. "He's my friend, Anya." My mouth works slowly, like I'm speaking underwater. "I'm not in the habit of trusting my trusting. Doubting them," I correct after a beat. "His uselessness—usefulness—doesn't dictate that."

"You're too drunk for this conversation, lightweight." She reaches for me with a sigh. "Which is fortunate for you, because I've been meaning to ask what in all the Mudda's Faces you thought bringing me along to meet with Madisyn's ex—" She stops, looks to the window once more. Her conduit lights up around her neck.

The din of the drinking house prevents me from hearing what she's muttering, and the alcohol, some distant logic tells me, won't be helping my concentration, but they'll be guzzu for something Stealth-related.

"Come." Anya snatches me to my feet. I stumble. The rum. It thrashes in my gut like a creature made of sludge. "We have to leave here, *now*." A shield swells from her conduit, engulfing us in its fizzing spark of protection. Several patrons are shunted away by its girth. There are grumbles, menacing glares. Anya hardens before me, calcifying into an unfeeling agent of the shadows who deal in secrecy and intimidation. All are quick to turn away. "Can't risk the chameleon guzzu," she grinds out. "I'm not carrying enough gold, and we still need to get away."

"Why?" A hand clutching my belly, I'm slow to move.

Dragging me after her, Anya curses. "Black River is under attack."

We burst out of the drinking house and onto the strip by the pier. A bone-shaking blast explodes a ship, launching splinters of wood that leave the alcohol-induced fog clouding my mind in tatters. Another wave of seawater barrels toward the drinking house. Anya's shield saves us, but my mind clears entirely now, as though the wave had actually hit me.

We duck as the sky groans—no, not the sky, a *mast*. Felled by the explosion, it falls toward another ship with a crunch, destroying another on its way down.

"Come *on*!" I take the lead now, yanking Anya toward Roje's stolen carriage. There's nothing for it. We'll have to face its owner's wrath if we return to Cwenburg—*when*.

Her conduit glimmers, freeing a prowler from its holdings. "Riding will be faster." She seizes a set of free reins, cooing in her throat to steady the great beast's growls. It tosses its lush mane, nervous amidst the surrounding destruction, but calms beneath her touch enough to permit Anya to mount its back. She tugs me behind her.

"What about the others?"

With a roar, five ships flying gray sails erupt in dazzling toxic green flames on the water. They are backlit against a starless night where only the moon looks on, pale and veiled by a netting of fire.

"There's no time to do anything for them, Jazmyne. I need to get you to safety."

I cling on for dear life as Anya digs her heels in, and the jungle-prowler races away from the Jade Guild's second attack. This suggests the first wasn't simply an act of vengeance. It suggests *planning*.

It suggests there are more to come.

26

IRA

The Bidding Circle of candles on my bohío floor sparks to life at midnight on the fourteenth and final day of my tenure training here at Cwenburg's estate. Thanks to the Mudda's Faces, increments of seven have always blessed magi with fortune. Obeah don't hold Their favor any longer, but I'm in need of all the help I can get tonight.

It's been twenty-eight days since my spectacle at Carling Hill. Four since Emissary Divsylar's threat. And not a single moment has passed with Delyse where I haven't caught her looking at me like I'm keeping something from her. Which I am, of course, but that's beside the point. Matters here are tightening, on all sides. That requires some creative thinking, an area in which I happen to specialize. If I can rid myself of these glyphs behind my ears, I won't need control. Unbound and limitless, I might be powerful enough to override the

Shook Bargain around my wrist, and kill Doyenne Cariot.

A little thievery of thread and fabric within the village resulted in the Deleterious Doll sitting in the center of the ring of burning branches before me. Every self-respecting Obeah knows how to weave a doll using wild cane. Crudely bound together and looped around the middle with strands of my hair, the pastiche looks eerily sentient in the dancing light of the fire. I splash what remains of a stolen skin of rum I took from a drunk busha on the doll, appealing to the ancestors. This enchantment is too great for my conduit alone.

I dip a finger into the chicken blood I liberated from the village kitchen after tonight's meal. Shamar nearly found me out on my way back here, but a well-placed hand on his arm and a murmured compliment about his performance in our morning training drills distracted him. I'm lucky Delyse didn't catch me. I can't help glancing over at the window, where I've staked my sleeping sheet as an extra barrier. She was put out tonight when I rejected yet another offer to eat dinner with her and the others. She might come by later, knowing her. I need to be fast.

"Obújufra. Bone," I murmur. The opening of the traditional greeting to the ancestors comes out hoarse. My mouth's unused to the deep patwah, their ancient tongue, after so long. "Ta'k na mi, arik na mi. Priiz." I'm sure to end with *please* as I implore the ancestors who linger on this mortal coil to talk to me, to listen, the first step.

The ring of fire ebbs, and then blazes bright.

They've heard. But will they come?

Though Mama always said the dead have a certain affinity

with Adair witches, given that we were chosen by the Seven-Faced Mudda to rule Aiyca, Delyse was right when she said using Spirit Magic directly from the source requires the utmost respect. While some spirits are always on hand to help an earnest Obeah, there's a risk calling on them, one many of my order have paid for with their lives. In Carne, there were magi who tried to summon the spirits to help liberate them. I thought about it too, but without the Jákĩsa, harder to come by than the other fundamental offerings of blood and bone, there was always the chance I would have been twisted inside out, just like those discovered by the guards.

With blood-steeped fingertips, I complete the second step, swirling whorls of deep patwah behind each ear. In the hut's tepid air, they dry fast. Other than sálo, I include wudu, ishó, kiir, and mínibo. The deep patwah promises strength, fluidity, care, and a grounding power. I already carved the same words onto the chicken bones, also smuggled from the kitchens. They're tossed inside the circle along with the doll, completing my vow with an intention of blood and bone.

The ring of fire sparks out before lighting once more.

That's twice.

The ancestors are here.

Wind whistles through the gaps in the thatched roof and the reed door as their invisible forms seep inside. The flames dance, casting distorted shadows on the curve of wall. My breathing quickens as my shoulders are clenched in claw-tipped gossamer again and again as the spirits mass around me, lending their strength via touch. A shiver sluices down my spine, both at the drop in temperature and fear as a vacuum of energy cyclones around me. It would be foolish to feel other-wise in the presence of such primordial power.

The hands around my shoulders force me to kneel and lean into the center of the circle. It's the strangest sensation to watch my hands reach for the Deleterious Doll, knowing that I'm not in sole control of my movements. It's a shared custody, an understanding of what must be done and a desire to see it through, something that's both beautiful and terrifying. Even if I wanted to stop now, I'm not sure if I could.

I don't think they'd let me.

The circle binds their control to what I want, and they'll see that through.

Whatever the cost.

Together, we hold the Deleterious Doll's head above the ring of fire until it smokes in its heat. The glyphs behind my ears heat up. Discomfort builds to a searing pain as the skin stretches into bubbles.

No. Too much.

I push back, but the spirits are immovable. Their clawed tips wrap around my wrists, holding my hands in place. The doll's head erupts into flame. My teeth sink into my lower lip, suppressing a scream as the bubbles behind my ears swell until my head feels ablaze with fire too.

Vomit erupts from me. My body convulses itself free of the spirits' grip, jarring my spine as I heave and heave. Weakened, I slam sideways onto the wooden panels of the bohío floor, my head throbbing and muscles spasming. The minutes pass slowly. I count each second, begging the ancestors to let me be as I wait for the sea of sickness to abate. Mercifully, they listen, giving my body the time it needs to calm down—but only just.

My chest still aches from heaving and fighting for air, my brow's slick with sweat, and the heat from the fire makes my head spin on top of its throbbing, but their grip tightens around me once more, forcing me to take up my conduit. With the little strength I've eked back, I squint down at the coin, imagine the rushing waters of the river, and will it to light.

It does in an instant.

The golden glow beaming from the coin belies its size, glazing my hands and forearms in a celestial lambency. The spirits don't give me long to bask. The cane walls tip as I'm lifted by more hands and forced into sitting position. Spirits sit at my back, keeping me upright. Their intentions are clear.

I draw in several breaths. The glyphs pulsate like tiny hearts. My stomach roils at the thought of exacerbating the pain, but there's nothing to stop the ancestors from coaxing my hands behind my ears, where the burn blisters are primed for popping. Splitting the skin there completely is the only way I can rid myself of the glyphs. I take a deep breath, two, before I press against them. A hiss snakes out from between my teeth. Stars spot my vision as I press harder. *Almost there, just a few more seconds*—without warning, the ring of fire is extinguished, plunging the bohío into darkness and freeing me from the ancestors' hold as though they were never here.

Relief and trepidation are equally felt at the presence of the three shapes that sift into existence before me, the magical teleportation abrupt and disorienting. My witchlight lamp flickers on to reveal they're Xanthippe. Oh. *Oh.*

I should have considered that there'd be an alarm on the glyphs.

My smile's tight as I rise, slowly, willing myself not to throw up all over them.

"Witches. You'll have to excuse the mess. I wasn't expecting guests this evening."

"It's *her*." The Xanthippe who spoke retreats. "I'll summon the doyenne." With a frightened look, her eyes roll back in her head and expose the whites.

Spirit Shunting. I always hated the idea of sending an ephemeral extension of myself away from my body to relay a message. It leaves the body too open for an attack.

With the glyphs stretched almost to bursting point behind my ears, I no longer need to visualize the Great River for my conduit to dazzle from my chest. The guards flinch from its brightness, hands thrown up to protect their eyes from the shine of my intentions, freed and eddying like a brewing tempest within a nebulous sky.

"That shouldn't be possible." Sweat trails down this Xanthippe's nose. She's smaller than her companions, jittery.

"First day?" I ask, my voice full of faux pity.

"Don't engage," her partner orders. Older, she does a better job at concealing her emotions. Her dark eyes, impassive, squint into mine. "The doyenne will be here soon."

At her threat—her promise—my conduit flares like a burning meteor.

The novice tightens her grip on her cutlass. "She's going to attack!"

"Don't!"

Faster than her companion's command, the novice's conduit emits an amber guzzu of suppression. I roll across the floor to avoid it. My head spins with queasiness when I right myself. The duo group together, stomping like a pride of prowlers right through my circle. *Gods-damnit*. I need to get my pastiche. Such magic, bound to me by my hair, can't fall into anyone else's hands. Especially not the doyenne's.

I fling my body at the one who's Spirit Shunting and bounce her head off the wall. She crumples in a heap at my feet. Outside, someone calls my name. *Delyse*. Her distraction costs me. Another amber spark flies my way; two, three more follow suit. There's no room to maneuver from my position in the corner. Magic surges inside me, splashing over its banks with eagerness. Pulling from its thrashing core, I will a wall of protection. The magic moves *through* me, extending from my conduit to grow between me and the Xanthippe in a shimmering golden manifestation. Though it's small, about the size of my torso, Self-Intent comes easily. The sparks smack against its translucent protection. I'm forced back a few steps. But I'm unscathed. The Xanthippe look on, openmouthed.

Now, this is what I'm talking about.

The smallest desire makes the shield zip forward. They meet my parry at the same time. Their larger intentions smash through mine like they're nothing. I fly backward, smacking into the wall with enough force to rattle my bones.

"Restrain her."

She's here.

Shackles bind my wrists and ankles. I strain against them. They don't give. The metal must be glyphed to suppress my magic. *Cha!*

"You were warned about protocol when handling this Obeah. Why would you engage in combat? Mengkeh! Fools! Lift her, so I can see her face."

I'm hoisted up by the shackles on my wrists. One of the Xanthippe grabs my braids, snatching my head back so I meet the doyenne's lone eye. It doesn't leave mine as she steps into my ruined circle. She dips, fabric from her golden robes pooling around her legs as she lifts my pastiche.

No. No!

"I gave you the honor of a warning. And you try this." Her fist closes around the doll. Without the protection of the circle's flame, her influence pervades. My ribs contract in pain as the doll's magic transfers the touch. She tugs on one of the arms, and my shoulder jars, bone grinding against the socket. My teeth sink into my bottom lip until I taste copper.

"A Deleterious Doll," she says, disgust in every syllable. "Dark magic Alumbrar were never foolish enough to tamper with, not when it had the ability to kill whoever it was rendered after if a needle was driven through its heart." She angles one of her dagger-sharp nails over my doll. Painted bloodred, it curves like a talon on the paw of a monster. "But you could bring the magi back to life if you took the needle out soon enough. Can you imagine dying and coming back over and over again? The pain, the anticipation, the *fear* that the next time could be the last?" She holds my doll against her chest, her arms forming a cage I feel press around me as sure as any bars. "Perhaps it is too dangerous to keep, hmm?" Her conduit blazes on her chest, mirroring the sudden swell of flames in the hearth across the bohío. She snatches away the curls of my hair I'd wrapped around its middle and then tosses the deactivated doll into the flames. "Needless to say, I'll have to find some Obeah to punish for your gall, for breaking your promise not to pop style." Firelight throws her face into cruel relief. "In the parish beneath this domicile, perhaps. And as for the glyphs. Well." She steps in close, enough that her dreadlocks brush against my tunic; her nails pierce my cheeks as she seizes my face and turns me left to right. "They're burnt beyond repair." She presses her fingers onto the tender flesh. My head swims. "We'll have to install more. Ones so deep, any attempt to remove them with another Deleterious Doll will result in its little head being burned clean off. Rebrand her," she orders the older Xanthippe. "To the white meat."

The hot poker feeling returns beneath the skin as the glyphs take effect. I grit my teeth at the doyenne's vigil, but the pain grows, ensnaring my entire head.

Heat grazes bone.

A scream rips through me; it takes too long for everything to fade to black.

JAZMYNE

"Two Jade Guild attacks!" Presider Antwi slams a hand on the table in the council chamber; her charm bracelet, adorned with acorn-size precious stones, rains down on the wood like hailstones in a gale. "How much longer will we continue to roll over and show our bellies?"

My head rings with her question, her demand. In the five days since the attack, I've considered every scenario in which the council converges around the doyenne for answers, as they are now. It's redolent of what Anya posed just yesterday, when she returned from the cleanup initiative I ordered the Nameless—now the Faceless—to engage in helping those in Black River.

She has to come forward with Iraya Adair's existence.

"First my beloved parish was subjected to their Spirit Magic," Mariama continues. "And now Presider Phelony's home too has been burned and charred!"

Wheezing into a bag across the table, Ormine has yet to voice her concerns. I'm not sure she'll have the chance. Not unless she knocks Presider Antwi off the soapbox she's stood atop this past quarter of an hour. In the month since her parish languished beneath the surprising might of the Jade Guild's first attack, her grief has boiled its way to ire—one with no temperance for respect.

"We cannot permit this gross hubris to continue, my doyenne." Palm greets wood again with an emphatic slap.

Doyenne Cariot's eye lowers to Presider Antwi's splayed fingers. "I understand you are suffering, Mariama," she begins, top lip curling. "But you'll do well not to take that tone with me again." The room, already cool, drops several more degrees. The presider is quick to snatch her hand back. "My cabinet of Sibyls is working tirelessly to help locate the insurgents. Imbuing themselves with the ancestors daily, they assure me the Alumbrar spirits will soon show them where we need to go to disrupt the Jade Guild stronghold. And then there are the patrols in the wetlands. The insurgents will be found, and once they are, there will be a public execution to deter further infractions."

Though no word has been mentioned about Iraya, my back, ramrod straight, doesn't relax. I can't see how the doyenne will work around her, and then the presiders will demand the Lost Empress's head to be spiked on a stake before the Obeah insurgents, leaving me without a means to get the doyenne off the throne; this time, there will be no other options. I'll lose.

"How can we deter further acts of insurgence if—please excuse me, my doyenne—" Presider Antwi trips over her words to ensure veneration this time. "If we don't know why they attacked to begin with?"

Mudda, go with me.

"Why did they choose *my* parish? Why Ormine's?"

Presider Caldwell clears her throat. "I think they're planning something."

Doyenne Cariot looks to her sharply. I do too. Ada might be her second, a witch sworn to put her safety above all others to the extreme that she has no pickney and no partner, but she's also a Recondite. If she isn't in the doyenne's confidence about Iraya, her training in the arcane means she'll be clever enough to suspect something's happening.

I've never longed for a blade before, wouldn't know how to use it, but I'd try anything to silence her.

"The escapees from Carling Hill, the first attack in Mariama's parish," Presider Caldwell says, her voice curling away from its typical warmth like a snake in the bush preparing for attack. "The destruction of the fleet of prisoner ships in Ormine's parish—"

"*Some* ships," Presider Magmire, Doyenne Cariot's first, corrects. "We have more."

"The destruction isn't what's important. It's what it symbolizes, Westira." Ada's conduit glistens around her neck, brightening as she retreats into her unique mind. "History understands the importance of signs. Especially those that preface war."

My chest aches, but I don't dare draw breath.

"For that is what this could become," Presider Lewis interrupts, and all at the table swivel to her in shock. The eldest witch on the council after Light Keeper's execution, she's often content to sit back and listen, her sightless eyes concealed behind stylish dark shades, her round face smooth and indifferent to all discussion. It's fitting that she interrupts now. As a Squaller, she understands a brewing storm even better than Ada does. "They're fighting back." Her voice, awash with calm, is sinisterly incongruous with her words. "They are ready to."

"Don't be stakki." Westira straightens, her face twisted with scorn. "They have too much to lose in fighting, with no gold themselves, and their magic wielders conscripted with too little."

"Tell that to my parish," Ormine croaks, her voice ravaged by tears and anxiety. "Tell that to the remaining parishes quailing in fear that war is flying on *jade wings* to our island." Drawing a stuttering breath, she wipes beneath her eyes; they look like two overripe June plums. "I mean no disrespect, my doyenne, but what can I tell those I was called to protect? What can *we* tell the entire island in the face of two attacks? People are afraid. They want to know why the insurgents are fighting now." She sobs. "*Why?*"

The weight of an executioner's scythe presses against the back of my neck, driving itself further in as the doyenne's silence ticks by. For surely I'm done. *Aiyca's* done.

It's not like I could have all the presiders killed.

"You forget yourself," the doyenne says at last, and in a tone that silences Ormine's cries. "Weeping and wailing like a fishwife, not one of my chosen custos." Her sniff is sharp. Ormine isn't the only presider who flinches from it. "Of course your parishioners are afraid; how could they be anything else when the source of strength they look to is bent and battered by a change of wind? What have you told them to allay their concerns?" She looks to Mariama, whose mouth opens before closing. "Just as I thought. It seems it falls to me to be the voice of reason. Blessings to the Seven-Faced Mudda, who knew Aiyca would need a steadfast leader, and not any of *you*. For as it happens, I've had a campaign in the works since the first attack. Though the Jade Guild are a mere fly in my glass, I am not ignorant to the opinions of my people, witches. Just wise enough to remain calm in the face of trouble, something you would do good to remember."

That was masterfully disturbing. She didn't need to mention Iraya at all.

Doyenne Cariot casts her eye across every face. The council shrinks before her, silenced. "You spoke of symbols, Presider Caldwell; then I will start a fire of my own that will cauterize what the insurgents have wounded."

All around the table look on, confused. Myself included.

The doyenne rolls her eye. "There'll be a tour."

"Really? You haven't toured the island in at least half a decade, my doyenne," Mariama says, something like hope on her face. "St. Ann will appreciate your appearance, I know."

"Not I." Doyenne Cariot turns to *me*, seated at the opposite end of the table. Her council follows her focus, almost as if they'd forgotten I was here. "Emissary Cariot will be my eyes and ears across the island, my mouthpiece while I remain here to oversee the Sibyl panel as they entreat the ancestors for answers."

Disappointment draws my features tight. It's as if she knows this is the worst possible time for me to go away.

"You can begin with Westira's parish, and end the tour with a speech in Queenstown. Take this." She slides a binder with notes my way. "I've prepared what you need to share with the parishioners. You'll do good to follow the script."

Spin her story, she means.

"The emissary will do your bidding, to the best of her abilities, I'm sure," Mariama says. "But she is without your magic."

"If I go, it will only encourage Alumbrar belief that this island is in danger."

"Perhaps then you can bless our parish perimeters with more first battalion soldiers?"

Doyenne Cariot's lips disappear, thinning along with her patience. "Fine," she concedes.

"Blessings, my doyenne. Blessing—"

"Emissary." My title severs through Mariama's ramblings. "Have your attendants prepare luggage for several phases of travel. Small packs; you'll be traveling by one of the Cariot sloops. Tell them to make haste. I wish for you to leave before nightfall."

"Will I have a guard?"

"Choose who you wish from the Xanthippe."

"What about bringing along some Stealths?"

She waves an impatient hand. "As you wish. Should I not see you before you leave, may Benito bless you on your journey."

I bow my departure, doing my best not to slam the chamber door behind me.

Kirdan and Anya wait in my suite, in the games room. Kirdan sits, one leg resting on top of the other, his cotton traveling cloak abandoned on the couch beside him, as he turns the pages of the book he's reading. Humor lingers on his mouth. No doubt that's down to Anya sitting across from him, her arms folded; eyes never straying from him. Their animosity is a perfume in here, and yet I breathe deeply, comforted by its familiarity after the shock turn of the meeting.

"Doyenne Cariot's sending me away."

They both start, Kirdan abandoning his book, Anya getting out of her seat. Her conduit flashes; a bubble of silence swells around us, keeping my tale from prying ears.

"For how long?" he asks.

"Where?" she asks.

"Almost a monthlong campaign of the island, to quell concerns that we're about to fight a war against the Jade Guild. There can be no more delays," I say, determined. "We ask Iraya now, before I go."

"That won't be possible," Kirdan says. "There was an incident, last night."

His words scoop through my stomach, hollowing it out.

"She tried to escape, didn't she."

"Something like that. Xanthippe apprehended her, and the doyenne issued punishment."

"What?"

"New glyphs," he expounds. "I was hoping Iraya would have woken by now, but she's in a deep fever sleep."

I fight for calm, resisting the urge to throw something.

When will it be my time?

When will I win?

"You'll need to write me, Kirdan," I grind out. "As soon as she wakes."

"I'll stay here, keep an eye out, and do just that."

"You can send me the fire message," Anya tells him, because of course she knows I want her with me.

"You'll come?"

"To every destination." She nods. "Once word spreads that you're away from the safety of the palace, the Jade Guild might make a move on *you*. What was the doyenne thinking, sending you when she's clearly too afraid to go herself?"

"Probably that she can always have another heir," I say, oddly unthreatened by the threat of the Jade Guild. It's not me I'm worried about them getting close to during my tour.

28

IRA

I wake shivering, but not with pain.

"Steady, Just-Ira," Delyse says. "Everything's well. Considering."

We're in my bohío. Cradling my head in her lap, she holds a cooling cloth to my forehead. I try to sit up, but she holds me firm.

"Don't dislodge the Bush Witch."

At the end of the cot, the Healer breaks her incantations to smile at me; she tucks a thick twist behind her ear; they're so long they brush against my hip. If her face was a little broader, with the gap between her two front teeth, she could be Kaleisha's sister. . . .

I dip my gaze to where she works. Both wrists are coated in a poultice of clean-smelling herbs. While bush herbs are temperamental in that they must be blessed by the ancestors, when they work there's nothing more powerful. Cool magic enters my veins via my wrists, steeping through my system until it reaches the place that needs it the most—my head. Though my throat takes close second. It's on fire, no doubt from the vomiting, the heaving, and the screaming. I *screamed* before the doyenne—a truth that hurts more than the new glyphs.

"Personally, I've never seen you look better."

I start at Ford's voice. He lifts a hand in greeting from where he leans against the hut door. "Didn't think we'd be waking together so soon. It's a shame about the circumstances."

"Drink this." Delyse forces a rough spout between my lips. I slurp down the cool coconut water. "You nearly knocked me out with that snare, you know." The torn sheets lie in a heap on the floor, the books I tied together to form the pendulum crowning them. "I'm not sure if you remember what happened. You were passed out when I found you. There were the remains of a Bidding Circle, rum, fire." Her delicate features draw into a scowl. "We don't labor out of choice, you know. Whatever you try, we've all done it before. Multiple times." She sighs. "I thought you smart enough to know that." She taps my conduit.

Parts are charred, dark. The shield. My use of Self-Intent has corroded time away from an already loaded countdown. *Gods-damnit.*

"Don't ride her too hard, Delyse," Ford interrupts. "Actually . . ."

"Don't even go there," she says. "Some things can't be healed. Remember *that*."

Ford straightens from his slouch with a wince.

"Pardon me." The Bush Witch's voice is a smoky rumble in her chest. "Not to take the heat off Ford, but I've done all I can to lower the body's temperature. It will keep the fever away, but slowly. You'll be sore, Ira, but I won't let the pain become unbearable. That I can manage. I'll return this evening to change the wrappings and poultice once more."

"Blessings," I manage to croak.

The witch bows her head before making her departure. Ford takes one look at Delyse and beats a hasty retreat to the sun-pervaded village outside too.

"Likkle more, Ira," he calls. "I'll tell the others you're still alive."

Delyse helps me sit, propping me up against the wall with a little bit of fuss. In contrast to her usual physical comportment, her hairline is mussed, and there's a suggestion of shadows beneath her eyes.

"Have you been up all night?" I can't keep the surprise out of my voice.

She settles in the chair by my cot, propping her legs up. Her feet are bare, dusty. Like she ran here without sandals.

"Nel heard fighting. You would've drowned yourself in sick if she hadn't found you."

Delyse, Ford, *and* Nel?

She fidgets with a loose thread on her pants. "The Zesian emissary came and sanctioned Master Agape's best Bush Healing apprentice in the infirmary, Fatou, and a day of bed-rest after the doyenne left."

He did?

"Why?"

"You looked near dead, Ira. How could she order him to impart anything else? He told me to stay and keep watch, in case you relapse." She twists on the hard wood of the chair. "Toss me your pillow?"

"I don't think so."

Delyse's smile turns sinister. "I can call Shamar to bring me mine; he's been anxious to know how you're doing every five minutes or so."

I tug my pillow from behind my back and fling it at her.

She makes a point to settle on it, laughing at the look on my face. I don't smile back, can't. I start training tomorrow, and my conduit's charred; I've new glyphs—more.

It was improbable before, but how do I stand a hope of killing the doyenne now?

Killing . . .

"Delyse," I say quickly, remembering the threat Doyenne Cariot issued, "is there any news about Obeah being punished?" I swallow. "Killed?"

Her face tells the story before her mouth. "No one has died, but . . . Xanthippe did visit one of the Obeah settlements beneath the hill. There's been talk of bruises, and a few broken bones. They go out and stir up trouble sometimes."

Not this time. This time that's all down to me. I slump further against the wall. The prickly reeds at my back aren't enough discomfort. I deserve more—to be flayed with them, a mark for each person who felt pain for my actions. A mark for each pickney who had to watch their parents, siblings, bredren, or sistren harmed *again* because of my idiocy.

"All isn't lost, mon."

"What?"

"You did a stupid thing, but you're not alone in making desperate choices." Delyse nudges me with her legs. "And we'll help you keep up with your training drills until you're on your feet, Shamar, Ford, Nel, and me."

"Why?" *I've done nothing but avoid you.*

"Because, Just-Ira, unity is the sweetest resistance in an atmosphere created to foster discord." She winks, ignorant to the fact that my heart just stopped.

She can't know—she couldn't . . .

Those words are from one of Mama's most famous speeches, one of her last.

"Now rest," Delyse says, retrieving a book from the floor. "I'm not going anywhere."

I'm surprised to find that I do.

29

JAZMYNE

"Your doyenne, devoted protector of this island, first wishes me to extend her apologies that she couldn't be with you this morning." I do my best to smile, even though I avoid looking directly at the crowd gathered in the town square in Port Airam, the capital city of St. Jayne Parish. Not only is this the opening stop, it's presided over by the doyenne's first. Westira Magmire stands close at my shoulder, enough that each time she exhales, I feel her hot breath against my left ear. "She remains hard at work on the Yielding in Cwenburg, ensuring our immediate and future safety."

"And do we have a future?" someone calls. "Or will there be further attacks?"

There are approving murmurs, demands for answers. Xanthippe jostle along the periphery ready to subdue the crowd if need be. My fingers curl around the wood of the pulpit, digging in to steady their shake.

"Answer them," Presider Magmire hisses through her teeth.

"I—that is to say—" My tongue trips as I make the mistake of looking at the faces gathered, far more than there have been when I've visited the city in the past. There are many Alumbrar, Obeah too, those who are conscripted and the free alike.

They'll all be my sole responsibility soon.

"Emissary."

Do I want to begin my rule by telling the doyenne's lies?

"It would be foolish not to prepare for further attacks."

Magmire pinches the underside of my arm; one glance at Anya and the presider's pulled back, whether by magic or physical force I don't know, or care. Turning Doyenne Cariot's directions over, I begin my speech anew.

"You are afraid, and I . . . I won't stand here and tell you your feelings are not justified. What I will say is that these are times to turn to sources of light." My throat bobs as I think of the resistance leader. "Find the beacons of hope in your communities, for they are ready and waiting to share these safe spaces with you, these oases of comfort." In the crowd, there's a Nameless member to every ten parishioners, at least. They might not be ready to seek out the resistance now, given what happened at the Yielding Assembly, but my people will be waiting for them when they do go looking. Because they will.

"Will there be war?" someone else calls.

I hesitate. I don't want to loop the Yielding into my discourse.

"There are . . . forces at work on this island, allies of those in the palace, and they're laboring to prevent further attacks. Know this, Aiycans"—I emphasize the island-wide title, not wishing to isolate the secular who too have gathered this morning, not when I am about to irritate the Order of Obeah members who stand stalwart at the edges of the crowd—"and I say it with absolute certainty: we will not capitulate to the insurgents' threat. Something they would do good to remember after ten years—something you shouldn't forget either." Several Obeah turn away, mouths twisting. I hesitate, falter, uncertain of my next words.

Someone applauds, most likely Anya rescuing me, but it picks up in the audience before me, and then the majority are clapping; only the Obeah bow their heads, leave. I'd meant to close with Aiyca's dictum, *Out of many, one people,* to foster the idea of unity, but perhaps now isn't the best time given tensions surrounding the Obeah and the Jade Guild.

With a final nod to the crowd, I turn for the stairs, yellow and gold kaftan held aloft. Presider Magmire isn't waiting with the Xanthippe. No doubt she's gone to send a missive to Doyenne Cariot; she was incensed enough that she might have sifted to the palace herself. But Anya's there to help me down, along with a cabal of six additional Nameless Stealths she handpicked, all shrouded in black like the shadows they usually operate from, not the high morning sun present today.

"Well done," Anya murmurs. "Someone needed to take a stand."

We exchange a loaded glance, both knowing it's one the doyenne will no doubt make me pay for when I return.

"I bet we'll see an increase in numbers from today." Filmore, one of the cabal, nods with enthusiasm. "*I* want to sign up for the Nameless," he says, his conduit lit to keep his comments from the Xanthippe. "And I've been part of the movement for years."

His energy is catching; I find myself smiling.

"To the sloop, Emissary?"

"To the sloop."

"We'll meet you there."

The Xanthippe form a wall around me and Anya, who stays close to me while her team moves ahead to assess for threats. The magical barrier holds back the flurries of citizens who shout their concerns, but there are also others who shout blessings—to *me*. They push against the magical shields with expressions of gratitude, adoration.

"Lower the shields."

"There are risks, Emissary," one of the coven cautions.

"Lower them."

The magical barriers shrink enough that I can reach out for hands, accept blessings, and look parishioners in their faces. Parishioners *I've* made feel better, and with something far closer to the truth than the doyenne wished me to share. Whatever she says when she learns I deviated, islanders here respected *my* words. My voice means something.

It's a much longer amble back to the private mooring in Port Airam's shallows, as we're orbited by Aiycans the entire way—which makes what's waiting for us even worse. There, splashed against the mooring house's street-facing side in bright green woad, is the message *BAG-O-WIRE*. The bodies of the Xanthippe who were guarding the sloop are left on the dock, abandoned to the carrion crows.

Anya grips my arm. "What color is that?" She nods to the message dripping down the brick.

"Jade," I whisper.

"Thought so."

Unlike the attack in Black River, there's no Witchfire this time, but the Jade Guild's name rips through the procession of accompanying Alumbrar all the same, scatters them, sends them fleeing back to the safety of their homes repeating the same cry over and over again—*war*. Their tone is far more incendiary than the word, and sure to spread like a blaze across the island.

Our exodus is a flurry of Xanthippe collecting the bodies of their sistren, others commandeering another vessel, deeming the one we traveled in unsafe, though it looked unharmed, Anya ordering the cabal of Stealths to stay behind in pursuit of answers, and me, staring at the bold slur on the wall until, hours later when Port Airam is well at our backs and we're on the way to the next parish, it's printed on my eyelids. The Jade Guild thinks *I'm* a traitor.

"They're the ones who attacked first," Anya murmurs over the roar of the sea beneath the hull. "I don't understand."

But I do.

"I didn't tell them Iraya lived," I whisper. "They heard it from the runaways."

The presiders were prescient, in the meeting that prompted this tour. Our order is afraid, and with no news from Kirdan about Iraya waking, I no longer feel confident standing before them and telling them to look for light.

Not when the Jade Guild have this island cupped in the darkness between their palms.

Within the hour, we've docked at the lip of a beachside eatery to take proper stock of our losses. At Anya's insistence, I leave matters to the Xanthippe and permit her to coax me into one of the metal shacks in pursuit of sugarcane, to help with the shock, and a hot meal.

The proprietor takes one look at the Xanthippe who accompanied us inside and leads our party to a private room without windows and only the single door. While I sit at the table, too numb to do much else, Anya walks the perimeter, conduit ablaze as guzzu flows freely from her mouth. The Jade Guild have proven themselves capable of dispatching members of the doyenne's coven; I put more faith in her enchantments than their ability to guard the door outside. She steps in coal dust before the hearth and tracks it behind her—fire.

Kirdan.

"I need to send a message."

"To the doyenne? I've been thinking the same. Tell her what happened. She should request your immediate return." Catching sight of my expression, Anya pauses. "You weren't thinking about the doyenne, were you?"

"I wanted to learn if Iraya woke."

She sighs. "We'll send two, and order some drinks while we're at it."

Kirdan's missive is quickly dispatched. I share our location and beg him to send news about Iraya. The doyenne's correspondence takes longer to write, with Anya magically striking my words out enough that I concede the breadfruit skin and writing tool to her in favor of sending one of the Xanthippe for the proprietor to take our meal order.

"She might already wish for you to return to Cwenburg if Westira has spoken with her," Anya says grimly, though not without hope. "It would be reckless to keep you here."

I don't know what I feel beyond the neck-snapping turn from jubilation to the cold fear at the Jade Guild's message. We expected their rancor, but not their retribution. Returning home might be for the best—and we receive an answer about it sooner, I think, than either of us expected one.

We both dive for the missive tossed from the fire. It's from the doyenne. Clutching a side each, Anya and I read quickly. Instead of the admonishments I expected for deviating from her script after the first stop, she demands that I continue the tour, regardless of the Jade Guild's threat.

Anya shakes her head, disgusted. "Just when I think she's done the worst thing anyone could possibly do, she proves me wrong."

Supper, red pea soup with thick bread, is eaten in tense silence. Every crackle and pop from the fireplace makes Anya and me abandon our spoons to look over until—another reply arrives.

Closer to the hearth, she beats me. "Kirdan," she says, passing the scrap my way.

His note contains only two words: *Iraya woke*.

Mercies bestowed.

It's the first and last piece of good news we receive for some time because, when we pull alongside our second stop thereafter, the rebels' message that I'm a bag-o-wire is already waiting for us. The woad, still wet, glistens like blood as the sun rises above St. Ann.

"They're anticipating our stops," Anya murmurs from where we stand on the sloop bobbing out at sea still. "I think we have to change course."

"I think so too," I whisper.

It's a tense voyage to the next parish, and a lengthy one since we have to go back on ourselves to loop the island in the opposite direction.

Anya sits by my side, where she has stuck herself since the second stop, as the narrow beam of the sloop kisses the delicate curve of neck arching out of the mountainous coast of Lawson Bay. In moments like this, gliding across the ombre wash of the Xaymaca trench, running the gamut from the deepest Prussian blue to a blinding aquamarine, my anxiety seems all but gone. But our sharks are on land, not at sea.

"What's the Nameless climate like in St. Catherine?"

Anya, watchful beside me, lightens up a little. "Filmore was right in what he said that day, before we found the first message in St. Jayne. Word has spread about the Jade Guild messages and Alumbrar across the island have been flocking to neighbors, or bredren and sistren they know were affiliated with the Nameless. Everything you said during that Genna meeting is coming true, Jaz. Our numbers are growing."

My heart swells, like the sails replete behind us.

"I do have some bad news I hoped wouldn't matter, but since we've had to divert here . . . The second trial took place yesterday evening and claimed a life, but not Javel's. Since you're addressing her parish, Presider Phelony will expect you to attend the supper she's throwing in his honor tonight."

My groan is swallowed by gull and sea. The Yielding has been easy to run from, touring the island, but having to see Javel will lay it all at my feet. Two trials, three Yielders dead, and more to come after this rite is finished if I fail to convince Iraya Adair to hitch her wagon to my prowler. In the time since she woke, Kirdan has sent regular updates. There is always the risk of her getting into further trouble, but it seems her last parley with the doyenne has cowed her rebellious spirit. For now.

"Tell her I can't do supper, please. Tell her that I don't have anything to wear."

Anya snorts. "That's a poor excuse, mon. We're in the sericulture capital of the island. She'll most likely have something made for you at her great house. So what's it going to be? Are we mooring close to town and picking something up ourselves? Or will you risk Javel walking in on you in your undergarments while you're being fitted in his family home?"

Less than an hour later, we dock at a public mooring. The number of Xanthippe accompanying our party has grown exponentially since the deaths of the first. That, at least, the doyenne said yes to in response to one of the missives Anya and I sent. They won't help with keeping my anonymity, but at this point I'll settle for coming and going without seeing any hint of jade.

The streets of Lawson Bay, the parish capital, are bright with streamers of fabric; they festoon from up high in a spectrum of grays for the Artisan métier. It's an homage to Javel, and I hate it. One conversation where I shock him into silence doesn't make up for years of cruelty; tonight I'll have to toast to his success, choke down food in his company. It will be worse than my talk with Iraya. She, at least, doesn't attempt to hide who she is.

"Let's pick something quickly and be done with this."

Magi have started to gather, drawn by the Xanthippe and word of tomorrow's expedited address. I don't have the energy to smile and laugh with them, not when I must act already tonight.

Anya is quiet by my side, scanning the crowd over her shoulder with an intense curiosity.

At once my heart races.

"Do you see them?" I murmur, panic mounting. "Is the Jade Guild here?"

"What?" She whips around. "No. I was, er, checking for Filmore. Why don't you try this store? I'll let the Xanthippe know they need to stay outside. Doesn't look big enough for all fourteen of them."

The bell over the door tinkles when I enter. The Alumbrar clothier, as elegant as Cardil back in Queenstown, bows her head in deference.

"It's an honor, Emissary Cariot. Is there anything in particular I can aid you with?"

"I'll call on you should I need to. Blessings."

She bows her head again, and I lose myself in the racks of kaftans. Her needlework is sublime, delicate and feminine. It will be a shame to waste one of these masterpieces on a meal I don't want to attend. In the storefront, the bell sounds again. That will be Anya. She can help me decide if the black kaftan with the gold edging is too somber and will offend Ormine, or if I should respect her hosting us with something gray. My hands trace over a fitted crimson marvel, complete with a train and gold beading that looks like a living flame.

"That color will suit you."

Drawing my hand back as though burned by the ensemble, I flinch around.

"Wahan, Emissary."

"Roje," I breathe.

He smiles with his eyes first, the twin golden sunsets. "Heard you've been having a spot of trouble." He rests a thick arm on the rack of kaftans; I take a small step back. "After Vea's unavailability, thought the least we could do is ensure you live to kill your mama."

"I'm not—that's not what I'm doing."

He tucks a lock behind his ear and laughs. "No judgment from me."

To the left of his bulk, at the shop front, Anya steps into view. Though she browses the tunics and accompanying pants, her lips press together in a barely contained grin. Did she know he was coming?

"How did you know I'd be here?"

"Some of the crew have been following you since you left your last stop. We were going to keep our distance, but your sistren made me out there." He jerks a thumb over his shoulder.

"Said I shouldn't follow without permission; it's . . . creepy."

Vea sent him to keep me safe?

"It's good of you to come." My shoulders relax a little. "How is your queen?"

The irreverence in Roje's face is exchanged for something subdued. "Not long left now, and she's killing herself faster to ensure all is right on the Iron Shore in her absence. I've practically had to tie her to her bed, mon, which wasn't as fun as it should have been." He scratches the stubble on his chin. "She's a fighter. You remind me of her, actually."

"I do?"

His face is serious as he stares down at me. "I've watched your order from a distance my entire life; I've endured their judgment whenever I've ventured ashore. Coming to us as you did, you're not like them. With you in the palace, they might become better people. And I trust you'll get there."

An odd feeling comes over me. I don't know what to say.

"So, are you good with a few of the crew keeping an eye on you? We're not in the galleon—don't worry, too conspicuous."

"I'd appreciate it."

Still sporting that serious expression, he nods, backs away.

"Tell Vea I offered my blessings? It was kind of her to send you."

"She didn't send me." Raising a hand in farewell, he leaves the store.

What did *that* mean?

"You can stop looking. He's gone." Anya seems far too pleased with herself.

"I—I wasn't. I was thinking."

"Sure, mon. Have you chosen something?"

More distracted than I'd like her to know, I hand her a charcoal kaftan and some coin to pay the clothier. We leave arm in arm, my new purchase wrapped, and carried by Anya.

"So, Vea didn't send him," she muses after I've filled her in. "I wonder what made him come."

"Your tone says you already know."

"Don't tell me you don't." She snorts. "He's a man, Jazmyne. They all want one thing."

I duck away from her prurience. We're in public, parishioners line the streets as we head toward a carriage the Xanthippe procured.

"Of course, it doesn't matter if you want it too."

"*Anya.*" It isn't the Alumbrar way to discuss such things.

I feel her eye roll rather than see it. She's always lived how she wants, giving her body to whoever she wants. Such indulgence, fear of reproach, is almost Obeah of her. Meanwhile I've never been kissed on the mouth, let alone anywhere else. My face is ablaze with my embarrassment at the thought of being intimate with someone. Since Madisyn's death my only thought has been Aiyca, preparing to rule, and working with the Nameless. I haven't put much thought into what my life will look like when all is said and done, who I'll want to spend it with. My sister always said women were soft, safe. Anya, for all her angles, encapsulates that for me—platonically. In a romantic relationship, I can see why it would be comforting to feel safe.

Roje isn't safe.

He is a current too strong to fight against, leaving you with no choice but to let yourself go. To let that power, that sheer force, overwhelm . . . I'm pulled out of my thoughts by the closing of a door. Somehow, we're in the carriage.

"I'll have to leave soon after supper," Anya says. "Work calls me back to Queenstown."

"I can't believe you're leaving me to Javel's mercy."

"You have protection. And I suspect you'll have plenty to distract yourself with when I'm gone." She lands another knowing look; my stomach flips. "Will you meet with your pirate? This bay is beautiful at night."

I consider her words as we rattle through Lawson to Presider Phelony's great house and the uncomfortable dinner that waits. How would it feel to let go after seventeen years of drawing myself in? To lose myself in someone.

Terrifying.

This close to returning home and engaging Iraya in our plans, I can't afford to divert from all I know, for the possibility of something I'm not even sure I want.

Aiyca is my only love, for now. My only obsession. As it should be.

30

IRA

"Drink this" is how Delyse has taken to greeting me since the Bidding Circle incident. Today she hands me a skin of guava juice, watching to ensure I finish it all.

After sitting with me all day following my failed attempt to remove the glyphs behind my ears, she's barely left me alone since, despite her official buddy period ending. It's a dangerous admittance for me, but . . . I'm grateful for her persistence. Without everything she's done for me in the past month—continuing to work with me outside official training hours, having either Shamar, Ford, or Nel partner with me during the drills so the busha wouldn't see how pathetic my guzzu are, even taking my watches for a time so I could sleep in late after my encounter with the doyenne—full recovery would be phases out instead of days.

"Classes have been canceled for the day," she says, taking back the skin. "The Masters have surprised us with a challenge course. It's something they do from time to time to assess how we're applying their teaching as well as the training drills."

"How many shields will participate?"

"All forty-nine."

Oh gods.

That's too many of my ilk who could either find themselves on the wrong side of my naevus, or—no. There is no right side to my magic exploding in the fields. Trouble, it seems, isn't done with me quite yet.

Shamar joins us as we leave the Cuartel, and round three of its seven sides to a copse of trees on the far east of the mount. I stay quiet, preoccupied by my worries, which grow at the sight of busha separating lined-up shields into two different streams of traffic. Delyse links our arms and makes to step past one.

"Hold." His eyes rise to our scarification and then dip to the coins around our necks. "Stealth, you're that way. You too, Poisoner. Warrior, you're this way."

"Why?" Delyse demands.

The busha's prowler shakes its auburn mane; yawning, its lips curl back from yellowed tusks the length of my forearm in a timely reminder of their threat.

"Delyse," I mutter. "Leave it."

"No. Why can't we compete together?"

"Your conduits have more char, so you'll engage in the challenge course that requires less magic." He nods at me. "But yours only has a smudge, so you get to do the heavy lifting, so to speak."

"This isn't char," Shamar insists. "It's dirt."

The busha clicks, and his prowler springs up onto its hefty paws, setting us all back a step.

"We're going now," I promise.

"Ira." Delyse's eyes bounce between me and the prowler, assessing, always assessing.

"Don't worry, mon. I'll be fine."

We all know it's a lie.

The challenge course I'm sent to isn't much to look at. About one hundred yards in length, the wooden apparatus varies in height. Some beams are strung up in the tree canopy, others low to the ground, separated by gorges of muddy water. With no rope to be seen, or ladders, I can't see how we—*born back a cow.*

We're to exert our will around us to get across.

My suspicions are confirmed when Master Fayard casts a Stealth-sharp look at the dozen of us gathered at the starting line. Of course he's responsible for this.

"Shields," he almost whispers, so we must all lean in. "Your objective is to get across the course by sundown without guzzu, only will."

"Forgive me, Master Fayard," one shield says, the silver hood that should be covering her shaved hair twisted between her fingers. "But are we forbidden from using guzzu to cut down some of the posts, to make it across?"

"Let me spin you this." His eyes, the brown hue tinted with the blue patina of age, narrow all the more. "You can protect Aiyca, or you can save it. You may think they are the same, but it is the difference between rescuing a drowning man by dragging him onto a bank, and rescuing a drowning man, and

286

then visiting him every day after to ensure he is well."

The Obeah-witch who posed the question doesn't stop twisting that hood.

I think that was the Master's way of telling her no.

"You may begin whenever. The busha will track your successes and failures." He waves a hand and hobbles away, cane before legs, until he is clear of the trees and out of sight.

My fellow shields scramble to start the course, conduits blazing bright as they summon winds to carry them across gorges, or will vines to enliven so that they can hoist them up and over obstructions. They all make great headway, and then there is me.

As the morning wears on, I only manage to light my conduit, a difficult task in itself with these new glyphs. Their presence is like a weight on either side of my head, and trying to draw on the winds to move builds pressure there, like surfacing too fast from the sea.

When the bells ring for lunch, I haven't managed to move past the starting line.

"Food will help," an Obeah-man promises in passing, his round face kind. "Summoning takes some getting used to."

"You go ahead. I'll catch up," I lie. I'm not eating until I've moved.

When I'm alone, I draw a grounding breath and then will the wind that even now stirs the leaves in this copse to carry me to the next station. I could cheat and attempt to leap over, but if I fall in the muddy sludge separating me from the opposite bank, everyone will know I failed anyway.

Come on. I push as my conduit flickers.

It doesn't.

I close my eyes.

Nothing.

I threaten the wind with mental obscenities.

Nothing.

I threaten it with *verbal* obscenities; it actually dies down in complete refusal.

Stubbornness courses through my insides, molten and searing. Heat explodes in a furious burst of lambent white light. The pressure behind my ears, in my head, is alleviated, and my body is unbound and weightless; my skin tingles with sensitivity in the heat, and I want to let go.

I want to let it all go.

No. *No.* Sense mounts, but extinguishing my naevus is like trying to slam down a lid with rusty hinges. I cover my eyes with both hands, blinking the light away until my face cools.

I brave a look.

A thick cloud of choking smoke rises from the burnt gorge. Its acrid remnants clog my lungs, burn my eyes.

"It's you."

I whirl, squint. The Obeah-man who encouraged me stands there with a fat patty in either hand.

"You brought me lunch," I'm quick to say, to distract. "Blessings, mon. I—I'm starved."

"You're here," he says, louder now, his voice quivering with—with reverence. "Empress."

I flinch at the title, like it's a slung stone. "Don't—don't say that."

"It's you!"

"Stop!" My hands push through the air, like I can stop the words from leaving his mouth, stop them from traveling over the Cuartel walls to where the others eat. "I—I'm not. That's not—"

A roar rips through the sky.

I duck as a prowler leaps overhead, landing before the Obeah-man with an earthshaking *boom*. One swipe from its mighty paw knocks him to the ground with a cry. The busha from earlier, the one who sent me to this course, stops beside me, a delighted malice in his eyes.

"Thought you'd be one to watch after this morning."

"Then watch me!" I shout. "And let him go."

Footfalls sound from behind. It's Delyse and Sham, their bredren and sistren. Did they hear the Obeah-man? They don't look at him. They're looking at *me*. The atmosphere changes. They adjust their stances, but not to flee—to fight.

They heard.

"Cooh deh!" The busha surveys the gathering Obeah. "What have we here?"

Delyse steps forward; I wave a hand in silent command to stay back. The busha sees.

"It's the Stealth and Poisoner from earlier too! What's got into everyone?" He's clearly smarter than I've given his bredren credit for; his eyes narrow on me, and the air thins. "Did you hear me, Warrior?" He nods at his prowler; it plants a paw on the struggling Obeah-man's chest. He wails, it's plaintive and resonant around the course.

Resonant in my core.

"Tell me what's going on. *Now*."

The Obeah-man could have been my age, but magical exertion has robbed his rich brown skin of its shine, his cheeks of their elasticity. Sympathy slips around my chest like a lariat, tugging and tightening. Some of my order have been here for five years. Waiting for the Vow of Peace to be broken.

By you, a quiet voice says.

I can't breathe.

My order has surrounded us. No matter how grayed they are, their eyes—they rage in the sunlight. The blacks and browns golden, splendid, fevered. I see the revolution that brews just beneath the surface. The Obeah are fearful, but ready to charge—at my call.

No.

Not *Ira's* call.

"Nothing is going on," I whisper, dropping my gaze. "I—I don't know why he started talking to me. I just want—I just want to get to the end of the course."

"Yeh mon? Then it seems to me the rest of you've forgotten we run the road!" the busha roars. His bredren reply with their own bellows to the sky. "Now dust from here!"

Delyse appears by my elbow as some of the shields swarm the busha. "Come with me." She leaves no room for discussion when she takes my arm and tugs me after her.

I pull against her, looking over my shoulder as the busha disappears in the middle of a crowd of Obeah, and his bredren shout for their prowlers—will there be a fight? But her conduit's lit, and magical strength must coarse through her, because I cannot break free.

"Wait, Delyse. Wait!"

She doesn't respond. We're walking fast enough that it feels more like running, away from the course and into the Cuartel, the village, to a bohío into which she drags me.

Seated on a chair in the center of the hut, Shamar nods at me, his expression grim. He must have run here, to beat us. I force my stiff muscles to relax, like nothing happened. Like I didn't leave an Obeah-man to a prowler's fate.

Like the Obeah didn't look like they were about to revolt.

"Kidnapping requires anonymity, you know."

Delyse smirks at me, her lips a soft pink against the white of her teeth. "You're the one who's done nothing but conceal your true self since you first arrived here. Not that it worked."

"We had our suspicions for a while," Sham admits, his face still serious, and almost . . . hurt? "Master Omnyra told us to be on the lookout for Iraya Adair several months back." He pauses. I keep my expression blank, disinterested, but it's like trying not to puff while racing uphill.

And my heart, it's racing, all right.

"Her visions aren't perfect, of course, no Bonemantis's are. And none of us could remember Iraya's actual earthstrong. Nor could we say for certain if she survived the Alumbrar raids after the Obeah Witches Council fell," Shamar says. "No one had seen her since she was a pickney. But when the Jade Guild informed us about what took place at Carling Hill, the Adair naevus, we knew it was her. Luckily for us, you were the only new conscript to arrive here. Keeping an eye on you hasn't been difficult. One of the first things you did was visit the resting place of your ancestors' bones."

My indifference gives way to fury. "You followed me there? How *dare* you."

"How'd you think that tree branch happened to grow over our side of the wall?" Shamar defends, but he still looks guilty. "Anyway, why did you hide? You arrive at Cwenburg Palace, where your mama, our empress, ruled. The estate you grew up in, before you disappeared. Now you've returned, and with the scarification of a Warrior, no less." His eyes rise to the line on my forehead; they're as acuminate as the blade that put it there. "Someone willing to take a Vow of Protection for their land. An empress willing to show her order she knows what it means to fight, even though she'll never need to."

"He might know who you are, but I want to hear it." Delyse is resolute before me.

The fight seeps from my shoulders.

"Yes, I am Iraya Cordelia Adair," I mutter. "First of my name, and only living heir of Empress Cordelia and Admiral Vincent Adair."

They bow before me. Circling their right fists around their hearts, they thump their chests once in Aiyca's salute of veneration.

"I called it first to Master Omnyra," Delyse says, smug once more. "Even before one of the Jade Guild's Gennas managed to send us a message."

"How did the rebels know?" I ask.

"They came across a group of Carne runaways in the fingers of wetland by Carling Hill."

Kaleisha.

Could she live?

"They told the guild everything. Though they were uncertain if you'd survived—do you know why Doyenne Cariot kept you alive?"

"My naevus, no doubt," I say, dismissive. "But that's not important. The busha will talk about a witch with Warrior scarification, and an Obeah-man willing to die to talk to her," I spit, in a bid to stop them looking at me like I'm some kind of deity simpering down at them from atop my pedestal. "The doyenne will hear what happened, assume you know who I am, and kill all of you." I expound on her threat.

Sham's shaking his head before I've finished. "We're taking care of all busha who saw."

"We?"

"About two-thirds of the shields here, like us, are part of the Jade Guild."

"Of course you are," I mutter.

"We've been waiting for you."

I trail my foot through the dust, tracing shapes. "Is that so."

"I trust that's rhetorical."

"Delyse, mon." Sham tuts at her, but I'd rather she keep her gall than switch to curtsies.

"It was more of a statement," I say. "When I was in Carne, the Jade Guild didn't make any progress. Before the attack in St. Ann, I didn't even know the rebels *could* fight fire with fire. Are you telling me nothing's changed because everyone's been waiting for someone they didn't know was dead or alive?"

"Not quite." Shamar bows his head. "After the Viper's Massacre, the Masters needed the time to rally, to come together, and then to form a plan of attack with us shields. It's also taken the Jade Guild longer than we would have liked to establish a presence, to build the trust of those who didn't think anyone was coming to help. And even when that was said and done, there have been other things we've sought, Ira, Iraya. *Empress*."

"Ira."

"Just-Ira, then," Delyse cuts in. "As much as I'm sure you'd like it if we waited all this time for you, we've been busy growing our numbers. But Cwenburg isn't the place for another Genna." She looks at me, really looks at me. "It's the place for an empress. One we hoped for but didn't allow ourselves to believe we'd find."

I knew this would happen.

They see my scars, know of my training, and yet they want me for my name—the very thing that propelled me to Nana Clarke as soon as I could choose a different métier. I always wanted to be more than a title, to do more than it would allow.

Sham stretches his legs, his feet close to mine. "You want justice, vengeance against the Witches Council, the doyenne. We want the same."

I stalk to a set of handmade shelves, run my finger in the thick coating of dust while I wait for my anger to abate. "But it's not the same."

"You're right, it's not. For us, it's worse."

I jerk around, fire on my tongue. Delyse holds a hand up.

"You lost your parents, yes. But some of us lost your parents and our own. Sham's dada died refusing to concede his gold to the Xanthippe, and you know about my mama. We're not claiming to love your parents as much as you, but we did love them. We still do, Ira. With you, we stand an even greater chance of avenging them."

"Doyenne Cariot threatened—"

"So what if she did? It's only because she knows that with you, we can finally rise against her. Who do you think crafted the words in the Vow of Peace? Master Fayard is responsible for: *to protect the named island from all threat, including the vulnerability of leaving said island bereft of its leader.* That doesn't have to mean Doyenne Cariot now we have Aiyca's rightful heir—*you!*"

Their faces are aglow with excitement. It doesn't even occur to them that I don't want to be the leader they're looking for.

"What *other things* have you sought?"

Delyse fumbles with her words. I took her by surprise, as planned. She exchanges a look with Shamar, shaking her head.

"Jéges," he expounds, and unwisely at that.

The magical artifacts from Anansi's story? Fiction? *That's* their big plan?

"Do you see her face?" Delyse kisses her teeth. "I told you not to share that part!"

"She tried to soften you to the idea, but you wouldn't bite." Sham chuckles. "We know you don't believe in them, but we thought they were why the doyenne didn't kill you after Carling Hill. Your naevus, yes, but it also makes sense to use you to find whatever jéges she doesn't already possess, and then use them through you." He nods at my forearm, the Glyph of Connection. "We think the missions none of us can recall have been the doyenne hunting for them, and that it's

295

only a matter of time before she takes you out to find them."

"Given that they don't exist," I say, pronouncing each word slowly, "we'll have to assume I put on a good show and she liked what she saw." I pause. "Or hated it. Either way, here I am." I don't share that I had my own suspicions about the doyenne. Not when they have nothing to do with fictional artifacts and everything to do with the very real Jade Guild.

"Do you know the song, at least?"

I rest a hip against the fireplace. "I'm Obeah, aren't I?"

Our order's oral history stretches back a meridian of time. I might not remember Mama's face clearly, but I can still remember how she'd sing tales of our past while I sat cross-legged on the floor between her legs and she braided my afro.

"I've never heard it from an Adair," Delyse says, her voice low. "Will you share it?"

My sigh stirs more dust. "The jéges aren't real."

"Like you're not?" Sham says quietly. "We heard the stories about you too, Ira. That your parents sent you away because they knew the Alumbrar threat wouldn't abate, no matter how those deceivers smiled and simpered. Griots tell their stories about you being hidden in plain sight, waiting for the moment you'd receive your magic to return and right the Alumbrar Witches Council's wrongs. How can you deny that those scars on your forehead show us you went away to train so you could return to fight for Aiyca?"

Because, I think, *I trained to protect Aiyca, not lead it.* Rather than wade into that, I recite the tale of the jéges. Something that will take far less time.

Words of magik, words of might,
Dolls, charms, and guzzu, a witch's delight.
To bear the book, to tempah the tome,
Results in a witch's dominion over all that looms.

The second now, while small, is great;
It grant witch magik that will incur much hate.
For though it offers momentary aid,
The bearer of the locket is one of whom magi need be afraid.

Jége three is more than it look,
Something greater than a guzzu in a book.
To look in two its surface won't reveal a face,
And what it shows is something magi can't erase.

While the last, the golden chart, will bring magik sublime,
Conduit. Weapon. Instrument, divine.
Avarice will see a witch's demise,
Just as too likkle gold doesn't permit the ability to trive.

To hold all four will bring much prestige to the master.
But such power isn't something that guarantees happy ever after.

"The Grimoire, the Amplifier Locket, the Mirror of Two Faces, and the Conduit Falls." Delyse's tone is one of awe. Not at my deliberately monotone singing voice, I'm sure. "The artifacts the Mudda bestowed to Aiyca's first doyenne. Come on, Just-Ira! They *have* to be the reason that Cariot witch is so powerful now. If we stole whichever ones she possesses and placed them in your rightful hands, we would turn the tide in our fight for Aiyca. With them, there'd be no question of our victory."

I laugh. I can't help it, it's so frustrating. "You're pinning your strategy to kill the doyenne on stealing magical artifacts that *don't exist*. None of Aiyca's previous Obeah leaders have ever confirmed the Anansi story is true."

"We'd hoped you'd be able to confirm rumors of a map," Delyse pushes. "You were to inherit, after all. With that we could search for all the jéges, find ones the doyenne might not have, use them against her."

I couldn't inherit anything when I spent the years I would've trained to become empress battling with my sistren in the mountains.

"The Jade Guild is hoping that it's here, in Cwenburg."

"They'd sooner hope for no rain during wet season. It would be likelier."

Shamar raises a hand; Delyse retreats, rubbing a hand across her mouth in frustration.

"The jéges aren't all we've planned," he says. "We still have the Black Moon."

At that my interest piques. Alumbrar might call the phase a New Moon, a time for offerings, worship, and other bores, but for Obeah, the phase's reprieve from the Mudda's otherwise omniscient eye allows for extra mischief. The heightened powers provided will make that moon phase an optimal time to strike. One, I must confess, I hadn't considered. Though it's not as if I had a lunar scope to watch the skies with, in Carne.

Could the moon be enough to override the Vow of Peace?

"Jade Guild operatives will attack during the blood sacrifice the Alumbrar have—"

"Alumbrar have a blood sacrifice?" I interrupt. "Since when?"

"Since our fall," Shamar says. "It's how the barrier around the island is powered, with the bones of pickney she kills in some sort of competition. I know," he says, at my raised eyebrows. "It's not a move you'd believe an Alumbrar would make."

It's not a move Obeah would make either. Sacrificing our own? Never. It's more akin to something Unlit would do in a desperate bid for power. Mama had a cousin deemed Unlit who tried to kill for magic, I remember vaguely.

"The doyenne's order don't object?" I ask, returning to our conversation.

"They love it." Delyse shakes her head. "And those who don't have no voice in their society. The Jade Guild have plans to attack during the sacrifice, the Sole. We're letting them in and then getting out, so the doyenne can't use us against them. But as soon as she's dead, we'll come back to fight. We're taking Cwenburg. Finally."

Mythical artifacts aside, the rest of their idea isn't terrible. But magical fatigue and limited gold won't make it a done deal.

"How can you be so confident?" I have to ask.

"There was some shifting in the hierarchy, and new faces gave the old Gennas the push they needed." Shamar says.

"Truthfully, our numbers don't touch the Xanthippe and Alumbrar on the estate, and the final third of shields who've yet to sign on are fearful to take the risk of failure. But if you asked them to fight for you, there'd be no hesitation."

Fight *for* me. Not *with* me.

"I won't send an order who'll fail into battle." Not for me, with me, or behind me.

"We're preparing to manage our shortcoming of limited gold. We can show you how."

"Hold fast." I shake my head. "I need time to consider all this."

Delyse's voice is low, but I still catch the words. "*You don't have any.*"

"We can give you a couple phases, but no later." Sham rises, unfurling his long frame. "We should head back. Master Fayard can't cover for us for much longer."

"Cover for you? Did he know this would happen?"

"We've all been waiting for your naevus to make an appearance."

Wonderful.

Walking back through the Cuartel, I see what the Jade Guild wants me to be: a figure the masses can worship and charge into battle for, like Mama was, and many of my ancestors before her. But I've always been too independent to be contained beneath a crown. Spending a lifetime pinned, like a butterfly to a board, seems like a waste when I was made to fly.

But with my magic harder to master now than before, and no way around the vow in sight, the rebels might be my best shot. Nana Clarke always advised that the first water you catch, you wash in.

Shamar and Delyse head back to their course without a word—not to me at least. When I return to mine the Obeah-man who outed me is gone and Ford's in his place. He welcomes me with a wink and a conspiratorial nod. Of course he knows too. They all had their suspicions this entire time I thought I was so slick.

"I understand you need sweeping off your feet," he says, gesturing at the gorge that has magically developed fresh soil and grass, hiding all evidence of my explosion. "So here I am, at the Masters' request."

Ford's grin, higher in the left corner, doesn't lend his expression to anything other than mischief. I might not be ready to smile, or have the capacity to ever again now that my secret's out, but I appreciate him, his levity.

It's one light in the dark sky that now lingers overhead.

Decisions, decisions.

I've stopped brightening the lamp in my bohío when the day ends.

Delyse and Shamar have taken to shadowing me everywhere in the Cuartel in the phase since our talk; they don't push for an answer, but their presence pushes *against* me, rubbing and irritating my nerves enough that when I come home, particularly during the dawning after a long and tedious night watch on the mount, I like to believe it's just me and the fading dark, even if the raised hairs on my arms tell me otherwise tonight.

"I'm not in the mood to spar, Zesian."

A sunburst flickers into being, illuminating the emissary beside the window; unbound, his hair falls around his shoulders, his chest, like liquid midnight.

"Has something happened?"

"Look around," I scoff, weary and irritated. "What hasn't happened?"

"Talk of a truce."

The fatigue in my body is sucked clean away by disbelief.

"What?"

A variety of emotions fight for dominance in Kirdan's face before his shoulders lose some of their rigidity. For the first time, he seems small before me. "That day in Carne, Carling Hill, I thought you stakki. I considered your arrival an unnecessary blight upon—"

"I assume this talk begins *after* you've finished insulting me, mon?"

"But watching you this past month," Kirdan continues, the harsh cadence of his voice somehow softer in the dark, "has been an education. One that's meant I have to consider that perhaps I haven't seen you as I should." He takes a step closer. "Perhaps I hadn't seen the real you at all, Iraya."

My name, my true name on his lips, makes the breath I release rattling and short, starved of air that's become inexplicably tight between us.

"You were serious about not sparring, I see." He takes another step, those intent eyes alight with faint amusement and focused solely on me. "I don't think silence has ever known such joy in your company." The timbre of his voice is a serrated edge against my skin. Confused and off-kilter, I fight an urge to take a step back. "If you're unwilling to talk, that's fine. You can listen." His hand darts out, quick as a hawk with its prey in sight, and grabs me. "I have something to teach you too." He's close enough to be a lover—or Death.

I've yet to determine the difference when my stomach lurches, and my bohío whirls around us as his magic tugs me away in a stomach-clenching, breath-stealing sift.

My only anchor, through it all, is the warmth of his touch around my wrist.

31

JAZMYNE

"This is where I leave you," Roje says.

We stand on the private dock at Queenstown Port, phases after our encounter in St. Catherine Parish. After many evenings spent laughing at his wild tales in eateries and drinking houses across the island, accompanied by Anya, members of his crew, and my cabal of Stealths, this parting feels incongruously somber, final. There's little cause for the two of us to interact again, and it makes me almost forlorn, as if I'm losing something.

"Unless," he says. "Unless you needed a ride to the palace with your sistren away for work?"

"Emissary Divsylar's waiting for me." By my request. I glance over my shoulder as though looking for him when, in truth, I'm eager for a reason to continue avoiding Roje's eye. Wind from the sea tosses my unbound afro across my face. A curl catches in my lashes.

Rough fingers brush it away, graze my cheek, tuck it behind my ear.

"It's been a surprising pleasure watching you work, Emissary."

I duck away from Roje's hand, annoyed. "Because you didn't think I could do it?"

"No, mon." His laughter rumbles in his chest. "Because I always knew you'd find a way to make things work."

I look at him then, at his unruly pile of dark dreads, his ever mischievous expression, and close the parts of myself that opened over the course of our time at sea. I am to be doyenne, and he a thorn in my side in typical Alumbrar-pirate relations. Enough lines have been blurred in my attempt to wrest Aiyca from its current leader.

"Blessings again, Roje, to you and Vea."

At the distant professionalism in my voice, the mirth in his expression gives way to something colder, hollow.

"Walk good, Jazmyne."

Thanks in part to him, I have been. Once he joined the tour, unofficially, I didn't see another message from the Jade Guild. And then there's the growing Nameless numbers, the parishioners who now know me outside of the doyenne's shadow—who listened to me. Not even that dinner with Javel, boastful and intolerable in the face of his second triumphant trial, could unsettle the confidence that settled across my shoulders like a mantle.

I had to become ready to assume the role of doyenne; now I know I am.

At the head of the dock, Kirdan waits atop a carriage. His

face lights up and he gives me a small nod, all we can get away with when there are Xanthippe around. Anya might not trust him, and it's true that somewhere along the way things have shifted between us, but the urge to run to Kirdan tells me that he's still family. He's *home*.

"Return to the others and take my luggage to the palace," I order the Xanthippe who accompanied me from the sloop.

"Emissary . . ." She hesitates, glancing at Kirdan. "At least two of us should accompany you back to the palace."

"I have Emissary Divsylar's magic for protection. I'll see you at Cwenburg." Her protestations follow me until I reach the carriage. "Wahan, Emissary Divsylar."

"Where's Anya?"

"She had a job." My hand hovers over the carriage door handle. "Don't tell me you missed her?"

"Jazmyne—"

"And why didn't you procure a driver?" I open the door as he hops down from his seat.

"Wait!"

My jaw slackens at the sight of who awaits on the bench inside.

"You look as surprised to see me as I was to find myself here," Iraya Adair says. Arms folded.

I slam the door, gape up at Kirdan.

"I was about to tell you I brought her with me."

"*Why?*"

"You sent that missive stressing the importance of meeting with her immediately upon your return." He shrugs, a little helplessly. "You don't have to sit inside there with her. It's more of a prison on wheels than a carriage; look." Kir shows me the small Glyph of Containment etched into the plain carriage doors; barely discernible from scratches.

Irritated that I have to ride outside, I grip the ladder attached to the driving bench and pull myself up to sit on the far side. What was Kirdan *thinking* bringing her along? I've been sailing all day, the silver coils of my afro are stiff with salt water, the hem of my kaftan encrusted with it too, from where it splashed into the sloop. It's hardly the impression I wanted to give Iraya Adair when I pose the offer of an alliance.

When Kirdan joins me moments later, he glances at me; I stare straight ahead.

"It wasn't safe to put this in writing."

"I know."

He sighs at my tone.

A shimmering tray of magic grows from his conduit before us, a shield to protect us from blood eaters that already buzz in preparation for attack. Kirdan flicks the reins and clicks his tongue. The sand-prowlers scurry onward, just like Joshial. Though I'm forced to grip the railing ahead, I bite back any further complaints.

We have Iraya Adair in hand, and we're asking her for an alliance, finally. There is the matter of the Vow of Peace, but a witch as enterprising as she is must have a way around it by now.

We're not yet an hour away from the rooms Kirdan reserved for our parley when we're forced to stop at a crossroad

juncture. Several palm trees lie across a fork in the Doyenne's Road, preventing us from taking either route. Jelly
coconuts, great green boulders, lie split and scattered amidst
the fronds. Their weight must have pulled them down. It's
happened before.

"Can't you just levitate the carriage over them?" I ask Kirdan as he slows the prowlers. We'd been making good time,
since we haven't encountered another soul out here in the
country.

"If you know a guzzu that will do it, yeh mon."

"Maybe *she* does."

"It'll be better if she stays inside." Kirdan passes me the
reins. "Those trees haven't fallen naturally."

His tone sets my teeth on edge.

"Bandits?" They've been making a nuisance of themselves
everywhere, but we usually have a Xanthippe escort to deter
them from stealing on this road. Usually.

"Perhaps. I'll find them before they make their way out to
us."

I grab his arm. "You'll leave me here? What if they're Jade
Guild?"

"The trap would have used Spirit Magic. They've made it
their signature. Just stay up here and keep hold of the reins. If
you see anyone who isn't me, turn around and head back to
the city."

"Why don't we sift?" I ask, hysteria raising the pitch of my
voice.

"I don't have the gold to sift all three of us and the carriage."

I almost tell him to leave the carriage, but the prowlers are tame. They'd never survive out here. My grip eases around his arm.

"Remember," he says, emphatic. "Don't let Iraya out. Here." Freeing his hunting knife, he hands it to me, bone handle first. "Just in case. Soon come."

Though it's too early to be evening, with the bush encroaching on either side of the dirt road and palms stretching up and overhead, it's darker out here than it was in the city, quieter. In the gloaming, I soon lose Kirdan to verdant surroundings that swallow him whole.

The snap of a branch ricochets through the bush.

"Kir?" I call, a reflex.

He doesn't answer. If it was him at all.

A prickling starts at the base of my spine, spider-walking its way to the back of my neck. Remembering the knife, I swap it to my dominant left hand, serrated blade turned outward. It feels as alien as an extra digit.

Don't let Iraya out, Kirdan said. Warned.

Time creeps on. He doesn't return. My hand grows slick around the hilt of his weapon. It slips; fumbling to catch it, I almost slice off a finger.

"Ah!" Blood wells from a long cut.

Don't let Iraya out.

Licking the blood from my finger, my focus dips to the carriage below. . . . I might stand a better chance with Iraya than a cloaked bandit after more than the coins in my purse. Standing before I can change my mind, I almost tumble off the carriage at the sudden egress of a flock of birds; they move in a dark wave from the dense copse of trees—trees that bend with a sigh to give way to something moving between them. Kirdan, making his way back? Or something else?

Something to explain the quietness choking the Doyenne's Road.

Something to explain why my heart quickens in my chest and my brow dampens.

Bandits aren't all there are to fear in the wild.

With a calmness I don't feel, I climb down the ladder, almost losing my grip twice thanks to my cut finger. Iraya merely looks at me when I open the door, sniffs at the blade I angle in her direction, and turns her head.

"Where's the Zesian?" she drawls. "I'm hungry."

"I—I'm worried something's happened to him. He went to look for bandits."

Stretching, she yawns, her mouth wide and her head flung back.

Prickling at her insouciance, I draw myself taller. "Both ways ahead are blocked. If someone comes for us, we have—"

"What do you mean, both?"

"The trees have fallen before a crossroads."

She freezes. "Crossroads?"

I nod.

"Gods-damnit," she mutters. "You need to ingest my blood."

"What?"

"Do you have a Glyph of Connection?"

"I—yes." The doyenne deemed it a necessity on the chance I needed to discipline a conscripted Obeah in my emissarial travels across the island. "But I can't ingest your blood."

"And I can't access the magic we'll need with my Impediment Glyphs." She leans across the carriage like she's about to try and take the knife from me, but she collides with an invisible barrier. "Blasted Zesian," she curses, and then, "I need that knife, Emissary."

"What's going on?"

"Didn't any of your family tell you stories about the deep, dark bush?"

Dread tastes bitter in my mouth. Madisyn did. I look down at the knife; my grip's made the tips of my fingers a deep pink with blood. I've never had to use my Glyph of Connection before, never had to exercise the control it provides me over one whose blood I have ingested. The thought of it has always made me sick but . . . better that than death tonight.

Though reluctant, I proffer the blade. I can't cut her.

"You need to bend past whatever glyph the Zesian put on the carriage to keep me in here."

"Don't try anything."

"Rest easy. You're not my type."

Scowling, I lean into the carriage. With deft fingers, she swipes the knife and cuts her palm without a flinch.

"Bottoms up," she says, before smacking her hand against my mouth.

I fling it away, my face smarting. "You did that on *purpose*."

"Saved our lives? I like to think so. Now, we need higher ground, a tree preferably. If you wouldn't mind wiping through whatever's on the door?"

Biting back my annoyance, I drag the returned blade through the circle, and then the cross, freeing her. She hops out of the carriage, straightening her long limbs. I step back so as not to look up at her too obviously. It's strange, to be with her like this, without Kirdan, without Xanthippe. I haven't the faintest idea of what to say.

Iraya's without such limitations, of course.

"You're a tiny thing, aren't you?" Her voice is warm, certain. She smiles, and her cheeks rise. They're fuller than they were in Carling Hill. Time away from Carne has restored her health.

"Small I may be, but I'm still your superior." I draw myself up taller. "Help me with the prowlers."

She dips into a mocking bow. Together we unfix the lizards and coax them up a tree; better trained than Joshial, they don't take to it naturally. Ira swings up ahead of them and makes a clucking noise in her throat to draw them toward her.

"Shall we wrap the reins around the trunk?"

"So they hang themselves if they jump down?" Swinging from a low branch, she lands in a crouch beside me. "No, mon. Come, let's take this one." At the base of a towering shade tree, she helps me latch onto the lowest branch. "Start climbing!" she orders.

My hands shake with such violence, I miss my next grip and scrape my hands on the bark. Agile, Iraya overtakes me with a wink. We climb until the ground's indiscernible through the leaves. Whatever moves toward us thuds the earth with a weight that can't be human. The gooseflesh peppering my skin, even in this heat, portends the arrival of some ungodly Aiycan beast. And several minutes later, it comes.

Bypassing the tree with the prowlers, it snorts and sniffs at the base of the one we hide in. My entire body stiffens. I can't see Iraya, but I feel her willing me to keep quiet and still. It doesn't matter that I barely breathe; the snorts turn into grunts, and the grunts turn into wild knockings that jar the mighty tree. I scream. I can't help it.

The knocking stops, and whatever waits beneath us sniggers with a chilling sentience.

Then the tree begins to fall.

Iraya's sigh is a blade from the dark. "If you want to call my magic before we fall to our deaths, that might be a good idea."

There were lessons I sat in alongside Alumbrar Conscription Officers but— "I've never done it without guzzu before," I say in a rush. "Just—wait!"

Summoning is a mental search in the dark for a glimmer of candlelight in response, I remember. Or was it visualizing a tapestry of magic from which you pluck one thread?

"Cariot!"

"Don't shout at me! I'm trying!"

At a tilt, the tree gains momentum, and the ground looms with too much speed to think clearly.

"Too late. We need to jump!" Iraya shouts. "*Now!*"

Stomach in my throat and air whistling past my ears, I

make one last attempt to will Iraya's magic to cushion our fall. Power hits me in a wave, and I'm heady with it until I collide with the earth, and air shoots from my stomach.

Mudda have mercy.

"Get up, Cariot. I don't think this beast will be fooled if you play dead."

Aching, I roll onto my feet within the tree branches with caution, checking for broken bones. I brush my curls from my face. Iraya's conduit illuminates the hewn tree. She stands on the other side of the damage. She's crouched, and her slick brow's furrowed in concentration, her focus on whatever brought the giant down. I force myself to face it.

It's a great shadow of a beast. A weapon of the night. Hulking shoulders crest horns with points so acute, the air must scream when it charges on its four powerful legs. In its wide face, brow bowed in a formidable scowl, narrowed red eyes bore into mine with a humanlike intelligence. My legs liquefy, and I almost drop to my knees once more.

It's a Rolling Calf. An omen of death.

Standing tall where the crossroads touch, it nods in recognition. In promise.

Iraya whistles, long and low. Eyes on me, it pays her no mind. The creature's tail flicks behind it, lashing the air with piercing cracks. Those eyes, as cutting as rubies freshly cleaved from rock, don't divert as the beast lowers its head and huffs two short bursts through its wide nose. A hoop hangs low on its upper lip. I remember reading somewhere that if you took a bull by that ring, it would comply with your every order. But that book didn't state how you approached the angry creature to get close enough to touch it in the first place.

Its front hoof drags through the earth once, twice.

"Cariot." Iraya's voice is hoarse. "Walk toward me. Slowly."

"I can't move."

"Listen to me," she grinds out. "Either we both make it out, or we both die. You can do this. Come *on*."

Before I find out if I can, the Rolling Calf charges.

Iraya shouts as its horns drop to gouge me. A low wall of fire springs up around me. It sends the beast bucking backward with a roar that rattles the stars.

"That deterrent won't last," Iraya breathes, now beside me. "And I can't do much else."

She saved me?

"You need to launch balls of flame at its neck and belly." Digging within the fallen tree, Iraya stomps through a branch. She tests the rudimentary spear. "I'll do the rest." The determination in her face is overshadowed by a sinister glint in her eyes.

She's *excited*, while I shake like a fledgling rocked in a storm.

"Cariot! Are you with me?"

The flames die, revealing the calf. With no preamble, it canters at us—*me*. Head lowered, its eyes are mad with rage. I draw on threads of magic in my mental tapestry, tugging on each until an alabaster fuse electrifies my thoughts. *There it is*. Pulling on Iraya's magic, her wealth of intentions, I ready myself for the deluge of magic and will a ball of fire.

Instead, a coruscating white-gold light ripples from Iraya and me.

Stealing my breath, it kicks back a gust of wind loaded with leaves, splinters of bark, and dirt. Arms raised to shield myself, I flinch back. Distantly, the apparition howls into the night. When I open my eyes, the light's rescinded. Disappeared.

The Rolling Calf's gone.

Iraya's looking at me—my neck, where my locket sits.

She wavers on her feet, blinking like she's fighting to remain conscious. "That power came from your necklace."

I shove the chain out of sight. "It couldn't have. Whatever you saw was just a reflection of your naevus." If she saw anything. She looks half dead. Proving my point, her legs give. I start as Kirdan sifts out of the night to catch her. He hoists Iraya into his arms; her head lolls against his chest.

That was timely.

"Where have you been?"

He adjusts his hold until he's almost cradling her. "Let's go to the room to talk. It's not far." Without waiting for a response, he strides to the carriage.

I watch their silhouettes in the dark, my stomach twisting itself into knots.

"What about the tree?"

"There are no bandits, so I can take the time to break it up with magic." He lays Iraya inside the carriage.

Is it my imagination or is he lingering a little too long? Placing her down with too much care?

"Can you coax the prowlers down, Jazmyne?"

"Yes, of course." My steps are jerky with leftover adrenaline—the calf scare has no doubt heightened my nerves, making me foolish. Kirdan's most likely checking that Iraya's still breathing. When I get to the tree, I look back at the carriage. "Would you like—"

Kirdan still stands there, staring down at Iraya.

How did he first say her name, phases ago now? Like it was both a prayer and a curse.

Right now it only carries the malignance of the latter.

32

IRA

The sharp sting of medicine rouses me with a jolt.

I force my swollen eyes open in time to see the Bush Witch, Fatou, slip through the doorway. She pauses on the threshold to wink at me, and then she's gone. The soft burn of her poultice makes the coated muscles on my neck and shoulders twitch and tingle as they relax, soothing away the fight with the Rolling Calf.

"Where am I?" I murmur.

"Above a taproom that asks few questions," Emissary Divsylar says. Swathed in black, he's barely discernible from the shadows. Just enough to notice that he's leaning against Fatou's point of egress. The only exit within view.

The Cariot emissary is seated by my bedside. Her dark eyes are wide with worry, with concern. I can't tell if it's for me, or because she's sitting so close to me. She twists a gold ring on her pinkie finger . . . gold. Something else was gold tonight too. Jewelry.

"The necklace," I croak. "Your locket. It lit up."

"That was your naevus, as I said."

The Zesian emissary clears his throat. "I'm sorry, Jazmyne, but she's right."

I wonder if Fatou added a little something extra to the concoction—a little something *green and leafy*—when she healed me, because the look the Cariot—*Jazmyne*—sends his way makes it seem like she has no idea what the Zesian—*Kirdan*—is talking about. He pushes away from the door, cloak billowing behind him and stirring the room's stale air.

"Pass me the locket and I'll show you. Please."

With another inscrutable look, she hands it over.

Curious, on all counts, I ease myself up onto my forearms with a wince. Kirdan drags a chair over to the bed and removes his cloak from his left shoulder before he sits. The wood creaks beneath his bulk. He holds the sturdy chain aloft. His conduit lights in the handle of his saber. As the pendant circles the air, incisions appear on both sides. From this close, the markings whorling across the gold surface look a lot like—

"Deep patwah," I breathe.

Kirdan looks at me, his gaze as deep and consuming as the darkness outside the room's lone window. "I think your magic, Adair magic, woke it during the Rolling Calf attack."

"How can that be if it's just a locket? And my locket at that."

"Because it's not." He looks at Jazmyne and then back at me. "It's one of the four jéges."

I blink at him.

Everyone on this estate has lost their gods-forsaken minds.

Except Jazmyne, it seems; she looks just as full of disbelief as I am.

"You don't believe me," he says. "But you already used it outside. Both of you."

The pendant still turns in Kirdan's scarred grip. Gritting my teeth, I prop myself up against the wall and draw on the air in the room; it washes over my body with a feeble touch. I aim a thread at the locket, all the energy I have to summon. It lights at once, with a white-gold sheen that makes me squint, and a gust of wind blusters, tearing at the sheets on the cot, at Jazmyne's and Kirdan's hair.

"What did you do?" he asks, eager, hands tidying his hair back as the wind dies down.

"I sent what magic I could, and it reacted almost . . . intuitively. Like—like it knew I couldn't spare much, so it gave me more."

"That's how the Amplifier Locket of legend should work with Aiyca's heir."

Holy hell.

The jéges exist?

"Wait a minute," Jazmyne interrupts, fingers scrabbling to draw her curls away from her face. "I've been wearing that for almost two years, and you're telling me it's something from an Anansi story?"

My focus shifts from the locket to the two of them.

"Where did you get it?" she demands.

"From the palace." Kirdan runs his tongue over his bottom lip. "I stole it. I . . . was sent from Zesia to steal all the jéges."

And the mask is shucked.

While I merely look on, satisfied with my early deductions, Jazmyne sucks in a breath. Did she really believe he was friends with her, an Alumbrar, because he *liked* her? Gods. It would be sad if it wasn't so pathetic.

Shooting up out of her seat, Jazmyne stalks across the room. When her words come, they're quiet, hollow.

"Are you even an emissary?"

Kirdan takes what I interpret as a bracing breath. "No. I'm a firstborn son, with sisters."

"Then you're one of the Simbarabo," I'm all too happy to pitch in.

I *knew* he was a Warrior, and one from Zesia's army of bastard soldiers at that. Jazmyne, her face tight with shame, can't even look at me. If I were her, I'd be livid too. No. If I were her, I would have known he wasn't to be trusted.

"You've been lying to me," she whispers.

Kirdan drags a hand down his face. "I couldn't tell you in the beginning, and by the time we became friends, it seemed too late. But come, Jazmyne. You should know I wouldn't have let the Rolling Calf hurt you. I only needed to see for myself if the locket reacted to Iraya's magic, and I was ready to step in at a moment's—"

"That was you too?" Jazmyne stares at Kirdan like he's a stranger. "You risked my life to test a theory?"

"That would be *our* lives," I interrupt. "Something I won't be quick to forget either, Zesian."

"No harm would have befallen either of you." He glances between the two of us, united against him for the second time in this conversation. "I can concede that it was cruel, perhaps, not to tell you, but I had everything under control." He looks to me, receives an eye roll, and then turns to Jazmyne, palms splayed and eyes shining.

She opens her mouth, presumably to continue moaning. I beat her to the punch.

"As heartbreaking as this all is, really, and as much as you should watch your back once we leave here, Zesian, I'd much rather you both get to the point of all this cloak-and-dagger stuff now. I'm sure Doyenne Cariot expects me back in the Cuartel tomorrow, and I'd like to heal unconscious if the two of you plan to continue sharing all your feelings."

Jazmyne stares at Kirdan a moment longer, teetering between tears and anger. I find myself almost rooting for the latter. Instead, she draws a deep breath, and visibly pulls herself together.

"We're overthrowing the doyenne," she says, her voice tight. "And I was going to offer you an alliance if you promised to kill her. Though how we can all work together now, I don't know."

"You *want* me to kill her? But she's your mama."

"Only by blood."

"Yeh mon. *That's the entire point*. I know why he'd want the doyenne dead." I tip my head toward Kirdan, quiet in his ignominy. "And now I suspect you do too. But why do *you* want that? Alumbrar always were fond of usurpation, but you've become rather murderous since I've been away."

"It's not murder. Ridding Aiyca of her rule will be the island's cure. One it needs. Surely you can see that, perhaps better than either of us—*me*." Her bottom lip trembles.

"I still see that," Kirdan murmurs.

And I don't know who to believe.

Jazmyne's motives can't be entirely altruistic. Hell, I don't think they're altruistic in the slightest. And Kirdan's just confirmed why he should never be trusted. This entire setup feels like a trap—or at least it would, were it not for the locket.

"However you justify it, I don't really care." A lie. But which of us here isn't a liar? "How do you plan on *doing* it? With the locket? How d'you know it isn't a fluke?"

Jazmyne struggles with words for a couple of seconds before deferring to Kirdan with a contemptuous head toss.

He shifts. "The late Empress Adair confirmed the jéges' existence to Zesia's doyenne, and the Skylands'. There was a covenant in place that prevented them from discussing the artifacts before her death—and even then, they still had to wait seven additional years before the magical gag order came to an end. Empress Adair was thorough."

That was Mama.

"I didn't know for sure that it was *the* locket from the Anansi story," Kirdan continues. "I'd never seen Doyenne Cariot wearing it, when she visited Zesia, but I did see a rendering of Empress Adair wearing it in a portrait in Cwenburg Palace. The only painting Doyenne Cariot was unable to remove when she moved into the palace. Empress Adair must have secured the locket inside the painting using a powerful guzzu."

For me? I think. *Could she have known that I'd return one day?*

"I commissioned a replica in Zesia, to put in the painting before taking the real locket, altering its surface to hide the incisions with a cloaking guzzu. Only an Adair witch can be connected to the Amplifier and the Mirror of Two Faces. The weapons' ancient knowing is dependent upon a nexus with your ancestors only, something you confirmed when the calf attacked."

I glance at where Jazmyne still stands, her lips pressed together like she's holding back questions, accusations—perhaps sick too, judging by the odd sheen to her skin. She's been carrying a legend around her neck this entire time. One her friend placed there without her knowledge. He might be worse than I thought.

"The spider mentioned that the jéges were used in times of war only," Kirdan says. "The Jade Guild has emerged from the wetlands and is engaging in magical warfare for the first time ever. I'd say this is a time of war."

There's one thing I can't wrap my head around, and I hate that I have to seek my answers in Kirdan, an unlikely savant in *my* family history.

"If Mama had the jéges, how did the Alumbrar defeat us?"

He leans forward, his long fingers splayed across the edge of the mattress. "What if they were waiting for a period of Obeah prosperity? What if Doyenne Cariot charged her order to fake compliance long before those years she served by your mama's side—"

"She was arrested for scheming against the crown," I interrupt.

"Another illusion," Kirdan explains. "So she could infiltrate the palace and lull Empress Adair into a false sense of security, knowing that if the empress wasn't imbued with the jéges' power, she'd have her greatest chance of winning."

She is a Stealth viper, first and foremost. It would make the artifacts a truth within a story, hidden in plain sight. It's just the kind of scheming typical of my order.

Jazmyne clears her throat. "So all four jéges are real?"

"As real as you and me," he says.

As real as a Lost Empress.

All the same, my eyes search Kirdan's for any sign of deception. I will not succumb to the same fate as Jazmyne.

"And if the Mudda gave this power to the Obeah," he says, "we know how They wanted to be honored when they used them. Blood sacrifices."

Jazmyne shakes her head. "But Alumbrar dance for offerings."

Nyába, I remember with a snort. What a waste of the ancestors' abilities.

"We don't offer blood sacrifices." Her brows pinch. "They're dark, they're—"

"Obeah rituals," Kirdan fills in for her. "And the Yielding might be the bloodiest I've ever heard of."

"*That's* what the doyenne wants?" she says, stunned. "It's

never been the Yielders' bones? She's been using the dead as offerings to work the jéges? My gods. Does anyone I know tell me the truth?"

Kirdan rises, makes to guide her back over to her seat by the bed. She twists away from him, whispering something under her breath. I watch their exchange, but I'm not really seeing them. Shamar and Delyse mentioned this sacrifice, this Yielding. How has the doyenne retained power when she's committing monstrosities Mama would never have done? What sort of people are the Alumbrar that they allow her to rule?

"We can't risk believing one jége will be enough," Kirdan says; taking the seat closest to me, he casts a tentative look at where Jazmyne still stands. "She definitely has access to the Conduit Falls, because in addition to limiting conscripted Obeah with tiny conduit coins, strands of gold are woven into her clothing, her head ties. She also has a catalog of malignant guzzu that can only be from an Obeah Grimoire. *The* Adair First Family Grimoire. Her use of the Glyph of Connection tells me that."

I glance down at my arm, where the triangles are scarred. It is an Obeah war ritual.

Kirdan's eyes are on my scar too, when I look up. "She's the most powerful Alumbrar in the history of the order."

So killing her will be tough, but not impossible.

"You've mentioned two artifacts she's accessed," I say. "The third is here. What of the mirror?"

"Finding the Amplifier and freeing it from its enchantment

326

took the better part of my time here." Kirdan looks at his hands. "I didn't get around to finding the mirror."

The locket's metal glints between his fingers. The very thing I mocked Shamar and Delyse for lies less than a foot from my reach. If they knew the jéges really existed . . .

I'd be trapped in a role I'm not made to fill. One that could result in their deaths if they're counting on the claim they think I have on Aiyca to override the Vow of Peace, and help the Jade Guild kill the doyenne. They don't need me the way they think they do. *I* need to seek my coven of Warrior sistren, and then be out there razing the Alumbrar rule, not getting a numb ass on a throne somewhere. If I worked with Kirdan and Jazmyne, a thought I can't believe I'm actually having, I could steal the jéges after Doyenne Cariot is dead, which would help the Jade Guild reclaim Cwenburg. Everybody would win.

Well, everyone who mattered would.

That is, if Jazmyne and Kirdan really mean what they're saying. Something I might be a fool to believe. For one, he's spent at least a year lying to her, and for another, she has yet to punch him in the nose. Though she hasn't looked at him since his revelations either. . . .

"Am I to assume everything is forgiven between the two of you? What's a little dishonesty between bredren and sistren, and all that?"

"Our relationship doesn't concern you," Jazmyne says, a little haughtily considering her self-respect is in tatters right now. "All that matters is Aiyca, and what you're prepared to do to keep your order safe. When I am doyenne, I'll reduce the conscription time, see to it that the magical among your ilk keep their conduits after their debt to society has been paid."

"If I help you kill the doyenne."

Stone-faced, she nods.

"And if I told you I don't know how to do it?"

"I will," Kirdan says.

Jazmyne turns to him sharply, opens her mouth, and then shakes her head and closes it again.

My brows have shot upward. "You will?"

He nods.

Why does this feel too easy?

"He will." Jazmyne waves a dismissive hand. "Fine. But *you* need to take the fall for it if you want to help your order, Iraya."

"I must have misunderstood earlier then. This isn't an alliance; it's blackmail."

"Consider your order insurance."

If I didn't despise her, I might have applauded. Still, she isn't the tactician here. I am.

"If the Zesian really kills the doyenne, and I want to be there to watch it happen, then their safety doesn't need to be contingent on my compliance. Once she's dead, I'll go."

Jazmyne straightens. "Just you?"

I nod. *Just-Ira.*

"You'll really leave?"

"Life here will be easier for them without me." Not a lie. "And I want to shake on it."

"A Shook Bargain?" Her expression's incredulous.

"If we shake, none of us can betray the other without a cost—our lives."

Kirdan's body tenses like a drawn bow string. "Jazmyne, we can't—"

"Actually, I agree." She doesn't spare him a glance.

Good girl.

"A bargain will ensure the dead are deserving of their fate." She twists her fingers before her, spinning and spinning her pinkie ring. "It also means you can't make a bid to lead, Iraya."

And thank the goddess for that.

I pretend to consider her words. Nana Clarke always said people prefer suggestions when they feel like they made them themselves.

"We have a deal," I murmur, after a while. Suitably torn, but noble, because it's something an empress would do. I think. What I *know* is that a student of Master Fayard's would make sure she crafts a bargain with enough loopholes to come and go wherever she pleases.

Precision is tantamount when wording a Shook Bargain. The doyenne's invisible oath already clings to my wrist, reminding me just how binding they are. It's a dangerous gamble, but one I have to make.

Jazmyne sits beside Kirdan and takes my right hand with quivering fingers. Despite the warmth of the room, they're icy. My conduit sparks to life; the glyph burns with a white-hot heat as she uses my magic to cast the guzzu.

"I, Jazmyne Cariot, agree to honor my end of this bargain. To work with you to kill Doyenne Cariot; after the named is dead, Iraya Adair has one moon phase to leave Aiyca."

Our skin sparks at her promise, a golden band looping around our wrists ready to ratify the agreement—something Kirdan seems to be in two minds about as his hand wavers before settling atop mine and Jazmyne's; the loop sparks around his wrist too. "I, Kirdan Divsylar, agree to honor my end of this bargain. To work with you to kill Doyenne Cariot; after the named is dead, Iraya Adair has one moon phase to leave Aiyca."

The loop tightens on his last word.

My turn. "I, Iraya Adair, agree to honor my end of this bargain. To work with you to kill Doyenne Cariot; after the named is dead, I have one moon phase to leave Aiyca."

The golden circlet tightens for a final unbearable moment, cutting into our skin like a vise—one last reminder of what we stand to lose—then it sparks out. The Shook Bargain isn't as big on being seen as it is on being felt.

"*And so we promise*," we say in unison. "*So things do*."

"Now all our lives are on the line," I say, "I know of a map to find the jéges. Sort of."

Kirdan leans back in his seat. "Well, do you or don't you?"

"Say there is one, and I look at it when the doyenne's distracted—"

"Like the All Souls' Night celebration, next moon phase," he muses. "With a copy of the map, we could locate the mirror, making it two-all. But when would we kill her?"

"The Sole," Jazmyne says. "She won't expect it."

Delyse and Shamar are planning to attack with the Jade Guild on the same night.

Though, if I have an in with the emissaries, it's almost a guarantee that I'll be able to help the guild infiltrate its golden walls—they could take the palace back.

"That's supposed to be a Black Moon," I muse. "Or New, for Alumbrar. It can provide the power we need on the chance we don't find the mirror."

"Why wouldn't we?" Kirdan asks. "Where is the map?"

"Presiders?" I parry. "I'm assuming you don't plan on keeping them around."

Jazmyne shakes her head. "I'll have a new council, but I don't want to kill the current one. Their roles will become advisory."

"Losing one or two will weaken the doyenne's reign," I push. "Think of it as a tower, one you'll be blowing holes through. The foundations wouldn't sustain with a couple of gaps."

"If we did this during All Souls' Night, she'll look to the estate first." The look Kirdan gives me is almost cautionary. He means she'll look to me, the Obeah, first. "We can't risk you."

And I can't risk the shields, something I'll have to consider.

"I'm a big witch, I can take care of myself. Anyway, if the doyenne has been waiting for me to find the jéges all this time"—something that explains her decision to spare my life—"surely she won't kill me before that happens."

"We can't guarantee that," Kirdan insists.

"No, Iraya's right." Jazmyne's forehead bows in thought. "Consider why the doyenne hasn't mentioned anything about Iraya to the Council, why she partook of the Shook Bargain along with the Conscription Officers at Carling Hill. It enables her to keep her hunt for the jéges quiet. She won't kill Iraya until she has what she needs."

"And while I'm living out my last days, I'd like them free of Magmire's existence." The doyenne's first shares her culpability, in my eyes.

"She'll be with Doyenne Cariot the entire night." Jazmyne shakes her head. "We have to start smaller."

"There's nothing small about death. It's why we have to take out those closest to the doyenne now, while she's unaware. Magmire dies."

Jazmyne gathers her robe tighter around her body. "Fine. I can get you into the palace on All Souls' Night, giving you access to whoever."

"What about you?"

"Me?"

"Are you planning on getting your hands dirty at all?"

She squirms in her gold. "I—I can't kill anyone."

"Well, I won't kill *everyone*. If you want more than one presider dead, you'd better make sure you kill the other yourself."

"For the gods' sake," Kirdan snarls. He shoots out of his chair and stalks back to the door. "The Obeah, the Zesian, and the Alumbrar might sound more like the beginning of a bad joke, but if we're working together, we have to *work together*. If you can isolate Magmire and one other, Jazmyne, *I'll* kill them after Iraya and I find the map."

"We will?"

"You can't honestly think we'd let you go alone?" He

snorts. Which he wouldn't have been able to do without great difficulty if Jazmyne *had* punched him earlier.

"I won't give Magmire up just because you want to spend some time alone with me, Zesian. Not when I can't kill the doyenne. We find the map, and then the presider is mine."

"Fine!" Jazmyne looks between the two of us. "We'll make it work."

We plot until the sky begins to lighten outside, bringing dawn on soft pastel wings. And with its arrival comes a reckoning from three unlikely allies:

The Obeah with lies in her eyes and poison in her heart.

The Alumbrar, foolish with desperation.

And the Zesian, who might snatch the entire foundation from beneath them all to take an island his country always coveted.

33

JAZMYNE

We sift Iraya right into her bohío in the Cuartel, before Kirdan's magic carries us away once more.

In my study, we stand in silence. Though the tile beneath my feet is solid, the surroundings familiar, I feel like I'm trapped in that World Between we traveled through. Somewhere familiar yet foreign.

"What just happened?"

With a sigh, Kirdan shrugs out of his cloak.

I continue, "You offered to kill the doyenne when I told you Zesia can't be implicated in an overthrow! Iraya might have been lying about the Vow of Peace, she might have a way around it, and you could fall foul of whatever nefarious intentions she has! And—" My voice tightens in an attempt to block tears. "How do you explain giving me a jége almost a year ago and not saying a single word about it? How do you explain what just happened above that taproom? Iraya could tell I had no idea what you were talking about. And why didn't I?"

"Would you have worn it if you knew?"

For a moment I'm thrown. That's not the apology I expected. "Does it matter?"

"When I came here two years ago, I watched you, Jazmyne." There's nothing repentant in his face. He looks like a stranger. "Magi treated you like you were soft, broken, and you let them. Your mama had no respect for you; neither did her council."

"I'd just lost Madisyn."

"Exactly." His face softens some. "You were in no state to hear about jéges. So I ask you again, would you have worn the locket if I told you what it was?"

"No," I whisper.

I push away from the door and cross my study on shaking legs to stand behind my desk, put some distance between the two of us. The wood presses against my thighs hard enough to bruise, but the pain grounds me. Loosening a breath, I sit. After a moment, he sits too.

"I am sorry." He sighs. "That wasn't the way I wanted to tell you."

"By scaring me half to death? Or in Iraya Adair's company?"

"Both. What I said in the taproom was true. I didn't know if the jéges really existed."

This doesn't count toward the betrayal Iraya, Anya, alluded to. He came clean.

It doesn't matter if he lied.

"Tell me about the Falls?" I ask, ready to go back to the way things were between us. "A waterfall made of pure gold can't actually exist, can it?"

"It's not made of gold," Kirdan clarifies, looking relieved. "At least, that's what my doyenne told me. She's never seen it. I don't know anyone who has, except, I suppose, Empress Adair. Over the centuries, explorers across the empire ventured into Aiyca's bush to find the infamous cataract of water that crashes into a pool of golden coins—an endless pool, the legend says. But it's never been discovered. Knowledge of its whereabouts is passed between doyennes on some kind of magic scroll." He rolls his eyes. "I don't know if I believe that last part."

"So you didn't find any magic scroll, or the Grimoire," I say, checking. "Just the locket that only responds to Adair magic?"

"Yeh mon." He drags a hand down his face. "I had no idea how I was going to return to Zesia. Then I found you crying into one of your sister's scarves, and here we are. You kind of saved me."

Then why, despite my best efforts, do I feel more distanced from you than ever before?

"You were right, in the taproom." He sits forward. "There is a strong possibility that the doyenne kept Iraya alive to use her to find the remaining jéges. I didn't want to say so in front of her."

"Fair. What I don't understand is that the Amplifier and Mirror of Two Faces will only work with an Adair. Why would she want them?"

"She could always use them *through* Iraya."

"But Iraya didn't know about the jéges."

"No." Kirdan's forehead bows. "Not until *I* confirmed their existence, however necessary it was. But over half the island hunts for them. Alumbrar and Obeah alike."

"If she tells the shields they exist . . ." I can't finish my sentence. "I shouldn't have pushed, back in the taproom. If she thinks she's safe from death . . ."

He shrugs. "We'll just watch her."

"Not me." I shake my head, making a quick decision. "You." Iraya is like lightning, and Kirdan doesn't seem like he's afraid of the burning caress of her strike. The witchlight lamp on my desk highlights how his eyelashes curl up toward his eyebrows, sooty strokes against the sun-kissed brown of his skin. His looks have never played a role in how I've seen him, but Iraya could be distracted. "If half the island is involved in the hunt for the jéges, and the doyenne already has two, the last thing I need is Iraya Adair making off with whatever's left. Become her friend, more, if necessary, to stop her looking too closely at what we're doing." It's my voice, but the intent behind the words is alien, bold.

Kirdan's neck turns a blotchy red. "I'll do my best."

"Good. Even with the Shook Bargain, trusting her isn't an option."

After tonight's revelations, trusting anyone doesn't seem particularly wise.

Within seconds of Kirdan's departure, I've summoned an attendant and requested Joshial to be saddled and brought out from the stables. I need to see Anya.

"It's rather late for you to be leaving, Emissary."

Doyenne Cariot sits astride a sand-prowler in the stable yard when I arrive. Dressed in a deep midnight tunic and riding pants, there isn't a drop of gold on her. She looks more like the shadow her métier trained her to be than Aiyca's leader.

"You didn't come and see me to debrief after your tour." She dismounts and passes the reins to one of the stable hands. Has she been riding around the estate, or off with ensorcelled Obeah from the shield hunting for the—

Mudda have mercy.

All this time I thought she went out looking for Jade Guild insurgents. What if she's been hunting jéges instead?

"Emissary?" The doyenne's brows raise.

"Forgive me."

"The Xanthippe said you went somewhere with Emissary Divsylar after your final speech, earlier today."

"I—yes." Off guard and out of sorts after my evening, I don't have it in me to think of a halfway decent untruth. "We were catching up after our time apart."

"You've yet to take my advice about relationships, as you neglected to follow my directions for the tour. While the latter diversion was a success, you won't find similar results in your relationship with the Zesian emissary. His land isn't one known for its loyalty."

Does everyone think me a fool for being friends with Kirdan? Or are they just jaded? Anya, who lost Madisyn; Iraya, who lost everything; and the doyenne, who keeps everyone at an arm's distance so she can't ever say she's lost anyone.

"You have taught me the necessity of keeping my enemies

close, Doyenne. It's a lesson I haven't forgotten. If you'll excuse me, I long for the feeling of land after close to a month aboard the sloop." I depart with a bow, conscious of the weight of her focus.

Within minutes I'm seated atop my prowler and the two of us are flying down the palace drive with a formation of accompanying Xanthippe on jungle-prowlers behind.

Anya lives close to the foot of the estate, enough that requesting a carriage isn't necessary, and I don't mind the winds that tear past as Joshial alternates between great bounding leaps and his scurrying sprint.

Her white stucco villa sits, half wild, on top of a verge in a small village. The lights flickering in the windows are all the reason I need to toss Joshial's reins into the hands of one of the coven before running up the concrete steps and stepping straight inside. The storm door slams behind me. Sweet vanilla and something more robust, plum perhaps, coil around me from the candles in the front room as I head through to her bedroom. Anya won't be asleep, not with candles lit.

I open the door and squint in the darkness at the mass on her bed. "Anya?"

She screams. I do too. A light bursts on overhead, forcing my eyes shut.

"Gods above, Emissary Cariot!"

That's not Anya's voice.

"No!" my sistren yells this time. "Don't open your eyes!" And then, quieter: "Go to the front room. I'll be along shortly."

A wicked heat blazes up my neck as I realize what I walked in on.

"I—I'm sorry," I stutter, tongue-tied.

"Don't think nothing 'bout it, Emissary Cariot," that first voice, Anya's date, says, closer than before.

A door closes behind me; it's followed by a wheezing I know all too well. I open my eyes to my sistren in her night shift, clutching her stomach in near-silent laughter. I throw my hands over my face, which only serves to make her laugh even harder.

"Oh, Jaz. Hasn't anyone spoken with you about what happens with two people who care about one another?"

"I know what happens!" I drop my hands. "Doesn't mean I want to walk in on my friend doing it!"

She wipes tears away, calming down. "Did you just fancy seeing me, or do I need to send Kenise home?"

Remembering what drove me over here, all humor evaporates. Anya straightens, concerned.

"Give me a few minutes to say goodbye, and then come through."

Moving toward the bed and thinking better of it, I stand, shifting from one foot to the other while I wait for the lovers to say their goodbyes. For the past year or so I've been encouraging Anya to move on from Madisyn, and here I am making her send her potential new girlfriend home. With a sigh, I switch off the light and seek her out in the front room with more caution than when I entered.

"She's gone."

Accepting a tumbler of coconut water, I sit in the love seat by the window. The Xanthippe aren't in the front yard anymore, but they'll be close.

"I'm sorry."

"Don't be." Anya curls up on the sofa before me, tucking her legs beneath her.

"Have you been seeing her long?"

"She moved to the village today." Though she tries to contain it, a self-satisfied grin soon dominates her face. "But enough about me. What's worrying you?"

"We asked Iraya. She said yes."

"That's good news, no?"

"I thought so. But—" I lean forward to rest the tumbler on the coffee table. "Anya, Kirdan's been lying to me." I recount everything about the jéges, his true reason for coming here, our conversation afterward. It isn't until I reach the end of my tale that I realize the locket is missing. He didn't return it to me.

"I *knew* he wasn't to be trusted," Anya bursts out. "He's *Zesian*."

"I know he came here to steal from us, but—"

"And *used* you to hide what he stole. That's sick."

My stomach still twists when I think back on all the times I clutched that gift for comfort—but it means something that he didn't secrete it away, surely?

"You can't honestly tell me that you're still comfortable working with him."

I hesitate. "What's my alternative? Vea said no, the Nameless isn't strong enough to fight, and we've already approached Iraya Adair." Then there's the long-term plan. "How can I keep Aiyca safe without the Simbarabo? Keep the Yielding?" I sigh. "It's not Kirdan, anyway. Not entirely. Everything was cogent before Iraya arrived."

341

"It wasn't. He was still hiding things from you." Anya exhales, long and loud. "I don't like this."

"And I'm liking it less and less, but I could like it more if you were in."

She sits up, blinks at me across the flickering candles. Surely she must have considered that I'd call on her eventually. She's a trained Stealth, my oldest friend, and untouched by the Shook Bargain. I want to continue trusting Kirdan, as I have done these past two years, but a part of me can't help wondering what else he might be keeping from me until he can't anymore.

"Light Keeper wouldn't like this either," Anya says, measuring every word. "But we can no longer afford to only take rooks now; we have to move for the queen."

"So, you're with me?"

"Always."

"And what about Filmore and the cabal of Stealths from the tour?"

"They'll stand for their future doyenne." She flips her loose sheet of silver hair over her shoulders. "I'll see to it. But there's not enough of us to defeat your mama."

In everything that unfolded with Kirdan, I forgot that she's lied to me too. Lied to Aiyca. Killed Madisyn and ten years' worth of Yielders under false pretenses when she *could* have sought another way.

"Jazmyne?"

"It isn't her they'll be fighting during All Souls' Night."

Before the queen is taken, I must first dismantle her tower, brick by brick.

34

IRA

As it's in the emissaries' best interest to keep me healthy for what is still to come, it takes less time than I anticipated to recover from the Rolling Calf attack, thanks to the Bush Witch, and Kirdan's healing touch later that night. I shake my head to physically dislodge the memory of his literal touch, and then do it again. A shield in the village calls out to check if I'm good. Somewhat mortified, I wave my assent and limp away faster.

Palliative magic aside, after a day of ensuring my naevus wasn't exposed during magical drills, classes, my body is tired. After what Kirdan said, that the doyenne would look here first when her presiders die, I've distanced myself from Delyse's and Shamar's orbit near entirely. No busha or Xanthippe will be able to tell the doyenne I've been close with them, if she comes looking for the presiders' killer in the Cuartel. While it's been easier without the weight of their expectations these past couple of days, there's a loneliness I didn't expect to feel without their noise, their jesting.

As All Souls' Night edges closer, the Cuartel prepares to welcome the two days of holiday provided by the Witches Council. Bohíos are adorned with streamers for the village's own celebration, one filled with music and dancing, food and stories. Shields will need to be ready, should the doyenne require any of us, but only Xanthippe will stand guard on the mount while the Alumbrar celebrate. I'm so busy thinking about all the ways the plans I share with Kirdan and Jazmyne could go wrong if the shields are called in to intervene, I don't notice Delyse leaning against my bohío until I'm almost upon her.

"Long time no see."

"Now, I don't believe that," I say, squeezing past her to open the door. Heat brushes my skin like a heavy pair of drapes as I enter. "Not with your network."

"I'd rather have heard how you are from *you*." Delyse pauses, looking hurt. "Why haven't I heard anything from you?"

Why indeed. Well, anger I could handle feeling; we're old friends. But Delyse's wounded expression? It dulls the strike of my tongue, loosens the knot of cruelty in my chest that drives me to repel anyone who tries to get too close. *This* is why she hasn't heard from me.

"I've needed space to think about your offer," I lie.

The toiletries I unpack are as loud as drums in the face of Delyse's incongruous silence. My mind jumps to conclusions, but I snatch those thoughts back and tether them to more rational ones. She can't know the plans I made with Jazmyne and Kirdan, not unless she was one of the planks of wood lining the floor in that filthy hole above the taproom.

"Shamar told me not to come to you until after the All Souls' Night celebration. He figured you needed space, but I have to say this now. We need you on the ground here, out talking with shields to convince them to fight, when the time calls for it." The words tumble out, like her mouth's been filled with them for days. "They're reluctant to trust that the vow will break—*is broken*, now that we have you."

I can't look at her.

"Not because they don't believe in you," she's quick to add. "There's just a lot to lose. Hearing from you will make them feel better, I know it. And there's training they need to receive, attack units they'll need to join. Hearing it all on the Sole will be too late."

Stealing time, I fill a pot with water and hoist it onto the hook over the fire. Crouching down to light the wood, I put my back to Delyse to hide how my fingers shake.

"The doyenne has me under constant surveillance."

"The Jade Guild can get you out of here."

I brush my hands on my dirty shorts as I straighten. "What about waiting for the power of the Black Moon?"

She throws her arms up. It's the most uncomposed I've seen her. "We don't feel good about her taking you on one of those missions no one can remember, all right? *I* don't feel good about it." Her face contorts. "We can't lose you if something goes wrong, like we have lost others—*I* can't." Her voice splinters.

I clear my throat and blink rapidly. Allergies. "Leaving wouldn't work for countless reasons. You're the one who told us about the Jade Guild's second attack at Black River. The doyenne will expect more." My early-morning excursions have taught me that Xanthippe now occupy the battlements around the palace. The Cuartel might be next after the presiders die. "It isn't smart to risk so much at this point," I say, cold and distant. Delyse withdraws. *Good.* "We agreed on a date. I still have time."

Forget the date, refuse her now!

"Just think about it. Please."

I don't respond. She doesn't stay, but her words linger like the tendrils of steam rising from the pot over the fire.

"Don't tell me you're having second thoughts?"

Kirdan's sudden appearance in my bohío makes me whirl around.

"And don't tell me *you* don't know how to knock!" My heart pounds as I take him in, all of him, in my bohío, hot with steam and only the one window, unable to think of anything other than the last time we were together in here. It's a distraction from what just happened with Delyse, but an unwelcome one. "Your timing seems a little convenient," I manage. "Right when I'm about to change."

A faint red speckles across his cheeks. "You didn't answer my question."

"Second thoughts about what?"

"Everything you agreed to with me and Jazmyne." His ebony tresses are swept back in a sleek bun, for once. The style emphasizes the edges of his cheekbones, the intensity of his expression. "That discussion with the shield looked serious. Sounded even more so. Do I need to remind you about the Shook Bargain?"

"The one *I* asked for?" A bead of sweat drips down the back of my neck. "No, Kirdan."

He blinks at my use of his first name. It does feel oddly intimate.

Gods, why is it so *hot* in here?

"I— All Souls' Night, I'll meet you outside the village by the tree you climbed down that first morning I caught you in the graveyard," he says. "Don't be late."

He watched me climb down from the tree too, that morning?

Is there anywhere I can go without him shadowing me?

"Don't tell me what to do," I snap. "I still haven't forgotten about your little trick with the death omen."

Something surfaces in his expression, something I can't quite name.

"I wouldn't have let it hurt you," he murmurs.

He said the same back in that hovel, but paired with this odd expression, it feels more earnest . . . *that's it*. He looks open—vulnerable.

My head tips to the side. "You actually meant that."

"I don't waste words I don't mean with you." That open, earnest look is still on his face when he disappears with the same suddenness with which he arrived.

I exhale, long and hard, staring at the place he stood.

I don't quite know what to make of him anymore, but I do know better than to even entertain a bag-o-wire such as he. So what if he doesn't seem to fear the strike of my tongue, or bow down to the prestige of my title? And who cares if, when he's not being flat-out rude, he treats me how—how I treat people. Like they're just *people*. How I always wished my order would treat me, if I was their empress. . . .

And he's sort of beautiful.

The sentiment of that thought makes my neck hot, my stomach curl in rejection of the feelings it stirs. None of that matters. He is a traitor, a means to an end—the hand I'll use to strike down my foe.

With him, all of him, gone, my thoughts clear somewhat, returning to the conversation I had before he arrived. Delyse's haste to incite matters is worrying. She's concerned, for *me*. And yet, I mustn't lose my edge, allow her feelings to blunt and file it away until I'm rounded like a ball and all the easier to kick about.

However difficult it has become to avoid, friendship is a noose I can't afford.

Not for my plans to be a success, or my order's safety here.

35

JAZMYNE

In the wake of the news about the Yielding's true purpose, it's as if I'm seeing everything through fresh eyes.

With the majority of the Order of Alumbrar members traveling to the villages and towns around Cwenburg to celebrate All Souls' Night at the palace, preparations begin early.

Overseeing the decorations for the past two years was a role I enjoyed. Now, watching attendants scurry about, spreading salt to control where spirits can enter and hanging garlands stuffed with wish-bags to prevent the more malevolent among the departed from invading, it occurs to me that I looked as they do—like if I just kept moving, I'd make it through the day; that if I stopped, I wouldn't be able to go again.

It doesn't make for an easier life, thinking for yourself, but it does make for a clearer one. How could I not have noticed that All Souls' Night isn't the doyenne's way of honoring the dead, as the holiday demands? She's *apologizing* for how she treated them while they lived, warding the more vengeful away lest they try to possess *her*.

It's viewed as the highest honor for my order, opening our hearts, our minds, our bodies, to the ancestors through nyába. For me, the thought of taking spirits in like invading crustaceans seeking to use my body as a shell makes me feel unsteady, ill. It's only now feeling under my complete control again as I experience everything anew, and strength has been elusive enough since the one-two blow of Kirdan's and the doyenne's betrayals.

Swamped in a gold kaftan, rings, and bracelets, I'm struck by the need to tear everything off.

"Soon come," I choke out to no one in particular.

The afternoon sun is without mercy, outside the palace. It beats down on my already fragile spirit as I walk the grounds and find myself standing before the stupa. Noise rings from the temple on the adjacent knoll, but here it is mercifully silent. Unsure which skull is Madisyn's, I circle the memorial and talk to them all. I ask for forgiveness, make promises.

During my sixth pass, Kirdan joins me.

"I don't want to hear anything about Iraya."

"We don't need to talk about anything," he responds.

We walk, for a time, in silence. It isn't awkward per se. I've accepted his betrayal the way one would a bruise. It's an ugly knock, but one that will fade to memory in time. He and I can move past this, we have to move past this, because in less than a lunar cycle I will have no dada, no sister, and no Doyenne Cariot, for all her sins. I can't lose Kirdan too.

"I forgive you." I glance his way, find him frowning at the stupa. "I didn't say it, after everything that passed, that night. But I do. I understand why you did what you did. You won't lie to me again, and I forgive you." Our eyes meet; he still frowns.

"I'm sorry, Jazmyne."

"Neither of us is experienced in ruling kingdoms. Mistakes were bound to be made."

"You sound better."

I shrug. "It isn't the end. Learning the truth about the Yielding hasn't made our path any longer. It's just given me another reason to go onward, because whatever lies on the other side of all this has to be better."

We fall back into silence. He knows the truth behind the doyenne's excursions off this hill and into the island below to find the jéges, and we've discussed that enough. I could tell him about the plans I made with Anya, but . . . he still feels distant. Things will improve.

They have to.

I slap a hand on the exposed skin of my arm, killing several blood eaters. Lit by witchlight posts and lanterns in its trees, Cwenburg's private gardens pulsate with insects on the evening of the All Souls' Night celebration. They buzz louder than the roistering from the drums welcoming riders at the front of the palace.

A low whistle peals from the vegetation. Iraya emerges ahead of Kirdan without a sound, like she charmed the leaves into silence. "Don't you look ready to cause trouble tonight."

Though I stand firm beneath her frank appraisal of my

dark lace mask and oxblood kaftan, her compliment incites a flush of pleasure that takes me by surprise. I could say the same about her. But I won't. Even though, adorned in a dark cloak Kirdan provided, longer than the capes favored by women, she wears the oncoming night like its darkness was created for her.

"Are you clear about tonight?"

"Find map, copy map, don't get caught. I think that covers it." She rolls her eyes. "Are *you* clear about tonight?"

"What do you mean?"

"You're facilitating the deaths of witches you know. Emotions can't come into play, or, map or no, the Sole will be messier than we'd like."

"Iraya's right," Kirdan says. "Are you sure you can isolate them on your own?"

This is the stance he's taking? I said I forgave him, not that I forgot.

"*Yes.*" I seethe, my jaw clenched. We'll have to talk about the timing of his flirting later. "I can do it."

"That's the spirit." Iraya claps. "On the chance you end up getting a little dirtier than your honey trap role requires, I find incapacitating an enemy easiest when I'm really committed to doing the best job I can. It doesn't even have to be with a blade. Smash a head against a wall hard enough and you can cave a skull in. There's even a pressure point in the center of the throat that, if you strike it hard enough, will stop a magi breathing." She offers her suggestions with a lightness I find sinister. My stomach twists at the thought. Just how hard would someone's head have to be knocked against a wall to dent *bone*?

"Stop that," Kirdan warns Iraya. "You just try and keep a low profile until I give the signal, mon." He gestures across the gardens, at one of the doyenne's study windows. "I'll be there in an hour. Less. Don't find yourself *committing* to any jobs other than the one tonight."

Iraya crosses her heart.

"And Jazmyne, it won't come to anything physical."

Indeed it won't, not with Anya and the Nameless Stealths in attendance.

"But if you need to convince the presiders to stay in place, here." Kir passes me his hunting knife. The metal's thicker than my wrists, and wicked sharp.

"Where will I put this?"

Iraya bends before me and tears a dangerous slit in the front of my kaftan to my lower thigh. "Holster, if you please?"

Kirdan's conduit winks beneath his collarless jacket. A dark leather strap appears in Iraya's hand. She shoves it at me and instructs me to buckle it to my upper thigh. With extreme care, I tuck the knife away. It makes me feel powerful, danger-ous, not blindsided and taken advantage of, as I did the last time we three were together.

"You good?" Kirdan asks; Iraya looks on, eyes alight with mischief.

"We meet an hour after midnight."

Night's imminent arrival is visible through the posterior wall of glass in Cwenburg's ballroom. Cresting the canopy of trees obscuring views of the Cuartel across the estate, the encroaching navy chokes the dying sun.

Benito, go with me. I need your fortune tonight.

Bedecked in decorations, the grand space sighs for breath. Gold drips from the ceiling, from the walls. Ceremonial Kumina drums reverberate through the dark tiled floor. Bodies draped in colorful fabrics writhe in the damp heat to their rhythm, invoking nyába to honor the Alumbrar ancestors. They contort as the spirits fill them, sending their eyes to the back of their heads, making them scream and shout with pain and pleasure.

Most wear grotesque masks with exaggerated features, the eye sockets gaping and consuming. In the smoke from the burning incense, their features become distorted and monstrous. Tonight is a wild dance where austerity tangles with indulgence. The masks allow my ilk to become someone else. Though I chose not to wear one, I feel different. More than a suggestion of my legs peeks through the slit in the front of my kaftan. Warmth caresses the exposed skin, a zephyr touch that tugs a shiver from me.

The doyenne oversees the party from her intricate throne of thorns. Now that I know the truth behind the Yielding, the crimson mixed with the black of her kaftan takes on a new meaning. It calls the towering golden crown that sits proud on her head into question. She isn't a loyal Alumbrar. She's a witch betraying our ways by using Obeah rituals.

She claps her hands twice. "Wahan, Alumbrar. From light we are born."

"*And to light we cleave.*" Fevered faces smirk up at her;

among them are her council.

"Tonight we take a reprieve from the Yielding to honor those who can no longer be with us, whether due to natural causes, or at the hands of those who once sought to rule us. But we shall not speak that name this All Souls' Night. Instead we will speak the names of the departed, over and over, as we open ourselves to receive them."

Xanthippe move from sentinel positions to control the crowd, who push closer to the doyenne, howling their approval like a pack of jungle-prowlers. How the timbre of their howls would change if they learned the truth about the ritual behind the Yielder guzzu.

"Without their sacrifice, we wouldn't be here. Tonight we thank the fallen for daring to burn brightly, however fleetingly. We will always remember them." The doyenne instructs the Kumina drum players, the dancers, to summon the ancestors in dance and music once more.

"Outside," Kirdan murmurs, appearing beside me, "I didn't mean to suggest you couldn't do it. I have my role to play with Iraya, as you well know. But if you are uncomfortable about luring the presiders away, you can tell me."

He wouldn't check if *she* could do it.

"I'll be fine." I push my shoulders back, dip my chin. "Don't you have somewhere to be soon?"

"Walk good." His blessings are a gust of warm air as he departs. He'll need to make sure he's seen around a little more prior to disappearing to meet with Iraya.

He'll be surprised when they come back and find I've taken

care of the presiders. They're already enjoying the festivities. Especially Presider Phelony. She stands with Javel, who is surrounded by adoring Alumbrar. I roll my eyes. He's become the island's favorite to be crowned the Yielded. Zidane stands by his side, his own smile less sure as they're congratulated on surviving their third Yielding trial, along with Raeni, beautiful in a trailing kaftan the color and texture of a storm cloud. I'm hoping she swipes the victory from beneath Javel's nose.

Making a slow prowl beneath the balcony, I seek out the evening's targets. Presider Magmire converses with a broad Alumbrar-man; Presider Caldwell stands off to the side, mask-free and stone-faced; no doubt she'd be happier with her books. Later I can draw her away under the guise of a rare collectible so Anya can *take care* of her in the library.

Heady with all that will happen tonight, the progress that will be made, I brush a hand against my thigh, where the blade is strapped. Anya wanders past me, masked, as per the plan I didn't get around to sharing with Kirdan, and wouldn't have with Iraya.

Tonight I will show them that they sit at my table, not the other way around.

36

IRA

My makeshift twig-dagger grates as it glides across my thumb, but out here a witch has to make do, and I'm anything but unresourceful.

The golden filigree on the palace is cool beneath my bloody touch. I hold my thumb there a moment, staining the intricate coils of conduit metal fortifying Cwenburg. "*Adair.*" I whisper the command for the tunnel to open and reveal itself, my blood working as the key. After what feels like an appropriate amount of time has passed, I dig my fingers into the wall, feeling for a door. There's no dip, like the last three times I tried this evening.

Gods-damnit.

If I can remember where the tunnel is, I'll have my way out of the palace after Kirdan's killed the doyenne. Whatever the Shook Bargain dictated, I'd be a fool to count on him and

Jazmyne playing fair. But, for the life of me—quite literally—I can't remember which part of the wall the glyph sits behind, not outside of. My ancestors couldn't have placed the glyph somewhere easily accessible, could they? No. That would be too easy, too Alumbrar. *Cha*.

There's no more time to search. The last thing I need is Kirdan learning that I didn't follow his advice about undertaking *multiple commitments*.

I race back through the gardens, past my favorite places to play as a pickney. At the roots of the familiar cotton tree beneath Dada's study window, I climb their gnarled tentacles where they jut from the paved border. Beneath my palms the bark's as jagged as I remember. I had a governess who told me to stay away from the cotton trees, lest one of the more malevolent duppies who enjoy playing by its roots stole me away and replaced me with a changeling. Though I haven't seen any spirits, I climb faster. Even now her warning holds fast.

The study window's propped open. Kirdan's face appears, his jaw tight. So I'm a little late. Ignoring the hand he proffers, I climb inside. This room's familiar to me, even in the dark. I can almost smell Dada's peppermints he kept in the top drawer of his desk, the sweet pipe Mama hated him smoking. I stumble as if the memory's a slap. A fist.

Kirdan takes my elbow. Electricity runs up my arm; I snatch it out of his hold.

"I've just spent a decade in prison."

"I heard something about that, yes," he comments dryly. "A regular tagereg, aren't you?"

"Exactly. A criminal. You should know better than to treat me like I'm helpless." I cross to the wall behind the desk. Kirdan follows, a shadow. "A little privacy?"

With a beleaguered sigh, he turns his back. "You wouldn't be immature enough to pull faces when I can't see, would you, Iraya?"

I drop the rude hand gesture. "Never." An eye on Kirdan to make sure he doesn't turn around, I press my thumb to the wall behind Dada's desk, making blood spill from the earlier cut. "*Adair.*" Releasing a breath and a prayer that I've remembered the right spot, I run my hands along the wall, feeling for the concealed seam of the tunnel. They catch. I dig my fingers into the groove and drag the door open.

Its inside is cool and smooth. Iron. That explains why it's so heavy. I huff with exertion. Kirdan helps; with his considerable weight behind me, we manage to fully draw it back. Stale air slinks out. Of course: no one's been here for ten years.

"Give us a little light?"

Kirdan's conduit flashes in his saber's handle; on the walls behind the secret door, intermittently placed iron sconces flicker to life. The witchlights glow a brilliant white, highlighting a flight of interminable steps. Memories tumble through my mind. Mama showing me the access points inside each tunnel. They're glyphed with symbols of Learn, Conceal, and Protect. I trace them, remembering the feel of her hand around mine. Am I really about to show a Zesian bag-o-wire her most prized possessions?

"Witches first." Nodding into the tunnel, Kirdan plucks

one of the sconces from the wall.

It's for her, and Dada. You don't have a choice.

"You'd better gather your skirts and hurry up, then."

He clearly thinks better of whatever rebuttal he was going to make as he shakes his head. The corridor's narrow and low enough that Kirdan's forced to slide his back against the wall, crouching slightly to edge past; his chest murmurs past my own.

I don't exhale. Neither does he.

The deeper we traverse, the older the walls become until the stone is ancient enough to predate the palace. The descent feels like I'm suspended over a declivity, awaiting a fall into a great unknown. I've been ignoring my stomach's protests, but something inside heaves, forcing me to grip the walls slick with slime on either side of the tunnel. With a rising nausea, I refuse to consider what horrors may be beneath my fingertips.

"I need a minute." I close my eyes to allay the sickness threatening to overcome me.

"Dizzy?"

Very, very much so. But he doesn't need to know how I feel about heights. "I didn't eat dinner." I fight a gag. "I'm a little light-headed."

"Too busy thinking about your revenge?" The words drip with sarcasm.

Breathing steadily to fight the bile climbing my throat, I can only give him a death stare.

"Don't you find it tiring? All the hatred and scheming—it doesn't wear you down? It's killing, at the end of the day. Even for Obeah, it takes its toll." His voice has a hollowness to it that speaks of his experience with the Simbarabo.

In the flickering light from the sconces, flames crackling as they combat the murky pall of this enclosed space, I run my eyes across the scarification visible above his collarless tunic. Preoccupied by deep scratches in the stone, he doesn't notice my focus. It's annoyingly easy to picture the rest of the midnight woad beneath his clothes, the way it squeezes the column of his neck before snaking over muscular shoulders and encircling his straining biceps. The very way they're mapped across his body mirrors the violence he had to commit to earn them— the very violence I'm counting on, seeing as I cannot kill the doyenne myself.

"Don't you get tired of the labels Obeah carry? Bloodthirsty, selfish, arrogant." He darts a look at me. "Especially that last one. Don't you want to be more?"

"You're so right," I muse, the threat of spewing all over him having passed. "What have I been thinking? If the Alumbrar had thought us soft, they wouldn't have attacked, my parents would still be alive, the magical among my order wouldn't be conscripted, and I wouldn't be down here, with you. *Obeah* are the ones who need to change."

"That's not what I meant. Don't be reductive." His voice dips and he glances at me, his stare weighted with meaning. "Did you ever consider that your fight's bigger than what's owed? Bigger than another Alumbrar-Obeah rivalry? You could have helped Jazmyne and me fight the Alumbrar Witches Council's injustice, changed how things have been, as your mama tried to."

"Are you regretting your decision to kill her?"

"Are you regretting your decision that you've thought of nothing *but* killing her?" he challenges.

My eyes race across his face, tracing every feature. Jazmyne's caveat in our bargain made it clear that she doesn't want any of the Aiycan Obeah leading the island her order fought tooth and nail for. So Kirdan's apparent wish for me to play a role in its revival—if that's even what he truly wants—makes his motivations even more questionable.

"I'm not being reductive. I simply have no interest in hearing about the empire's politics." I stand, forcing him to back off. "We should get moving. We don't have much time." I squeeze past, half prepared for him to seize my wrist and pull me back. Instead he falls behind, silent once more. I tell myself it doesn't disappoint me, knowing fully well I'm lying.

Though, he is too.

I'd be a fool to think his actions, his words, tonight and otherwise, are anything other than some sort of trap. This I tell myself with every descending step, ignoring the unified beat of his tread with mine.

But then, which of the two of us is the spider, and which the fly?

37

JAZMYNE

When I was younger, pickney would play a game during breaks in the yard in front of our villas. As the smallest, my sistren and I were often prey in their hunt.

Hide, the bigger pickney would order us. *And we'll see how fast we can find you.*

As recently as this year, the memory of that visceral terror, the pounding *everything* and shortness of breath, still submerged me until I was back stuffed beneath our porch praying for Madisyn to come home and scare the pickney away.

Tonight's the first time I understand the allure of being the hunter.

It's about the power.

Moving around the ballroom, tallying the additional Xanthippe on duty, more than ever before after the Jade Guild's attacks on the island, and nodding urbane greetings to those who recognize my station as the doyenne's redundant eye, faculty electrifies my limbs and everything seems to sharpen. All this time I thought myself lame, a toothless prowler not ready to lead. It's only in this past month or so that I've learned I have the claws to tear apart the doyenne's rule, to put an end to her corrupt council, to sit upon the throne.

As midnight approaches, I'm tracking a giddy Magmire around the ballroom, her third glass of rum in hand, perhaps her fourth, when she turns and I let her catch me.

"You are without your shadow, Emissary Cariot." Her eyes are unfocused; she wavers like one of the palm trees on the palace lawn. "I know you defend him to the death," she slurs. "But don't you suspect his motives at all? We all know Obeah loyalties lie with their own, ultimately."

"Actually, there was—I saw something. Something suspicious earlier," I blurt out. "I wasn't sure if it's worthwhile. We don't want to anger Zesia, on top of everything else."

Magmire's head bobs in what I *think* is a nod.

"Perhaps you could come with me? You can help me decide if it's worth showing the doyenne or not. I never know with these things."

Your mama had no respect for you; neither did her council, Kirdan said.

I will take their underestimation and use it against them.

"In truth, sometimes I find my role as emissary overwhelming."

"Of course you do." Westira waves the hand clutching the rum. It sloshes onto the floor. "I'll just inform her that I'm leaving."

I grab her wrist. "There might not be time. If what I saw is incriminating, the doyenne will only blame you for not coming with me when you had the chance, won't she?" I tap my thighs seven times, waiting for Magmire's eyes to focus.

"You're right," she finally says, and hiccups.

"Meet me by his rooms, and tell no one."

Forcing my way through the bodies in the ballroom, I'm sure to greet magi on my way to the privy. *It's important they see you going somewhere far from where the bodies will be found*, Anya advised earlier today. She passes, taps me on the shoulder to let me know she's stoppered Westira's tongue. Now she *can't* tell anyone I told her to go upstairs, should her rum-loosed lips attempt to proffer the information. Only when the crowd thins do I divert up a service staircase to the third floor.

On the landing, I lie in wait until Westira stumbles into view. No one else will come up here, not after the cabal of Stealths cast a guzzu of disorientation that will make any magi who might think about coming up here forget why they did so and return to the party. With murmured worries, I slip behind the presider and lead her away to one of the spare rooms several halls away, spinning lies about her accidentally stopping outside the wrong room.

"Now, where is it, Emissary?"

Able to speak now we're in the room, her voice is my guide in the darkness of the quarters as my eyes adjust. Although the heavy fabric curtains are thrown back, a bank of clouds obscures most of the moonlight. In the dark, the room feels more like a nightmarish chamber in which bulky shapes lurk.

Presider Magmire trips into one with a thud and curses. "I need light to see what you mentioned. What was it again? I don't—I can't recall. Too much rum." She titters.

The clouds clear, flooding the room with light from the moon. When she catches sight of the blade I've freed from my holster, Presider Magmire gasps. But no one hears her. And no one will again. Filmore darts in from the shadows, releasing an ominous purple disk from his conduit. It rotates through the air like a spinning blade to slice across the presider's throat.

Hands gripping her neck like she hopes to hold the split skin together, Westira drops to her knees, looking up at me in shock, betrayal. Vomit lurches from my mouth before I can stop it. My throat's set alight with its bitterness. I shiver, twitch . . .

"We couldn't use a cleaner guzzu," Anya says, also appearing from the darkness. She rubs my back. "Sorry, Jaz. We need Doyenne Cariot to believe the Jade Guild are responsible for this."

"They could get their hands on a knife, easy," Filmore says.

They're both largely unaffected, but even with Anya's hand at my back I quiver and sweat. I didn't like Westira—she was nothing more than the doyenne's puppet—but I can't pretend to be inured to her death. It takes longer than I thought it would. It's noisier too: the bubbling of blood, wet gasps of breath.

"Mudda have mercy!"

Anya, Filmore, and I twist around. Presider Caldwell stands in the open doorway, her mouth agape as she takes in the body. Her small eyes dart to the blade in my hands.

"I watched you lead her in here," she says. "Murderer."

"Shield!" Anya barks at Filmore.

Her conduit projects a golden net that slinks over the two of us just as a suppression guzzu, bright as a sunbeam, shoots from Ada's conduit. I scream at the smashing of glass, the splintering of wood. Something thuds against the shield—a body. Filmore slumps to the tile, unconscious.

With a final fierce look at us, Ada turns and bolts.

Back to the party. To the doyenne.

"Tell me there are other Stealths up here," I breathe.

Anya grimaces. "Filmore was too slow with his shield, so now there's only me." Her own protection falls from around us. "I guess Ada will be death number two."

"Wait! What about the bodies?"

"Stealths have a homing glyph. Filmore will disappear on his own soon if he doesn't wake. I'll come back for the pre-sider." Leaping to her feet, Anya runs for the door.

Gathering my kaftan in the hand still clutching the knife, I wipe my sticky mouth against my sleeve and hurry after her.

38

IRA

After what feels like an age, Kirdan and I finally alight at the bottom of the staircase in the secret Adair Chamber. Like mine, his senses will be wired for the faintest sounds. We both noticed the dust coating the upper half of the staircase did not occupy its lower half. With the labyrinth of tunnels snaking throughout the palace, it would be foolish to assume the doyenne might not have found another way down here.

More sconces light with a gleam from Kirdan's conduit blade. In the low-ceilinged space, their muted glow isn't strong enough to reach the corners. But they are bright enough to illuminate piles of bones randomly discarded on the floor.

For a terrifying moment I'm transported back to Carne.

Memories float to the surface unbidden, like waterlogged corpses. Large hands, cruel faces, a cold cell. Blood. A perennial flow of it snaking through the O Block like an artery—

"You good?" Kirdan's voice draws me back.

"Yeh mon."

Get it together, Adair.

More rattled than I thought I could be at my early memories of Carne, I edge away, taking a torch for myself. Its weight's reassuring as I weave between squat stone pillars, wielding it like a bat around the truncated cavern. This isn't how I remember it being.

"This can't be it." Mirroring my thoughts, Kirdan keeps his voice low. "There are other chambers branching off. One of those is most likely where your mama kept her trove, but I think we should take a thorough look before moving on. Don't shout if you find anything. I— Something's not right."

His is a feeling I share.

Eager to look and be done with it, I tap walls, checking the earth for hollow places the map could be hidden; using the butt of the torch, I knock aside piles of bones to unearth any trapdoors. Something scratches against stone behind me. I jerk around, torch aloft. It's just Kirdan, scouring bones on the other side of the crypt.

That's what logic and reason try to make me think, anyway.

But they can't displace a decade of learning to trust my instincts in Carne, understanding the ways my body senses a threat before my head registers it. The prickling of fine hairs sensitizes my skin, transforming the very air in the room into something acute and coarse as I'm awash with a predatory knowledge that we're no longer alone down here.

If not the iron door, the sconces, or the absence of dust on the lower half of the staircase—where the reach of the iron from the door and the Glyph of Protection would have been weak—then the memories of Carne should have tipped me off that something was hiding down here—not an antechamber. A *security* chamber. I sealed all those Carne nightmares in a mental vault no magi's magic can penetrate.

I didn't think about any monsters.

Steel whispers through the dark as Kirdan draws his saber.

I send my weight to the balls of my feet as a bulky shadow pulls away from the others in the corner closest to the stairs. It drops onto all fours with a weighty *thud* that echoes across the cavern. Blood pounds battle's rhythm in my ears, heightening my senses, honing them for survival. Eleven—maybe twelve— hands high, the creature's hairless; its pygmy flesh anemic. It lifts its wide rutted head to the air and inhales the chamber's musty scent. *Blind*, I remember. I saw enough boddlelice in Carne. The mountain beneath the prison was flush with the vermin that dwell wherever it's dark and cold, emitting a scentless secretion, a poison of the mind, to evoke the fear it feasts on as an appetizer to flesh.

The boddlelice's lips peel back, exposing thick saliva trailing from a crooked fence of teeth as it lowers its head, preparing to attack.

"Probably some form of security," Kirdan whispers, closer now. "But what is it?"

A not entirely unwelcome image of those teeth clamping onto his arm and dragging him down a spiky, bone-infested road to death manifests.

"A boddlelice," I murmur. "It has a hard outer shell, but it's soft underneath."

He grips his saber in his left hand and frees a plainer thrusting knife from his hip with his right. I lower to a crouch and grab the first bone my fingers wrap around—something's skull. My fingers curl into the eye sockets. We look at one another in silent communication, almost like we've done this countless times before.

I chuck the skull at the creature, aiming for the softest part of its head—the fleshy sockets in which its eyes don't rest. I make my target. The boddlelice screeches, rearing on its hind legs. Kirdan darts in and slices its raw pink underbelly from its hind legs to throat with both blades in an impressive move that reminds me why I suspected he was a Warrior in the first place. Few emissaries could handle their blade like it was an extension of themselves. Jazmyne is a case in point.

"A hard outer shell but soft underneath," he repeats, wiping black blood from his blade on the inside of his jacket. More gushes out of the creature as it moans its way to death.

"Don't you dare compare me to that thing."

"I wouldn't dream of it." The hint of a smile lights Kirdan's face.

In an adjoining room, more sconces awaken with a gleam from Kirdan's conduit blade, illuminating a vast cavern felled into the rock—Mama's cache of riches. Mounds of conduit coins and weapons gleam beneath suspended witchlight pendulums. Priceless artifacts spill from trunks and straw baskets positioned atop thick handwoven rugs.

"There's a chance the mirror could be down here too." He pivots, taking everything in. "Can you recognize it?"

"Have I suddenly developed the ability to see through wooden chests?"

"A moment without your claws and fangs, if you will." Folding his arms across his chest, he cocks his head at me. Muscles bunch up beneath the sleeve of his tunic.

Heat stabs low in my stomach—leftover adrenaline from the boddlelice attack.

"The jéges are connected to the Adair ancestors," he says. "So asking them for a guiding hand might be a good idea, no? I believe you're comfortable communicating with them after that incident with the Deleterious Doll."

That heat travels up to my neck. He saw me passed out, possibly drooling.

"I'll look through the trunks and baskets in the meantime." He doesn't say what we both know: there isn't enough time to get through everything in this cavern tonight, never mind the additional rooms beyond where the light reaches. The ancestors will save time.

A conversation doesn't require blood and bone, just manners and the little Jákīsa he hands over with a knowing look.

"Ta'k na mi, arik na mi," I murmur. "Honti yu ye?" *Are you here?* I ask the spirits, splashing rum from the skin on baskets and jewelry boxes, in cabinets and drawers from armoires I rifle through, repeating the deep patwah again and again.

"*Na hunty yu cohn yeh fi?*"

The trinket box's lid slams shut before me; witchlights blink in the cavern. Once. Twice.

"Iraya?"

"Wait," I tell Kirdan.

"*Na hunty yu cohn yeh fi?*" the hive of voices repeat, slithering against the wall of my thoughts. *Why did you come here?*

"Mi no no onti fi jéges." My memory of deep patwah isn't what it once was, and my tongue sits useless. "Can you show me where?"

Though braced for it, the familiar hold of claws clamping onto my shoulders still takes me by surprise. The ancestors' touch imparts thoughts, images, impressions, feelings that overwhelm at first. I close my eyes, scrunch my forehead against a headache, and then their influence lightens, and they encourage me to look . . . up.

"Iraya?"

The fingers rescind, and the impressions fade. I whisper my thanks.

"Iraya, are you good?"

"The jége isn't here," I say, opening my eyes. "But I know where the map is."

"Where?"

"We're standing in it."

Arrayed like stars on the domed ceiling and the walls around us, hundreds of illustrations narrated with an old Aiycan dialect are incised into the stone. My skin pimples into gooseflesh.

"Can you read what's up there?"

It takes close to half an hour, skipping through legends about enemy witches and their beastly pets, before I find the section with jéges in it.

"This is the part. You'll need the breadfruit skin and coal."

Carvings and faded splashes of paint pay homage to the fallen empire. Ornate whorls map the Seven-Faced Mudda's arrival, Their creation of the Obeah and Alumbrar, and the gifting of my order with four jéges. Though, as with all Anansi stories, there seems to be a catch. The inscription looks too short to detail where every jége is, as Delyse and Shamar hoped—but still, they weren't entirely wrong about the map being on the estate. And I laughed at them.

"Does it say where the map is?" Kirdan asks, pulling me out of my head, my shame.

"I'll need books to translate."

"I can provide those for you." He follows the stick of coal as it moves across the breadfruit skin as though held between invisible fingers, rendering a perfect copy of the map. "Who painted this?"

"It would have been my ancestors." Some parts are newer than others, the pigment brighter, carved by a different hand. Could Mama and Dada have contributed to some of these stories?

"Are you . . . artistic?"

"They held painting classes every Tuesday in Carne."

Kirdan raises his brows.

"I wasn't a painter before prison," I admit, suppressing a snigger. "I did enjoy creating as a pickney, though; music in particular."

"What did you play?"

"I sang." Hosted concerts for my parents whenever I could pull them away from their duties. Only the gods know if I was

374

any good or not, but Dada always applauded and whistled, begging for encores. "One day, I'll sing at your funeral."

"Are you talented?"

"If you wake up reeking of decay and wondering why you're lying eight feet under dirt, then you can safely assume my lullaby had the opposite effect than intended."

He throws his head back and laughs, a real, deep, from-the-belly sound. It's loud and entirely unexpected from him. My face must convey my shock, because he laughs harder. His eyes crinkle in the corners, the lines deep enough to indicate that in another life, he was happy.

No.

Spinning on my heel, I take one step before his voice stops me dead.

"Iraya."

Low, it sparks across my skin like a static shock.

"No more lectures about revenge, thank you," I say, brusquer than necessary. "You should quit while you're ahead, Zesian." I might sound somewhat out of breath, but it's just my allergies. There's a lot of dust down here. "I didn't say when that funeral would be." I wander away from him on legs that shake just a little, needing space, but his shoes brush against the carpet in pursuit.

"I was going to ask," he's foolish enough to continue, his words a caress against the back of my neck, "for answers to my earlier questions."

A shiver trails its traitorous fingers down my spine. Desire isn't foreign to me, after too long without touch. All I'd have to do is arch back, bend my head to the side a little. Indulge. Obeah are used to taking what we want, after all. And what I want is for him to stop talking; I can only think of one way to do that right now. But the rational part of me, the side not preoccupied with wondering how his scarred hands would feel around my hips, hates him and his for all that's been done to me and mine.

"Is an equally yoked Alumbrar-Obeah world one you think about?"

"I think about a better world."

"Really? I wasn't sure if you were allowed thoughts of your own as an Alumbrar pet." I turn just as Kirdan rears back, and launch my second attack without delay. "Is this where you say you were wrong about me again?" I mock. "That I'm every bad thing you thought I was?"

Recovering, he laughs. This time it's artificial, cold. "I wish."

What does that mean?

No. No more of this, whatever it is.

"I hate you." I breathe the words. "I *hate* you."

The chill in his expression thaws into something I don't quite understand.

"The copy should be done soon," I say, short. "How about you keep to that side of the cavern, and I'll keep to this one?"

"If that's what you want."

"It is."

39

JAZMYNE

I've been pacing Cwenburg's upper landing for the better part of half an hour—prowling like a great cat in the bush, but a predator I am not.

Hopeful, I glance at Anya, but she's still unconscious and propped up against the wall where I found her when I caught up. I'm not quite sure what happened, but her breathing is steady. I'd give anything to trade places. The bloody truth to hunting even now turns my stomach. Talking about killing is one thing; its reality is an awful exposé into the fragility of human life. I don't want to endure that again tonight.

I don't want a reminder of how easy it is to live one moment and to die another.

Presider Caldwell has locked herself in one of the suites in the west wing. My only security lies in the fact that her lone escape route's down the staircase behind me, and sifting within the palace is magically embargoed, even for presiders, so she'll have to come out at some point. As for what I'll do when she does . . . She's had enough time to ruminate over every guzzu in the encyclopedic mind her métier affords. And what happens if the celebration ends before she vacates the room? The doyenne may come.

Benito, I beseech the Mudda's Face of Fortune, *have you forsaken me?*

I grip my borrowed blade so tightly, the incisions on the hilt emboss my palm. Peaked to a fine point, the dagger winks in the iridescent shimmers of witchlight cast by the chandelier suspended over the palace vestibule. A sage voice, *Madisyn's voice*, orders me to jimmy the door open with the blade's tip. To force myself inside. To *survive*. I look down at the blade, remember the feeling of its cool metal against my thigh when I first strapped it there.

Two presiders do need to die tonight, Kirdan, Iraya, and I agreed.

But must I be the one to do it?

Must.

I swallow the acrid taste in my mouth. Lest my earlier sickness rise again. Tucking the blade away for a moment, I hoist my arms beneath Anya's armpits and drag her with as much care as I can into a curtained alcove.

Returning to the presider's hideout, I draw several shallow breaths before dropping to my knees and jamming the blade in the door crease. Silent and unforgiving, it slices through the metal lock. Her back is turned when I edge inside. Any traces of footfalls are swallowed by the plush carpet. I draw the dagger back, pull in a breath as I've seen Xanthippe do during training, and will myself to let it fly—but I can't.

"I know you're there, Emissary."

I'm frozen. Ensorcelled by a guzzu.

"I've been waiting for you to muster the confidence to enter and face me." Ada turns with a mellifluous jingle of her jewelry, reproof in her frigid stare. "My beloved doyenne chose me to be her second, to know what she cannot." She rests her thin form against the large wooden dresser at her back. The silver stubble atop her shorn head glints like shrapnel in the glare cast by the witchlight lamp. It's eclipsed only by the glower on her face. The disgust there—for *me*. "What I have observed in the almost three months since the infamous Carne transfer on September first, the one none of the Conscription Officers present that day can speak about, is that you have lost weight. Magi not of my métier might rationalize that away as the development from girl to woman, not seeing as I have your increased confidence, surety. Your sister was much the same as she prepared to flee the palace."

Her reference to Madisyn lands like a knifepoint against my heart.

"And so I have kept an eye on you, and what I saw tonight will turn Doyenne Cariot's stomach. The heir she has groomed to replace her at a time she deems fit has killed one of the Mudda's chosen, and arrived here to try and kill another."

Under her thrall, I cannot object. I cannot tell her that I haven't killed anybody—that I don't think I'm capable of it.

Her chin tilts upward. "Once in possession of that knowledge, she'll thank me for taking your life. She might even regret not killing—"

A blade shoots past me and embeds itself in the presider's chest with a dull thud, an inch or so above her conduit. Darkness spools beneath her abaya, growing as she looks down at the protruding dagger.

"That was *almost* a bull's-eye," Iraya says. "Not bad for my first throw in a while."

My knees give as Ada's do. She splays across the carpet like a discarded breadfruit skin; her conduit dims, now a regular coin in her death.

"We would have been here sooner." Kirdan strides to my side, proffering a hand to help me to my feet. "But the stairs, we had to use the tunnels and find another way. You good?"

Nodding, I blink at Iraya. "You saved me."

"I killed *her*." She draws her braided ponytail over her shoulder like a whip. "Is Caldwell the first presider?"

"The second. Westira was first. Sorry."

"At least you got one." She shrugs, unbothered by the body between us, as well as the first body I left behind.

When sleep comes, I know I'll have to fight away the image of Westira drowning in her own blood.

"Did you find the map?" I look to Kirdan for an answer.

"Yeh mon. Copied it too. Most of it will need translating."

Iraya yawns, her mouth stretching wide. "I'll need access to the library."

"We can do that." Kir looks to me.

"We can ensure you have books, yes," I correct. "We'll have to work fast, and it will be tight—"

"To avoid the chance of a funeral."

Iraya smirks at Kirdan. "That promise was just for you."

380

I look between the two of them. "What promise?"

"It's nothing. It was a joke."

A *what?*

"At Kirdan's funeral," Iraya expounds. "Don't ask me to sing."

He clears his throat. "It really doesn't matter, Jaz. What does is the jége. As soon as we know where it is, I can retrieve it."

"Then it's decided," I say, with some caution, still looking between the two of them. "We can begin as soon as the books have been gathered."

"Your mama didn't throw away the Obeah tomes?"

"Not to my knowledge. Though—"

"Wait." Kir cocks his head to the side, hearing something I can't. "Someone's discovered the first body already, and here in the palace. Jazmyne—"

The Stealths' guzzu must have ended, or been broken.

"There wasn't time to hide it."

"And now there's no time to lose." Iraya crosses the room to draw the sash window upward. "Has she summoned the shields?"

Kirdan pauses, listens, and then shakes his head.

"Then there's still time," she says. "Who's first?"

"Me." I edge forward. "I need to find Doyenne Cariot and make sure she suspects the Jade Guild."

Kirdan whispers a guzzu that enlivens the ivy clinging to the side of the palace, manipulating the green vines into a lattice ladder for me to climb down.

Cast in shadow by the towering guard of guango and palm trees nestled close to the palace, the garden below is free of revelers. I wait until my feet are secured before I address Kirdan, my voice low. "Private jokes? Is there anything you need to tell me?"

"Have you forgotten what you asked of me?"

"*Shh*," I hiss. Iraya has a conduit and intentions as mercurial as the tide. "I remember."

"Do you? Do you also remember when we planned for me to take care of the presiders?" His face is almost hurt. "Though I suppose Anya did a good enough job."

"How do you know I didn't do it?"

Kirdan leans back, withdrawing into shadow. "I suppose I don't."

"Can we move this along?" Iraya calls. "I'm tired. And bored."

"Just—be cautious," I beg Kirdan. "Take care of Caldwell's body, and then come back as soon as you've escorted Iraya to the village. The council might raid."

He nods his farewell.

Overhead, a half-moon spills light across the stretch of grass between the garden and the border of trees. Magi hurry away from Cwenburg like a fire blazes within and the long-feared Aiycan night's the only refuge. Where laughter and music sounded, only the slap of feet, the rush of bodies, and the murmurs of fear rend the evening now.

The remaining presiders are already assembled around the conference table in the doyenne's study when I fly through the door, breathless.

"Let us not forget that the Obeah were master war tacticians once," the doyenne muses, not sparing me a look as I take my seat. "The Jade Guild's evasion should be reminder enough."

Good. She doesn't suspect Iraya. Or me.

"Killing presiders to force the council's hand to drastic measures could have been the insurgents' plan all along. We won't retaliate until we know more. We won these seats by playing to our strengths," the doyenne says. "We are not soldiers, witches. We are patient. We'll award a holiday in honor of Presider Magmire at the start of the next moon phase, delaying the final trial. The Obeah may think we're using this time to mourn our dead, and while this will be true, the reprieve will also provide the opportunity to watch them. I want those responsible for Westira's death found before the Sole." The doyenne looks at her lap, mouth puckering. I suppose the two of them were as close as she'll ever be with someone again, after she manipulated Empress Adair through their friendship. "When I learn who killed her, I'll take care of them personally."

I worry about Anya, vulnerable in the alcove on the second floor.

"Will we raid?" Presider Antwi asks. "Frighten the Jade Guild sympathizers among the shields? They might be hiding the killer."

"No. They'll expect us to act tonight. I want them fraught with anticipation. That's when they'll become careless, and that's when I'll catch Westira's murderer. Until then, the moratorium on sifting within the palace will extend to the entire island, not unless my permission is granted. See that the guzzu is set, witches. And someone find me Ada. She left the celebration not too long after Westira."

My breathing shallows.

"She mentioned following signs before she left the celebration," Mariama says, in reference to the last time we were all gathered. "Whatever that means."

It meant following *me*. But as the other presiders shake their heads, more than used to the distance Presider Caldwell's genius provokes, I rest easy.

"Tonight it isn't prudent to disappear. Find her for me," Doyenne Cariot orders the attending Xanthippe by the door. "Ensure she comes, with haste."

We are dismissed.

I make my way back to where I hid Anya, before the Xanthippe searching the palace find her. Kirdan still has to hide Ada's body, but my earlier trepidation about the doyenne blaming Iraya is nothing more than a fading aftertaste. Though it's necessary that she continues to evade Doyenne Cariot's suspicion, she will need to take the fall after the doyenne's dead.

After seeing her with Kirdan tonight, I'm reminded that pushing her is a task I look forward to.

40

IRA

Kirdan and I conceal the presider's body in the private gardens, shielded by guzzu from patrolling Xanthippe while laying her to rest amidst lush foliage, not a bad grave, before he sifts us into my bohío.

It's disconcerting to find that it now feels more like *our* place instead of *mine*.

"Blessings, mon." I might have put on a show to poke at Jazmyne's insecurities, back at the palace, but I've had enough of Emissary Divsylar tonight. "I'll be seeing you. Hopefully not soon."

"You said you hate me."

He stands far enough away that his features are indiscernible in the dark. I wish I could turn on the witchlight, but Delyse or one of the others might be watching elsewhere in the village.

"I do."

"Why?"

"Zesia stood by while my parents were killed and my order conscripted, as if the Alumbrar's avarice was our fault. Now, if that's all—"

"That explains why you hate my island." His jacket rustles as he shifts. "Why you hate Doyenne Divsylar, the Witches Council. But you said you hate *me*, and I want to know why." The weight of his focus presses against my body. "Because I don't hate you, Iraya."

Warmth spears through my lower stomach.

In disgust.

There he goes again, saying my name like he has a right to.

"I hate that you're determined to walk one path," he continues. "And I hate that you're allowing the past to dictate your future. But I don't hate you. So why? Why do you hate me?"

I fumble with words, with understanding, off my game and unsettled by him.

"*Why?*"

"I—I don't know."

"Consider, then, that it isn't hatred you feel," he says, almost smiling. "Goodnight, Iraya."

The door closes, and he is gone.

I sink onto my cot feeling oddly bare. I stay that way for a long while, part of me wanting Kirdan to come back, part of me fearing what might happen if he did, because—what if it *isn't* him I hate? And that's not to say I like him either.

But what if the only thing I hate is the way I feel when I'm with him?

* * *

An hour or so before sunrise, the next day, consciousness comes via the hairs standing on the back of my neck, a sure sign something isn't right in my bohío.

Facing the reed wall my cot leans against, my back tingles with vulnerability. Someone else is in here. Someone who knows how to measure their breathing for maximum stillness.

If it was Delyse, she'd be fidgeting with my things. Hell, she'd have snatched this pillow from beneath my head to wake me up. Ford would have settled behind me and laughed the moment I woke and kicked him to the floor. Sham and Nel would never enter if I didn't answer, which I would have, had someone called me. No, this interloper isn't someone I'd call bredren or sistren.

I let a sigh escape, a winsome sound of someone lost in the throes of slumber, not about to enact a nightmare. Stretching a hand under my head, I retrieve last night's twig-dagger from beneath my pillow. In one maneuver, I roll and lash my arm out like a whip, letting the twig-dagger fly—at *Kirdan*. His conduit flares, almost lazily. An inch from his face, the wood dissolves into ash.

"Did you realize I didn't bring breakfast?"

Falling back against the cot, I expel a breath of relief. I'd envisioned a magic-stealing busha waiting to pounce, or even Doyenne Cariot, after all that happened during All Souls' Night. Kirdan being here, though, is worse.

"Why are you here?" I swing my feet out of the cot and stand. "Again?"

"Presider Caldwell has been found." He stands too, ducking as he moves farther in where the thatched roof peaks. A waft of heady incense, spiced with cinnamon and bay leaf, roils from him.

"Well?" I wipe my mouth; try not to adjust my askew sleeping scarf. "How did the doyenne react?"

"Jazmyne isn't around this morning, and for obvious reasons I can't sit in on council meetings without invitation." He toys with the bone hilt on his hunting knife. Between his fingers it seems impossibly small. "But last night there was some talk between the presiders. Jazmyne thought they might raid—"

"Raid?"

"It was dismissed by the doyenne."

All the same, I knew there was a significant chance she'd blame my order here. Why didn't I warn Delyse? How could I have left the shields in the Cuartel unprepared for a potential *raid*?

"It's in everyone's best interests that you keep a low profile today," Kirdan says. For a second it seems like he means to say more, and I'm reminded why I didn't want him coming back last night, and that I haven't cleaned my teeth, and my undergarments lay in a pile on the floor by my feet, but his conduit beams, and with another secretive almost smile he disappears in a whorl of dark fabric.

Good. I exhale. There are other matters to deal with, this morning.

Ripping off my hair scarf, my nightgown, I wiggle into my uniform, not having anything else to wear for the day of rest we've been granted by proxy, after All Souls' Night. I make quick work dismantling the snare to open my door. Outside, I'm stopped short by Delyse, Sham, Ford, and Nel.

"You're in a rush," Delyse says, eyes scanning every inch of me. "Is something wrong?" Behind her, the others tense for threats.

"I was coming to see you. Come in. I have my answer."

Shamar exchanges a quick look with Delyse; panic's mirrored in the dark hues of their eyes.

"If you'll forgive me, Empress," Ford says, closing the door behind him as he's the last to enter. "But D and Sham said you're worried we're too weak to fight."

Not with words, that's for sure.

"You know my name, Ford."

"I was trying to be respectful." He shoots Delyse a look that screams *I told you so.* "Since we're being ourselves, your reason is stupid. We're tougher than Alumbrar think. And you, apparently."

"Don't make a decision yet," Sham begs, in the face of my silence.

"I told you we've been preparing long before you," Delyse says. "You can't deny us the chance to show you why Obeah are stronger together."

Actually, I can. And I should, but last night, my carelessness could have ended lives. I've been so busy fighting for the dead, I haven't paid attention to the living. And the foursome before me epitomize life, sparring and caring for one another in equal measure. Fighting for this island—fighting for me. I meant to keep my distance, and yet here I am, *feeling* things.

One chance.

I owe them that much. Then I'll tell them no once and for all.

"My mind won't change, you know. But . . . show me what you will."

"Maybe later." Ford shrugs. "I've never been one who takes my intimacy with an audience. A man has to have some standards."

Shamar and Nel gape at him. I can't help but laugh.

"I'll tell you what you can do with those standards." Delyse steps menacingly toward him.

With a parting wink at me, Ford bolts through my bohío door.

Obscured by a heavy cloud bank, sunrise is muted in the village this morning. Magi lean from windows, whispering behind their hands, staring.

"Delyse," I hiss through the side of my mouth. "What did you tell them?"

She doesn't bat an eyelid at the harshness of my tone. "Only that there's going to be a competition. One with a prize they have to see to believe." Humming, she smiles in a frustratingly knowing manner.

Her words, and that out-of-tune humming, wind me tight. Enough that, when we alight in the center of the village, if Ford or Nel look at me one more time . . .

"Welcome all." Sham throws his arms out. "I told everyone here that you thought we were past it, Ira." His eyes glitter with a dangerous promise. "And I have to say, they were more than happy to prove you wrong."

The magi crack their knuckles with a light-hearted menace, jeering with good humor. It's an atmosphere I know well from my days training with my coven in the mountains.

"What's the game?" an Artisan of Cloth calls.

"Bull Inna Pen."

I fight a smile. "I haven't played that game since I was a pickney."

"I'll keep the rules brief then." Sham explains that the game centers around four roles: the mother hen; her chicks; and their adversaries, the Bull and his partner, Bredda Hawk. It's the mother hen's responsibility to protect her chicks from an attack instigated by the Bull and Bredda Hawk as they journey back to their coop. "We can take turns playing the mother hen, Ira; it'll only be fair that we give you the chance for redemption when we beat you."

Nana Clarke made her Warriors-in-training use Bull Inna Pen to practice team leadership skills while under enemy siege. Shamar doesn't need to know that, though.

"I'll remind you what you said when you're licking your wounds later."

That challenging glint in his eye flares. "Minor combat and magic use are permitted to disarm." He waves a witch over; she sports a rolled-up bandanna tied across her forehead. "But we need to be cautious with our conduits. Your objective is to release these." He snatches away the bandanna. An iridescent powder falls over her face. She collapses into his arms, eyes rolling back.

"Sleeping powder." Though the wonder in my voice makes Sham look far too pleased with himself, I can't hide it. I'm impressed.

"It'll only last for thirty seconds. Once your tie's been pulled, you're out. Victory comes when the mother hen and all her chicks make it back to the coop. Think you can handle that?"

"Like most things," I say, "winning is something I do well."

My words are met by a raucous amount of cheering.

We commandeer the entire village to play Bull Inna Pen. Its wizened land and close confines make for the perfect adult playground. With my group of chicks assembled, an assortment of experienced and newer shields, I edge past bohíos filled with observers watching from windows. In this game, as promised, it's me and a small team of chicks against Sham, Delyse, and their allies.

With a cry of triumph, an enemy witch—identified by the bandanna tied across her forehead—charges from the slip of space between the bohíos to my left. I whirl on her, barking orders that my chicks cluster together.

My conduit flickers, fades, my magic skittish at the chance of exposure. Looks like I'm doing things the old-fashioned way. Charging at her before she's had time to draw breath, I kick in the backs of her knees and pin her to my chest. With one arm around her neck, I release the tie across her forehead. The beads shimmer in her lashes, across her nose; faster than she would have if I'd suppressed her airways, the witch collapses. Sleeps.

Checking the way ahead is clear, I order the chicks to walk on. They're immersed in the fantasy of the game. I am too. It's as if the world outside the village doesn't exist, and I'm back at the mountain bohío, competing with my sistren. I double back to loud protestations from more Obeah spectators. They shake their heads in that infuriating way of one who believes they know more than you.

In this moment, though, they might have something.

A shrill scream sounds ahead. Laughter. I weave through a cluster of huts and emerge behind the attackers dragging two of my chicks away. Nel and Ford.

He pushes his chick to her. "I was wondering how many of your team we could take before you'd get here." A wall of air knocks me onto my back. Skidding across the dirt, I will my own to block Nel from leaving with my chicks. It doesn't work. Of course.

Rolling onto my side, I dodge another fist of air and send a cloud of dirt at Ford with my hand. He chokes, face twisting. My laughter is genuine as I kick off the balls of my feet to hook my left leg around his neck, using my right as an anchor to swing him down. At least, I intended to. With both of us snorting like a couple of swine, the move isn't executed as smoothly as it once was. I might catch my toes in the dirt as I kick up; my knee might knock him in the side of his head; we roll, tears streaming, relatively unharmed. He pouts as I snatch his bandanna away. My grin slides off my face when I rise to find my chicks surrounded by the rest of the enemy.

We've been corralled into a trap.

"S'how we do it!" Sham boasts, emerging from behind a bohío. Those hanging out of their windows applaud. Nel shouts commiserations at me. I wave her away. I won't lose this.

"The game isn't over." I will a shield of wind to be erected around my chicks. I will it to force their captors back. Magic thrums through my veins, drawing on the surrounding winds, but it's not through the conduit that my intentions manifest.

An ebullition of white light emanates from my face.

Its heat is both cool and warm, all-encompassing as it spreads like a wave, zinging out and upward until everything is bathed in a supernal light. Unlike the times before when my magic exploded, the urge to rein it in doesn't come. The release is like breathing after an age underwater. And the light—it's like breaking the surface and seeing again.

Far beyond the village, the banana tree fronds magnify as if they're right before me. I catch hints of ochre, mustard, amid their green folds. Geckos scurry up their trunks. One flicks out its tongue; I could count the raised bumps on its surface. And the *smell*. The cleansing salt from the ocean mingles with the estate fruit grove's ripening produce: plantain and mango. Sweetsop and cocoa bean.

When the light clears, blinked away, the game players are on one knee before me, their heads lowered in veneration. Observers from the surrounding windows stumble from their homes and fall before me too. Tears stream down their faces. My own eyes fill with tears too. Last night, this number of magi before me could have been slaughtered in their beds.

In coming here, I always thought I needed to keep my distance—to get in and get out so I could protect my order the only way I know how. But if my distance lands my fellow shields in another situation like last night, avenging Mama and Dada won't make up for the pit their deaths will leave behind.

I know what I have to do.

"I am Iraya Cordelia Adair. First of my name, and only living heir of Empress Cordelia and Admiral Vincent Adair. In another world, I would have been your leader." I draw a shuddering breath. There it is, out in the world. "That world was snatched from us by our enemy, and I mean to make her pay." A low hum of fervor thrums in the packed earth beneath my feet. "I know there'll be magi here wondering why I didn't say anything when I first arrived. Or why I didn't find a way to send a message to the Obeah to keep their hope alive, while I was in Carne." The words pour from an unknown well deep within me. "You lost your leaders. But I lost my family—my will." Tears sting my eyes. I blink them back. "All I can say is, I'm here now, and I mean to bring this palace to its knees. But I can't do that without your help."

Shamar stands and slams a fist over his heart; others follow.

"For you, we'll go into battle, Empress," he vows.

The Obeah don't cheer or applaud, but the determination in their expressions, the passion there, grows like the silent build of a storm in the sky. They view me as their mother hen. Yet I can't help feeling like the jungle-prowler who killed her and donned her flesh as a disguise to walk among them.

I need to control their movements to keep them safe.

Pretending to be Empress Adair is the only way to avenge the dead and protect the living. My order will hate me for my deception when they learn the truth, but by then they'll have the palace and I'll be gone.

Just-Ira.

41

JAZMYNE

"Two cheers for two deaths is a little macabre for Alumbrar," Anya calls from the hearth in her front room, evoking many titters from the gathered Nameless members. "But last night's successes are worth celebrating—our future doyenne is worth celebrating." She turns to me, sitting in pride of place on the love seat before the bay window in her villa. "So here's to Jazmyne Cariot; not only did she save my ass with her quick thinking, but she's saving all our asses." It's with much laughter from her guests that Anya raises the flagon she swiped in place of something smaller. She might be a little inebriated. "To Aiyca's future doyenne."

"To Aiyca's future doyenne!" is returned by all.

Though I raise my tumbler, exchange nods with the exclusive gathering of Nameless Gennas: Stealths, Recondites, and Sibyls, I don't drink from the heady concoction Anya mixed. My stomach still turns at the memory of my last, and I don't believe those gathered would be as forgiving as she was when I threw up down her back miles from home when we fled Black River.

"I'd also like us to raise a glass to Light Keeper," I say. Meritha's name instills a silence, one weighted with respect. "Without whom none of us would be here. And for whom many of us founding members stayed." There are murmurs of agreement; hands are raised in veneration; heads are bowed. "Her death wasn't given the acknowledgment it should have received." My voice grows stronger. "But we know the truth, and we won't allow this island's frustrations to be silenced for much longer. In two phases, I hope to have you all gathered at the Sole, and ready to stand behind me when at last this island will be cleansed as I usher in a new reign of peace. To Light Keeper." I raise my glass. "To you, dear Nameless Gennas, and to the new Aiyca, where Alumbrar need not fear the Yielding."

All in attendance raise their glasses in silent tribute, drinking to Light Keeper, to success, to the fruition of everything we've worked toward.

"Do we still have an audience?" Anya says through her teeth.

"Yeh mon," a Stealth named Winston replies; one of my cabal of six from the tour, he stands with the others around Anya's villa casting a unified guzzu of something close to silence, prohibiting my Xanthippe escort outside from hearing the true extent of our celebration. "They haven't touched their drinks, but the day is hot."

"And young," Anya returns. "All right, turn up the music."

A quartet of magi return to their drums, pans; one player, an Alumbrar-man, blows sweetly on a tiny wooden flute. Guests smile and relax, enjoying curried goat and roti, jerk chicken cooked out back, and caramelized plantain and rum sauce for dessert. Followed by a paean of blessings from my fellow Nameless, I meet Anya in the study at the back of the villa.

"That was well done, sistren." Leaning against stacked crates of books, she sips from her tumbler. "Now that business is over, what did you think of Julie?"

"Which one is that again?"

"The secular Grower, with the big . . . teeth." Anya's grin is wolfish.

"You've started making your way through the new members?" Following the tour, there's been an influx in secular Aiycans joining the Nameless's cause, my cause. "Don't run them off with heartbreak," I warn her.

"Well, so far she's turned down my offers to meet for drinks, for prowler rides, everything." Anya sighs. "I must be losing my touch."

"At least you have a touch."

Definitely tipsy, she does her best to focus on me. "Didn't look like you were doing too badly with the pirate during the tour. What's his name again?"

"Roje."

"Got you." She winks.

My cheeks heat in the face of it.

"It's a shame it's too much to be queen and doyenne."

"You think I could have been Pirate Queen?"

"After all I've seen you accomplish these past few months, I believe you could be anything." Anya salutes me with her drink, before disappearing behind it.

"And I believe that this time," I say to myself, "it's you who has had too much to drink."

Doyenne has proved itself complicated enough without adding queen and the Iron Shore to the mix, I think, when a crash outside makes Anya splash her drink down her front; the music stops. Before either of us can open the door, a knock sounds outside; whoever it is doesn't wait for an answer before coming inside.

"Forgive me, mon." Filmore, one of the Stealth cabal, winces. "Emissary, your Xanthippe guard barged their way in. They're demanding you leave with them, now."

Anya sobers fast. "What is it? What's happened?"

I already know.

"There's been a third Jade Guild attack," he confirms.

IRA

After an afternoon of greeting shield members I'd yet to meet, visiting bohíos, and being robbed of every win in subsequent games of Bull Inna Pen, I find myself alone with Delyse, who dresses me for an evening of food and dancing in the village.

"Quit fidgeting. I'm almost done," she mumbles through a mouthful of pins.

Her fussing isn't the cause of my discomfort.

"Something will happen soon," I murmur, unable to leave her in the dark any longer after a day of light in her company. "Don't ask me what it is, or for more information. It's better I don't tell you." I look away as she pauses to peer up at me. It was she, after all, who told me about the jéges I now seek.

"I wish you'd tell me what ails you." Delyse hesitates for a moment. "Don't you know by now that you can tell me anything?"

I can't decide if I feel relieved or flush with guilt, regardless of my intent.

"Just remember my word."

Needing to move, to get away from eyes that would fill with disappointment if she knew the truth about my plan to leave after the Sole, I cross the small space to stand before the mirror. I still look a little hungry, but strong. Especially since Delyse has dressed me in white—the color of Obeah. Worn for battle, matrimony, death. It's the color of home. She wears it too.

"Where'd you get this?"

"Not everyone dyed their white fabric when the doyenne made that decree."

The slip of material she's tied at the nape of my neck skims mid-thigh, accentuating the length of my legs, their scars. I feel no shame. They show that I've survived, I've fought. A white scarf is wrapped around my braids. Gold bells hang from the fabric, tinkling with my every move. My eyes look large and deep. My brows aren't lowered in a scowl, for once. If I could remember Mama's face, I think she'd have looked like this.

"Come on." Delyse grins over my shoulder in the mirror. It doesn't meet her eyes. "I'm about as starving as Shamar and Ford are going to feel when they see you in this."

Outside, Obeah line the paths at every turn; they too are bedecked in white. Their conduits glow as we walk through the village, meandering beneath the jars filled with witchlights that glimmer like trapped magic.

"I do believe I said I had some things to show you, mon." Delyse loops her arm through mine. "We've had to be smart about our operations here, so everything is hidden in plain sight." She gestures at the bohíos.

"You haven't?"

"The Masters knew you would come. They wanted to be ready for you, and they've made sure we learned what to do too. We conceal weapons, made from scraps stolen around the estate, in the thatch of the roofs; there are maps of Cwenburg, compiled with information from the Masters, rolled tightly and slotted inside hollowed reeds that line walls." She laughs at my expression. "Shamar has a stock of that sleeping powder we used during the game and other more *incendiary* concoctions. It's as I said: we haven't been sitting around waiting for you."

"You knew about Night Prowler, didn't you?"

"Yeh mon." Her voice turns wry.

I laugh. "I never stood a chance at hiding my identity here, did I?"

"I only wish the doyenne never made you feel like you had to."

Liar that I am, I let her believe that was the only reason.

Delyse's arm tightens around my own. "With your naevus, this palace will tremble beneath the Jade Guild's might."

Uncomfortable, I seek distraction from a gathering of Obeah seated before a bohío.

"What are they waiting for?"

"The griot," Delyse says. "You should listen to her. I'll find you later."

Sweet incense coils from the doorway of the bohío as I take a seat at the edge of the gathering. I'm nodding at magi, even smiling a little, when a tinkling sounds from the shadowed mouth of the hut and the griot emerges.

Stooped with age, the witch makes a slow descent down the three steps, lowering her body to sit like she's lived hundreds of years and is approaching her last. She arranges her long salt-and-pepper dreads on the steps beside her, where they drape like a thick rug.

Without warning, her eyes flicker to mine. Pinioned against the sky, even the stars' dominion has to concede to their luminescent coloring. They look like dual moons in the dark plains of her face.

My stomach flips.

She's not just a griot, she's a Bonemantis. Her third eye scarification seems to stare at me from its place between her brows. Dada would tell me bedtime stories about the scrying of her ilk. It's alleged that the ancestors themselves whisper tales in their ears, often enough to drive many of them stakki. There isn't a trace of insanity in this Bonemantis's noble brow, though; she looks learned, sage.

"Tonight," she begins, in a voice that seems both prescient and innocent at once, "I wish to tell a story where the past and future collide." She lets her shawl slip, revealing a dark bosom painted white with deep patwah.

Magi gasp, whispering among themselves. I know some of those whorls. Those deep patwah words of violence, of death, foretell war—a sign? Or is the woad merely part of her theater? There's no way to tell with a Griot-Bonemantis, a magi

403

grounded in fiction but connected to fact.

Her conduit illuminates around her neck. She twists her hands before her, drawing forth a small group of blank-faced magi from its golden light. Her limited magic doesn't allow for any distinctive features, like the griots from my childhood, but seeing her story is such a throwback, I can't help being excited by it.

"As most cautionary tales begin, my story starts with avarice." She draws a gong from a gaping sleeve and sounds it. Its ominous ring reverberates through the earth. "It was first born in the bitter secondary métier to our Adair first family for the power the Mudda bestowed upon them."

So this is a story of fiction. There is no second métier to my family's. Aside from the Adair title, all Obeah scarification is considered more or less equal.

"Overshadowed by the combat between the Obeah and our silver-tongued cousins"—the crowd hisses and spits at the suggestion of the Alumbrar name—"this secondary family's hubris has been lost in the histories of the Adair family's greater witches." A vicious swipe of her hand sees the group of blank-faced magi disintegrate into golden sparks. Magi cheer at the theater. "Though the rule of the first family's matriarchy has been an inimitable one, there have been instances throughout the epochs in which it has come close to permanent collapse. Its maintenance is solely due to two Obeah-witches. The first belongs to the past." The griot winds her hands in elegant shapes, drawing a girl from fizzing sparks. "We refer to her as Boatema, 'she who brings strength.'"

My smile slips.

"A fleck of gold born to the Obeah in the later days of their creation, she grew up alongside a girl who would inherit Xaymaca." A second figure is cast to stand beside the first. "The two remained close as they reached adulthood," the Bonemantis confirms. "And when the empress passed the torch down to her pickney, one of her daughter's earliest acts was to make Boatema her first. Unfortunately, the new empress's reign began during a time of turbulence between Obeah and our silver-haired cousins. Taking advantage of the distraction, the rival family rose against the crown."

The Bonemantis doesn't move, but the atmosphere shifts, tightens. My body draws in. I don't want to miss a thing even though I know this story well now.

"But while the empress was cast from power and exiled to Aiyca's peripheries, she didn't capitulate to the threat of the second family, or the threat of the Alumbrar who sought to take advantage of the fractious relationship between the two families. Not with Boatema as her first. A skilled Warrior, she rallied in the face of the impossible, recruiting from their stronghold of the Blue Mountains." The figure of Boatema multiplies tens of times over, creating hundreds of shimmering figures, Warriors. "From there she created armies, but it was her personal cadre who drew the most fear." The Warriors combine, twisting into a symbol that makes my breath shallow. "Carrying the sigil of bravery, the Aeng horn, this elite band of Warrior witches' name was the Virago."

I feel light and heavy all at once. Dada raised me on stories about the Virago. Mama never liked for me to hear about them and the clandestine role they played in protecting our order. Living in the bush, their time spent fighting and training, they weren't the role models she wanted an already rebellious heir to have.

"Over a period of three years, Boatema spent her time building and training her forces until they were ready for an attack." The Aeng horn expands until it bursts, each bead of light popping to reveal a warrior crouched for attack. "One of such cleverness, the Alumbrar and Obeah family of usurpers did not see it coming. With the empress's position restored, and the family and Alumbrar warned about the dangers of their avarice, Boatema's elite fighters guaranteed years of peace in Aiyca. Though all too soon, that would be challenged once again."

Someone sobs; I blink back my own sudden desire to cry, emotional for reasons I can't think about. Not now.

"Our hope for our future now lies with the second witch—one of bone and briar." Boatema's forces dwindle back down to one witch. This golden figure seems to stare right at me, with her blank, featureless face. "The former haunt her; the latter grow thicker each day. This witch must exercise caution, for when the time comes, she'll be the one atop wings of obsidian who will cast out the malevolence that creeps around this island, eager to choke with its poison of conceit and greed once more."

I swallow. Every magi in attendance is looking at me. The Obeah man beside me, his eyes a beautiful amalgam of green and brown stare up into mine in wonder, in awe. A golden spark flashes on his face. He blinks with a cry, hands leaping up to his eyes. That spark jumps to my face, dazzling me. What is that? Squinting, I look into the village. Gold light flashes from a rooftop in the distance. Once, twice. Once, thrice. My stomach bottoms as I recognize the code. It's a warning. It's a *raid*.

The doyenne's coming.

"Raid." I jump to my feet. "A raid is about to happen! Run, *now*!" My order look back at me with confusion. "The doyenne's coming." I force my voice to stay steady, clear. "If she finds you out here with me, she'll kill you." A few of Shamar and Delyse's bredren and sistren sit among the listeners; I direct my orders to them. "Spread the word, quickly. Make sure people get inside." Springing to their feet, they bound over to where the food is being served, where the music sounds. "What are you waiting for?" I ask those who remain behind.

"What about you, Empress?" a witch says.

Not this. Not *now*.

"I'll leave too." I clasp my hands before my chest, ever the humble monarch, not a witch with claws and fangs.

I walk in the direction of my bohío until I'm out of their line of sight. Breaking into a run, I navigate sharp turns and narrow pathways. The doyenne will send the Xanthippe first. I have to meet them, buy some time for my order to hide the celebration and get inside their homes.

A hulking shadow drops down from the roof ahead of me.

I skid to a stop. Dust plumes around Kirdan's ankles.

He jerks the hood of his cloak down and closes the distance between us with stomping strides.

"Did you really throw a jump-up after our talk this morning?"

"You said the doyenne didn't suspect me."

His brows sit so low over his eyes, I can't tell if they're black or green. "After Presider Magmire's body, the *first*. We didn't have any intelligence on her reaction to Presider Caldwell!" He kisses his teeth, every line in his body taut.

I should have known better. I *do* know better. Gods above. I can't win. If I focus on Mama and Dada, I neglect my order. When I focus on my order, I make mistakes that could cost me avenging Mama and Dada.

"I hate that you're so *reckless* with yourself."

The words pull me out of my head, so similar are they to those he uttered last night.

"If I weren't here, the Xanthippe might have—" He breaks off, steps forward, hand outstretched like he means to touch me, to hold me. "They're closing in on the village." He pulls his hand back. "You need to get back to the bohío, lest she comes and finds you."

This is another game of Bull Inna Pen. One with real threats this time.

Kirdan and I cling to the shadows, pausing at every sound. We're close to my bohío when the first shouts rend the night. *Please*, I offer up, to whoever listens. *Protect my order*. Sandals rustle atop leaves above us. Kirdan places a finger on his mouth in warning.

He can't fight them all without losing his anonymity. But if we wait here, we'll be found. Either by the coven, or the doyenne.

"Be ready to run the moment the last one falls," I whisper.

He reaches over and tugs my hair tie down over my forehead. "We don't want them seeing your scarification." His eyes roam over my face, dip to the white on my body. His throat bobs. Mine does too.

Skin tingling where his calluses, and eyes, brushed, I emerge from the cover of the huts. One of the three guards opens her mouth to warn the others. I fly at her, knocking her unconscious with the hilt of her cutlass. Snatching it from her weak fingers, I set its length across my body as the remaining two size me up.

And then a fourth drops down from the roof with a cry. Stupid. Why give warning that you're landing a sneak attack? She's silenced by a hit to the throat, and another to her stomach. An amber spark of suppression zips past my elbow. I use the cape of the fourth to block a second spark from the watching Xanthippe. The guzzu-limned fabric rebounds the magic. It catches the one in the stomach. She falls and doesn't stir. Kirdan steps out of the shadows, conduit aglow; the last falls to the ground too.

"Go now," he orders. "I'll take care of these bodies. You're not to get in any more trouble." His eyes, black from where I stand, glisten. "Not tonight, at least."

"Thanks."

He nods.

I sprint the last few yards to my bohío. Swinging in through the window, I land in a soft crouch.

"You have less than five minutes to get out of those clothes." Delyse stokes a raging fire in my hearth. She's shucked her whites for her conscript uniform, and there's a determination on her face that doesn't bode well for either of us. "Night watch reported movement up at the palace. She'll be here soon."

Tossing her the fabric she draped over me with such care, I can't watch her throw it to the flames.

"Is everyone all right?"

"You tell me." Delyse leaves the fire to sit on my bed, positioning a board and pieces. "Why are the Xanthippe raiding? Have you done something?" She glances at the door. I feel it too. The prickling against my skin, the sharp tang in my nose. She's almost here.

"What game are we playing?" I ask, ignoring her questions.

Delyse's eyes flit between my own. "Cat and Mouse."

The door to my bohío flies open.

Doyenne Cariot has to tip her head to fit her tall crown beneath the doorway. Three Xanthippe enter behind her; they dominate the tiny space.

Delyse drops to the floor, knees tucked under her chest, hands thrust before her, the back of her neck exposed. I scramble to join her.

"An intruder broke into the estate, infiltrated the palace, killed two of my presiders."

Beside me, Delyse stiffens.

Heels click on the wooden planks next to my ears. "No shield would be stupid enough to challenge my council. Not

410

with the knowledge that death would find them, and any magi helping them, no matter where they sought to hide." The doyenne's shoe presses onto the back of one of my hands, driving my fingers into the rough wood. My teeth sink into my lip in an effort not to snap her foot clean off her ankle. "My coven and I are checking that this intruder isn't being housed anywhere on the estate. You were playing a game, I see." Her foot lifts, and the point of the heel takes its place, plunging into the back of my hand. I whine into my lip. Delyse shifts.

Don't you move, I will her.

"And have you both been playing all day?"

"Not this game, my doyenne," Delyse falsely simpers. "We were with others, in the village, before coming here after dinner. I'm playing the cat, and winning."

"And you, little mouse?" Doyenne Cariot asks me as her heel sinks in farther. Blood pools between my fingers. "How are you taking your loss?"

Pain shoots from the puncture, blitzing up my arm and straight to my head, where it pounds behind my eyes. "With my usual grace," I force out, every word an effort.

"But not with much modesty." The heel drives down, drawing a cry from me. "Be sure to exercise that, little mouse. A sore loser isn't often invited to play any more games." Her heel is freed from my wound with a squelch. I swallow a moan. "Be warned, shields, my guard will comb through every inch of this estate to determine which tagereg killed my presiders. If they suspect one of you to be responsible for risking Aiyca's safety, *all* of you will suffer for it."

The door closes, and once again Delyse is faster than me.

Her brow furrows as she checks my head, my face, before cradling my punctured hand. "I'll get Fatou."

"Just—wait." I could do with the Bush Witch, but what Delyse did, her performance . . . "You lied for me. You risked punishment, death, for me."

"Did you doubt that I would? Even if you weren't my empress, I thought us sistren." She flashes a smile, but it's jittery, forced. "What she said about the presiders . . ." Delyse sucks in a breath. "Did you—"

"Forget what she said." Today reminded me about the thrill of being part of a team, of feeling connected in a fight for something greater than yourself. I won't let my order fall victim to Doyenne Cariot. "Do you remember what *I* said, about being ready to run?" Delyse has had my back since I arrived here. However irritating it's been, *sistren* . . . it would have been an honor to call her such. "Don't ever forget."

43

JAZMYNE

I should be working. After the third attack, and in Light Keeper's parish—a stampede of prowlers who tore through an entire village, trampling tens of magi—Doyenne Cariot decided to appoint three new presiders, lest Ada's and Westira's parishes suffer the same exploitation in their deaths. She wishes for me to weed out the best candidates from a series of applications, but I can't tear my eyes away from Kirdan and Iraya, the thorn growing between us.

They're translating the map on the table in the center of my study with books sourced from the palace library. Days have passed like this; they've barely exchanged words, don't even look at each other, but the tension between them is palpable. Whether it's hatred or more, I can't quite put my finger on. It's said the line is indistinct.

I abandon work in favor of joining them. Iraya's cursive curls and loops across the paper, making it difficult to read.

She said the injury she incurred after that reckless jump-up with the shields is responsible—one she wouldn't let Kirdan heal—but she has other intentions, I'm sure. Like all bandulu, she's never guileless.

"Doyenne Cariot will be visiting another parish the day after tomorrow, making it an optimal time to look for the jége."

Iraya looks across at me with those bottomless eyes, so deep they seem to leach all the light from the room. *She doesn't look at Kirdan like that*, I think sullenly.

"Do you think you'll finish translating the map in time?"

"I'm done now."

"Really?" I reach for the locket around my neck, forgetting I haven't worn it since the taproom. "Where is it?"

"Not on the estate," Kirdan answers, his body stretched across the table to read Iraya's writing for himself. "It's somewhere in the Salt Woods."

Bordering the coast below us in St. Catherine Parish, the Salt Woods consist of mangrove swamps and wetlands. It's about a long jungle-prowler ride from Cwenburg.

I peer at the map, understanding nothing. "Why would it be there?"

"If Anansi is to be believed . . ." Kirdan continues reading from Iraya's notes. She doesn't stop him, I notice. "Someone stole the mirror, and the empress before Iraya's mama obliterated them. She buried the jége beside the thief, cursing their bones to guard the power in its reflective surface."

"How does the mirror work?"

"Like a sentient shield," Iraya says. "If you launch something at it, it rebounds the strength of the magic ten times over."

It will be invaluable in the fight against the doyenne. "I'll have a Healer on standby for when the two of you return."

"You're not coming?"

"When the doyenne is away, I must be her eye here."

"I'll come for you in the night, Iraya," Kirdan says. "It'll be as though you never left your bed."

"Is that so?"

"That's so."

The air becomes charged. I look between the two of them again, oddly uncomfortable.

"I do believe that's all, Iraya. If you go out into the hall, Xanthippe will escort you back to the Cuartel."

She leaves without a word. Kirdan watches her go.

There are cases I studied when I was training to become a Healer about victims who became infatuated with their kidnappers. While the two situations aren't the same, the look on his face reminds me of the drawings in the study book. Her beauty isn't something many magi can ignore, her wide-eyed innocence—however misleading—emphasized by her bridgeless nose, a full mouth always quirked in some smirk or other. And then there are the rings of amber fire around her brown irises—ones in which Kirdan seems to have trapped himself.

It's my fault. I asked him to flirt with her. I thought he'd be stronger than this. No matter. I've done things I never thought I could to secure Aiyca. His infatuation for Iraya won't make those acts be in vain.

I'll take care of whatever is between them myself.

44

IRA

The setting sun stains the surrounding grass crimson with its dying light. The stems sway in the breeze, brushing the tips of my ears where I sit in a crouch.

"Shamar's close," Delyse murmurs beside me. "What are you going to do?"

"Move."

"Can you move and maintain your magic?"

No. It'll dislodge my concentration.

"Thought as much," she chirps in the face of my silence. "You'll have to think of something else. And fast."

Air shifts against my cheek. Its gossamer touch is beset with a warning.

I roll away in time to avoid a flying baton of sugarcane. It smashes against the earth where I just was; pulp and juice glisten like precious stones in the waning light.

"What a waste."

"Really, mon? It doesn't worry you that you're compromised?"

I rise from the stalks. Shamar stands less than twenty yards away. "If that hit me, it would have bruised!"

Conduit shining like a searchlight in the dark, he harnesses his will to pitch another baton my way, then two. They tear through the air, fast. Twisting away, I only just dodge them.

Delyse edges out of the danger zone. "Are you only going to evade?"

"I'll attack you in a minute."

Her laughter coaxes a smile from me as my conduit illuminates. Breathing steadily, I summon my own baton of cane from the pile we're using for target practice, willing the wind to lift my weapon. It does. But rather than zooming toward Shamar, the cane hops and stutters through the air. He runs to meet it, sweeping it aside with a large hand. The scars on his chin stretch with the size of his grin. I can only fall back when he swipes a longer baton at me. Evading, just like Delyse taunted.

But I *can* attack. I'm a Warrior.

Sham's leg snaps forward. I catch it with my good hand. Winking at the surprise in his face, I twist with my hips, forcing him to fall or suffer a dislocated kneecap. He drops. I do too, thanks to the shunt of air behind my knees.

"Cheater," I grumble into his sweaty chest. Rolling off, I stand and dust grass off my legs.

"You started it. We said no combat, bag-o-wire. Only magic."

"Hush, you two," Delyse chastises. "That wasn't bad, Just-Ira. You summoned successfully, and your magic didn't break its banks and nearly blind us this time."

"But it's not enough. You saw."

"This is about control. We'll need your naevus when we attack on the Sole, and you'll need to make sure you don't burn out, that you draw your magic slowly. I'm pretty sure I've been telling you that this past phase." She loops an arm through mine.

Shamar lopes alongside us with an easy gait. One I envy. Everything about me has to be so damn *light*, carefree, lest they suspect anything. The fact that both sides' plans are happening on the same day, at the same time, might turn me gray-haired when all is done.

Beneath Delyse's arm, my Glyph of Connection lights with a sudden bite of pain.

"Trouble?"

"Oh, no." *Only that Emissary Cariot has developed a taste for my blood.* While it saved us from the Rolling Calf, there hasn't been any need for her to use it since then. "The scar hurts sometimes," I lie to Delyse and Shamar. "I have a balm back in the village. I'll see you both in the morning."

Eager to meet Jazmyne, on the chance something has changed with the plan tonight, I break into a run up the hill. Delyse shouts something after me, but I'm too far to hear. Palm trees bend, creaking like old bones as I run along the path snaking around the estate. At the west gate, Xanthippe demand to know my business, and insist on escorting me when

I tell them I'm being summoned by Emissary Cariot. As we walk the estate, Alumbrar pack their things and hurry pickney inside. Overhead the sky's awash with hues of nebulous pewter. There's going to be a storm. Although few in number, when the tropical forces hit, they leave the island bruised and battered all over.

Jazmyne's magical summons directs me to the stables. Inside, jungle-prowlers whine in their stalls, unsettled by the weather. She saddles a sand-prowler near the back. Its clawed feet are the size of its feeding bucket, with nails the length of my wrist. Jazmyne whispers to it, running a hand across its scales. They glisten in a spectrum of yellows, some so pale they're almost silver, others so deep they rival an Aiycan afternoon.

"You summoned, Emissary?"

Jazmyne dismisses the Xanthippe before addressing me. "I'll be off the estate for a while tonight." She gathers her kaftan in a tie, making her legs more accessible. "I wanted you to know in case you and Kirdan meet trouble and can't find me when you return."

"What would you do if you were here? Find someone else to help us? That Healer you promised?" I bypass her indignation to feed her prowler a lettuce leaf. Its tongue coils around my wrist as it draws the vegetation to its mouth, leaving a loop of saliva dripping from my arm. Nice.

"I didn't call you here for *this*." She seems to battle with herself, her words. Which is normal, for her. But in this instance, her face isn't pinched with the usual irritation I like to think she stores just for me.

Inhaling through my nose, I ask the goddess for patience. "Then what?"

"Be careful, tonight. With Kirdan. There's something I haven't told you. I—I didn't think you'd trust me right away, but Kir, well. You've seen him." She breathes; it's replete with girlish want—whimsy.

"This is something you should record in your diary, Emissary."

"What I'm saying is, I wanted your help. As one of your ilk, I figured Kir would be the one you'd feel most comfortable listening to. Perhaps falling for. He agreed. Since All Souls' Night, the two of you have looked close, and I thought I should remind you about that warning you so generously bestowed on me, that night in the sentry bohío."

"Oh, you did?"

"Yes. Whatever Kirdan did to make you feel like you could trust him, forgive him. Forgive me."

She meant for him to seduce me?

This, from her, is a surprise. I'm almost impressed.

"I like to think my taste is more refined than Zesian bag-o-wires, Emissary. So you can abandon the false apology. Whatever your true motives were—embarrassment?" I take a step toward her; she backs up, almost losing her footing to the bucket. "To catch me off guard?" Another step makes her dodge the sand-prowler's head to put herself on the other side of its body. "To make me bemoan the times he and I spent together that meant so much to me?" I snort. "Whatever they were, you've failed. I suggest you leave the scheming to those who have a better propensity for it." I spin on my heel, leaving without dismissal.

Outside the barn, away from her eyes, shame flashes red-hot across my face.

She almost had me.

There were moments when Kirdan would look at me, and it felt like the start of something significant. That evening, after hiding Caldwell's body, had I let myself . . . *Cha!*

Jazmyne would have had a good laugh. And that, really, is what stings most about the entire affair. She thinks she's made a mockery of me, thanks to *him*. I picture his duplicitous face and wonder what sounds it would make if I smashed my fist into it.

Girlish want?

Whimsy?

The Salt Woods might be an excellent place to find out.

"You found the clothing."

Having sifted into my bohío behind me, Kirdan doesn't see me wrest to find the control I've been searching for since leaving Jazmyne in the stables. When I turn to look at him, standing in the place he's stood so many times before, looking at me in the way he's started to recently, it's a struggle for me not to punch him in his silver-tongued mouth.

"Are you ready?"

"Are you?" I pose.

"Can't wait." His mouth lifts in a small, secretive smile that makes me want to burn this bohío down with him inside. How many times has he laughed at me? "Have you said anything to your fellow shields?"

"Are you really questioning how many faces *I* have?"

"No, I was—they could come looking for you."

"Don't worry about my order." Striding toward him I proffer a fist. "Let's go."

Opening his mouth as if he means to ask me what's wrong, he seems to think better of it. One of his hands encloses my wrist. The gleam of his conduit illuminates the concern in his expression before we disappear. The magical leap is disorienting enough that I grip his forearms with my spare hand impulsively. Losing hold of your anchor during sifts can disintegrate limbs, or leave magi trapped in the folds of space the magical transport takes us through. We reappear on a dark road, overgrown on either side with bush. Immediately I shove away from Kirdan.

Giving me an odd look, he whistles. A thicket parts, and a great cat slinks out—a Zesian shadowcat, and a female, the marks behind her ears tell me. I don't have to stoop to inspect them either; she's taller than me; and her tail lashes the air above my head. Richly obsidian, she could be a living shadow with teeth and claws. The iridescent variants of aubergine in her glossy coat indicate her coveted thoroughbred status as one of Zesia's Panera felines. She's stunning, and I instantly want to stroke her.

Still—

"We're not riding all that way on one mount?"

"I don't have the gold to sift us there, and I couldn't take any prowlers, or a carriage, from Cwenburg's stables without incurring suspicion. But Niusha's strong enough for four magi." At the sound of her name, the feline turns her great head to look at her master with loving eyes the color of pewter, unfurling a great pink tongue to lick him. "Her name means 'good listener.' You can take the reins."

That's not the problem.

When I swing my way up on top of Niusha's back using the stirrups, Kirdan sits behind me. Too close behind me. The rough cotton of his cloak flutters over my bare shins; it takes every muscle in my body not to shove him from atop the shadowcat, follow, and beat him to a bloody pulp for trying to play me at Jazmyne's request.

For still looking at me like he sees all the parts I hide from everyone else.

"You're trusting, giving me these," I say, holding the reins.

Kirdan shifts behind me; his thighs brush against my legs. "Am I?"

"Yes," I grind out, my entire body stiffening. "Blood beneath my fingernails is always a bother; with these reins I could choke you to death without getting a drop on me." I dig my heels into Niusha's flank, tugging her around toward the Salt Woods before her wide paws break their stride.

Let him think about that for the next few hours.

45

JAZMYNE

Beneath me, Joshial plods steadily onto Main Street in Ol' Town. Though we're followed by Filmore and two additional Nameless Stealths from the cabal, they keep their distance, and their jungle-prowlers' paws are quieter against the stone, making this visit redolent of the last Joshial and I took close to two months back now. After three Jade Guild attacks, fear lingers on these streets with the pressure of the rain that will soon fall overhead.

When we arrive, I tie Joshial's reins to a witchlight post. His pink tongue unfurls at the sight of giant moths divebombing the bulb. Trusting the Stealths will catch up, I check the stretch of abandoned avenue before I take off like a duppy in search of a host.

Muted yellow witchlights blink sluggishly from the windows of my destination. The entirety of Ol' Town's missing patrons seem to be jammed inside the drinking house, playing cards, gambling. My shoulders lower from my ears; the tightness at the base of my spine eases. Here I am one of many, and numbers will help should this meeting turn disastrous.

I elbow my way through magi who are sloshing watered-down alcohol over their companions, skirt puddles and choking clouds of smoke until I reach the booths to the left of the grime-coated windows. My guest's already waiting, convivial grin and tankard in tow.

"Emissary." Roje rises with a swish of leather. Though he smiles, it doesn't meet his golden eyes. The black mourning band around his arm makes sure of that. "Care for a drink?"

"No, thank you." Sliding into the booth, I wish there was a more elegant way to scoot across the cracked seat. My cape catches under my legs, tugging my hood down. Freed, my curls spring around my face. "And call me Jazmyne. Please. I've told you that before."

"As you wish." Roje sits. Beneath the narrow table between us, his knees push against my own. I scoot farther into the booth, my cheeks prickling with heat. "Though first names feel a little informal considering the conversation we're about to have. I always preferred surnames in a fight. Speaking of, where's your Zesian ally? Waiting to ambush me outside?"

"What?"

"Your missive was kind enough, but I'd rather we just hashed it out now so I can get back to the Iron Shore." Roje grips the tankard between his fingers but makes no move to drink from it. "We're spitting pirates from our teeth like sweetsop seeds." His words are harsh and confusing, given where we left things, but his eyes . . .

"When did she go?"

He leans back with an exhale. "Too recently."

"Loss is lonely, but you're not alone."

Kirdan told me that one of the first times he found me crying into one of Madisyn's scarves. Disloyalty worms through my core at the thought of him. He won't approve of what I'm about to do.

"Chance would be a fine thing." Roje snorts. "Where's the Zesian? And your Stealth sistren?"

"Not here. I wanted to talk with you alone, about the race for Pirate Queen."

"Listen, mon; I'm sorry. I had no idea what Vea's death would incite. If it helps, you have a couple of months to ready yourself for the siege. But if I were you, I'd—"

All noise in the taproom fades. "I'm sorry—siege?"

The table creaks beneath Roje's weight as he leans forward, scrutinizing me. "You don't know, do you?" He glances around. "That Zesian really isn't waiting for me. I thought you called me here because you knew about the storm brewing in the wake of Vea's death."

My stomach jolts at the grim look on Roje's face. "Tell me."

"She spent the past few years protecting Aiyca. I thought it was a matter of pride over its proximity to the Iron Shore. Turns out it was one of your sister's wishes that should anything happen to her, Captain keep you, and in turn Aiyca, safe."

My eyes fill with tears. "I didn't know."

"That makes two of us. Vea left a letter, to be read after her passing. It contained a warning." His face becomes graver. "Now she's gone, Aiyca's no longer under her protection, and the waters' most notorious pirates, many of whom already dwell within the Floating City, have plans to plunder this island for the Conduit Falls as soon as the new queen sanctions it. She'll be elected in months. Maybe sooner."

I grip the edge of the bench so hard it's a wonder it doesn't snap off and disintegrate into pieces in my hand. "But—" *Doyenne Cariot is the only one who knows where the Falls are.* I almost reveal what Kirdan told me. "No one knows where it is," I amend. "What makes you think you'll find it?"

"We're in the business of gold. And an endless waterfall filled with it, or made from it, depending on the legend, might as well have *pillage me* carved all over it."

"Does Doyenne Cariot know?"

"Why would she?" His upper lip curls in a sneer. "Sorry, mon. I know she's your mama. But as far as she's concerned, the Obeah are the threat who have kept my ilk away. She'd never have thought of Vea helping to keep Aiyca safe." Roje lifts the tankard to his mouth. I watch his throat bob as he pulls and pulls from its depths. "There's no love lost between the Obeah and my bredren and sistren, as you know, but when the pirates flood this island, it's unlikely that they'll object. Not if we can give them magical freedom in exchange for fealty." He lays a rough hand atop one of mine where it grips the table. "I'm sorry, Jaz. I wish things could be different, but you have time to get away."

"I'm not running." My voice sounds far away, muffled. "Back me."

"What?"

I'd planned fancy rhetoric to dazzle him, but Aiyca under siege? Pirates allying with Obeah? Alumbrar—what, run out with their tails between their legs? No.

No.

"Back me, for queen."

Roje's features soften. He takes back his hand. I grab it, pin it between mine. "Next moon phase, I'll be doyenne of Aiyca. Regardless of what you think the Obeah will do, those with magic will be under my control. Imagine meeting that power in battle, as you will, should you stand against this island. Or, imagine allying with that power, as you could, with me as your queen." It seemed an unnecessary complication in my quest for doyenne, but Kirdan's loss of focus is a risk I can't afford. I must guarantee Aiyca for myself, and Pirate Queen will do that. "Let's not be enemies, you and I, Roje."

His fingers twitch beneath my own. "I've given the crew's backing to someone else. Someone who knows our ways."

"Rescind it."

"What do you have that would make me?"

"I told you, Zesia. Obeah—"

Roje's hands engulf mine, tug me forward. "I came tonight because I do not fear the Zesian," he murmurs. "And I told you how the Obeah will react. What can you give me?" His eyes dip to my mouth. For a reckless moment, I consider throwing myself at him. I've already allied with my family's greatest enemy, made threats against her ilk to force her into compliance, and sentenced others to death, including my own mama. What's my body?

I only hope the Stealths heeded the order I gave them before we left Cwenburg to stay outside. I don't want them to see this.

"The Falls. When I'm doyenne, I'll—" *Receive a magic scroll with details about where the conduit gold is sourced from?* "I'll know where they are," I lie, a professional now. "I can give you gold. I can give you a seat beside me on my council." My heart thuds, my legs are water, but I look at his mouth too. "There isn't anything I wouldn't give to protect my home."

His thumb drags a rough course across the back of my hand.

I shudder, feverish. "Will I have your backing?" We're so close now, I taste the rum on his breath. A warning of the last time I allowed myself to become intoxicated. I lean in all the same, close enough now that all he'd have to do is—

Roje stands abruptly, sidesteps out of the booth. Those golden eyes are more alive now as they take in my hair, the rise and fall of my chest. Does he see my desperation? Is that why the corners of his mouth curl up in a smile that promises dark, wicked things?

Or was it me promising dark, wicked things?

"I'll be in touch."

46

IRA

Niusha slows with my gentle croons, purring in response.

A bone's throw away from the Salt Woods, Carne Sea ripples silver in the moonlight. From our vantage point at the maw of the towering tangle of bracken and roots, we're hit by the spray from its waves as they smash against the sand, restless in the stirring winds of the squall that has yet to break this rainy season.

With some coaxing, Niusha enters the mangrove swamp. Her paws move silently through the waist-high grass. Whiskers twitch on either side of her wide head. I too am alert for gators. The stink of death's ripe in here. Kirdan unsheathes his blade behind me. I take the witchlight lantern he proffers without a word. There's been little conversation since we left Cwenburg. The Warrior must be smarter than his past actions suggest.

We ride past tree trunks twisted like faces frozen mid-scream; when birdsong sounds, it's shrill and sinister.

Although Kirdan's muttered guzzu keeps the eyes following us at bay, the jungle on either side of the overgrown path seems to ululate. I wonder if I'm the only one unable to determine if the cries belong to the hunter or the hunted.

"We'll need to leave Niusha here," Kirdan says when we're deep enough in that I can't hear the crash of waves any longer. "The ground's suction will become too much for her with our weight."

We dismount; I withhold my screams of agony at the burning between my thighs. It's been a long time since I've ridden, and I can't say I've ever had a hulking soldier pressed against my back for the duration of the journey.

I held myself away from him as best I could, but the motion and pace soon forced me back into the hard wall of his chest again and again; it could have been my mind, but I thought his legs squeezed closer at times, and his arms on either side of my body, hands gripping the saddle pommel between my legs, enclosed me in an embrace that felt too intimate after everything Jazmyne told me.

Kirdan takes in how I stand, on the balls of my feet, the right ahead of the left. With a sigh, he gathers his hair in a tie at the nape of his neck. "She told you what she asked of me."

"I'd give you a treat if I had one."

"Iraya—"

"So you're not only an Alumbrar lapdog, but you're one of their whores as well. A *gallin*." I spit the slur at him. "I could have saved you the embarrassment and told you you're not cut out for romance and seduction. Not when you're plagued by the overriding stink of your treachery—*that's* what I hate about you. You are a *traitor*."

Kirdan averts his gaze, his mouth a thin line. "There's that infamous Obeah tongue, and it's still as hypocritical as I remember." He tugs his cloak's tie, letting it fall to the earth behind him. "I wasn't going to defend myself, because you're partially right: I have acted as Jazmyne asked. But—did you think I wouldn't find out about you, Iraya Cordelia *Boatema* Adair?"

My ancestor's name rings like a herald from the Aeng horn she carried into battle.

"I know you shirked your responsibilities to your mama in favor of training with your dada's family, the Virago."

The Salt Woods seem to fall silent at that final revelation.

How does he know the secrets I alone have carried like a weight these ten years? That it isn't enough to be the daughter of an esteemed empress, I am also a great-granddaughter of an acclaimed Warrior and protector? That I have disappointed my family in all ways?

"Don't," I whisper, maybe even plead.

No mercy is visible in Kirdan's face. "Imagine the stories I heard when I spent my youth training in Zesia's military. The matron in charge of my cabal would go on, at length, about the group of elite girls in Aiyca who trained with a legendary coven of Obeah Warrior witches. She always warned us that they'd hand our asses to us, should we ever be unfortunate enough to meet one, never mind a coven of them. When the Obeah ruled this empire, the Virago personified the very best part of them. Their drive, honor, and vow to protect made them unassailable—goddess-like." He charges forward, posturing like the giant ape crabs that dwell in these wetlands, large enough to swallow a magi whole. "So my question to you, Iraya Cordelia Boatema Adair, is that if you were willing to abandon your role as empress to live a life in the shadows, protecting your order in a coven your ancestors created, how could you have sworn into the doyenne's Shield Initiative, and then turned your back on the very magi waiting for you to free them from the Vow of Peace?"

My mouth's dry, enough that the stagnant bodies of water around us look appetizing.

I could tell him, now he's said their name, figured out my role within my ancestors' legendary coven, that I was silence-bound by an oath, one that forbade me from discussing my covert role as a sistren of shadow and staff.

But then he speaks again.

"Imagine if your parents lived."

My burgeoning urge to share shrinks.

"How would they feel?"

"Don't you dare."

"What, challenge you? Or get close to you? Close enough to see that it's never been me you've hated, Iraya. It's *feeling* that you hate, because with feeling comes guilt. And two months of living with an order you forsook, an order who look to you to lead them out of their service to her, that guilt twisted its way to hatred. You hate yourself." The emerald in his eyes cuts right through me. "Perhaps you always have."

With a snarl I force him back with my fists, blocking his attempts to attack with quick hits to his ribs and abdomen. His body's hard, but I will see it give. Between the thud of flesh, the whirlwind of elbows and knees, he looks at me with something like pity. Incensed enough that he blurs before me, I release a little more, pushing forward, swapping between my left fist to hit with my equally strong right.

Kirdan draws his saber. I cartwheel away before the song of silver can touch me, but I land badly. My ankle goes over and I fall flush against the sodden earth. Air whooshes from my lungs. Muddy water splashes on my face, reeking of sour rot.

"Do you feel better now?" Kirdan exhales, looming over me with the malice of the storm brewing in the sky. "Does fighting me make your lack of fight for the Obeah easier to bear?"

I'm humiliated by the traitorous tears that prick my eyes. "You have no idea what it feels like to—" I cut myself off. "You know what? I don't owe you a damn thing. Zesia didn't help us. You didn't help! You left!"

Kirdan's facial expression switches between contempt and pity. I'd rather have the former. "You speak like you can't see you haven't helped either. Not on the estate, and not in Carne. Stick within a hundred yards all around. The mirror's here, somewhere. We need to leave before first light." His footfalls are heavy as he strides away.

It takes every ounce of latent strength I possess to stand, breathe myself calm, and dismiss the memories Kirdan no doubt sought to raise to distract me. I could kill him for that. I could strip the skin from his bones without the aid of a blade.

I might just do it, kill him, as soon as I unearth the mirror.

As I did in the Adair tunnel, I call on the spirits connected to the jéges. "Ta'k na mi, arik na mi. Honti yu ye?"

This time, they answer without delay. "*Na hunty yu cohn yeh fi?*"

"Show me the Mirror of Two Faces. Please."

The Salt Woods' heat intensifies, a film of sweat coats my body. Something stirs within my core. A magical pull, like a hook burrowed in my stomach.

The ancestors who battled here, they're drawing me to the jége.

Locating the mirror is a race against Kirdan rather than the departing night. That tether looped around the core of my magic gives a sharp tug. I splash across the saturated earth, climbing roots that twist and curl until hands force me down. Dropping to my knees in waist-high grass, I dig and exhume a circular wooden box; within it, protected from damp, an antique golden mirror sits. The handle is delicately incised with tiny renderings of the same dialect from the map that led us here. I peer into its dull face; my reflection doesn't appear. From within the box, something calls to a part of me I didn't realize was absent. It hums an intricate weaving of sharps and flats, haunting and resonant.

I slide a hand underneath the layer of velvet. My fingers scrape something else—

"Iraya!" At the sound of Kirdan's voice, I start, almost dropping the box. "Small up!"

A bolt of wind slams into me, knocking me across the ground in time to miss the cutlass that zooms past my face. The momentum knocks me down a swampy verge; between rolls, I notice a gathering of shadows at the top of the hill.

"Anansi got it wrong." Kirdan appears across from me, his magical sift reducing distance to nothing more than a fold in a map. "There's no undead guard here. These magi are zealots hunting for the jéges."

"How'd they know to find one here?"

"Does it matter?" he breathes. "Just get the mirror back to Niusha." He hands me a thin rod about the length of my forearm. "Press the tip!" he shouts, running to meet a parry from one of the masked assailants.

The tip of the bat dips with the force of my thumb, expanding to a staff. There's a shout. Two more masked assailants, shrouded in gray, bear down across the marshlands. Tucking the box under my arm, I use the staff to vault myself across a body of stagnant water; gators' eyes follow, their mouths open in anticipation. Landing with a roll and a crunch, the bones in the acquisitive earth spur me onward just as much as the momentum of the move.

I feel the closeness of my pursuers in the agitated cries of the bough-prowlers living in the canopy. The earth rears upward. My calves scream in protest as I force myself to sprint the slope, zigzagging a tangential course through the bracken to avoid any further weapon throws, but my legs tire. They catch up. One charges. I snap the metal of my gifted staff into the center of their chest, gritting my teeth at the contact reverberation traveling up my arms. They stumble back, narrowly avoiding their partner. I'm granted the time to dart to higher ground before they both dart in, cutlasses wielded with a wild zeal.

I drop, rolling across the damp earth. On my knees, my elevated staff meets metal with a double *thwack* that jars my shoulders, my back. Another blade whistles past my head. Too close. They dance back. While I can't see their eyes, I feel the hunger of their focus. Zealots, Kirdan said. Delyse spoke about a hunt for the jéges—but how did they know to find one here when we have the map?

Were we followed?

A stone rolls across our paths, delineating a line in the spindly stalks of grass.

The magi communicate with urgent hand signals before the stone explodes, its bang deafening. I'm flung backward, ears ringing. Strong hands seize my arms and tug me to my feet. Through my muffled hearing I register a familiar voice. When he takes my hand, however much it pains me, I don't let go.

Coughing doesn't help the ringing in my head as Kirdan and I sprint back to where Niusha awaits. Astride her back, we spring and bound through the long grass like a fired arrow with Cwenburg in its sights. Who were those magi? I didn't see any gold on them, but only Obeah could fight like that.

"You good?"

By my ear, Kirdan's breathless question is hot and close, and then I can't think of anything else but him at my back, his body low against mine as he urges Niusha on, his arms around me like I still mean something to him—no. I didn't mean anything to him.

"Iraya?"

"Do not," I bite out, "say my name."

Though his weight is still there, his breath, inexplicably I feel Kirdan pull back as my words sever whatever nascent tie might have connected us.

* * *

This time it seems my request that Kirdan leave me alone sank in.

We spoke only once more, during the ride back to St. Mary, when I asked him not to sift me into my bohío, and he agreed. The moment we bounded up to the estate, after he settled Niusha with a bowl of water beneath a lid of stone, he sifted us to the Adair Graveyard, where he merely held out his hand for the box with the jége. Once I dropped it into his waiting palm, he blinked back out of sight.

Not disappointed in the slightest, I slip out that which I stole from the box—a second mirror. It's hardly my fault if Kirdan didn't interpret Mirror of Two Faces correctly. I place it in my running bag I've stashed in a shallow grave beside one of the tombs, and cut through the grass for my tree.

My bohío is in sight when the first Xanthippe steps out of the darkness in the village.

More surround me from all sides, conduits aglow and cutlasses raised.

"Doyenne Cariot wishes to speak with you," one witch says.

"About what?"

"Your role in the bruckout that happened here, this evening."

47

JAZMYNE

After my parley with Roje, Joshial and I ride back to Cwenburg with the cadre where we learn a bruckout occurred. The shields rose against the Xanthippe, one of the coven informs me, in an unexpected attack with several casualties. I am stunned stupid. Did Iraya order this?

Kirdan isn't in his rooms, or mine, when I hasten upstairs in the palace. What I do find on the console table in my foyer, though, is a note from Anya. Wild-eyed and breathless, I meet her in the Corridor of Power, a narrow stone aisle between Doyenne Cariot's study and the Witches Council Chamber.

Tense on a stool before a golden vent embedded in the wall, she chews on sugarcane with a furious zeal, spitting the remains into a bowl before popping the next piece in.

"Doyenne Cariot arrested Iraya, for the Cuartel bruckout."

"*What happened?*"

"With the shields? No idea." Anya peels her focus from the vent, the view it provides over the doyenne's shoulder. "Something set them off though. The council has been going back and forth about what to do with Iraya for the past hour. They're holding her responsible."

"Doyenne Cariot actually said her name? She said *Iraya*?"

"No, but she can't. Not with the bargain she made after Carling Hill, right?"

"Right." I'm the one who told her I suspected the bargain of stoppering the doyenne's tongue. "Then how can you be sure they're discussing Iraya?"

"Listen for yourself."

Snippets of conversation float through the vent.

"—know she was alive!"

"Carne is a vast place, my doyenne."

Anya and I stare at one another; my heart sinks.

In the same breath, I'm so confused. Why would Iraya arrange for a fight the night she was away from the estate with Kirdan? Was she hoping to use the jége against the doyenne? Against him and me?

"We weren't to know one survived," floats through the vent.

I recognize Presider Antwi's whiny voice.

"Vast it may be, but this is why I have a council, so mistakes like this aren't made!"

Something smashes inside.

Anya and I, shoulder to shoulder, push our faces closer to spy.

"In those early days, we were busy settling in the parishes,"

Presider Antwi stutters. "W-we missed her. But it isn't too late to rectify our mistake."

"Mariama is right, Doyenne," Presider Lewis croons. "Now we know she lives, we can kill her."

I grip Anya's hand.

"A message does need to be delivered." Doyenne Cariot's chair drives away from the table, screeching against stone. She's forgone a crown tonight and instead bears a headdress of antlers draped with golden chains. "Leave me now, sistren. I have work to complete tonight."

The presiders file out of the chamber behind her, exchanging worried looks—Anya lands one of her own.

"Will the doyenne kill Iraya?" she asks.

"She can't." My voice is hoarse, pleading. "Not until she has all the jéges."

"That still seems like an awfully big gamble, Jaz. Are you *sure*?"

"I'll go and talk with her," I decide. "I have to do something, say something."

"Wait—maybe you don't have to. How did the conversation with the pirate go?"

The one where I learned the entire Iron Shore will set sail for Aiyca in several months?

"It wasn't a no, but it wasn't quite a big enough yes to mean we don't need Iraya."

Her disappointment makes the outcome of my conversation with Roje even worse. The current Yielder guzzu will hold, for several additional months, but under constant attack? And then I don't know what Vea might have prevented the pirates from firing at the Defense Force's ships.

"I'll meet you in my rooms."

Fleeing the Corridor of Power, I intercept Doyenne Cariot around the corner from the Council Chamber. "I just learned about the bruckout," I breathe.

"Then you already know you failed to watch Iraya. I'll deal with you later." Imperious, she makes to sweep past me, but I block her again.

"I have watched her. She's been searching for something."

The doyenne stares down at me; her eyebrows raise in surprise.

"You were told to inform me of her actions."

"I was waiting to see if I could learn what she sought," I lie. "Do you have any idea what it may be?"

Her eye edges past me, staring off somewhere far. "A weapon." Her focus flickers back to me, probing and alert. "It took the Xanthippe a while to find her, tonight. . . . Are you sure she's been searching the estate?"

I nod, not trusting my words.

The crack of palm meeting flesh makes my head fly to the side and steals my breath away. My hand flies to my face; my eyes fill with tears.

"You should have mentioned this earlier, Emissary."

"F-forgive me."

"I need you to prepare a statement about what happened tonight," she orders, her voice barely above a whisper. "A fire broke out in the Cuartel. It wasn't an attack. It wasn't the Jade Guild."

"I will." My face aches. "And Iraya?"

"I alone will deal with her," Doyenne Cariot says, and then she takes her leave.

On the long walk to my rooms, cheek smarting, I ask the first attendant I come across to bring a bowl of ice chips and a cloth to wrap them into my rooms. She meets me just before I enter, not ten minutes later. Weary, I press the cold compress to my throbbing cheek. It's been a long while since the doyenne's hit me; I'd forgotten that the lingering sting is far worse than the initial shock.

In my receiving room, Anya and Kirdan stop their arguing when they catch sight of me.

"That bitch." The former peels the compress away from my face. "What happened?"

"I told her Iraya was looking for the jéges, in fewer words."

"A truth within a lie," Anya says. "And maybe the only thing that will keep Iraya alive."

I have to believe I've done enough.

Kirdan stands away from us. "Your cheek?"

"It barely hurts anymore," I lie. "Do you know what happened with the shields?"

He shakes his head.

"It wasn't Iraya?"

"When I picked her up, all was well."

"Did you get the mirror, at least?"

He removes a box from inside his cloak, places it on the coffee table.

Thank the goddess.

"Will you go and learn Iraya's fate?" I ask Kirdan. He

grimaces; it's faint, but I catch it and it makes my heart sing.

"If she's responsible for what happened tonight," Anya says. "She's a fool."

Kirdan gathers his cloak to leave. "If she's responsible for what happened, she's dead."

48

IRA

For as long as I'm sat in Cwenburg Palace's holding cells, the glyphs zapping my energy with every minute that passes, I don't come any closer to figuring out what bruckout the Xanthippe were referring to when they stole me away from the Cuartel.

It might not matter, in the end. Not when the Shook Bargain around my wrist congratulates me for my forethought. Jazmyne has to come. She doesn't have a choice until our agreement has been met. As if spoken into existence, some distance from my cell a door bangs open. I settle back, pick flakes of dirt from beneath my nails. But it's not Jazmyne's quick steps or Kirdan's steady tread echoing down the stretch of cells. Four Xanthippe march into view. In the center of their quad, spite demonizes Delyse's appearance as she spits slurs and struggles against invisible bonds. Sham is compliant beside her. The guard locks them in separate cells opposite mine.

I wait for the thud of the closed door before I force my glyph-weakened limbs to crawl over to my cell's bars. Delyse does the same; her eyes are puffy bruises, and something about her shoulder isn't quite right. My stomach lurches. She's been in a fight—the bruckout is real.

"What happened?"

"Where were you?"

"What?"

"Where. Were. You. Tonight? We couldn't find you, assumed the worst—that the thing you told me would happen happened, and you'd been *taken by the doyenne.* So we fought." She shrugs, and then winces.

I can blink at her, blindsided.

My tongue's dry when I run it across my top lip; the skin there's salty. Bitter. "How are the others?"

"Being punished, because they rallied against Xanthippe at your cry."

"I didn't ask any of you to rally." As the words leave my mouth I'm disgusted by them, but that doesn't make them any less true. "In fact, I ordered the exact opposite."

Delyse's laughter turns to a damp-sounding cough. "You're not that stupid, Ira. What did you think would happen when we couldn't find you?"

"I imparted an *order.*"

"One an empress would never mean," Sham adds, his voice husky like he's catching a cold. Or he's been choked. He sits beyond the reach of the dim glow of the witchlight sconces. "No shield was going to let any harm befall you. Least of all

446

me. We live to protect you, to protect Aiyca."

"I was protecting *you*!"

"Then you should have told us the full story. Whatever it is." Delyse levels me with a look of disappointment that's so heavy, I feel it rest atop the left side of my chest. "I knew it was strange when you arrived here and didn't tell us who you were, even after you told us about the doyenne's threat, but I didn't listen to my own instincts because I was so damn happy to finally have our leader here. I should have listened, though, shouldn't I, *sistren*?"

The endearment is wielded with an edge this time.

"What is it?" she pushes. "What aren't you telling us?"

I've told so many lies, I don't know how to navigate the truth. Do I tell them I was trained in war, not court etiquette? Am I supposed to share how it felt to be born into a life that meant I'd grow up to inherit an empire? How do I tell them that in becoming empress, I would've had to send my soldiers out to die but I wouldn't go myself? How can I convey the weight of that expectation? The pressure of all those lives across my shoulders like an inescapable yoke.

The only family member who understood the freedom my blades afforded me isn't here, and neither are the Virago sistren who shared my affinity.

"Iraya!"

"It doesn't matter," I finally mutter.

"You owe us the respect to try and explain."

The holding cells' door bangs open once more. Delyse and I retreat from our respective bars. Six Xanthippe come to a stop outside my cell. Two tug me out.

The glyph-incised walls aren't solely responsible for my body's heaviness, nor are they entirely to blame for my inability to look at Delyse and Shamar as I'm dragged away.

They take me to the doyenne.

Inside Dada's study, she stands at the side of his lignum vitae desk, staring out the bay window behind it. Dada adopted that position more often than not. He always loved the views of the gardens from this window. I doubt Doyenne Cariot appreciates the Strawberry Hills rising like a herb crust in the distance. The desk's monolithic slab of wood is from a tree Dada and I felled where they grow at the base of those hills. That day, my fingers and mouth were stained with berry juice while he told me about the strength I could seek from my family tree. Whenever I felt lost, he said, or unsure about who I was, I could anchor myself to the knowledge that I was a giant among magi. Limned with more strength than I ever knew.

Drawing myself up to my full height, several inches taller than the doyenne, I hold on to his words now, anchoring myself like the sacred giants outside.

"This might surprise an arrogant Obeah, but I'm not so naive as to think that you're wholly exempt from what's plagued this island since your arrival: death and insubordination. Even though you might not have perpetuated any acts yourself—" She turns and stares at me, as though half waiting for a confession.

I stay quiet. Of course she'd suspect, but she has nothing concrete on me. Jazmyne and Kirdan would have sequestered me away if she had facts, if only to save their own necks.

"I can't help questioning the timing," the doyenne continues, her eye still boring into my own. "I wasn't ignorant about what it would mean to have you here. I have always known your motives, Obeah. Revenge. Retribution. Puerile notions of heroism for your order." She makes a slow prowl across the study to stand by my side. "If you were able to see beyond the end of your own nose, you would have remembered that I promised you death would not be your release, *tagereg*."

With her final word, control seeps from my limbs like blood from a wound too quickly to stanch. It burns with magic, but what? Which guzzu has she cast on me?

"Bring them in."

Shields I recognize from the Cuartel file into the study along with more familiar faces. All twelve or so are bruised or bloody from the fight they led in my name. The line extends beyond the door and into the hallway. Somewhere deep within my consciousness, my internal self screams as the doyenne's punishment becomes clear. She means for me to watch her harm them. Possibly *kill* them.

My shoulder jerks, as though it has a mind of its own. Absentmindedly I rub it, trying to think of a way to free my order. Then my leg kicks out, twice, almost taking me off my feet. Is this the guzzu? Which enchantment would do this?

Oh.

Oh no.

"The loss of control is never a pleasant feeling," the doyenne says, with an unbearable sweetness as her enchantment locks its claws in my mind and hastens to take over.

It's the pinnoco guzzu.

She's not going to kill these shields—she's going to make *me* do it.

"The number of your ilk before you is a great one, as I promised it would be."

Desperate, I lash out against the crawling snares her guzzu has planted in my head, but where I manage to cut one, more spawn like multiple heads of a beast. They twist and turn, choking off my ability to fight.

"Some of these shields were party to the events in the Cuartel tonight," the doyenne continues, indurate and merciless. "The rest confessed to their roles in deaths of my council. Though they say they acted alone and don't have any knowledge of the Lost Obeah Empress, I can't help wondering . . ."

The Bush Witch who tended to me after the Bidding Circle, Fatou, blinks with a recognition that goes beyond a Healer and one of her patients. *Don't fight this*, her eyes say—beg. They're trying to protect me, but I don't want it. Not like this.

Supreme Being, Clotille, it's been so long, but please, forgive me. Help me.

My internal self's screams are quieting.

The guzzu is winning.

"Those who swore they'd killed my presiders were very convincing. They could tell me about the wounds that wrought the presiders' deaths. They told me where the first body was found, my favorite place in the garden where the second had been dumped like chattel."

How did they know . . . *Delyse*. She must have dug up information after the doyenne threatened me during the raid. My chest heaves. I think—I think my heart's breaking.

The shields before me look on with pride, stoic through their sorrow. Control is like trying to catch water in my hands. But I have to, because if I don't—

"I want those ill intentions to rise like the tides." At the doyenne's command, my magic roils within me. "I want them to eddy and boil as though contained in a great cauldron of ire. And then I want them to spill, and all before you to drown."

There's a commotion in the hall outside; the line of Obeah are shunted to the side by more Xanthippe elbowing their way into the crowded study.

"And here are the final two."

Delyse and Sham are shoved from their embrace. She won't look at me. Chin high in the air, braids swinging, she aims her furor at the doyenne.

"Kill them."

A solitary tear rolls down my face. It's the last expression I have as the witch I am ceases to exist, and a caged creature to which the doyenne alone has a key moves to the forefront.

The world speeds up.

Intentions appear as dark sparks of death igniting only to diminish the light in others. The Obeah don't avoid my magic. Their silence amplifies every broken bone, every last gasp of breath as it escapes; they don't run when someone outside my vortex of death and destruction hands me a weapon. There's so much blood, my feet slip and slide in it. But I know only one purpose, one design, and so I continue to whirl and spin, a top of death the doyenne's using in her own personal game.

She finally stops, rescinds her curse, and returns my consciousness. The horned vines of the guzzu slink out of my head, clearing space to think, to feel; my senses return with a lilting familiarity. I'm breathing hard, exhausted, in the vestibule, where a graveyard of Obeah lie at my feet.

No!

I slam onto my knees, and everything blurs.

"What Obeah have always failed to understand is that being a leader demands sacrifice." The click of Doyenne Cariot's heels on the tile echoes like cannon fire. "Sometimes it's the sacrifice of others, but ultimately it's the sacrifice of one's self. Obeah only know of indulgence." She stops before me. The hem of her kaftan is dark with blood.

My order's blood.

Sham's and Fatou's and Delyse's blood.

"I suppose you're wondering what happens now."

Pain shoots through my glyph as the doyenne uses my magic to raise my chin, so that I might look at her, this witch who's taken so much from me. The very core of me strains against the compulsion to fly at her, to beat her with everything I am. But I'm exhausted. I'm broken.

"You can live with your mistakes, as I live with mine." Blood spatter speckles the left side of her face. "Perhaps they'll teach you something."

That I was a fool to think I could pretend to be my order's empress? That my folly is the reason fourteen lie dead at my feet, and more fell afoul of my choices earlier this evening?

Lesson received.

I shouldn't try to be anything other than what I am—a liar, a runaway, a Warrior.

And now it's time to teach a few lessons of my own.

PART III

WHOEVER THE TITLE FITS, LET THEM WEAR IT

JAZMYNE

The fourth and final Yielding trial is a flickering labyrinth of fire in a field of wild cane on the palace estate. Aside from the very first, it's the only one that's permitted an audience, though there hasn't been much to see since the Yielders began—happenstance that's not necessarily an issue, as long as I witness the victor when they emerge.

Being here this evening isn't entirely due to emissarial responsibility.

It dawned on me that in all that's happened, the reveals, the schemes, I haven't considered what I'll do with whoever is crowned Yielded. The way Kirdan, Iraya, and I have planned our move during the Sole, their sacrifice won't happen. At least, it doesn't need to if Raeni or Zidane is triumphant tonight.

Part of me hopes Javel walks out.

Movement in the mouth of the maze draws the crowd's focus—my focus. Hours have passed since Javel, Zidane, and Raeni entered, tasked with combatting unrevealed tasks within.

"Can you see who it is?"

"You already know who it is," Kirdan says, hands gripping his saber's guard where the weapon stands between his knees.

Bursting from the maze, arms aloft in victory, is Javel.

Around us, Alumbrar explode in riotous applause, vacating seats to be the first to congratulate the next Yielded. Kirdan and I remain seated.

"Do you think he killed Zidane or Raeni in there to warrant all that blood?"

In the firelight, it glistens on the curls of Javel's mohawk.

"I doubt he would have left this moment to chance."

"Never thought I'd praise this rite after learning its true practices." In my peripheral vision, Kirdan shakes his head. "But no past Yielder has ever deserved death as much as this one. You good?"

I nod my reply, my focus pinned to the spot Javel disappeared beneath the swell of bodies eager to glean luck from touching him, eager to impart their blessings for his sacrifice—an act that has little to do with altruism from him. This, their adoration, their praise, is what he's craved. I find that I don't care if he dies a hero to the island. Two years on from Madisyn's death, he will finally atone for what he said about her.

Circumstances on the Sole will need to change, but I'll make sure of it.

Kirdan and I slip away when the parade begins. Javel will be carted down to Queenstown, where islanders from all seven parishes wait to honor his victory and his final night of life before the Sole tomorrow. I'm still no closer to a decision about how to see his sacrifice through without telling Kirdan, and risking his condemnation, when we enter my rooms and he flings an arm out to keep me in place.

"Someone else is here."

"An attendant."

He sniffs. "No."

"Don't tell me my scent's that unforgettable?" Iraya drawls, sauntering from my sleeping quarters.

Without any Xanthippe.

"How did you get in here?" Kirdan murmurs, as stunned as I am.

Iraya runs an idle hand up and down the wall of the archway. "This was my childhood home." Dark eyes dart to my face, appraise me in a second. "How'd *you* get in here, Emissary?"

"Iraya—"

"Kirdan." She sashays into the sitting room and drapes herself across one of the velvet couches. "Did the two of you miss the Xanthippe standing outside?"

"No guards were there." I speak for the first time.

"Well, their slack security is something you should take up with them." She stretches like a shadowcat flexing sharp claws, looking every bit at home in *my* room.

And worryingly unaffected.

I know the doyenne made her kill almost a quarter of the shields not even three nights ago, yet she's acting like nothing happened. A pointed glance at Kirdan reflects the same confusion I feel, the concern. Iraya's body crackles with unspent energy. It surrounds her like a corona, pulsating like something living and sentient—something eager for release.

"If you came because you're mad about what the doyenne made you do," I'm quick to say, "if I hadn't acted on your behalf, you'd be dead too."

Menace glitters in Iraya's eyes. "Would you like my blessings?"

"I'd like to know why you're here."

"I came to confirm details for the Sole, of course."

She sits up, swinging her legs around fast enough to make me edge back a step, and Kirdan's blade to grind against its sheath.

Her mouth casts the shadow of a mocking smile.

"The biggest task left is to catch the beast we're setting loose during the celebration." Kirdan looks over every inch of her, scanning for weapons, threats, concealed beneath her scrapes and bruises. "I'll do that tomorrow."

"And me?"

"You'll come to me first and I'll give you the jéges." *To borrow.* "In the evening, you'll wait in the saferoom for the doyenne," I tell her. "And Kirdan will meet you as soon as he's set the beast loose."

Iraya nods, looking thoughtful. "And after, I leave. Everything sounds faultless."

"Good." Kirdan strides for the door. "Then you can go. I'll retrieve two Xanthippe."

Before I can make one sound of protest, he's out the door in search of the guards.

"Not a fan of music?" Iraya asks.

"I—what do you mean?"

"This room used to house my instruments. I'd sit practicing for hours."

"Music is only to be used during nyába, for the ancestors."

She coughs, but I hear her laughter, how she ridicules Alumbrar customs.

"I'm sorry for the deaths of your order members." Not sorry at all, I will every word to sting, to swarm her like a flock of carrion vultures, to peck and slice until the dark beauty of her skin is nothing but ribbons of bloody flesh. "Killing them yourself makes the act all the worse."

Her expression grows distant. "Your mama is many things, Jazmyne, a murdering, duplicitous, power-hungry witch who ruined the lives of her own pickney and countless others. But she's never concealed who she is from your order. You've all known the scope of her depravity, long before my sect did, and embraced her for it." She drags her focus back to me. "When they see your true face, I wonder if they'll accept you too, or feel like you've fooled them. Kirdan I'm sure will berate himself for underestimating you all this time."

"As you did?"

Her laughter is soft, as the kiss of a blade is before it presses into your throat. "I didn't underestimate you. I didn't think of you at all."

I rear back as though she struck me.

"And now?"

"And now," she repeats, her voice softening, "I wonder what would have happened if you weren't raised to hate me."

461

My face contorts with confusion.

"If, instead of keeping our backs *from* one another, we'd turned them *to* one another." Iraya leans forward and rests her elbows on her thighs. "Someone has made us enemies. Perhaps they feared the damage we could do together would be far greater than what we could ever do apart."

What is this line she walks, with those rings of fire in her otherwise dark eyes? Another trap? More lies? Of course. She means to throw me off as she did that night in the sentry bohío. Kirdan's weapons clink against one another as he enters the room. Realizing my mouth is hanging open, I close it, sit back, and shake my head slightly.

"The guards wait outside."

"Until the Sole then, allies." She tips her head with a wink and leaves.

"You good?" Kirdan eases himself into a seat.

"Of course," I lie. In truth, I'm shaking.

"The deaths of her order have no doubt unhinged her."

"Not unhinged." What she said was articulate, well considered. She's thinking about this, about me. Perhaps it was unwise to want such a thing, to find myself between her paws like a plaything. "She's tethered. I think she's planning something." I *know* she's planning something. "I think she has been this entire while." Just as all prowlers must hunt, and wildcats must scratch, Adairs must scheme.

It's why I have been too.

"I can sift her straight to a port the moment the doyenne's dead, and make sure she boards a ship sailing far from here."

With his usual foresight blinded by her, Kirdan is a few steps behind.

"Or we could do something else." My voice shrinks. "The bargain doesn't say how she must leave."

"You want to kill her."

I trace the twisting pattern on my kaftan with a finger. "Would you be on board?" He is the only one with access to enough gold, enough knowledge to do it, as one of the Simbarabo.

"Why wouldn't I?"

I thought she'd gotten to you, infected you, like her family got to so many others.

"Last time we spoke about her, you didn't want to dirty your hands."

"A lot has changed since then. You and I most of all."

I reach for his locket, forgetting again that I no longer wear it. His eyes linger on my neck, a physical reminder of how far we've come.

"Then it's decided. We'll kill her during the Sole too."

50

IRA

The third mistake Kirdan made was selecting only the two guards to escort me away from Jazmyne's rooms. I suppose he thinks I won't try anything after what occurred in the palace with the doyenne, my order, mere days ago.

Miscalculating my feelings was his second.

His first is my favorite. It goes back to an early encounter between us, when he showed how little he respected the Xanthippe. It's the only reason I knew he'd believe me when I lied and said they'd escorted me to Jazmyne's rooms.

His disdain for them isn't unfounded, though. Which experienced member of the doyenne's private coven would place their charge ahead of them, unrestrained? It isn't until after a few well-timed stumbles, pretend breaks for freedom, and a coughing fit wherein I turned our little party onto this abandoned hallway that one of the guards catches wise—well, almost.

"We've come the wrong way." She and her companion are so busy cursing about the number of dead ends in the palace that neither of them notice when I slip three of Jazmyne's hairpins from my bun.

"What if we—"

The first pin plunges through the skin and muscle in her neck before she can finish her thought. She trips backward with a cry, a hand flying to the wound. A spark flies from the second's conduit. I twist out of its trajectory, lunge, and drive the second pin in.

"I wouldn't do that if I were you." At my warning, the first guard's hand stills on the pin in her neck. "You'll bleed out in seconds, and all over this beautiful rug too." I snatch their conduits away, pocketing them. "If I can't find what I'm looking for, I'm sure your sistren will ensure you get these back."

Sixty seconds.

That's all I have to find the Adair tunnel, hide the guards, and get out of this hallway.

The third pin glides across my palm, splitting the skin to form my own bloody inkwell. Avoiding the temptation to smear my hand across the fabric on the wall, I leave thumb-size stains amid the floral mural in my search for the tunnel. It was an emergency exit for our immediate family. Losing access to the tunnel I took to Jazmyne's rooms—once *mine*—was a shame. She and Kirdan returned from the final trial sooner than anticipated.

Thirty seconds.

At the clank of metal, footfalls, I whip around. My guards now lie slumped on the ground, blood trickling into the collars

465

of their uniforms, half-lidded gazes on me as they lose consciousness. That noise wasn't from them. I force my breathing to calm, my hearing to stretch without magic. One explosion from my conduit, and I'll never make it out.

This dead end lies around the corner at the bottom of a long hallway on the second floor. There's no reason for any Xanthippe to patrol so far down here.

Unless they saw two of their sistren head this way with a shield and fail to return.

Twenty seconds.

Muttering my family name until it becomes a garbled mess, I dig my fingers into the wall until—*yes*. My fingers catch. Leaning my shoulder in, I push until the door gives with a low groan. A bead of sweat runs down my back as, closer than the previous sounds, someone draws breath.

Ten seconds.

I drag the first Xanthippe to the door and shove her limbs through the narrow gap. Spiderwebs cling to my face, slick with sweat. The scurry of legs sprint across my scalp. Biting back a scream, I haul the second into the tunnel as the glow of conduit light touches the corner of the dead end. With two seconds to go, the door closes without sound beneath my trembling fingers.

Both witches have lost consciousness as I drag them farther into the tunnel, fumbling my way through the dark. They can keep the hairpins. They won't wake now. Their capes I do take to bundle along the bottom of the door, just in case their blood seeps through.

Removing a witchlight from my pocket—also stolen from Jazmyne—I clutch the orb to warm it to life. A dim passage stretches before me, endless in the dark. Clotille's name is on my tongue, her favor carried in the scarification on my forehead, as I plunge into the shadows without further delay.

The air is damp down here; musty enough to give the illusion that I'm suffocating. I push on, doing my best to ignore the hitch in my breathing. More light would help, but I won't risk the torches. They might wake something else. I don't fancy fighting another boddlelice.

A fork in the tunnel materializes in the dark. We were in the west wing; I need to get north to find the tunnel I accessed from the fields, so right it is. I undo my vest in order to unbind the head tie wrapped over my tunic beneath. Even beneath the cool blue glow of the witchlight orb, the golden detailing across it is beautiful. Dancing girls spinning around giant winged creatures. Biting down on the edge, it's with mild regret that I tear it into strips. Needs must.

The gold is like a flame against the dirt ground. I stake it at the corner with another of Jazmyne's hairpins and move on. At each crossroad, I repeat my process with only the click of insects in the dark and the squeaking of rats to accompany me. Every step feels like too much and not enough time.

At the next intersection I inspect all three rounded tunnel mouths. A gray flag is tucked into a crack in the wall in the last one—the first path I traveled earlier tonight.

It's with a renewed frenzy that I claw cobwebs out of my way, waving the witchlight at the ground to catch the last few markers until my feet hit the stairs I climbed down hours earlier. I ascend at a sprint, breath thundering through my mouth. When my thighs burn enough to make my knees knock, I drag myself up each step, crunching roaches and only the goddess knows what else beneath my palms. Then my hand scrapes ceiling. It's wedged open, permitting a slither of real night to enter. I push the lid up an inch, peer out—it flies open. Hands reach in and haul me out.

"You said a few hours, mon." Ford squeezes me to his chest. "I thought something had happened to you."

"Something else, you mean."

At Nel's cold voice, he releases me. She's lying on the other side of the tunnel flap, now melted back into the earth. She doesn't look at me—hasn't, since.

I clear my throat. "Busha?"

Ford raises his head above the grass before dropping down again. "No signal. It's clear. How are the tunnels?"

"Perfect." For Delyse and Shamar, sharing my escape route is the least I can do. To say it's been difficult for me to accept help would be an understatement, but as it turned out, I didn't need to break past the various rings of protection around the palace to access the door I discovered as a pickney. This more accessible route, one I wouldn't have found alone, was discovered in a matter of hours once I told Ford what the Jade Guild needed to get inside the palace during the Sole. "They'll give you access to everything you need."

Ford clenches his fists in silent celebration.

"If that's all, I'll go to the cartographer." Nel doesn't wait for a reply. Peering above the stalks to check the coast is clear, she leaves without another word.

"She's grieving," Ford murmurs. "She doesn't mean any offense."

I'm impressed she's kept so quiet. I suspect it's because she has lots to say—to scream. Memories resurface of walking into the village after what the doyenne made me do. There were so many tears and questions. It didn't take long for faces to twist in disgust at the blood on my uniform, my face and body. I beat the images down, secure them in a far corner of my mind.

No one has come outright and said it, but I know my order here blames me for what happened. How could they not? Everyone knows an empress is to be protected at all costs. It's a rule as old as this island. It's *the* rule that sent me to the Virago. But in that moment I left the Cuartel with Kirdan, I didn't think about what those I left behind might do.

"You good?"

At Ford's question, fatigue hits me like a convoy of fists all over my body, but I must rally. A Warrior doesn't mourn until the battle is over, and the fight for Cwenburg is just beginning.

"Yeh mon. Now, the gold flags lead to the west wing, white to the kitchens, and gray to Emissary Cariot's chambers."

"Come and tell the cartographer yourself?" Ford suggests, his umpteenth attempt to immerse me in their operations since he stepped up to take over Shamar's Genna vacancy. But Obeah died the last time I played empress.

"The doyenne's watching me" is my excuse, and one he

can't dispute after what happened over a phase ago. "I don't want to endanger anyone." Neither of us says *again*, and Nel isn't here to do the honors.

"I'll tell them." He sighs, burdened with a responsibility that should be mine.

The morning after the vestibule slaughter, Ford found me, in a daze, to tell me he was leading the attack during the Sole.

"You still haven't told me what your plans are. I'm not going to deny you the doyenne's death," Ford insists. "But you can't be alone when it happens." He fidgets, clearly uncomfortable with dictating terms to me.

"I'm playing things by ear," I lie. "But I'll keep out of the way." Peering above the grass, I check my way out is clear.

"Iraya." Ford's face is grave when I glance down at him. It's hard to believe he's the same irreverent jokester Delyse introduced me to. "I can't lose anyone else."

I resist the urge to issue promises I'm not sure I can keep.

"For the record, your leadership is much better than your jokes."

Almost as soon as he grins, Ford's forehead bows in confusion, like the action has become as foreign to him as it has to me.

"Don't linger," I tell him, nodding my departure.

I run up the mount in a crouch, the witchlight clasped in my fist, ready to take up a night-shift watch until it's safe to re-enter the Cuartel. All starlight is snuffed out in the sky looming over the estate, like the heavens themselves have forgotten how to smile too. Not for the first time since the vestibule, I contemplate what it would mean to join the Jade Guild's fight after killing the doyenne: a lifetime of being unheard, coddled, and forced to delegate . . . I can't stay. Leaving will free me to answer the song contained in my bones: returning to the Blue Mountains to find my family, the Virago.

If it turns out they're not there, and all were killed as my parents were, I'll still take up my old mantle. Virago: Witch. Warrior. Weapon. One who swears on her scars to protect her order.

Until the very end.

51

JAZMYNE

"You're early." I can't keep the surprise out of my voice when I find Kirdan inside my study. Closing the book of guzzu I've been studying, I come round from behind my desk. "How did the jége exchange go?" He left a few hours ago to lend them to Iraya on his way to the wetlands. After her last attempt to play games with me, to unsettle me, I couldn't meet with her. In this final stage, another wrong look between us could dismantle everything I've worked for, and I'm not sure if it would come from her or me. "Was she still tethered?"

"I don't think she has any other settings besides being ready to cause trouble. Where's Anya?"

"Outside with my cabal of Nameless Stealths. They're watching the Cuartel." At my instruction. I'm not leaving tonight's security to busha and Xanthippe alone.

A large crate jumps and rattles on the floor by the window, interrupting whatever Kirdan had been about to say next.

Unperturbed, he shoves a hand into his pants pockets.

"The sukuyan?"

He nods. All he has to show from his hunting expedition in the wetlands is a shallow slash across his left cheek. "Didn't take too long."

Indeed, he's already changed into his smart tunic, to match his pants; a vividly patterned scarf spliced with gold sits across his shoulders instead of his cloak.

"Have you ever seen one?"

"Never."

"Brace yourself. It isn't pretty."

The crate jolts again, as if in outrage. Kir's conduit flares. The wooden planks disappear, revealing a creature inside a barred metal cage. Humanoid in anatomy, the sukuyan's gray skin is naked and raw looking, like it scratched every inch of itself with a scouring brush. It stares me down with pits of bruised skin for eyes. Stretched against bone, its face is a nightmarish distortion of what a human's should be. I flinch as the Aiycan monster opens its lipless mouth, but no noise escapes.

"Thought I'd spare you the sound. I think I perforated an eardrum before I managed to mute it." Kir pokes a finger at the bars. The sukuyan leaps at it, hooked gray claws clinking against the metal as it holds itself aloft horizontally, its mouth wide with another silent scream. "It's most comfortable in vegetation; in all the chaos that's going to unfold, you need to get inside with as much haste as possible, you understand?"

"I've waited two years for this, Kirdan. I won't be making any mistakes." That was all I could think about last night, this morning. When tomorrow dawns, I won't be an emissary any longer—I'll be doyenne. Albeit one of an island on the brink of war. "I need you to do something for me." I draw a bracing breath. "Don't release the sukuyan until after Javel's blood has been taken."

"After?"

I turn to the bay window, unable to look at him. "It seems wasteful not to use the Yielder guzzu after the others died for this moment." Especially with a fleet of pirates eager to pillage Aiyca, ones I need to keep away until I've ushered the Simbarabo in.

"Javel will die, then."

"It's what he wanted." I shrug, turn. "Are you ready?"

Kirdan's nod is solemn. "Promise me you'll walk good, Jazmyne."

"All will be well."

I squeeze his hand; he flips the hold so we're grasping one another's wrists.

"The red suits you."

He leaves via the rear of the palace to situate himself for attack, the crate floating beside him. I glance at the ornate mirror outside my study. My kaftan is a rouge flare, a smoldering ember, one I ordered from the silk spinner in Lawson after Roje admired it. Its design isn't one I'm used to, with a fitted bodice and clinging sleeves, but it's one for a leader. Someone who knows the meaning of sacrifice as well as survival—a person I have become, these past two months.

"I want you by my side this Sole." Doyenne Cariot's voice echoes through the palace eaves.

I jerk away from the mirror; my legs tangle in the kaftan's

train as I try to find her. I'd thought her outside already. Did she see Kirdan, the crate?

"Hopefully you'll exercise more grace out there than you've shown just now."

She emerges from around a corner to the left of my study, something clasped to her chest, and glides down the hall, sleeves and train trailing behind her. I squint as the gold of her ceremonial robes, the rising sun of her headdress, draws the light from the candles, the witchlights.

"It's more important than ever to ensure that you absorb my customs, child." She raises the hand not clutching her journal, I can now see, and I flinch; she cups my cheek. "They will need to continue long after I am gone."

My face burns beneath her touch.

"You wish to keep the Yielding?"

"Indefinitely."

Breath sours in my mouth. "Then why did you renounce it in the first place?"

"Because I'd hoped we no longer needed to resort to such measures." Releasing my cheek, she wipes her hairline, where beads of sweat gather. "But it was a fool's hope, and one that's cost our order, this island, enough."

"The Jade Guild."

At their name, her hard exterior slips, revealing a vulnerable slither not unlike that fear I first saw in Carling Hill when Iraya revealed herself.

"The Yielding must continue," she murmurs. "Perhaps even twice a year."

Twice?

"More Alumbrar will die, more pickney will need to be born, and you, my child, will need to prepare to continue this legacy. That means it's time you stop messing around with the Nameless."

The world rocks beneath my feet.

Doyenne Cariot's chin tilts upward. "I see now that you were foolish enough to believe I wouldn't know you and the Divsylar emissary have been working with them. And to think, I was almost impressed with how you rallied the resisters after Light Keeper's execution. It takes a strong force to lead, but an even stronger one to assemble. This island will need that, in my stead."

Heat rushes to my head. She knew. She knew this entire time.

Could she know about tonight?

Bright against the shadows behind her, the look she gives me, if not fond, is proud. Just as I predicted. "Perhaps it's your turn to make the incisions to draw the blood this evening. I'm sure Javel will be thrilled. Come, daughter."

There's no option but to follow her out into the night.

Beneath a shimmering web of witchlights, the Kumina pulse charges the stone of the rear veranda beneath my sandals; the slabs feel sentient and wild, just like the frenzied beat that gives them life. Feet stamp, arms whirl, and sweat flies as Alumbrar gyrate in honor of the Seven-Faced Mudda in the palace gardens, sending their magic to the skies in plumes of golden sparks.

Benito's fortune is more necessary than ever for me, after the doyenne's revelations.

As for my order . . . however pretty the scene below is, no amount of delicate finials can mask the underlying tension. Magi may smile and laugh, glasses of rum in their hands, but their eyes dart about with apprehension, no doubt remembering the last time we were all together in the Yielding Assembly.

Spotting Doyenne Cariot, hordes of magi flock to the bottom of the dual-fronted staircase to meet her. Their utterances of gratitude and praise grow louder, almost drowning out the drums' refrain as they slow.

It's time.

Xanthippe utter guzzu to part the crowd, revealing the sacrificial altar atop a dais nestled between clusters of poinsettia trees at the end of the aisle. Long enough for Javel to lie across, it's draped in a variety of animal skin casting cloths. Spiced ginger incense curls with indolence from the inside of dull wooden bowls. The night's heady with jasmine and lavender too, to lower inhibitions.

It's not working.

Uncertainty slows my movements, thickens the air until I feel like I'm wading through cane syrup. The doyenne already stands behind the altar. A blade glints in her hand; bowls are stationed under the table to catch the blood she truly desires, not Javel's bones. Her eye bids me to hurry so he can come out and undertake his figurative journey between the Alumbrar, one meant to mirror his walk in death on the Bone Road to Coyaba—the afterlife.

I falter at the sight of her unexpected shadow.

Iraya.

She stands to the doyenne's left, dazzling in her silver and black uniform. Is this Doyenne Cariot's doing? She's meant to be in the saferoom waiting for Kirdan. Our eyes meet; her head tilt is limned with ill intent.

As much ill intent as the sukuyan's eldritch cry as it tears the sky asunder.

The crowd's reverent silence shifts to something redolent of an animal crouched in a glade, its ears cocked for predators. The hairs on my body jerk from my skin, one by one.

What's Kirdan doing? This is too early. Javel lives; he hasn't even started his walk yet.

The Xanthippe shift cutlasses they've taken to carrying from holsters at their backs in one uniform move, looking into the dark cluster of trees around them; the crowd too looks to the trees. But the sukuyan doesn't attack from there. It emerges from the left, adjacent to the congregation, slamming into their midst with an ululating screech.

I hoist my kaftan up in one hand and run for the altar.

Blood spatter, ripping skin, and cries for mercy rend the night as the screeching beast leaps from victim to victim. No, not one beast. *Two.* Another screech rips through the night to my right. There's another—and *another.* Did her nest follow Kirdan here?

Kirdan.

Anya.

My Stealths.

Please, Mudda, let them be all right.

The Alumbrar disperse in all directions. In their fear, they forget about the sifting restrictions. Magi disappear only to reappear with missing limbs; for some, great chunks of flesh blink back into sight before they do. Their blood will only make this hunting frenzy worse. I dodge screaming Alumbrar who reach for me, and bloodied body parts scattered about like macabre confetti, tripping over my own feet to reach the altar.

Breathless, I jockey with my elbows, pushing the final ten yards to the protective circle of Xanthippe. They part to give me entry.

The doyenne clutches the journal to her stomach like a shield, and Iraya before her like a saber. "What's happening!"

"A sukuyan colony," I pant. "They're attacking the Alumbrar." I hadn't planned to say anything to her. She was meant to run, not stand as she is now, her lone eye wide with a potent terror. In this moment, poised to lose everything, her order screaming in fright at the sukuyans' attack, she looks fragile. Old.

"Guards—" She breaks off as one of the Xanthippe before us collapses. Within two seconds, those on either side of her collapse too. "Hold fast! It's only wild vermin!"

The guard closest to us turns, her mouth flailing like she's choking on her words. "There's too many of—" Her words cut off as she too collapses, a wedge of metal lodged in her neck.

The gap her absence creates reveals the attacker—*attackers*.

"Honor demands blood," intones an Obeah-man fronting what looks like—like every single one of the doyenne's remaining shields. At his words, even with the sukuyans still tearing through the Alumbrar, the clash of guzzu as the Xanthippe try to kill them, silence falls. One that's so weighted, I feel trapped beneath it.

Rather than the black and silver of their uniforms, the Obeah before us are bedecked in stark alabaster cloth; it's almost luminescent against the rich gleam of their skin. This is why the doyenne feared the color. It's like a beacon, a call to war. My eyes dart back to Iraya. Her face is as impenetrable as always, but this turn of events has her name all over it.

Has she found a way around the Vow of Peace?

"You ensorcelled our empress, Judair Cariot," the Obeahman says, freeing a rod of wood from behind his back. Like it's a sign, the Obeah surrounding him reveal planks of wood, splintered staffs, strips of metal. "You forced her to kill our kin. And now we're here to kill yours."

The Xanthippe look to their leader for an order, but she's frozen before the Obeah.

My eyes dart back to Iraya. She isn't the only one with a surprise tonight.

Her magic comes at my call. Drawing that tumult from deep within her, I bellow a guzzu to split the Obeah. She cries out as the depth of her power makes her order fly apart and swell upward on two sides before us like dual waves of water; another guzzu freezes them in position.

"Go on!" I shout at the doyenne, rousing her. "Get to the saferoom! It won't last long."

After a beat she drags her eye to me. It's wild, manic. "They've come to reclaim something I took." To my surprise, she thrusts her journal into my hands. "You can't let them. Promise me you'll fight, Jazmyne. Promise me!" She takes a step toward me, curls her hand over my own as it holds the slim book.

However sobering her fear is, I can't feel pity for her. Not after all she's done.

"Everything will be fine." The lie glides off my tongue. "I'll keep the island safe. I promise." That vow, however, I did mean. "Now go." I prize her hand away.

With a final nod, she hurries through the bisected crowd, a phalanx of Xanthippe and her death sentence following her. I don't watch her leave. Stealing a breath, I take a step toward the awaiting Xanthippe, ready to issue orders. Their eyes go to my shoulder. They raise their cutlasses with a cry as, quicker than I can turn around, a hand clamps over my mouth, and an arm snakes around my middle, trapping my arms between my back and their front.

An axe juts past my head. Angled at the Xanthippe, it serves as a warning to keep them back as I'm dragged away, screaming into a hot hand, to the vegetation behind the altar.

The sukuyan's hunting ground.

52

IRA

Oh, Ford.

When the second Xanthippe fell, revealing a sea of Obeah ready for war, I thought my heart might beat its way out of my chest. He was supposed to infiltrate the palace. Instead he endangered all those magi to save his empress. Foolish, loyal Obeah-man, believing in me instead of the bargain . . . If he dies, I will paint this estate red.

Starting with the doyenne.

For all her frenetic haste to flee my order, the sukuyans, she pauses outside the fortified saferoom door in the basement, her head cocked toward the stairs she just dragged me down. Even here, in the palace belly, the creatures' cries echo in a paean of pain. As do those of their victims—Alumbrar only, I hope.

I fought Jazmyne and Kirdan doggedly for a sukuyan,

knowing that even if the doyenne didn't appreciate the irony of a beast who started its life as a witch, I would. But that decision was made with the mindset that there would be only the one, and the Obeah would be safe infiltrating the palace via the tunnels, not executing a coup—and a poor one, no less, in my name.

Lit by the cold hue of the witchlight-garlanded walls in the basement, the doyenne's shadowed profile is a painting of fear. If I were feeling picky, I'd want her to have more fight in lieu of what's to come.

But I'm not above kicking a witch when she's down.

"Guards here," she orders the phalanx of Xanthippe who accompanied us.

The fortified saferoom door shuts on their stoic expressions without a whisper, its handle magically transferring to the inside, preventing entry from outside. Kirdan will need to knock. Loudly. Cool stone and sparse furnishings populate the series of dark chambers; decanters of liquor sit on a shelf built into the wall in the first room. It's like a den, cozy with fat seats, footstools, and low lighting that's slightly incongruous with murder, but I'll go with it.

Doyenne Cariot sinks into one of the plush wingback seats. "Bring me a glass of rum."

As per her compulsion, I pour and distribute. She rolls the glass between quivering fingers. Aside from our breathing, mine steady, hers short, the clinking of the tumbler against her rings is the only sound.

"Pour another glass." Her eye is on the bottles littering the shelves. She hasn't emptied her tumbler. I'm careful to keep my face blank as I follow her instructions.

"Drink it."

I knock it back, wince. Her eye widens, roves all over me.

"After what you did to my parents, did you really think I'd put poison *inside* the glass?"

Not when she'd hold the outside between her bejeweled fingers long enough to ingest the debilitating tincture through her skin. Right on cue her conduit flickers, dwindles. Sleeps. I anticipate her throwing the glass and duck. Her jaw falls open as I reach down the front of my vest and free a perfect pastiche of her.

"And did you really think I only made the one doll? Look, I even removed one of its eyes."

"My hair—"

I drag a chair before her and sit down, crossing one leg over the other. "Keepsakes after all the times we shared together."

Her eye darts from the doll to the door and back again; her panic's so palpable I could stick my tongue out and taste it. "You don't have the magical capacity to manipulate that doll in full without weaponizing the ancestors. And you can't kill me," she adds, though it's with less certainty.

"This saferoom has plenty of Jákīsa, items to burn, should you refuse to play nice." In truth, I'm conscious about time. The poison won't last long. I have a half hour, at most, to get answers about what happened to my parents a decade ago before Kirdan comes to kill her. "I'm here to collect what's owed."

484

She swallows. I follow the movement beneath her throat's thin skin. "And what's that?"

"Before your head? Answers."

Doyenne Cariot swallows once more and then *smiles*. "So you've executed this elaborate scheme—escaping Carne, inciting a rebellion among my shields—to interrogate me about the role you believe I played in your parents' demise?"

"I might not have seen their bodies," I concede, "but I heard from enough magi what they looked like when you strode from Cwenburg and pronounced yourself doyenne of my ancestors' domicile."

She settles back in the chair, looking far too pleased for one toeing the line between a quick death and torture. "Do you really think Alumbrar were the only ones annoyed with how your order treated those they viewed as ancillary?"

"Someone helped? Who?"

"Your order."

I laugh; her smile turns supercilious at the challenge.

"I sought the assistance of a family of Obeah notorious for their attempts to rally forces against your family. They're magi my order has had cause to empathize with, throughout the years. Dismissed as badmind, both of us, we were relegated to a life we never should have lived. Although I did spend over a decade adding poison to your family's meals, the actual tincture was provided by that same cohort of Obeah to weaken your order so *they* could replace them."

"I don't believe you."

"But you choose to believe that the Alumbrar were able to

defeat an indefatigable sect of magi of skill we do not have with poison alone?"

Her words are bitter, a reflux of thoughts I've had before. What she's insinuating about Obeah traitors would be a betrayal of the highest caliber. It can't be true.

"By your silence, I assume you have some doubts."

I make a clucking noise with my tongue, chiding her. "I don't doubt my order, mon."

"That may be so, but such conviction isn't borne from loyalty. It's borne from conceit cultivated among the Obeah. Remember, the estate wasn't walled a decade ago. Inside security was lax to nonexistent. Why would the Obeah need protection from themselves? Or from the secondary Alumbrar? This underestimation meant that I was able to escort my Obeah allies into the estate with little fuss. The fight that took place was one to behold, lauded Obeah Masters falling. Your mama cried out when your dada's throat was—"

"Stop," I grind out.

"He didn't even think to fight back, he was so stunned. He just sat there, trying to shield against the monsters I unwittingly unleashed," she continues, her voice a claw tearing and scratching with no give. "You'll be pleased to hear that your mama was as wild as any of them. She killed many before she eventually died. By my hand."

"Stop *lying*!"

"I used her blood to make my bid for doyenne to the Seven-Faced Mudda. Right upstairs, in the palace. And They accepted. They didn't object that your mama—" She breaks off with a gasp, clutching at her chest.

My fingers crack, my grip around the doll is so tight. If I had the fire, the blood and bone, the ancestors, my clench could have crushed her insides.

"Why would I believe *you*?" I spit. "No Obeah would have stood against Mama and Dada. They were loved and revered by my order across the empire—even the Zesian bag-o-wire knew better than to bring war to their feet. If there was ever a group who felt rancor toward them, they would've been small, insignificant. They would've been—"

I almost leap out of my skin at the *boom*s that rattle the door.

Has Kirdan come, or are the Xanthippe outside signaling the all clear?

The doyenne chokes out a hoarse laugh. I whip around to catch her conduit flickering. A small spasm hits my stomach. Her compulsion. It's strengthening already.

I call my magic, reaching deep for it.

There's no response.

Touching the glass and ingesting the poison myself was a small price to pay, I thought. The gold she bears, on her head, in the fabric of her clothing—I should have made her shuck them. She's channeling at a faster rate than I can, and it's not as if I can attack her.

Outside, the *boom*s double in intensity.

"I am no griot," the doyenne begins, calm in the face of what may be her rescue outside. "But I have a tale I've shared with very few. As a pickney, my family moved us to the coast, where we lived to avoid Obeah oppression in the parishes. It could have been a good life, had Dada not neglected to consider who else would seek refuge from the empress who lived in the grand palace on the hill." The memory draws lines of sorrow in her features. "The Unlit came in the night. They took from us just as their magic and status were taken from them by the Obeah Witches Council. They abused Mama, me. She opted to take her own life afterward, rather than living with the shame of being ravaged by a beast, as I did."

Obeah exiled from Aiyca, the Unlit failed to abide by my order's primary rule—don't kill your own. The moment they lost their magic, they stopped being one of us. But to Alumbrar? They already think us merciless, lawless. The Unlit would only justify their hatred. If this family the griot spoke of, Doyenne Cariot speaks of, exists, it's one thing. But if they're Unlit, there's no limit to what they'd do to get what they hunger for—status, power. Even revenge. And it would all be against my family.

BOOM-BOOM-BOOM.

If it's Kirdan out there, I need a minute.

"Never did I think that I would have to ally with the fiends who tore my innocence from me, but who better than they to understand the plight of one trying to claw her way to a position in life that was stolen from her?" A shadow falls over the doyenne's face. "And while nothing saddens me more than the realization that I've become like those I loathe"— her conduit's light flutters, like an eye blinking in the face of the sun—"for power, acceptance, sometimes we do what we never thought we would."

An amber spark of suppression shoots from her conduit, and I dive from my seat, whipping out the Mirror of Two Faces concealed in the loose sleeves of my tunic. The intention rebounds. In the flash of light that follows, lambent white and blinding, I roll into the neighboring room. Back against a wall, tucked just out of the doyenne's sight, I squeeze my eyes to clear the spots of light dancing on my lids. Did I hit her?

"The moment I saw you in Cwenburg, I knew you'd make it your mission to find the jéges."

Shit.

My back twinges where I slammed into the wall; I shunt the pain aside to focus on the Great River, summoning the image of the flow of water in my mind. But—where a limitless stretch of water should be, only a dry bed appears. The poison is still repressing my magic.

"You're a relatively smart witch; you must have known I wanted them, kept you alive after I made the public declaration to execute you in order to use them through you." Fabric rustles. She's out of her seat. "Iraya?"

I can't respond. She'll know where I am, and I need time.

"Sulking, are you?" She pauses. "No matter. What's about to take place isn't a conversation. It's a chance for you to slide the Mirror of Two Faces across the floor, and come out from where you're hiding."

I swipe a hand across my brow. *Think, Adair.* She needs to attack me for the mirror to work. Suppression sparks I can handle, but what if she manifests weapons, beasts?

Compulsion wraps fingers around my spine and jerks, almost strong enough to pull me away from the wall. The Amplifier hanging around my neck is useless without Kirdan, without magic.

Double shit.

One drop of magic. I only need one drop to defend myself.

"You were never the threat I feared. Those Unlit allies I spoke of? We made the agreement to rule Aiyca side by side, when all would be said and done." She scoffs. "Have you heard anything as ridiculous as Alumbrar and Obeah working together? I knew the moment one of the jéges was in their possession they'd betray me. So I acted first. For the past decade they've sought to punish me for it in various ways that required I get a little . . . resourceful regarding how I protected my order."

One. Drop.

"Will you protect yours?"

Even the Seven-Faced Mudda has to see that I'm trying to do just that.

"Or is that mirror worth their lives?"

Perhaps They have . . .

There can be no more deaths in my order, and the solution is so simple, I can't believe I didn't think of it sooner tonight—I can't believe I didn't *solve* it sooner.

"Iraya?"

The mirror grates across the stone floor as I lean around the wall to push it into the den.

"There you are." The doyenne's brows raise in triumph as I

emerge from behind the wall.

But she isn't the only witch with something to smile about.

Her focus dips to my chest as the Amplifier warms there, magnifying my insignificant drop of magic into something far greater. The doyenne's eye bounces between the jége and my grin.

"You found the Amplifier too?"

"You didn't ask." I shrug. "As you said, this wasn't a conversation."

"Have you forgotten that you cannot attack me?" Her conduit blazes with a light that spreads, shooting through the threads of her kaftan right up to her headdress; its spokes glow with the molten intensity of the sun. Fanned around her head, they gild her silver dreads, making them seem alight with flame. She could be a sun goddess, one another witch might take the knee before to beg for mercy.

But I was never made to kneel before her ilk. Bargain or no.

"I won't kill you," she says, almost managing to keep her voice steady. "But you'll wish you were dead when I'm through with your order."

A spark of suppression flies from her conduit, as I was hoping.

I Summon the mirror. Aided by the Amplifier, my will is absolute, fast. I catch it in time for it to rebound her guzzu, aiming this time around. Face contorting with fury, she makes a dive, but the yellow spark smacks into her stomach. She falls back with a cry, freezes in that position. Her body at my mercy while her mind, I don't doubt, can only scream and scream.

"I imagined the ways I would kill you every night, in Carne." I stop before her, savoring the fear in her eye. "Recently though, there's only been one way I've wanted to end this." I place a hand on either side of her face. "And that's holding you," I whisper. "Your life between my hands while I tell you that you stabbed my family in the back, robbing a once great nation of its grace, and I have come for reparations." My hands slip down to her neck. "No doubt you're wondering how I can believe myself capable of killing you when the Vow of Peace forbids me from leaving Aiyca without a leader. But I won't be." I've been a leader ever since that morning I woke in the Cuartel and discovered those footprints. Even as far as deceiving my order after Bull Inna Pen to keep them safe, warning Delyse not to get involved, plotting with Kirdan and Jazmyne, I was leading whether I thought it or not—whether I wanted to or not. Only, not as a doyenne or empress. I acted as a Genna, for good and bad. But that's not why I can kill the doyenne. At least, it's not the only reason. Delyse and Shamar, Ford, Nel, and the rest of the shields here secured that when they believed in me, fought for me, died for me. "Fool's Bargains," I tell Doyenne Cariot. "They're hard to make watertight."

She trembles before me, the very picture of prey in its final moments before death. One of the earliest lessons Nana Clarke taught me during my training was that the toughest kill wouldn't be one made in survival mode; it would be the one where I had the choice between mercy and ruthlessness. It would be this one.

She was wrong.

The twist is abrupt. Doyenne Cariot crumples. As she falls, I am lifted—freed of the weight I have carried since I was eight years old. *For you, Mama, Dada*, I think, bending to remove the doyenne's crown. Now she is as she was meant to be, a moon whose only job was to make way for the sun.

It is done.

Making my way over to a chair, I sit and stay like that awhile. This entire time I thought I needed to be alone to see this through, to forsake friendships, relationships. My gods . . . If things had gone my way I might not have succeeded tonight. But succeed I did, and now I have to make sure my order is successful here too.

Startling me, the saferoom door flies open without warning, slamming against the wall. A cloud of smoke rushes in from the explosive used to break in. Rising, I choke in the pluming smoke, and stumble into someone's waiting hands.

"Wait," a familiar voice intones from the doorway.

The smoke clears, revealing Jazmyne. And the hand I took, the scarred fingers gripping mine, belongs to a leering *pirate*. One of many filing into the saferoom.

"Should we take her to the study with the other one?" a large sea snake questions. He leans against the doorway to Jazmyne's right, watching me with narrowed eyes the color of nectar.

"I don't think so," I manage to splutter. "We have a deal, don't we, Emissary?"

Taking quick steps across the room, she picks the mirror up

from the floor and then snatches the Amplifier from around my neck. It swings in her hand as she looks at the doyenne's body.

"Killing the doyenne is a crime punishable by death."

"Bargain," I force out, my jaw clenched.

She looks at me then, cold with triumph. "It never said you couldn't leave Aiyca in a bone bag."

She outmaneuvered *me*?

"Bring her upstairs," she orders. "And prepare her for the altar."

JAZMYNE

An Hour Earlier

Darkness engulfs as I'm drawn back into the bush. I smack the doyenne's journal onto the arm around my middle and sink my teeth into the rough hand over my mouth until I taste blood.

"*Cha mon!* Jazmyne, it's me!"

Freed, I spin to find Roje's grinning face in the moonless night.

"Sorry we're late. Parking a ship around here is a nightmare."

"You're here! Does this mean you'll back me?"

He bows with a flourish. "My queen."

I fling myself into his arms. His chest shakes with laughter.

"There'll be plenty of time for you to thank me later."

Dark, wicked things.

Squirming away, I put some distance between the two of us. "Why didn't you lead with the queen thing instead of scaring me?"

"I like the drama. What can I say, mon?" He dismisses my indignation with an insolent shrug of his shoulders. "Listen, there's something you should see—"

"Show me later. I need to look for Kirdan, Anya."

Roje draws me closer. "You should see it now. You won't believe me otherwise."

"But I—" *I what? I'm worried neither of them can handle the sukuyans?* "Can the crew go after Iraya and the doyenne?"

"Yeh mon. We're here for you."

"They'll be in the saferoom in the basement. Tell them . . . tell them not to let it go on for too long."

Roje whistles. A thin pirate appears from the trees as if conjured. He repeats my request, and then together, we edge around the Obeah, sticking to the line of trees to avoid the sukuyans. One digs in the bowel of a vacant-eyed Alumbrar-man. I avert my gaze as we creep around it, taking a wide berth. On the palace steps, we break into a run. Something whistles an inch from my face. Roje grabs my shoulder, forcing me back; the wall where my head was explodes, showering us with debris and dust.

The guzzu—they've ended.

Consecutive weapons whistle through the air toward us, accompanied by cries of dissent. Roje shoves me ahead of him, shielding me with his body. The explosives, blades, eat the palace's fascia, narrowly missing us. I fling open one of the doors. Turning to ensure Roje makes it in behind me, I glimpse an overflow of Xanthippe crashing into the white wave of shields.

In stark contrast to the melee outside, the palace is silent when we barrel through the doors, coughing dust from our lungs. Roje issues orders to attending members of the crew, who snap into guard position in the vestibule. I open the security panel by the door.

"Blade, please."

I'm presented with at least seven. Taking the cleanest, I prick my finger to smear across the Glyph of Containment inside the box to enliven the filigree on the palace, awakening the guzzu-incised gold to protect us from outside attack. My thoughts return to Anya, the Nameless. They won't make it inside now. I have to trust that they're safe. That the Obeah haven't harmed them.

"Some of the crew are still out there," Roje says. "Do you want them to help the Alumbrar?"

"Hold off on that for now."

"As you wish."

We reach my study; Roje knocks twice before opening the door. Distracted, it takes me a moment to realize that they have Kirdan, bound in rope, before my desk.

"What are you doing?" Discarding the journal, I run to his side. "He's meant to be elsewhere." Iraya is alone with the doyenne. "Untie him!"

"That's not a good idea." Roje flips open a ratchet. "Do you want to tell her who you are, or shall I, Prince?"

"Prince?" I look between the two of them. "Kirdan, what does he mean?" I reach for his arm, to loosen the rope, and he leans away like he can't bear to be close to me. "Kirdan?"

"Last chance to try talking with your tongue in your mouth, Prince."

"Why do you keep calling him that?"

"I always check who I'm getting into bed with." The white of Roje's teeth gleams in a small, satisfied smile. "There is a Kirdan Divsylar who's distantly related to the royals, but according to my sources, he's a wiry shrimp who'd have trouble looking my knees in the eye, and he's not an emissary. *This* is the Zesian doyenne's *son*."

At Roje's admission, Kirdan's mouth tightens.

My knees weaken.

"And if he's been concealing that from you," Roje says, "what else is he hiding?"

"Leave us."

"But—"

"The theatrics aren't necessary," Kirdan says, in a voice unlike any I've heard him use before. "It's not like I can attack her."

Her?

"Not now that you've been caught out, you mean," Roje snarls. "I'm right outside, Jazmyne," he says, the warning in his voice meant for Kirdan. The door slams behind him.

"Is it true? Are you Zesia's prince?" The questions spill from my lips with the bitterness of vomit. "Have you been lying to me all this time?"

"Yes."

"Yes, to what?"

"Yes to all of it." He adjusts beneath the rope, like it's an inconvenience, an ill-fitting jacket that he can't wait to shuck.

Words die on my tongue, crumbling into ash and swirling in the silence that grows like a wall between us. "You don't even try to deny it?" I finally manage to whisper.

Kir shrugs his shoulders. *He shrugs his shoulders.*

"But you—you didn't help the Aiycan Obeah during the usurpation. You hated them."

"Because we were on the same side, then. But now? This has nothing to do with them and everything to do with *you*." Kirdan straightens in his chair, and I'm hit with the full intensity of his gaze. "You spoke of Iraya's misanthropy, Iraya's attitude, Iraya's whatever you could find to pick at. But never once did you consider yourself, or your actions. The quest for power is like a singular winding track. One that's as thin as a blade, and as unforgiving as the sheer drops on either of its sides. The moment you vowed to let the Nameless kill your own mama, I knew your promises to lead a better island were empty. The Aiycan Obeah were a lot of things, but they never killed their own for self-gain."

He swims before me as my eyes fill with tears. "And by the *Aiycan Obeah*, you mean the Adairs. *Iraya Adair*, specifically." It always comes back to her with him. "Why? Why *her*?" *Why not* me? "*I've* done nothing but fight for Aiyca!"

"And we both know how you've done that, why. Will you kill me too, Jazmyne?"

That gives me pause.

Should I?

Instead of the revulsion I expected to feel, would have felt months ago, the idea purrs against the places I hurt. The places his betrayal has bruised.

I could.

I could call Roje in here. He'd split Kirdan down the middle with little persuasion. That would serve him right for lying to me for all this time. But . . . the thought of erasing him makes my stomach turn, my limbs seemingly lose bone and muscle. He was family to me, whatever he's done, and I've lost enough.

I sniff, wipe at spilled tears. "If you believe I would do that to you," I whisper, "you've never known me."

"And if you believed I'd side with you after you've become the very thing we vowed to remove from Aiyca, you've never known me."

"In that we agree."

In the hall outside, Roje stops his pacing to assess me when I dart out and lean against the closed door at my back.

"Whaap'm?"

"He lives."

"For now," Roje growls.

Freeing a kerchief from down the front of my kaftan's bodice, I wipe my eyes.

"You kept it."

Roje's face clears of all malice. He looks almost . . . dumbstruck. Unable to deal with any more emotions, I draw in a rattling breath and tuck the cloth, his cloth, back down by my heart.

"The crew—"

"Will return with the Obeah-witch soon." He clears his throat. "They're waiting to see if the previous doyenne still lives."

"Where are the sukuyan?"

"All caught."

"And the Alumbrar? The Obeah?"

"Some of the latter escaped, but those that are left have been locked in the holding cells by some Xanthippe and a cohort of

Stealths led by your sistren from Black River."

Anya is well. Thank the goddess.

"The crew haven't revealed themselves to her yet, but she's seen me. She has questions."

There are so many important decisions to be made—by me. Just as Kirdan purported, I feel the danger of the sheer drops on either side of this road I'm still on. I only have to cast my eyes around to see what power did to Mama. To fall would be tragic.

But what if, like the great avian combatants of old from Anansi's stories, I rise?

I take a deep breath; my lungs swell like wings. "Tell the crew to stay hidden, but to be ready. And have someone bring me Anya." This New Moon will still see a sacrifice.

"What do you need *me* to do?"

I stare at the door as though I can see through it to where Kirdan sits, Zesia's prince, one of the defunct empire's first family members, with all the powers the title suggests.

"Do you still have that knife?"

Roje removes it from his boot and flips it open into an angular smile.

"Prince Divsylar requires your immediate attention."

54

IRA

Obeah helped the doyenne kill Mama and Dada. *Aiycan Obeah.*

It's a refrain that loops around and around in my head. Not even the dull clang of pirate cutlasses from Jazmyne's convoy of sea snakes can drown it out. They escort me through a still palace. A distant part of me remembers my order, how Ford sacrificed his opportunity to gain a stronghold to save me. Goodness does still exist here. I cling on to my memory of the determination in his expression and knit myself back together once more.

I'm bundled through a doorway, shoved into a seat before the desk in Dada's study. A pirate ensconced in a cloud of rum so pungent I'm amazed she can stand, ties me in place with thick rope. Jazmyne stalks inside. Shoulders thrown back, she radiates confidence in a stunning scarlet kaftan that dances around her legs like a living flame.

"I grew up thinking I'd become a Healer," she says, stopping before me.

I close my eyes with a groan. I don't want to hear any more gods-damn stories.

"Though my path changed, it's clear that the Supreme Being saw fit to prepare me to purge the greatest disease that would attempt to destroy the land she forged. For the longest time, I thought it was Mama. Then I met you." She pauses. "Look at me."

A slap connects with my cheek. I cough spit. The pirate who hit me, who just signed her death warrant, winks as she takes another swig from a skin.

"Your family is a parasite. One that drove Mama to madness, and this island into disrepair. I will not let you continue to infect." She turns to the hulking pirate who hasn't strayed too far from her side since they apprehended me in the safe room, the one with aureate eyes. "Someone needs to stay with her while I go and address the Alumbrar."

He clicks at members of his entourage, imparting orders in his strange accent.

"Are you ready for them to see you without your mask?"

We stare at one another. Prowler to prowler, for that's what she has become.

My comment about us uniting was of course said to disorient her, but for a moment I consider the threat ahead and almost imagine her by my side to defeat it. . . .

Gods.

That slap must have knocked something loose.

"When *you* next see me, Iraya, I will be doyenne, and you, the first sacrifice this Sole." She leaves in a whorl of scarlet silk, the pirate behind her.

Five of his crew stay behind. Two sit to the left of me, two more to the right; the last lounges against the study door.

"How's that mouth?" the slugger asks with a smile.

"It's always been a bit of a problem."

Her eyes run a slow trail down my body. "Maybe it needs kissing better?"

"Maybe."

With an eagerness that would have made me laugh under different circumstances, the pirate leaps from her chair. My naevus swells against its dam, pushing, surging—

BOOM.

A blast from the hallway outside rattles the study, dislodging books and accoutrements from the built-ins around the door. Has Ford succeeded outside and managed to penetrate the palace after all? The pirates fly to their feet, weapons in hand.

A second blast launches the sentinel by the door across the room; its solid wood lands atop him with a thud. He doesn't rise. Three blades fly through the destroyed doorway and find homes in the necks of three more pirates, bar the one who hit me. She presses a trembling cutlass to my throat, forcing me to tilt my chin upward.

"Steady," I warn.

"I have your empress!" she calls. "Show yourselves!"

Heavy treads fall in the hall outside, but not the sound of many. Only one.

Kirdan crosses the threshold, his hair hacked to his shoulders, which might explain why he's wearing an expression Death Herself would admire. His eyes survey the room, assessing for threats, before they meet mine. The storm there intensifies.

"Roje will make you regret this, *bag-o-wire*," the pirate at my back says.

Traitor? That's *my* nickname for him.

"Roje can get in line." Kirdan loosens both his hunting knife and his saber. His gaze shifts back my way. "Are you hurt?"

Me? He's asking me?

"Drop your weapons, or I'll cut her head clean off her neck."

"And then you'll still have to deal with me, sea snake." Kirdan's gait adjusts as he spreads his weight and raises those weapons like he—like he's ready to fight. For *me*.

Very deliberately, I dip my gaze to the rope binding me to the chair. Half a second passes before Kirdan's magic makes it loosen and fall, freeing my arms and legs.

The pirate's surprise makes her blade lose some of its pressure against my neck. Enough for me to knock the handle away and twist her fingers hard enough to break bone. She howls. Shooting to my feet, I bring my other hand up to her head and smash it into my knee. She hasn't even collapsed when hands seize my shoulders and spin me around. Kirdan scans every inch of me with an intensity that borders on manic.

"Did they hurt you?"

"Hands, Zesian." I shrug out of his grip, concede a few steps.

"Answer me."

Bewildered, I shake my head. "I'm fine. I'll be even better when you start explaining what the hell is going on. You can start with the hair, if you'd like."

The concern in his expression darkens, twisting into something menacing. "Because now you want to listen?" His conduit lights. The study door lifts and flies backward, wedging in the doorway hard enough to unsettle what remains on the shelves. "Not before when your ilk here had things to say?"

"I don't speak vague and confusing. Elaborate."

"We've been working together."

"I—I don't understand."

"How could you understand when you didn't allow anyone to tell you the full story?" Kirdan's shout echoes off the high ceiling, rebounding like a volley of blows. "And now look at how things have turned out." He strides to the windows, peeling back a curtain to look at the gardens below. "Pirates," he mutters to himself. "I didn't think she had it in her."

"Wait!" I'm shouting too. This is bizarre. Like I've floated out of my body and I'm watching two strangers interact with each other. "You say you've been trying to help?"

"There's no time—"

I take a step closer to him. "Do you know about the Unlit? Did they help the Alumbrar usurp my order here?" He hesitates long enough that I shout again. "Tell me!"

"Yeh mon."

Oh gods.

"Only the Zesian first family knew." He pivots from the window. "That intelligence was gleaned from Doyenne Cariot in the process of forming an alliance against your order. We wanted to know what we were dealing with."

"Can you tell me who these Unlit are? Did any of them survive the Viper's Massacre? Could some be here, in Cwenburg?"

"You're thinking about revenge *again*?"

"They helped kill my family!" The words explode from me, spewing out like fire.

"They killed your family after Judair facilitated it, and you've killed her, I presume?" He pauses. "You must have, unless Jazmyne?"

"I did."

"How did you navigate the bargain?"

"It doesn't matter."

"No? Well, you took what was owed." Kirdan's voice is low, short. "If you retaliate with more death, you continue the Unlit's cycle of Obeah killing Obeah. You don't—" He whips around, head cocked toward the window.

Outside, roars sound, chants—Jazmyne's name. They're calling her . . .

They're calling her doyenne.

"There's no time for this," Kirdan says.

"Fine. What of my order outside?"

The reproach in his eyes ebbs. "Moved to the holding cells."

My stomach turns. "I can't leave them there."

"If we have a hope of saving them," Kirdan says, reading my expression. "We need to get away from here before we end up joining them."

"How do I know I can trust you to get me out, Zesian?"

"Calling me by my proper name might be a good start." He straightens; the soldier before me transforms into something regal, esteemed, butchered hair aside. "It's Prince Kirdan Divsylar. Firstborn and only son of Doyenne and General Divsylar, commander of Zesia's Simbarabo Fighters."

Goddess have mercy.

"I've crossed deserts amid sandstorms, sailed seas ravaged by monsters, endured suspicion under the Alumbrar rule in this land, where I've risked torture—death—if my first family status was discovered, because this empire has been doomed long before you instigated a fight in Carne Prison." His eyes bounce between mine, the green near glowing. "You weren't my first choice to save this land for countless reasons, the least being because you were only ever a story told to me as a pickney. But sometimes there's truth in fiction, and I need the might of the Witch of Bone and Briar."

My breath catches.

The Bonemantis, griot, whatever, used that same title.

"As a pickney I could only dream about what she would mean to this world—to my world. As a man, I have to believe it's possible, because without her the citizens of this dissolved empire don't have a hope of surviving." He prowls closer, his voice a soft rumble. "It might not always have been you, Iraya, but choosing you was a decision I made alone. Not Jazmyne. If you don't want to take my word, ask them."

His conduit beams; two figures pop into existence beside him.

Sham. Delyse. Bruised, just as they were when I saw them last. But alive.

It can't be.

"I know what you're thinking," Delyse says—*it* says. A duppy. Guzzu. A trap.

"But I'm real, Just-Ira."

"*We're* real," Shamar corrects. "The night we saw you in the holding cells, Prince Divsylar helped us escape. He printed our faces on two Xanthippe. It was them you killed, not us. We've been hiding in his rooms for the past few days."

"The others?"

"Dead." Delyse's voice is choked sounding. "Why didn't you tell us what you were planning?"

"Hey now," Sham coaxes. "There's no time."

"You could have told me anything," she thunders on regardless.

I can only stand and stare, at a loss for *everything*.

"There are many conversations to be had, but later," Kirdan interrupts. "We need to get out of this palace, now."

You saved them, I don't say, because he's right. Now isn't the time.

"What's the plan?"

"Leave the estate and lie low for a while," Shamar explains, not quite looking at me.

I understand his trepidation. They've all only seen my actions as attempts to separate myself from my order. But watching Delyse and Shamar die, or the magi charmed to wear their faces at least, shifted something for me. I lost Kaleisha because of my choice to work alone. I don't want to lose the friends I've come to know here too.

"All right," I say. They visibly relax.

"Follow me," Kirdan orders.

We take one of the rear exits out into the estate overlooking a courtyard, along an arcade and out past the fruit groves close to where the temple sits. All Xanthippe we encounter are taken out by guzzu from Kirdan, sparks that fly so fast even I don't see most of them until the guards are on the floor. He'll tire fast, without more gold.

A copse of trees in the public gardens is all that stands between us and the palace drive. In here, only our conduit coins' golden light and sporadic bursts from the stars slicing through the canopy overhead guide us through the dark. Rain, largely held at bay by the leaves, patters against them as the storm that's been threatening to break for phases now seems to have decided tonight is the best time.

Kirdan and Delyse walk on either side of me, with Shamar bringing up the rear. All her unspoken words buzz like the insects in the bush around us. Try as I might, the words to explain my actions, to justify what I've done these past few months, don't come. The thought of anything I say disappointing her further is terrifying. Heavy in spirit, I drag my tunic sleeve across my wet face.

Not looking where I'm going, I collide with Kirdan's flung-out arm. "Wait," he mutters, squinting into the shadows ahead of us.

Something silver shoots out of them.

The pirate's lack of magical visibility must be the only reason the flung blade bounces off Kirdan's shoulder gauntlet instead of plunging into his heart.

"You're fleeing with my doyenne's sacrifice, bredren."

Kirdan swears under his breath as Jazmyne's new guard dog strides out of the darkness toward us. He clutches a brute axe across his chest; the blade's bigger than his head.

"Roje," Kirdan growls.

"And guests," he adds with a charming grin.

More pirates emerge from the foliage around us; some drop from the trees, like bough-prowlers, forcing our foursome to cluster closer together. I wipe my face again as the rain bows trees, freeing space for the sky to fall through. As wild-looking as their giant leader, they handle brutish curves of metal, cutlasses, and glinting sabers—in gloved hands. Most of those weapons must be cursed. To be touched by one might mean death.

"Weapon?" I mutter to Kirdan, my eyes on what hangs around the neck of Jazmyne's shadow, Roje. The shriveled mass makes guzzu out of the question. The others wear them too. Pirates might not be able to will magic, but whatever we launch at them will be trapped in those sea slugs and returned tenfold.

"*Prince?*" I hiss. Eyes on Roje, Kirdan doesn't acknowledge me. Fine. I'll handle this another way. Stepping forward, I give the large pirate a little wave. His grin widens, exposing the sharpened incisors on the grill lining his bottom teeth. "I'm sure Emissary Divsylar's flattered you think so highly of his skills that you've come armed to the teeth—and with armed teeth too. They're very . . ." I take my time running my eyes down to his boots and back up to his face, hopeful that the other three are taking advantage of my distraction and picking their opponents. "Large."

"As fun as a dance would be, my fight isn't with you, Obeah-witch." He levels the mammoth axe at my head. The corded muscles in his arm don't quiver beneath its weight. Slick with rain, its sharp edge glints. "The loss of a beauty such as yours would be a shame, but I won't hesitate to cut you down if the Zesian's too afraid to fight me himself."

"Well, let's go then, prick," Kirdan says. "I am, of course, referring to your teeth."

With a laugh, Roje charges, swinging wide. Lunging before me, Kirdan deflects the powerful blow with his saber and hunting knife, gritting his teeth at the contact. The blades ring like a call to war, shedding their silver to reveal gold—*conduit gold.*

"Take care of them." Kirdan tosses me the conduit weapons.

I'm so stunned I nearly drop them. I haven't held a conduit weapon since my training days at the mountain bohío. Carrying one would make him powerful, but Kirdan has *four*—twin golden daggers slide from each of his vambraces. They spark with light as he channels his ancestors' magic to meet Roje blow for blow.

He is one of *the* royals. And a Simbarabo general at that. I don't know where to look. His cut hair is plastered to his skull, in the rain, but the loss of the power of its length does not hold him back; his muscles bunch beneath his shirt as he parries with Roje. A legend made flesh, he looks every inch the fabled soldier.

"Watch your side!" Shamar warns.

I spin. Two pirates approach. Twins, they perform the dance of battle in sync. Too in sync. One swipes low with a wicked shard of metal, and the other launches an arc overhead with a spiked bat. I concede the hit to my shoulder to keep my ankles, snarling at the tens of tiny blades ripping through my skin. A fist slams into my open mouth. I stumble back, coughing my tongue from my throat.

They dance toward me again, and magic percolates unbidden. Kirdan's blades ignite as my magic leaps for the excess of gold. No. *No.* A succession of red sparks shoot from either blade's tip, straight to the trappers around the twins' necks.

I run for cover. The tree explodes as I dive behind it. More splinters shoot into my tender skin. I surge to my feet again. Dazed by the sound of the blast, I slam into another tree. One I vaguely recognize by its narrow leaves. I know where we are, what we're close to. Drawing on latent strength, I shove away from the tree and lunge farther into the bush, narrowly evading the second suppression spark as it obliterates the tree I was just clinging to.

"She's running!" Delyse yells, cursing in patwah.

I don't have time for indignation, but *really*?

I battle through a thick patch of brambles, taking each lash from a branch, every slice from a scion in silence as I trace familiar steps—easier steps than the pirates will be able to find. Their struggle through the knot of vegetation behind me should guarantee enough time to do what I need to.

When I reach the Adair Graveyard, I gather discarded fronds and arrange them in a pyre as I make my walk around them. During my sixth turn, the brambles rustle in warning.

The pirates.

The deepest cuts in my shoulder scream as I plunge my fingers inside and smear the blood on my face. I swirl wudu, ishó, kiir, and mínibo. This time I don't use sálo. I need possession, and that requires máial.

"Obújufra. Bone. Ta'k na mi, arik na mi." After greeting the ancestors, I chant the deep patwah from the tomb under my breath. There's just one last step to complete the enchantment. I need to light the circle of leaves.

Rustlings from the snares are louder now. The twins will make it through at any moment. The coin around my neck splutters, the light ebbing. *Come on.* One of the pirates stumbles through and reaches back to help his brother. I renew my focus, appealing to all seven of the Mudda's Faces, to Mama, Dada. The brother's almost out of the brambles now.

I make one final plea.

The pyre goes up in flames, goes out, and then lights once more.

That's twice.

"Fire doesn't scare us, Obeah." The second twin pops out. Together, they advance.

"Then you're in excellent company. It doesn't scare them either."

The tomb's lid cracks, like the earth beneath our feet has split in half. The twins stop. I retreat from its side as the casing yawns wider like the hungry maw of a creature woken too early from slumber. Within its shadowed depths, a primordial groan resonates through the stone. Lit only by the flickering pyre now suspended in the air above the tomb, the graveyard assumes a nightmarish tenor. Even my breath catches when my ancestor's skeletal hand grips the side of the stone basin. She pulls her bones up; they clack like steel pans. Her skull turns until she finds me, the summoner, eye sockets endlessly empty.

"An Adair's under attack," I exhale, sure to exercise a respectful tone. "Cwenburg's Obeah are under attack. Help. Please."

The empress of old rises from the dark depths of her chamber with stilted, jerky movements. And she's not alone. There may be dozens of tombs in this graveyard, but entire families are buried inside. I don't need the magic for all of them. Awakening one will be enough. The ancestors will do the rest. I owe them an entire vat of rum for their aid.

Generations of pickney, siblings, cousins follow the empress. The pirate twins bolt back through the foliage. With one nod from me the skeletons charge after them with a melodious clack of bones.

When the twins' screams fade, I follow, my running pack

slung over my shoulder. Preceded by a cluster of skeletal pick-ney who tear down the snares and brambles for me, I step over torn parts of the twins scattered for the carrion until the fight is before me once more.

"Hey!" One by one, the pirates catch sight of my Army of the Dead.

Roje whistles. It's shrill and loud—a call to retreat.

"Go on." I gesture with Kirdan's saber. "I'll give you a head start."

They flee into the trees.

I hold out until the leaves still, then my legs give. Weak with magical exertion and woozy with blood loss, for a moment there's nothing but the rush of warm air, the feeling of weight-lessness, and then—arms. They cradle me against a chest damp with blood and sweat.

"This doesn't count as swooning."

"And this," Kirdan returns, "I hope you'll forgive me for."

Something cool hooks around my wrist, locking in place with a click. Its weight's familiar—it's a *fetter*, connected to a twin around Kirdan's wrist.

"What the hell is this?"

Sham and Delyse raise their weapons. "*This* wasn't the plan," the latter says.

"No. It's the way things must be."

I tug against the shackle and almost pass out at the zing that flits through my body. My bag slips from my shoulder. Kirdan's arms tighten around me.

"I wouldn't move again if I were you. The shackles are

glyphed. Aside from muting your magic, any resistance and they'll shock you." For a moment, apologies brim in his gaze, but they're quickly replaced by the unflinching glint of duty I know too well from him.

"Bag-o-wire," Shamar spits. "You told us you'd help keep her safe!" He starts for me.

"Don't," Kirdan cautions. "There's been enough bloodshed tonight. Be grateful I'm giving you this choice."

"And my choice?" I whisper.

Kirdan leans in close. "War makes killers out of most, and heroes out of few." His eyes dip to his wrist, where our bargain still sits. "I won't let you become the former."

"You're making a mistake." I try to squirm, to fight. "I'm no hero."

"Not yet." His eyes harden, like a crust of skin over a gaping wound, before we sift.

55

JAZMYNE

Javel's exsanguinated body is left out for viewing in the Temple of the Supreme Being's Chosen.

At least, that's who his family believes they mourn when Anya and I leave them sobbing around the altar, touching his face, his curls, holding his hands while trying to ignore the bandages around his wrists and neck from the incisions.

"You're sure the guzzu will hold?" I murmur, gathering my kaftan in hand as we descend the golden steps into the lamplit gardens lashed by rain and wind.

Anya casts a shield around us both. "As long as they don't check the center of his back for the Illusion Glyph, they'll never know that body doesn't belong to their son."

Who is probably kicking and screaming in the palace holding cells as we speak.

"I feel a little sick using one of tonight's dead like that." Anya sighs.

"Don't remind me." I had to slice the flesh, press the knife into skin, and then bleed the corpse before what remains of the council, Javel's family.

"I'd almost feel bad for Ormine too, if Javel wasn't such an ass."

I feel worse for myself.

If Kirdan had waited to release the sukuyan, I wouldn't have found that sacrificial blade in *my* hand, and most of the island's Alumbrar looking at me to protect them after I announced their doyenne was killed by her Obeah shields. But of course, he never intended on helping me with the Yielder guzzu. He stopped being helpful long before tonight. Thank the Mudda for the rain, for the excuse it provided to move to the temple, where Anya's quick thinking helped me save face.

She reads my silence as only she can. "You knew he wasn't to be trusted."

"*You* knew." My voice thickens. I'm not ready to talk about Kirdan yet.

"At least you don't need him now. Roje's intervention couldn't have been timelier." Anya glances at me. "Do I want to know what you promised to get him here?"

Almighty.

The jéges.

I don't know where the doyenne—*the late doyenne*, I mentally correct, suddenly queasy—left them.

"Anya—"

"Doyenne!"

The bellow is followed by crashing through the bush. Roje

thunders out, followed by a phalanx of pirates. All are soaked through and bleeding.

"What is it?" Anya demands when they just stand there, panting and exchanging looks amongst themselves.

Oh no.

"Don't tell me they got away."

Anya swears. "They didn't get away. These dunce bats *lost* them!"

"Shh!" I snipe. "Not here." Not where the council might listen. "Come to the palace."

Xanthippe still clean up bodies and body parts from the sukuyan's attack. I nod my thanks, ever the benevolent new ruler, when all I want to do is scream and scream into the night. At least I won't have to deal with the Witches Council on top of everything else. We're all meant to be in mourning for the doyenne—the late doyenne. But they'll come back tomorrow, and for the eight days following. I can't dismiss them until after the Nine Night, which must be planned, then there are the jéges to locate, and now—

"Tell me what happened to Iraya and Kirdan," I demand, the moment the doyenne's study door is shut. "Tell me they didn't escape *together*."

Hands gripping the handle of a mammoth axe, Roje can't look at me. "With two others."

I turn away, lest the screams I suppress erupt in his face.

"My doyenne—"

"She doesn't need your groveling, *sea snake*," Anya hisses. "She needs details."

"They don't matter," I say to the window, unable and unwilling to turn around. "Roje, ensure the crew are in the defense positions the shields would have taken, Filmore's around somewhere, he'll show you where to go, and then I need you to go to the holding cells."

"Forgive me," he says with a nod. "I won't disappoint you again."

When the door closes, I turn to Anya, my face crumpling. "I've done something foolish." And with that I confess, telling her everything about my encounter with Roje, the promises I made and the lack of intelligence I have about all jéges bar the locket and the mirror—ones I can't use, not without Adair blood. She's horrified, and rightly so.

"What can we do?" she whispers.

She'd do better asking, *What have I done?*

"I'm going to tear this palace apart." I rub my eyes, smearing shadow and kohl across my face like war paint. "And neither of us will mention any of this to Roje—to anyone."

"I think that last part goes without saying. . . . Are you sure you don't have an idea where any might be? The doyenne didn't have many, did she?"

"Only the scroll containing the location of the Conduit Falls and the Grimoire."

"A map and a book," Anya corrects. "There's a Stealth exercise where you reduce items to their simplest selves to help recall where they are." She strides over to the desk and begins rooting through the missives there. "Can you remember the doyenne ever consulting a map, or perhaps using the same book more than once?"

My body is awash with a chill.

"She gave me her journal tonight. . . ." The battered book she turned to whenever there was a problem on the estate, entrusted it to my care in her final hour when she believed the Jade Guild were coming—the Adair Grimoire, it could only be. Gathering the now ruined hem of my kaftan, I hasten toward the door. "If I'm right, it will contain the Yielder guzzu. We can sacrifice Javel, protect the island. Thank the gods. With me, Anya, quick!"

We race through the palace to my study; it's a ruin of woodwork and pages from books I'll mourn later.

"I dropped it here. Help me!"

Her conduit lights, and the large debris is raised into the air. We sift through the mess on the floor once, twice. And then again, more fervently.

"Jazmyne—"

"Something exploded in here; the blast could have moved it."

We destroy the study further, combing through everything until even I have to admit defeat—and my own stupidity. She *gave* me the journal, the Grimoire, and I threw it to the floor for Kirdan to steal. For surely that's why it isn't here any longer.

My wrist twinges with the phantom weight of the bargain.

"He has it, doesn't he."

It isn't a question.

"The last Sole was . . ." Anya conducts a mental tally. "Nine months ago. It lasts a year, so we have—"

"Three months before it falls, and the Iron Shore attacks, if I lose the race for queen, or Zesia comes knocking, possibly with the Lost Empress leading the charge." I scratch at the invisible bond connecting us. *Seven days to leave* . . .

Anya and I stare at one another in silent shock. *Give up*, that small voice I thought had silenced begs. *Give up and run.*

But I can't. Not now. *I wanted this*, I remind myself, in a louder voice.

And now I must do whatever it takes to keep it.

56

IRA

We whorl into being on a hilltop, a stone sibling amidst others surrounded by Carne Sea.

Kirdan's grip saves me from slamming onto my hands and knees. Sifting is awful at the best of times, but worse when you're not expecting it.

"You're bleeding. I'll heal you."

"Let go of me." I stumble out of his grasp, only to be zapped by the cuff. My wet skin intensifies the pain, as well as my temper. "And get these off me. *Now*. I won't ask so politely again."

"If that's polite," Delyse says, "something went wrong with my upraising."

I twist around to gape at her, Shamar, standing on the craggy rock with us.

"You're *here*?"

She merely sets her mouth and looks on; so does he.

"What's going on?"

"Do you feel like your hand's about to fall off?"

"N—"

"Not *you*. Prince?"

"Give me a moment."

My eyes flicker between the trio, united in something they haven't shared.

Minutes tick by, punctuated by the roar and crash of waves against the bluff peppered with black sand. This archipelago might be volcanic. How fitting. If my questions continue to go unanswered I'll have an eruption of my own.

"If one of you doesn't—"

"It worked." Kirdan nods at the other two. "No pain, and as you both heard, Iraya's in fighting form."

"I'm sorry?"

Delyse snorts. "An apology. Shame it's not genuine, mon." With an abruptness only lent to a slight, she turns to Kirdan. "We'll head down to base camp while you tell our dear empress how sorry she should really be."

Shamar jerks his head, as though he thought about bowing and he changed his mind, before following her. Then it's just Kirdan, me, the sky, and the sea.

The cuffs connecting us vanish.

"You're not a prisoner," he says, by way of explanation. "Just a fool." He flips wet hair out of his eyes. Though the sky is steel-colored, angry, no rain falls out here. "You suggested a Shook Bargain to Jazmyne after I'd already forged an alliance with Delyse and Shamar."

"And I was supposed to know this?"

"You might have," he snaps back, "if you ever listened a day in your life. Because that never happened, we needed you to think you'd been kidnapped in order to prevent the bargain's completion. Though at this point I don't know if you plan on returning to Aiyca." He huffs a humorless laugh. "I don't know if you've planned much beyond punching me in the nose and taking it from there."

"You're warmer than you think." I take a moment to assess him, the fatigue beneath his eyes, the cuts and bruises on his face, the tears in his cloak. He fought against Jazmyne's allies, stole me away from Aiyca. He's allied with Delyse and Shamar—the Jade Guild too? Only days ago he admitted to fabricating the heat that even now simmers between us with a stubborn insistence. But then, he made that comment back in the study that he chose me. "I'm listening now, Zesian." Our eyes meet, crash, like wave against rock. "I want to know everything."

He stares at me a moment longer, emotions warring across his features—fury, disappointment, and several others I find it harder to discern.

"Only if I can see to those wounds simultaneously."

"Fine."

He shucks his cloak with a wince. I commit the injury to memory, just in case. He advances on me; I stiffen, but he passes me and sits on the edge of the hill, legs dangling over the jagged teeth of rock rising from the sea below. After a moment, I join him. He doesn't touch me, but a comforting warmth spears through the wound on my shoulder, dulling the sting of my skin rejecting splinters and knitting back together. Once again I can only marvel at his power, even without the length of his hair. Though he is carrying that surfeit of gold I always suspected he had.

"Better?"

"Yeh mon."

"Good . . . I didn't want you to exist," he says to the distance; I reel at the abruptness of it. "I didn't think it possible to change Xaymaca if part of its history remained to remind the empire of what it had been. This island needed to change. It needed to grow for people like me and the Alumbrar to have a chance."

"What of the Obeah? Didn't we deserve a chance?"

"I haven't condoned what Doyenne Cariot has done here, mon. But I didn't believe my ilk in Aiyca wanted anything other than to return to their former way of life. They hadn't learned from the Alumbrar rising against them. It was just another game of possession, to steal the ball back from the pickney who took it from them. So I aligned myself with Jazmyne."

I snort, unable to help myself.

"She was different in the beginning," he argues. "We shared a vision, a hope. But things changed, these past few months. She courted power, and it corrupted the good in her."

"And you blame me for that?"

"I'd like to, but I've had to concede that I might have wished for Jazmyne to be someone she wasn't."

He says her name with something like tenderness.

"You care about her."

"She was my only friend here for two years. Those feelings don't just go." He sighs. "And then there was you, wildly different from your stories, secretive and distant from your order. It was confusing. You were confusing. Even as you hid, you sought to keep them safe. Until it came down to them or the advancement of your own plans." He shakes his head.

I tell myself his observations don't hurt.

"Did you pull me out of there just to insult me again?"

"I pulled you out because you've run from power and position since arriving from Carne, before even. I remember the shock on the face of your sistren at Carling Hill."

Kaleisha.

"You hadn't told her who you were. You hadn't told anyone. While I'd soon learn it was to protect your own interests, mostly, with Jazmyne more concerned about keeping Aiyca from your clutches than raising a different land, our interests became aligned."

So that's it.

"You want something from me."

He looks at me, and I feel it as sure as any touch. "You'll want something from me too when I tell you what I know. Timbámbu isn't the first instance in which the Unlit have turned to the ancestors." His eyes gleam with all the dangers of Witchfire.

"You mean the Jade Guild."

"I think we might find them one and the same."

Almighty. "No," I whisper.

"Jazmyne and I had an alliance with the latter that required some meetings for negotiations. I followed the envoy back to the wetlands once, and I saw . . ." He shudders. "I don't know what I saw. But they weren't from this side of the veil." His words elicit a shiver from me. "Do you know that every time the ancestors are used, it leaves scratches in the barrier between the living and dead? Most are tiny, inconsequential in the tapestry that keeps us safe from things best unseen, but other guzzu demand a higher price. They blast gaping holes that permit all sorts to slink through. And I think Timbámbu is what they're using to usher primordial creatures onto this island."

"Monsters?" Was the late doyenne being literal when she spoke of who attacked my family?

Kirdan nods. "You can't tell me you don't know what they're for."

War.

I grip the stony hill beneath me, but the pebbles of earth slip through my fingers. The Unlit, the same Unlit who helped kill Mama, Dada, plot to take Aiyca once more under the mantle of the Jade Guild. And they have creatures. Gods above. Conscripted Obeah across the island have rallied in their name.

"With the Simbarabo," Kirdan continues, "I'll help you banish what slithers, even now, toward your home."

"At what cost?" I manage to murmur.

"If you won't lead, decree a successor—an empress—who will abolish the laws preventing doyens ruling in Zesia."

"Why?"

His jaw clenches into sharper definition as he wrestles with a cost himself. "Mama is sick, my sisters younger than me, untried and foolish. They're not ready to take on an island locked in the past that faces conflict from those determined to control the future. Yes," he says, answering the question that rippled across my face, "those ungodly beasts dwell in Zesia, and I guarantee you they plague the Skylands too if the Jade Guild have been smart enough to immobilize my island with them. They're cutting us off from one another to make their victory here easier. And once they've taken Aiyca, its conduit gold, nothing will stop them from coming for my home." He stares back across the waters, far from an island he's desperate to save because those same walls I've run from, he's willing to find a way over.

I don't expect a hot wave of shame to submerge my protests, challenges. But it does.

"How long do I have to give you an answer?"

"Until first light."

"Then I suppose we should return to the others."

"Wait—" His hand reaches for mine.

Our fingertips graze.

"I let you believe that Jazmyne made me seduce you, in the Salt Woods. She did ask, but . . . by that time I was already losing against the indifference I wanted to feel toward you." My heart stutters. "You're Obeah; can you honestly tell me we're an order who do things simply because we're told to? Even now, I want to be distant. To feel nothing for you." Kirdan's voice grows hoarse and my body tightens. "It would make whatever comes next easier, but this entire time I've been fighting against doing the one thing I truly *do* want."

I want to look at him.

I don't want to look at him.

"Iraya . . ."

Gods.

My name on his lips has always threatened to undo me.

"No," I murmur, incongruously afraid. "No. I can't do this." This, this *thing* between us that's as bracing as the waves that curl at our heels, and I—I can't drown in him. "If what you say is true, there's much to prepare for and I can't—I can't think about this right now."

In my peripheral vision I see him turn away and nod at the sky. It's an oddly defeated move. I don't want to think about the warmth of his fingers against mine. And yet the entire walk downhill, exchanging the sea breeze for the barrier of heat from palm and bush, it's all I do. I think about Kirdan's shoulder brushing against my own when the ground dips and brings us together, the distance between our fingers as they swing at our sides.

I think about the world he wants and ask myself what it would look like, if it could be possible—if change is possible.

Delyse and Shamar sit in a clearing around a fire; a tray of snapper sits to the edge. Separating to sit on opposite sides of the flames, neither Kirdan nor I make a move to serve ourselves.

"Now you know the entire story, the depravity of the Jade Guild, our deteriorating situation here—what is to be done,

Empress?" Delyse's voice drips with sarcasm. She doesn't expect me to have a plan, and I'm not sure I do exactly, but I have an idea.

"I propose we travel to the Skylands, win over their aerial army, and fly back to Aiyca to destroy every one of the Unlit's pets."

That makes them all sit to attention.

"You'll rule?" Delyse breathes. "Just like that?"

I'm hesitant to say no, not wishing to disappoint her further, but one look at Kirdan and I find I don't have to.

"It's not about ruling," he says. "It's about surviving to see what comes next. And I think I have something that might help." He digs around inside his cloak and removes a slim book. "One Adair Grimoire."

Delyse and Shamar gasp; I stare at the book, its dull cover repelling all light.

"How'd you get that?"

"Jazmyne." He shakes his head. "She dropped it and it opened. I recognized the deep patwah. So she has the Amplifier Locket and the Mirror of Two Faces, and we have—"

"About that . . ." I interrupt, reaching for my pack one of the others must have carried over from Aiyca. Nestled between my stolen clothing for disguise, rations, is the second mirror, which I brandish. "She has *one* of the mirrors. Turns out they're a pair."

At Kirdan's raised brow, I shrug, not sheepish in the least.

"Then we are evenly matched," Delyse says, once the mirror has been passed from hand to hand. The Grimoire seemed to have skipped my inspection, though.

"Not quite." Shamar tosses a stick into the flames. "She has a fleet of pirates."

Outside the fire's minatory might, the bush is pitch-black. It seems to presage the darkness that will come, the future that Bonemantis warned me to be ready for, in her own way.

"We can have an entourage of our own too," I remind him quietly.

"The Skylands have never involved themselves in matters of the empire before."

"No." My mouth twists in a smile not unlike the first I gave Kirdan all those months ago in Carne. One that welcomes challenge with a fighter's nod. "But they've never been asked by me."

Not the hero my order wished for, but not the villain I thought I needed to become in order to win either. Forged by my past and fortified by my mistakes, I'm something of my own making.

And this empire will tremble with the knowledge that Iraya Adair comes, at last.

‖≂⁊ MÉTIERS ⸗⁊◐
Familial vocations undertaken by firstborn daughters at birth

OBEAH
~~

Artisans of Cloth
Scarification: A diagonal white line
on the left or right bicep, three for Masters

Artisans of Metal
Scarification: A pair of crossed white hammers
on the upper arm, two for Masters

Artisans of Wood
Scarification: Crossed white clubs
on the upper arm, two for Masters

Bonemantis—Seers
Scarification: A white eye between their brows,
three lines within the iris for Masters

Bush Healers
Scarification: A white bowl on both palms, with a cloud of
smoke above it for Masters

Growers

Scarification: White vines crossing the fingers on the dominant hand, multiple leaves for Masters

Poisoners

Scarification: White dots horizontally set across the chin, three for Masters

Squallers

Scarification: A circle on the back of the dominant hand, three interlinked circles for Masters

Stealths

Scarification: A white line horizontally set beneath the right eye, three lines for Masters

Transmuters

Scarification: A white alchemical symbol of transmutation on the back of the neck, a triangle within two circles for Masters

Warriors

Scarification: A vertical white line between the eyebrows, three for Masters

Wranglers

Scarification: White paw prints above the heart, three for Masters

ALUMBRAR

~

Artisans of Cloth
Color: Peach

Artisans of Gems
Color: Pewter

Artisans of Wood
Color: Steel

Erudites
Color: Sapphire

Growers
Color: Emerald

Healers
Color: Maroon

Sibyls
Color: Scarlet

Squallers
Color: Arctic blue

Stealths
Color: Black

Transmuters
Color: Umber

Wranglers
Color: Sand

SUPREME BEING
The Seven-Faced Mudda

FACE OF AURORE	Goddess of Creation
FACE OF BENITO	God of Fortune
FACE OF CLOTILLE	Goddess of Warriors and Might
FACE OF CONSUELO	Goddess of Consolation
FACE OF DUILIO	God of War and Blood and Metal
FACE OF MERCE	Goddess of Compassion
FACE OF SOFEA	God of Pathways

Acknowledgments

It's a strange and wonderful thing to have a ten-year-old wish fulfilled.

As soon as I knew books were written by people, it was the only thing I wanted to do, and I owe thanks to so many people for helping to make it happen. I'm going to issue them chronologically to try to include everyone. While it's clear to all who've read this book that I can't tell a short story, I'm going to try not to rhapsodise too much—here we go.

The first thanks are for my parents, who gave me my early love of books, and always encouraged my creativity. To you both, I will forever be grateful. My mum has always been my first reader and biggest champion—I want to thank her for believing in me and my writing when I couldn't, for supporting my sabbatical so I could finish this book, and only yelling about the chores a handful of times. You're the bees' knees, Mel; this book might not exist without you, though without those chores I might have finished sooner. My big brother Chris gave me my love of fantasy. I was way too young to appreciate *The Hobbit* during my first read, but I read it so he would have to wait a turn, and inadvertently developed a love for winning and sprawling worlds. Calvin. I'm tempted to leave it there since he hasn't read this book yet, but I guess I can say that, though he's my little brother, his heart has always been huge. They've both suffered through my rambles about publishing woes with little complaint which makes them all right, for brothers.

Though vast, my extended family has always played an intimate role in my life. My Nan, whose sense of humor is as sharp as her hearing. Josie, Megan, Clive, and the many other aunts and uncles and cousins whose homes I've run through, and whose food and stories have kept me full. While across the world, the Jamaican contingent has never been far away. Aunty Sandra, to whom this book is dedicated, Aunty Maxine, Daniesha, and Dave, who helped me authenticate this world, and took me to the places that helped inspire it.

Mrs. Gilbert and Mr. Cousins were my favorite English teachers when I was in school. They both saw something in my creative writing, and pushed me to become better at it. Mr. Cousins was the biggest inspiration to my sixth form class, and in addition to giving me my very first entry form into a writing contest, he also gave me the biggest appreciation for the nuances of literature; his are lessons I still carry a decade on.

Witches Steeped in Gold has been championed by many over the years—Davinia Andrew-Lynch, the first publishing professional to read this book and tell me it had potential.

Cassie and Piera, who managed to fit in reads between essays when we were at school and, later, life. Charlotte, my sounding board and one of the best people I know, who has also made sure I haven't turned out too badly. Shahima dragged me across East Asia, showing me a bigger world and teaching me how to laugh at every scenario whether good or bad, even while scuba-diving eight meters below the ocean. Ackeba inspired the sass. No surprises there. She's also been my big sister and first call in all aspects of life. Tracey and Louie rescued me with that Jamaican Bible! And the frequent patwah helped too, T. Harps, our unofficial book club started late and thank goodness for that otherwise neither of us would have completed any work. She dropped real life to read this book when I needed it most, and has flooded it and me with an overwhelming deluge of love and support. She's an amazing human and kindred spirit. I'm waiting on her book next—get a move on, will you? While on the topic of not completing any work, Alex and Aaron were on hand to help in that regard. Though their taste is sometimes questionable when it comes to movies and TV, in this case I can't fault it. Dee Brady has been a mentor, a second mum, a fierce advocate, and the person who inspires me to do and be better. Thank you for all the love, support, understanding, and writing snacks. You are the cat's pajamas.

Before 2017 I didn't know any other writers, and now I am lucky enough to be part of several communities filled with the best, like the 21ders, the class of 2k21 books debut group, the Black Mermaids, and the Pitch Wars Class of 2017. There are too many of you to name, but I am appreciative of my interactions with all of you, and the motivation and inspiration you've provided over the years. Huge thanks to Brenda Drake and the tireless efforts of the Pitch Wars committee for creating an environment where books can grow and friendships flourish. Thank you to Adalyn and Tomi for the tough love I needed to go away and finish this book—I've lost count of which draft this is, but it is, and that's all that matters. I'm especially grateful to know Jade Loren and Kylie Schachte. All the thanks for the endless conversations, jokes, and lamentations about this weird publishing gig. One of my earliest readers, Fallon, a fellow advocate of fierce weapon-wielding girls, provided enthusiasm and feedback that was invaluable—thank you. To Rena Barron, Alexis Henderson, and Shelby Mahurin, thank you for your support during Pitchwars and in the years since. I love that *Witches Steeped in Gold* gets to share shelf space with your wonderful works.

There's a reason my world is a matriarchy. I am surrounded by the best women, like the Afro-Caribbean Avengers, Deborah F. Savoy, Abbey Okubadejo, and Roseanne A. Brown, who Assembled throughout Pitch Wars, and in the years since. Thank you for being there in those early days; I've been so happy witnessing you all shine, and look forward to all the great news coming down the pipeline.

A special thanks also to Dhonielle Clayton and Samantha Shannon for the early love, enthusiasm, and support for *Witches Steeped in Gold*. Wishes are a strange thing, but an even stranger thing is to work with the people whose writing has inspired your own.

While books take the village I'm blessed to be part of, they also demand a partner in crime. Deborah F. Savoy is mine. Both a brilliant and sage friend, she has held me down on deadline, been a sounding board for the important things, like whether Sebastian Stan is finest in Gossip Girl or the Marvel Universe—we'll agree to disagree—and the other important things, like writing, self-care, careers, and whether salt lamps or humidifiers are the better choice. Dee. I am so grateful to know you, and to be seated beside you on this roller coaster.

Back to that village: I'm overjoyed that mine keeps expanding to welcome new, wonderful people, like Kat Dunn and Faridah Abike-lyimide—though, Faridah, I'd appreciate if you stopped terrifying me with the floating heads in my messages. And Kat, I'm not sure you're meant to encourage me to start new TV series while on deadline. All the same, meeting you both has been a highlight in this reel of wonderful moments. Kaymara, the CEO and lead curator of Decentred Lit, the ineffable Jamaican book box—thank you for you early love and enthusiasm, and for connecting me with Akilah White, whose sensitivity notes were thoughtfully rendered with the beautiful cadence I associate with home. Thank you to all the bloggers and booktubers who have expressed early enthusiasm about *Witches Steeped in Gold*, who have posted stunning photos, talked about it on their channels, and written reviews. Very bizarre to have something created in my head discussed, in the best of ways.

Landing at HarperCollins has been a dream come true, and

I am so thankful for the amazing teams working behind the scenes in editorial and marketing to bring *Witches Steeped in Gold* out into the world. Lots of love to Clare Vaughn and the creative minds flying the Epic Reads banner; same to the awesome teams in Marketing and Design: Ebony LaDelle, who injected the cover with Jamaican flair, and Chris Kwon, Jenna Stempel-Lobell, Alison Donalty, Nick Oelschlägel, who then captured this story's essence with their stunning design, as well as the incredibly talented Ashley Straker, whose illustrations of Ira and Jaz could have been plucked straight out of my head. Bethany Reis, Jessica Berg, Sonja West, and Dan Janeck held their microscopes to this novel—thank you for suffering through all my in-line repetitions, and for buffing and polishing this story until it shined. I look forward to meeting you all one day soon to express my gratitude in person.

I've been fortunate enough to land among more industry gems at my UK publishing house, HotKey Books. Thank you to my editor, Carla Hutchinson, for embracing my book and me with such enthusiasm and warmth, creating the best home for Black creators in the UK market. Thanks to the tireless efforts of Molly Holt and Amy Llambias, *Witches Steeped in Gold* has been given wings (all the way to Jamaica, in some cases); thank you for your creativity, acumen, and wit as we've launched this book. Isobel Taylor and Sophie McDonnell provided lambent designs that married so beautifully with the original illustrations on the US cover—thank you both. To Kate Griffiths and Victoria Hart, the secret keepers of the bunch. I can't say what I'm thanking you for at the time of writing this, but your work securing You Know What has made multiple dreams come true.

And of course, dear reader, I want to thank you for picking up this book; if you've read it already you'll know how much I love a corker of a chapter ending, and the closing of these acknowledgements will be no different with these final heavy hitters—thank you to Taylor Haggerty, and the entire team at Root Literary, who believed in this book and me as a debut. I am so appreciative of all your work, and that you paired me with Alice Jerman, editor extraordinaire and fellow dessert lover, who read this twisty, dark book, saw its heart, and helped me see it too.

THE DOYENNE IS DEAD, AND THE THRONE IS EMPTY.
THE WAR HAS JUST BEGUN.

Turn the page for an excerpt from

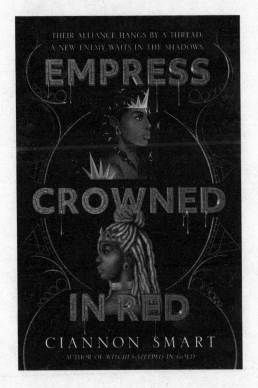

JAZMYNE

Knowing how heavy the crown would feel still doesn't prepare me for its weight.

"On tonight's coronation eve, we bestow this cradle of riches upon your head," the Alumbrar Seer before me intones, setting the gold circlet atop my curls, "to represent Aiyca's greatest treasure you will serve and protect: its people." Her movements are unsteady, bafan; withdrawing clawed hands, the witch steps aside as she says her next words. "Never forget that they, and they alone, are between you and the Supreme Being."

Beyond the Seer, on the dais steps below the throne, stand her fellow witches, the cabinet of fourteen who have served the crown for a decade. The wall of windows in the throne room behind them showcases cold teal light from a steepening dawn. As it bleeds through the vestiges of the rising sun, it stains the Alumbrar faces in the crowd gathered to witness my ascension, casting their wariness, their fear, in a lattice of shadows. Not even twenty-four hours earlier, their last doyenne fell—was *felled* by an axe that may swing at my neck too, yet.

Swallowing, I focus on the Seer, who steps back into my line of sight.

"All decisions henceforth must respect your people them, you understand?"

An internal war is fought. Fear versus fervor. The former cannot have an inch.

"I understand."

If the warning of the Seer's words isn't enough of a reminder about how my past decisions have impacted my order's present, or the tried prescience of her métier reflected in her milky eyes as the spirits of the long dead commune through her, the scarlet kaftan she wears is more than sufficient. Last night, before the events of the Sole, that color mirrored fire; my plans were set to purify an inflicted isle. Now it slinks down the dais steps like blood—in addition to mine, my order's is in danger of being spilled if I make the mistake of faltering for even a second.

"We place this scepter in your hands," the Seer goes on to cantillate; her salt-and-pepper twists quivering with her intensity, "to remind you that your reach alone is limited; seek out additional hands in your plight to keep Aiyca, its people them, hale and protected." She places the baton of gold into my waiting palm. "Never forget to pursue those hands should you need them."

A shadow catches my eye beneath the east mezzanine. Anya, dressed for Stealth in obsidian silk, is ever stalwart, like the pillars to her left and right. Her silver ponytail bobs in a proud flag of victory; light catches the unspent tears in her eyes as the intention we set for me to take the throne, so long ago now, comes true.

"Upon this night," the Seer continues, the rhythmic cadence of her voice a lullaby to soothe the roiling unease in my belly, "we pronounce you, Jazmyne Amancia Cariot, former emissary to the crown and second-born pickney of the late Doyenne Judair Cariot, Regent of Aiyca and all its territories."

A bolt of shock electrifies my insides—disbelief.

Regent?

Stunned, I look up into the white eyes of the witch leading the coronation. In the polished mahogany of her face, they are consuming. *Doyenne.* My frown castigates where my words cannot. Not before an audience of Alumbrar, including what remains of the Witches Council, who stand vigil close to Anya. *I told you to crown me* doyenne, *not a glorified babysitter.*

"Until such a time as when you inherit your magic," the witch continues, "meeting the eligibility to become doyenne of this great and noble land." She pauses as though in explanation, in a face-slapping reminder that I am still not enough. "Do you accept?"

Even as my cheeks burn at the slight, how public it is, my world narrows down to those three words in the Seer's question. With Iraya out there somewhere, allied with Kirdan, the rebels, pride would be a fool's error.

"Yes." A gelid determination replaces the hot flare of

my embarrassment. I draw myself up taller in the throne. "I accept."

"And do you promise to protect this island, its territories, and its people to the best of your ability, even if it means giving your life to do so?"

That determination morphs from ice to steel around my bones, and something more intrinsic—my will.

"I do."

The witch retreats down the dais steps to join her sistren; they stand in a line, arms aloft before them. "*And so it is promised*," the cabinet say in unison, "*so things do. Long live Aiyca's regent, Jazmyne Amancia Cariot, Favored by the Supreme Being, Healing Hands of Aiyca, Watchful Eye of Carne Sea, first of her name, and sole living heir of Doyenne Cariot.*"

Though the Sibyls and I crafted them together, with Anya's aid, hearing them called by my order transcends me from myself, from emissary to the crown.

"*Long live Aiyca's regent*" is returned by a crowd that isn't as sure as I need them to be, yet; my titles follow.

Standing, I allow myself one shallow breath, one moment to mentally savor the bittersweet paean of a title I never wanted, knowing it's the final hurdle before the one I've fought for and sacrificed in the name of. As my order will soon learn. A declaration of gold, my kaftan glows in the growing dark. More of the conduit metal graces my feet, neck, fingers, and finally crowns my head in an obscene finale of power and wealth. Word will spread, and my enemies won't remember that I

4

cannot summon, that as regent I have yet to inherit my ancestors' magic, this morning.

"Wahan, Alumbrar," I call. "From light we are born."

"And to light we cleave."

"Yesterday eve was one of loss," I begin, aware of the mount I need to overcome. "But we are no strangers to dark skies. It is the time our naysayers see how incandescent our shine truly is." Dawn blooms outside, a flare of a triumphing sun. My chin rises in acknowledgment of the Supreme Being's blessing, Their support as I attempt to shift the winds in this throne room from hesitant to confident. "While this morning we usher in a new era for Aiyca, it does not mitigate who we have been in the past: leaders, healers, protectors." Some in the crowd nod. Others only stare with hard expressions, doubt. "We walk into a future shadowed by our past. To that end, it is incumbent on us to be a shining light, to expose our enemies who would rather rely on that darkness, hide in it. Can I place my faith in you, Alumbrar? Can I, in doing all that I can, trust you to do the same? Not only for your families, for our rule, but for Aiyca?" The angle, the threat, is a gamble, one Anya didn't wish for me to make when I scrambled to formulate something inspiring for this moment. *There will be no reward*, I told Anya, *without showing them they are at risk too.* There is no time to earn my order's admiration, and hereafter, the island's. I must incite their fear instead. I'll show them that while I am their sole option, standing alone does not lessen my suitability for this position. "Will you stand with me, for our home?"

I'm met with silence. One so deep that, for a moment, I wonder if I might drown in it.

Was Anya right? My titles, my clothing, everything crafted to cast a greater shadow than I can at this time, after being swallowed by the late doyenne's, aren't enough to intimidate them into taking the knee. They won't follow me. They don't—

"In your words, Regent" is called from the crowd. "We do not fear dark skies!"

One. Thank the gods.

"It's true that we own the night, Alumbrar." There are more cries of affirmation, but they're hollow. I need *more*. "However much our enemies may think themselves comfortable there. Which is why we will defeat them! We will defeat them as we have done for the past decade. As we will do for decades more!" The cries of the crowd finally reach a pitch that makes me feel shot as high as the stars I can no longer see, thanks to the dawn. Is this how the late doyenne felt? Despite the pounds of gold around her neck, her wrists?

The thought of her, Mama, encases my ankles, drags me back down to earth in a breath-stealing jerk. She had the jéges. Magic. None of which saved her, in the end. Six phases stand between me and my inheritance. Compared to eternity, it is but a blink. This I tell myself as the crowd continues to holler and bellow. A time Aiyca will survive, with the aid of Roje, standing guard in the palace grounds with the rest of the pirates.

But we cannot grow complacent.

I cannot.

My left hand is held aloft; the crowd cows before it, row by row. "Victory, Alumbrar, may not look to you as it always has done, but while I sit on this throne, in Aiyca's Golden Seat, I assure you death's shroud will not find its resting place here again. Tonight, we mourn the late doyenne, as we will for the next nine. Thereafter, we live, Alumbrar." I look to Anya, still crying silent tears. "We do more than survive. We triumph. We thrive."

My sistren sinks into a curtsey first, and though the movement brings her forward, the action travels back. Warmth spreads from my chest and through my limbs as, row by row, Alumbrar in the throne room sink into a sign of estimation, with the exception of the Sibyls, who are too old to lower more than their chins, which they do. The three remaining Witches Council presiders also remain standing, their faces tight. We four will need to talk, later. For now, I open my arms to my kneeling order. The line has been cast, the bait taken.

"Rise, Alumbrar. Rise and honor me by honoring the late doyenne."

To their riotous applause, I pick my way down the steps with care, kaftan in hand. Anya meets me at the dais base.

"Regent," she says with a bow.

For all my earlier bravado, the title rips through my belly like a hot knife.

Catching my reaction, of course, Anya edges closer, lowers her voice. "I'm sorry, Jaz. I didn't know."

"Not now," I murmur. Alumbrar edge close, waiting to address their new leader. "Sister Grenich, how lovely to see you." Anya falls to my side as I approach the Alumbrar Healer

I remember well from my time training at Sanar, Aiyca's Alumbrar medical alcázar, the frontrunner in our order's healing. In fact, many Healers approach to bid me good fortune, to take my hand and bow their heads. They are a welcome salve to the late doyenne's court, one filled with vipers whose tongues birth poisonous comments about my succession and lack of magic.

"Will you wed?" an uncle asks. The surviving husband of one of the late doyenne's first cousins, I've never warmed to him. Or the slight daughter standing in his shadow; both watch me with narrowed eyes. "I'm sure you think I'm too old," Ivan goes on to say. "Even though we aren't bound by blood." He rubs bejeweled fingers across a rotund belly. "But my daughter is close to your age, you know."

Demar *is* my blood, though, and strange enough that not even Anya has invited her to bed. I used to see her in the gardens, unsmiling and all but mute, burning ants with glass.

"If it is attraction that concerns you," Ivan says when I am silent for fear of shouting *no* in his face, "or the bearing of pickney, there are matters we can discuss."

"Um. I will take what you've said into consideration, Uncle."

"About both of us?" He makes to step closer, but then Anya is there.

It is but a casual shoulder she angles Ivan's way, but with a wary look in her direction, he keeps his distance.

"It was good of you to come" is my verbal dismissal.

And as if that harrowing conversation set the tone, the

next are just as unpleasant when Alumbrar begin to inquire about the next Yielding. Mention of the sacrifice, their willingness to send their firstborns to slaughter, severs through my already-thin patience. I turn to find Filmore; always close, he's become the right hand to my left, in Anya. With a nod that has him brushing his twists out of his face, he imparts a murmured order, magical, by the faint illumination of the conduit beneath his tunic. The remaining six Stealths in my private vanguard disperse; trained wraiths, they intercept the stingers the doyenne populated her court with before their tips can sink into all the places I am soft.

Taking up a glass from a passing tray between well-wishers, I turn to the wall of windows to seek out another sign from the Supreme Being. Peace rests two hands on my shoulders as the teal light brightens outside, like the opening of eyelids, its color strengthening into something luminous. Something . . .

Something *jade.*

Witchfire.

My throat constricts around the drink at the familiarity, as if its murderous flames have drawn away all moisture from my mouth. For there, a faint growth across the horizon, nascent flames flicker their way to a dangerous maturation.

"Did the drink go down the wrong way?" Anya queries as guests turn to ascertain what's wrong. "Or does your throat burn? Tell me quick. We have an audience."

"Not poisoned," I force out, spluttering. "*Window.*" The green light begins to seep across the sky, like poison oozing from a gash; it will touch those around me first, however distracted they may be by my choking. Though the light will be without the heat of the Witchfire it no doubt belongs to, it will burn away any hard-won belief in my capabilities as a leader. "Anya," I say, my voice barely louder than a whisper for my Stealth-trained sistren. *Aiyca's insurgents*, I cannot say. *They're mounting an attack outside.* "I need the curtains closed. *Now*."

Turning to the glass, her face blanches as her magical will makes the fabric swing closed with a muffled thump.

"Send one of the Stealths after the council," I say, my voice low. "They're to extract the witches clandestinely, and fast."

My sistren imparts the order in a low murmur, conduit alight, so she doesn't need to leave my side. The Xanthippe keep those gathered at bay as we cross the throne room. I share polite nods, comments that I'll return soon; all the while sweat runs down my neck, and my hands, which hold my kaftan, shake.

"I need four of the Stealths to remain inside," I tell Filmore once we're in the quiet emptiness of the cavernous marble vestibule, with only the statuaries and gold-gilt-framed art to overhear. "They're not to let the guests near any windows. All curtains must be kept closed."

"Why?" Ionie Lewis snaps upon approach, her infamous Squaller temper blustering already. A gray cloud that accompanies her everywhere and takes up residence above my head too, since I can only blink at her, at Mariama and Ormine as they join us in their finery. Bangles and chunky necklaces clink like the shackles we might soon find ourselves bearing.

I am without the words until I know—and that knowledge is sought from a vantage point north of the throne room. I head there without further delay.

So rarely was this observatory used by the late doyenne, it's garlanded with cobwebs thick enough that the accompanying Xanthippe must use magic to clear them away. She didn't need this outlook, not when with the one eye she possessed she saw everything. Well, almost everything.

Once the golden hands extending from all seven Stealths' conduits have rescinded back into their coins, wind gusts through the ragged tendrils of dust, and my stomach lurches. Spherical, with teeth of stone connecting roof to floor, Cwenburg's Eye provides a panoramic measure of Aiyca—and where magically impotent sight fails, there are several telescopes infused with guzzu to see the distance.

I don't require the latter to discern the bowls of jade flame on undulating rooftops across the parish. The bright flame is alive and growing more audacious by the minute. My hand goes to my neck, where the locket—the Amplifier I haven't the magic to use—lays.

The Jade Guild are here. Obeah. Insurgents. Drawn arrows aimed at this Golden Seat, at me, which can only mean one thing. *She* is here too.

2

IRAYA

By dawn's light, a crimson wound that takes its time bleeding through the enormity of dusk, the Deleterious Doll takes its form between my fingers.

Half my focus is on the grass I weave, strands of hair hastily plucked from my head dispersed throughout. The remainder is on Delyse, the slow pull and give of her breaths. It isn't our earlier trek of the peninsula alone that tired her. Slumped against a felled tree in our camp, hers is a plant-induced slumber.

If I were a gods-fearing witch, I might have believed the dogwood I came across earlier, endemic to coastal zones such as this craggy peninsula, was put before me by Sofea, the Mudda's Face of Pathways. Either way it was a stroke of fate that enlightened me as to how I should step: as we set our guzzu to protect our camp for the second and final night, I fumbled enough that Delyse added poor dexterity to the list of grievances she has with me, leaving her to work alone and thus inhale the sedative flower I concealed in the grass. It didn't take long for her to fall prey to its debilitating, but otherwise harmless, spores. Ones, I find, with a shake of my head and widening of heavy eyes, I'm fighting the effects of myself. A small price to pay when, should I step quick, most of the Impediment Glyphs Doyenne Cariot incised deep behind my ears can be burned away before Delyse wakes and Shamar returns from his watch to find me missing. As for Kirdan . . . though I cannot see him, I turn to where he's spent almost two straight days resting above this verdant declivity, atop the rocky ledge overlooking the sea where I dashed whatever we might have been to the mercy of the rocks and waves below. With the strength in his hair reduced after Jazmyne had it hacked away, he should sleep awhile yet.

I haven't.

Each time my eyes close, I'm plagued by one thought: *They know how this will end.*

Them. The shadows in my periphery. Always there, but never discerned. Not even now, no matter how closely I scour my memory. For Them. The nebulous clouds that hid themselves in skies they were aware I've only ever known to be stormy. Obeah, once. Ilk, once. . . . No more. If the insurgents wanted to tussle for Aiyca, they needn't have twisted my arm with a force of monsters from the other side of the veil. Aligning themselves with the Alumbrar to kill my family was more than enough to coax me into the ring—where I won't simply bring them war. I will introduce them to Death.

Slipping away from the camp, I fold myself into the shadows within the knot of dense vegetation. At once my skin becomes damp beneath the weight of the oppressive heat beneath the canopy. In the dark, I will my conduit to light. After several tries, returning to Delyse's fundamental of imagining my magic as Aiyca's Great River, golden light spills across the floor, only just illuminating my path. A further push of will, of want, incites a tendril of cool breeze to brush across my temple. Busy weighing the time I have left until Shamar returns from his watch, where I might find a beast to bleed to summon the ancestors, and my distance from the camp, it takes a moment to realize something is amiss. The hairs on the back of my neck rise as my survival instincts tell me I am no longer alone. That, perhaps, I never was.

"You'd make a lousy Stealth," I say.

Made, Shamar steps out of the shadow of a trunk to my left. My relief that it's him, not Delyse, is extinguished by the tautness in his body; he stands tall, ready for battle.

"That depends on what I was keeping an eye on."

Who.

The smile I flash Shamar is more a show of teeth. "I wasn't going to run, back at the palace." It's the first time I've been able to explain myself to any of them since arriving here, against my will, in Kirdan's arms. I tried with Delyse, but she's ignored me since I told her of my plan to head to the Skylands two nights ago. Not even my intention to recruit their extensive aerial army to fight the Unlit has unthawed her. "You didn't figure that out when the army of the dead came? You know, the skeletons I raised from an ancestor's tomb that saved our lives and enabled our escape from the palace?"

Shamar's face doesn't budge. "And now?" he asks.

"Now I was—I was trying to free my magic." The truth is light in a way I've never known it to be before. But then, what use are lies when we face the possibility of war? And Shamar has always appreciated the need for soldiers.

Folding his long arms across the dark tunic on his chest, he nods for me to continue.

"I can see why you'd doubt my intentions when I've done nothing these past few months but fight to avenge my family. A personal vendetta? Yeh mon. A selfish one?" I swallow as the truth finally weighs what I always thought it would. "Maybe. But I'm not myopic by nature. You know that. My plans for after the doyenne's death would have helped Aiyca."

Curiosity softens in Shamar's expression, maybe some guilt too. "What were they?"

"I would have searched for my coven, rejoined them. If they still lived."

"And if they didn't?"

Guileless, a rare occasion, I shrug again. "I still would have helped my order, *our* order, regardless. You see my scarification; you saw me fight the pirates back at the palace."

"You'll fight for us, I understand, but what about leading us?"

Grateful for the darkness, I turn from him, from a truth unlike the others; if I buckle beneath it, Shamar would break. "You don't need an empress now. *We* don't. For one thing, there's no throne to keep warm." At that, Shamar huffs a small laugh. Progress. "Doyenne Cariot had Aiyca, ruled Aiyca, and the Unlit still came." The enemy she allied with to kill my family, before betraying them and setting us all on this bloody course. "Politics can do little against a sword when it's already falling." I take a step closer to Sham, allowing the glow from his conduit to illuminate my sincerity, rather than knocking it into him. "Though it looks different to what you want, helping our home has always been in my plans. I overcame the Vow of Protection to kill the doyenne. If you won't trust my words, trust that action. We need a Genna. We need to raise a sword and parry, or face losing Aiyca to the Unlit." Being stripped of their magic doesn't mitigate their threat. They're Obeah. There is no greater threat to my parents' legacy.

Surveying me, Shamar rubs his chin, fingers dragging back and forth across the horizontal row of scars there. Is he trained to identify poison in words too? Can he tell my intentions, this time, are pure? Mostly.

"You're not wrong," he eventually says. Dropping his hand, he sighs. "I'll help with your magic."